NEXT OF KIN

BOOK 1 OF STARDUST AND ASHES

MELINDA MITCHELL

ARUS
ENTERTAINMENT

Published by ARUS Entertainment (Seattle, WA). This book is catalog #ARUS5001, and has ISBNs of 978-1-954394-10-0 (ebook) and 978-1-954394-11-7 (print)

Edited by Scott James Magner

Cover art and design by EyeQueue Media

ARUS
ENTERTAINMENT

www.arusentertainment.com

NEXT OF KIN

In loving memory of David Van Brakle

1

The last conversation I ever had with my husband was in the bathroom.

The room had an angelic haze in the morning as our sun was in a high period of sunspot activity, but after the minute passed, a negative sign appeared on the test. It felt like another cruel joke by the gods. Or payback for the war, and all the lives lost because of me.

I tossed the white plastic stick in the trash. It clinked against the empty drum, hollow as my womb. Max waited on the other side of the doorway, one eyebrow raised, while I washed my hands. I shook my head.

"Come here, Ami," he coaxed. My husband wrapped his strong arms around me, holding me as if I might collapse. I drew in a deep breath and pulled away. "Next month," he whispered, touching his forehead to mine.

I nodded, blinking back tears. He'd said the same thing after our miscarriage, seven months ago. He stooped to grab his lunch.

"Call me when you take a break," I said.

"Can't. The receiver busted again."

"Give me five minutes, I'll—"

He grabbed my hand, pulling me back to him. "Ami, you're always tinkering with things. It's okay to let things be. You can fix it later, after supper." He motioned with his chin to the stairs. "Check in on Mara, if she's not up in the next hour."

I caught my bottom lip under my teeth. "It really would take me just five—"

He quirked an eyebrow. "Your five minutes always turns into forty-five. Because then you'll hear something on the engine you don't like, or a fan belt, or something else that needs fixing. I have to go. I love you. We'll talk when I come home, okay?"

Max pressed his lips to my cheek before he carried his lunch out the door. I leaned against the door frame, waving as my golden-haired farmer climbed aboard his tractor, smiling to assure him I was okay. I'd been through worse in the military, but I hoped to leave those days of loss behind.

Golden heads of grain rippled while the tractor pulled away, and I dreamed of imaginary golden-haired children. Twin crescent moons hung low on the horizon as Max's tractor faded in the distance, like my—*our*—dreams of a large family running the farm.

I tied my hair up and grabbed the laundry basket before climbing the stairs. Mara grunted as her feet hit the floor above me. Lately, my mother-in-law struggled to get out of bed in the mornings. Soon we'd have to move her downstairs, to the bedroom that was supposed to be a nursery.

"I brought your wash up," I called from the door. Mara sat on the bed, holding on tight with wrinkled hands. Her pastel yellow nightgown clung to her bony figure; her limp, gray hair was just long enough to brush her shoulders. The shades were drawn, and an eerie glow from the active sun framed the dark window.

"Do you need any help?"

Mara didn't answer.

I breathed out through my teeth, set the basket inside the room, and returned downstairs. My sister-in-law would be over soon, and Mara responded better to her.

While I waited for her, I finished folding our laundry, and was about to put the kettle on when the low *beep-beep-beep* of the alarm sounded. Dibon orbited its star at the edge of an asteroid belt, but our Asteroid Defense System meant meteor showers were rare. The ADS used military satellites to trigger explosions, obliterating small asteroids and diverting larger ones away from our planet. Sometimes a tiny one slipped inside, triggering the signal. The rest of the time, the system warned us of dust storms or major changes in the forecast.

Looking out the window, I knew it wasn't a test—since Max drove off the sky went from blue tinged with gold to the yellowish-gray of a major dust storm. I wrinkled my nose and began closing the windows. The house didn't have the push-button technology to automatically shut windows and air vents, let alone a central home AI. All we could afford was to upgrade the alarm system.

I finished securing the downstairs windows when the alarm changed pitch and my heart skipped a beat.

The last time I heard that sound, my brother and sister were killed.

All our lights flashed.

"ASTEROID COLLISION EXPECTED. FIVE MINUTES TO IMPACT. REPEAT, THIS IS NOT A DRILL. ASTEROID COLLISION EXPECTED. FIVE MINUTES TO IMPACT..."

I flung open the window I just closed, scanning the fields. Where the waving grain met the sky, a dark line formed, and the ground trembled beneath the house. Meteors were falling over the arc of the world.

There was no sign of Max.

Panic gripped my chest. I threw open the door, but stopped, hands on the door frame. No. First priority for a soldier—save the civilians who cannot save themselves.

"Mara!" I turned back, leaping up the stairs two at a time. "Mara! We have to go. Now!"

My mother-in-law's eyes glazed over. I didn't wait for a response, pulling at her arm until she stood, throwing her arm around my shoulders.

"Move!"

"FOUR MINUTES TO IMPACT..."

I half-carried, half-pushed her down the stairs and out the door. My brother-in-law's truck peeled out of the driveway. I spotted Sheya at the emergency hatch next to the garage, flipping her tight curls away from her face. "Chip went for Max," my sister-in-law shouted as she took Mara's arm, pushing her toward the ladder inside.

"We heard the alarm on our way over. He didn't respond to his comm."

"Go. I'll hold the door. Get Mara down," I ordered.

"THREE MINUTES TO IMPACT..."

White lines streaked across the yellowish sky, blossoming into brilliant fireballs as they crossed the crescent moons. I fumbled for the comm in my pocket, but the signal was out. The receiver on the tractor was still broken.

"TWO MINUTES TO IMPACT..."

I scanned the field, though the dust clogged the air, blocking my view. There was no sign of either Max's tractor or Chip's truck. I held the lid open as I crawled in the hatch. He couldn't have gone far. Any second now, Max would be driving up with Chip.

"ONE MINUTE TO IMPACT..."

A shower of rock struck the hatch. I wrenched my arm under the heavy door, keeping it up to spot my husband. Even if Max was at the edge of our farmstead, Chip should've found him by now.

A dark shadow passed over our home. A meteor, large as Max's tractor, was headed toward our farm. Dust penetrated my mouth and nose, the taste and smell of death.

Second priority for a soldier—save the ones you're with.

I pulled the hatch, spinning the wheel and sealing us in from the raining death.

"Go-go-go," I huffed, more to myself, but Sheya and Mara were only on the third landing. My foot hit the first—

Everything shook. Dust and small rocks shook loose from overhead, the emergency lights flickered. I coughed, dust in my throat and eyes. My mother-in-law grabbed the railing an arm length away, my sister-in-law ahead at the landing for the next floor. The older woman froze, her fingers wound tight around the railing.

"Mara, look at me." I palmed her cheek, peering into her empty gray eyes. Her mouth hung open. I pried her fingers from the railing. "You have to keep going. We have to get to the bunker. It isn't safe—"

Another impact knocked me into her, both of us tumbling down the stairs. My shoulder popped, my temple banged against the floor. Sheya grabbed me by the hand, and I shrieked in response to the sharp pain—she didn't see my shoulder was dislocated.

"Get her out of here!" I screamed. Sheya placed Mara's arm around her neck, and continued down the stairs, leaving me on the landing.

I twisted my body over, reaching for the railing with my good arm, and crawled to the stairs like a three-legged dog. Gasping, I pulled myself up. I expected another impact to knock me over, but the metal stairs only vibrated.

When I reached the final landing, I pulled the bunker door behind me, turning the wheel to seal us in again. I leaned forward, clutching my useless arm. Something warm and wet traveled down my face. I tried to wipe it with my sleeve, but the pain was too great. After a few breaths, I gathered enough strength to walk down the ramp into our village's bunker. The doors providing access hatches for other farms were already sealed shut.

Though I'd never been down here, I'd seen the design of the bunkers in the emergency procedures for our community development. The cavernous top level was the assembly area, containing only immediate emergency supplies and a triage station. If the danger passed, we'd never have to go below into the survival quarters.

I shuddered at the thought. No. We'd just be here an hour or two. That's all. It couldn't be that bad.

"Ami!" a neighbor cried, calling my attention back. She pushed through others crowding the line for supplies. Her eyes narrowed when she saw my arm and face. "Medic!" she called, and a white-clad woman made her way over to us.

"Anyone after you?" the neighbor asked, as the medic examined my face.

I shook my head. "When I looked back, it was raining rocks the size of tractors."

"Yours was the last—"

Another impact rocked the bunker. The ceiling lights flashed, and the emergency generators ramped up as the people screamed.

The medic ordered me to sit. She cleaned the head wound, sealing it with liquid stitches. Then she examined my arm. "Dislocated. Going to pop it back in, okay? One, two, three."

I bit my bottom lip until it bled as she pushed my shoulder back into place. Pain seared along my entire back and neck. She pulled a sling from her bulky medical bag, adjusting it around me.

"Are you pregnant?"

I blinked. "What?"

She leaned in, her gaze stern. "I said, are you pregnant?"

"Oh. No."

The medic slapped a bottle of pills in my hand before moving on.

Sheya spotted me, her perfect ringlets bouncing on her face as she jogged over, her warm complexion glowing in the emergency lights. Even at the end of the world the girl looked beautiful. "I've got cots for us. Mara is—well, Mara."

My sister-in-law and I might be as opposite as can be, but our mother-in-law had no favorites between us, only her sons.

They were gone.

The reality hit me as another meteor pounded the surface, shaking the supports in the bunker. Cries and shrieks echoed around me.

There was no way our men had survived.

That couldn't be right. I waved goodbye not even an hour ago. No. The world did not just end. It was only a dream.

My arm wouldn't hurt this bad in a dream.

Sheya spoke to me, but the words were a jumbled string I couldn't untangle.

"No survivors," I mumbled.

Sheya brushed a curl from her face, shaking her head. "Don't give up hope yet. They might've taken shelter in another village's bunker."

My head and arm throbbed. Sheya handed me a canteen and I popped two painkillers from the bottle. Peering inside, I counted six more pills of the same kind I gave to wounded soldiers during the war. Enough to make me loopy if I took them all, but not enough to do long-term damage. Not enough to make it so I didn't wake up. There was no pill to swallow to relieve that pain.

Someone came around with rations—mine stayed on the tray, untouched. Sheya tended to Mara, who rocked in her bed, bony hands clasped together in prayer to her god. If I didn't hurt so bad, I would curl up and rock with her.

Hours passed below ground in a blur. I guessed it was evening. The lights were a steady white, meaning the power was stable. I wanted to take that as a good sign, but there was nothing good about our situation. Rumors were already spreading like bacteria.

"The ADS should've warned us," an old man said to his daughter.

"If it was operating properly, we would've been in the bunker since yesterday," she retorted.

I frowned, scooting closer to listen. For any of us to have survived, the asteroid must've already broken into smaller pieces, so something worse happened when the alarm went off. Something caused the ADS to fail and for the alarm to kick in right before it struck.

"Maybe the system shorted out," a neighbor at a nearby cot suggested. "Sunspot activity could've done it."

"At the same time as a giant asteroid happened to exit the belt and head right for our planet?" another countered. "No, this was an attack."

"The Modes?" a younger woman asked.

A neighboring planetary system known for their cyberattacks, the Modes had shut down the ADS last year to blackmail Dibon and other planets, but a peace deal—and a hefty bribe—got us back online.

"But they would've sent a demand ahead of time, or at least warnings with hacks. There was no warning, nothing. Only the dustbowl alarm, and then the universal."

"It's the gods-dusted Twelve Rebels again—they must've sent the asteroid to us."

I shook my head, unbelieving. Twelve Rebels was the slang name for the Nacaen Group, a system at the reaches of wild space from which Mara and her sons fled as refugees ten years ago. The Outer Systems of the galaxy were often torn by war or simply ran lawless with no authoritarian government, the Nacaen Group was the most notorious of them all.

"It wasn't the Twelve." I gritted my teeth against the pain in my shoulder, grabbing the bed railing with my good hand, and stood. At one and three-quarter meters, I wasn't the tallest veteran in our community, but I wanted them to stop the blame game nonsense.

"Hey, we mean no disrespect, but the Twelve are at war again."

"And I said it wasn't the Twelve. I know the Twelve's work—"

All heads turned as chattering voices turned to gasps. I spied the door across the bunker. The red light blinked twice, turning to green.

Someone was on the other side.

I pushed through the crowd despite the pain, despite knowing that the distance from our field to the next access point was too far for Max to have made it. Maybe I was wrong.

Instead, six pilots in flight suits came through the door, followed by Marcus Vance, my old captain.

His eyebrows raised as he caught my gaze. "Lieutenant."

I snapped to attention, despite being out of the service for three years.

"At ease, Ami," he said, almost laughing. "It's damn good to see you."

"What are you doing here?"

"Low altitude training exercises, practicing field landings. No time to return to base, couldn't outrun the rocks. Ditched the birds and got in the first hole we could find. Had to climb through a half-caved-in tunnel."

"Was there anyone else?"

Vance shook his head, his joy at seeing me fading. He took in my injuries: arm in the sling, cut on my face. "Are you all right?"

I nodded, though my tongue caught in my throat—if it loosened, I might've screamed.

My Max was gone.

My neighbors began asking questions all at once. "How bad is it?" "Did any houses survive?" "Are there any other survivors?"

"Listen up," Vance addressed the crowd, raising his hands to motion for silence. "The largest rocks have either struck or passed. Comms to the surface are out for now. What I can tell you—the good news—is that the underground development has worked. This sector has full power and life support.

"The bad news is that based on what we saw before the hatch closed, the surface is no longer viable. Not for a long time, possibly ten to fifteen years."

Gasps, cries, shrieks and moans clogged my head, but there was no arguing with facts. I closed my eyes instead.

I knew Vance was being generous.

"Ten to fifteen years?" someone repeated.

"No, no, that can't be," the old man said, beginning to weep.

Regardless of all the technology we helped develop after the war to speed a planet's recovery, atmospheric conditions were still unpredictable. A piercing wail rose above the murmurs, the mourning cry of someone whose hope died.

As all our hope died.

"What about...what about those who didn't make it in? Is it possible there are survivors?" Sheya asked, her eyes pleading for a glimpse of hope. "Perhaps they made it to the next village bunker?"

Unlike Sheya, Vance and I knew the reality of mass destruction.

Even if they managed to figure out the dust storm was the precursor to a meteor shower, the next village lay several kilometers away. It was a false hope. Besides, the gods-dusted radio on the tractor was still busted. He might've started back when the dust storm began rising, but he wouldn't have received the alarm warning. It was only the backup emergency alarm that had saved us. Me.

Max. With his golden hair and deep-set blue eyes. The boy who'd taken my heart forever.

Now gone. Forever.

The captain bowed his head before answering.

"Even if anyone managed to survive the impacts, the air is unbreathable, and we have no working comms. Dibon, for now, is dead on the surface."

Shouted questions competed with one another as if someone's brother was more important than someone's friend, lover, niece, or mother. Vance did his best to control the crowd, as the only authority figure present. The shouting faded to a dull, throbbing ache.

I swallowed a couple more pills. The medic was smart to put only eight pills in a bottle, because I would've swallowed anything to take away the pain now.

A sharp ache, like a knife wedged deep, spread across my chest. I'd never taste his kiss again or smell the scent of sweet grass that always clung to his shirts. Feel his strong arms wrap around me, hear him whisper my name.

My mother-in-law's chanting murmur pried through the noise of collective grief, sounding more like a lullaby than mourning. She didn't understand what was happening.

"Mara," I said, moving to her cot. "Mara," I repeated, my hand on her shoulder. She stopped, her eyes fixing on me, the same deep-set eyes of my beloved.

"They're gone."

2

I rolled over in the bed, reaching for him, but all I found was an empty blanket and the edge of the metal cot. The farmstead was gone. Max was gone. The wooden ceiling of our bedroom was gone, replaced by the cold stone and metal of the bunker.

The kettle whistled, signaling my sister-in-law was up. My mother-in-law sat in the corner, her eyes closed, repeating the Mourner's Prayer of her people. "Blessed is the one beyond blessing," Mara muttered. I caught Sheya's eye from my cot, and she shook her head. No change. I closed my eyes for a moment, wanting to go back to the dream, but Max was gone, and I had to get up for my shift at comm.

Our quarters in the bunker were small as one might imagine—we called them cubbyholes, and we'd been here for five weeks. The walls were carved from stone with steel supports, built ages ago before the ADS came online, well before the last war. On one wall stood a cooking station and small cupboard, with a shower and toilet in the corner. Embedded in the wall next to the door was a small comm screen, listing schedules for Sheya and me for the next seventy-two hours.

Our three cots barely fit on the floorspace. We were lucky—because of my previous military service, we were given private quarters. Others were grouped two or three families to a cubbyhole or stuck in the larger bunk rooms.

I didn't grieve like Mara, wailing and crying, nor like Sheya, sharing memories while scrolling through photos on the viewscreen. Instead, grief hung on my shoulders, ached in my joints, caused me to fall asleep at the table during supper if I didn't keep busy. Most of the time, I kept going because I pretended he wasn't dead.

"Blessed is the one beyond song," Mara continued her chant. I folded my cot and set it against the wall, while my sister-in-law unfolded the table and our three chairs for breakfast.

"I see they moved up your shift at comm," Sheya said as she removed the covers from our steaming gruel.

"Yeah. They asked me yesterday." Basic comms were restored two weeks after the blast, but damage from the initial impact had limited their use to military personnel. Now that it was repaired, civilian comms were allowed. "They're backlogged and need help."

She tugged on a curl hanging by her ear. "Glad they asked you, instead of ordered you."

"What do you mean by that?"

"I mean, this martial law thing is getting old."

I rolled my eyes. "We've had a military regime since the war. It really isn't much different."

"I never saw so many soldiers until they opened all

the connectors to the other bunkers. Like they all flooded in."

"Everyone received new assignments once the passages were safe to open," I replied. "There are no more soldiers here than anywhere else. Besides, Captain Vance has things under control."

"Marcus Vance doesn't know us—our village."

"He knows *me*. Until we can have elections to replace the officials who died, he's in charge of our sector now. But everything is still on a volunteer basis. No one is being forced to do anything that wasn't their job before."

"For a bunch of farmers, there's a lot of us unemployed, and not enough military to run things," she said. "I'm just saying where I come from, we'd be watching out."

"We're used to it. Not a single family without someone in the service. Your system hasn't had a war in decades," I reminded her.

"Maybe because we disarmed."

I let out a breath. I didn't want to argue with Sheya. The Ramaen System neighbored the Noma System, of which Dibon was one of four habitable planets, each with its own governance. Ramaen biodome planets, moons and asteroids were united under one government. It was like comparing trees to rocks.

Sheya pushed a comm drive across the table to me, a plastic-encased, thumb-sized circuit board in which one could record messages or upload files. Comm signals couldn't reach this far below the surface, but we could upload messages to the comm station several levels above to send signals off-world now that civilians were able to. "I recorded that this morning for my parents."

I pocketed the drive. "I'll send it." She'd received messages from her parents recently. I hadn't. Mine left Dibon after the war and stopped speaking to me when I married Max. Diboni prejudices against Nacaens at the end of the war had broken my family, just like Nacaen hatred against Diboni had at the beginning, when my brother and sister were killed.

In the first few days after the sky fell, I'd put my military training to use assisting in surgery, but the post-disaster injuries were cleared out now. Five weeks in, all we dealt with were colds, fatigue, depression, and PTSD. They didn't need a worn-out flight medic for that. I didn't need to be pacing the floor waiting for someone to be hurt so I could help. I knew how to send comms. I knew how to fix receivers.

I should've fixed the one on the tractor.

Mara joined us at the table, sipping rationed gruel. For a moment, I spied a bit of Max in her, the way he'd sit in silence at supper when we had guests over. When we first started dating right after the war, I thought my new love was shy. Later I learned he was quiet-mannered like his mother, preferring to observe others over their idle chatter.

The chime of a news bulletin broke the silence as our screen shifted to the Dibon Shield—three stalks of grain behind two arms clasping each other at the wrists, circled by our planetary motto of, "One planet, one people: One Dibon."

After a few seconds, the shield dissolved to reveal Admiral Emil Donovan, dressed in a white uniform and sitting behind a desk in a room of similar shape and size to our cubbyhole. His full title was Admiral of the Dibon

Military Force and President of the People, but Emil Donovan had governed Dibon for the last six years, during the war and beyond, and I couldn't remember the last time someone referred to him as president. His hair was silver, and deep ridges lined his forehead. Medals adorned the left side of his jacket, just like when he'd first addressed us in the days after the meteor strikes.

"My fellow Diboni, all survivors of the meteor: with military satellites and orbital stations secure, we have lifted the ban on civilian communications ..."

Sheya leaned forward, ignoring the admiral's announcement. "Layla said she overheard some soldiers talking about the Modes, that they know something about the ADS failure."

"About what?"

"They are insisting they had nothing to do with the ADS, but for the right price they'll give more information."

I glanced at Sheya sideways. "Rumors are lies and lies are useless." I motioned back to the screen, wanting to hear the Admiral's speech.

"This has been an unprecedented time," Donovan continued. "The bunkers you—and I—now live in were designed before we had the Asteroid Defense System. The investigation into the ADS failure continues, but at this time, we can only confirm that it appears accidental."

"No one buys that," Sheya said.

I glared at her across the table. "Don't be like them."

"Like what?"

"Conspiracy theorists. Causing divisions, taking

sides, blaming others. People will start getting singled out, and someone will take matters into their hands." I leaned toward her, whispering so Mara couldn't hear. "You know what people can be like. You need to drop it."

Sheya gave me an incredulous look and turned her attention back to Admiral Donovan.

The leader of our planet stared straight into the camera. "I know many of you hope to connect with relations on other planets. We urge patience and a sense of calm and order as it may take several days to route comms beyond our neighboring systems.

"Right now, our Noma neighbors have closed their borders. There are currently no large vessels in the system capable of mass evacuations. Until we have more options, arranging transportation off-world will be made with private contractors and by a lottery basis for availability.

"Diboni citizens and immigrants, the bunker system is functioning, our air cyclers are working perfectly. We have supplies en route from the Ramaen System including food and medicine. We urge you to continue to maintain our unity as one planet, one people: One Dibon."

The admiral signed off. Sheya raised an eyebrow. "Air cyclers working perfectly?"

I'd made the mistake of telling her about the two families who died the second week in the bunker, poisoned by CO_2 in their sleep. Eight of them, including a child.

"How *bad* is it?" she asked.

I stirred the gruel in front of me. "Nothing bad. We'll be fine."

Mara looked at me, but I avoided her gaze, staring at my bowl. I couldn't let them down. I could barely manage one day to the next, but they needed something to hope for, something to live for.

"What I wouldn't give for good, fresh bread," Sheya said, changing the subject. She lifted her spoon and watched the gruel slowly plop back into her bowl.

"Thought you hated baking."

"I didn't say I would bake it. Just said I missed it. Chip always did the baking."

I almost choked on my gruel. Sometimes, it was easy for me to wallow in my own grief and forget what everyone in this room had lost. I didn't lose just Max. I'd lost Chip, my brother-in-law. Sheya had lost her husband and brother-in-law. And Mara had lost her sons.

"He made that amazing root bread," I remembered. "Said it was a family recipe."

"It was," Mara said, startling me. "My father used to make it, and I taught the boys once I learned what roots grew here."

We fell into an awkward silence. Mara hadn't spoken conversationally since the strikes, and even before that, we hadn't talked much. I finally responded, "I didn't know that."

"Remember the dinners we used to have?" Sheya jumped in. Despite our earlier conversation, I was glad she had the sense to turn things around when words failed me. "Chip would always bring a basket of bread, and I'd bring a bottle of Ramaen sweet wine."

"Max and I would cook together," I reminisced, as if I could recreate the aromas our kitchen instead of the steaming gruel in front of me. "You know why we invited you over all the time?"

"To convince me about farming," Sheya responded. I almost dropped my spoon. "Yeah, that's right, I was on to all three of you. Didn't think this city-raised, biodome Ramaen girl had it in her."

"Well you couldn't cook, that was for sure."

Sheya smirked in response.

Mara folded her napkin. "Chip really took to baking," she said. "But I always preferred the three-grain bread. Smothered in olive oil."

Sheya's eyes glistened.

"I miss the smell of bread," I said as I spooned up the last of my gruel, bringing myself back to the present. Our husbands, our bakers—even our bread—gone.

———

AFTER BREAKFAST I left our cubbyhole and headed for the lift to the comm station, which lay at the same level as the original assembly bunkers, now used for supply organization and storage.

Two soldiers in uniform stood in a corner of the lift, their voices low. In the other corner was a woman, maybe eighteen or nineteen, just younger than Sheya. She had a volunteer badge, granting access to the comm station and other places previously limited to military personnel. She shrank into the corner, as if she didn't want to be seen. Her hair was wrapped up in a scarf, like I'd seen other Nacaen refugees wear theirs, although Mara did not. The two soldiers kept glancing her way, until I stared at them. "Problem?"

"No, sir," they said. The veteran's seal on my volunteer badge still commanded respect, though it had been years since I left the service. The young immigrant exited the lift at supply storage, a level below the comm station. The soldiers got off with me.

I scanned my badge at the entrance, a large octagonal room facing the stems of the comm antennae that pierced the rocky layers above to the surface. After weeks of repairs the station was a jumble of new and old tech—with motion-sensing screens and old analog keyboards on countertops, a mess of black and orange cables snaking across the floor and...

"Ow!" I stubbed my toe on a cable, tripping forward to bang my knee into a military issue metal chair stacked high with yellowing repair manuals.

"Watch your step," a woman said from under my workstation waving me unseen to take a seat on a slightly less ancient chair. On the floor beside her was a bucket full of comm drives like the one I carried in my pocket from Sheya. Her boots were general issue, and the repair kit was a near-twin to the one I carried around during my years in service. Another uniformed technical specialist worked on the other side of the room, unplugging some cables and rerouting others. With everything that had failed since this station came back online, I could see why the military was eager to move out, leaving the scraps for civilian comms.

The woman slid out from under the table, dusted herself off and saluted me with a pair of wire strippers, "Ok, that should do this bank. Sorry for the inconvenience. We had a short overnight that fried a bunch of stations, and we've been working all night to get them back up. You should be fine, until the next major malfunction."

Less than a minute later she'd packed her gear and powered up my station, and indicator lights started blinking as the system recognized I was back online.

Instead of taking any live communications, I got to work on the bucket of pre-recorded comm drives, inserting the small circuit units into a port in front of me, uploading messages to the satellites above, and dropping the drives into a different bin for reuse. I slipped Sheya's out of my pocket and loaded it after the first few, to make sure hers got through.

"No, not nuclear," another comm volunteer replied to an incoming transmission. "No traces of Baratanium or any other radiation. All we know is an ADS failure. Yes, quartz was mined here."

I rubbed my temples. Similar conversations over-lapped throughout the station, as corporate developers responded to my displaced neighbors attempting to sell off their land. Even though Dibon would be a dustbowl for many years, it had become prime real estate, espe-cially for miners, and for those interested in the decades-long planetary recovery. The Near Side systems, including Noma and Ramaen, supported a hefty population, which meant any planet that lost a third of its population at once, even if the surface was dead for now, was an investment in the future.

"Here you go," a voice with a slight drawl called at my shoulder. I spun my chair around—the young Nacaen woman from the lift smiled and refilled my coffee.

"Thank you," I replied, smiling warmly. "I appreciate it."

She turned, pouring coffee for another volunteer.

As she started to leave, I caught the eye of another volunteer, who'd been listening in.

"Shall I pull your chair closer so you can hear better?"

She angled away, leaning closer to her screen, typing fast as if she didn't hear me.

When my people heard Nacaen accents, they stiffened. People dropped their voices and whispered. I know because I was once that way. Before I met Max. Back when I blamed all Nacaens for starting our civil war.

I downloaded messages to the personal comm drives, coded their destinations, and passed them along through other volunteers. Some messages were offers of transportation or work; others were families who still hadn't learned of their relative's fate. Sheya's family was probably figuring out how to send help, maybe even resources for her to get off-world.

I had nowhere else to go. Dibon was home, even underground, even with no hope. Besides, someone had to care for Mara, especially now. I remembered the soldiers in the lift reacting to the Nacaen refugee earlier. Sheya might not be the only one obsessed with conspiracy theories, especially now.

"Damn it!" the volunteer next to me shouted, knocking me out of my thoughts as she removed her headset. "It's gone out, again!"

"What is it?" I asked.

"We keep losing connections."

Sure enough, my live feeds had dropped, and a rotating circle appeared on my screen.

A uniformed tech moved to my station, unplugging some cables on the other side and rerouting them. "Try that," he said, and my screen blipped. The circle went away as the connection restored.

"How often have you done that this morning?"

"Sometimes every half-hour, when it's bad," the tech said.

"Let me take a look," I replied, pushing aside the bucket of used drives below me and crawling under the counter. Even though someone had just been down here making repairs, they were focusing on individual problems, not overall solutions. Lying on my back, I followed the wires with my eyes as they climbed the walls and into the pipe stems of the antenna array, rising up above us, through the rock to the surface. Right at the ceiling, the fans from the air cyclers were whirling. "Stardust and ashes, did no one clear this out?"

"What do you mean?" the tech asked, peering underneath.

"Do you have a light?"

The tech crawled under the console and lay down next to me, giving me his light, and I pointed it up. "See? All that?" I waved the light around, and dust particles swam a couple meters above me. "The air cycler is pulling all of that out. This needs to be cleared regularly. Meteor dust from the surface is finding its way in, and the cyclers are pushing it in here. It's corroding the cables in the pipes."

"Are you sure?"

"This isn't like dust that accumulates in your home.

This is shrapnel from a meteor, particles of metal and rock. It's gonna eat this up," I added, holding a discarded cable toward him, showing the corrosion.

"Dusted ash," the tech swore. "Get me a vac," he called out to another tech. "How did you know to look here?"

I pushed myself out from under the console, wiping dust that had settled on my eyebrows. "The last big dust storm—you know, before everything—we lost power at home, and it turned out the air cyclers were running overtime. Had to install a backflow unit to clear out the dust. Wasn't nearly as bad as this."

"Backflow unit?" The tech palmed his forehead. "These are top of the line air cyclers, Ramaen-built, tested every year for emergencies. They shouldn't need a backflow unit."

I stood, stretching my back. "They probably were built for people living down here a couple of days at a time, not for five weeks of accumulated particulate."

Later, as the Nacaen volunteer brought me a bag lunch, I slumped back in my chair. If our leaders hadn't thought about the lasting, cumulative damage, had anyone?

We weren't much different from air cyclers, having never been tested in quite this way before.

———

I FINISHED MY EIGHT-HOUR SHIFT, took the lift back down to the cubbyholes, and joined a crowd of people passing by me, carrying their dinner rations and grumbling about how the meat ran out weeks ago. I caught snippets of complaints about how other supplies were coming up scarce as neighbors made their way to their holes.

Vance was waiting at the bottom of the ramp leading to our section. New lines had developed on his forehead and at the corner of his eyes. The responsibility of supporting our new underground civilization and maintaining order weighed on him.

I leaned against the railing. "Hey Cap, what's the word?"

Vance raised his eyebrows. "Official word: everything's running as it should. Unofficial word: I needed a drink yesterday."

"That bad, huh?"

"You don't even want to know. We don't have enough soldiers to run things and keep order."

I glanced around, frowning. "I haven't seen much disorder."

"You're on the veteran's level where you all have your own hole. We've had fights in the shared cubbies and all-out brawls in the bunkrooms, emergency evacs—"

"What evacuations?"

He motioned over his right shoulder. "Twenty clicks south. Pressure valve malfunction on the whole unit. They managed to get it shut down with no explosion but about a quarter of those residents are being moved here. Still figuring out where to put 'em."

My former commander held out his tablet. "My offer still stands. Full rank, a real one this time, not the kludge we did to get you flying. And after two years, settlement on any world in the Ramaen System. You know you miss it."

He could still get a smile from me. I was proud to have served under him, but I shook my head. "When I left the service, I left for good."

"Even now? After all that's changed?"

"I can't. You remember how it was." Though the temperature was regulated in the bunkers, I shivered, gooseflesh rising on my arms. I pushed away the visions of bodies burned by rainfire, which wasn't even the worst of what I saw. Rows of wounded soldiers, most of whom I could barely help ease their pain. Body bags stacked like logs. The bombing of Nebo at the beginning of the war by Twelve Rebels. Mass shootings in retaliation by the paramilitary Dibon Renegades.

"I do remember. You were one of our best pilots, then the best flight medic in our division. I remember your determination, your energy. We need that right now."

I'd joined the war to avenge my siblings. I wanted my parents to be proud of me. I was only sixteen—the age for service was lower then. But when I left it all behind, and married Max—I lost everything I fought for. The soldier Vance knew didn't exist anymore, but he couldn't see that. He just saw me as a kid: Ami, the eager and loyal recruit he plucked out of the motor pool. At twenty-two, post-war and post-meteor, that kid was long, long gone.

"We sustained heavy losses from the disaster. Dibon is defenseless right now. The rest of the Noma System is maxed out for resources, and we can't trust the ash-dusted Modes. The Ramaens are just waiting for us to fail before they petition the Noma Council to annex us. Give them another system to control against the Modes.

Donovan won't go to a draft, but we are boosting our recruitment efforts."

I crossed my arms. Dibon already had a bad reputation in the Noma System. Our military regime had been in power ever since our king's assassination decades ago, but it wasn't a dictatorship. We'd taken in Nacaen refugees when no other planet would. But when we went to war, our military used horrific weapons of mass destruction against our own people—refugees, too— that were later banned by all planetary systems on the Near Side.

We'd crawled out of that war attempting to restore our reputation as an orderly, loyal people, with human rights declarations and our new motto of "One Dibon."

"We're still not in their good graces, after all the negotiations following the war?"

"Ramaens had to agree to banning some of their prized weaponry in the peace accords, because they'd armed us. They're still not happy about that, though they are agreeing to resettle our veterans, and they're our largest emergency supplier. But that's not why I'm asking you to sign on again." He leaned in. "We can get your family away from here. I know what the rumors are."

I caught my bottom lip under my teeth. "Vance..."

"We've confiscated weapons from at least six individuals who've threatened to find those responsible." The captain pursed his lips, and I knew he was about to tell me something he wasn't cleared to do. "We had our first murder last night. A Nacaen refugee."

I gasped, pulling away from the railing. "Who?"

"Still classified while we investigate. But they were Dahan."

My shoulders sank. "Damn." I didn't know them, but still, one of Mara's people, one of the Twelve of the Nacaen Group.

"Ami, we need you. We can get your family to safety."

When I met Max, right after the war ended three years ago, I knew I had changed. I vowed never to return to the military, and I couldn't break my promise.

"No."

I brushed past Vance, heading back to my cubbyhole. The industrial lighting was a bit dimmer for the evening hours, trying to mimic what the surface used to be like. About this time the two moons would be off-cycle, one rising as the other was at its zenith. Time to get in the second planting before autumn.

But there was no more planting, no more soil to till. Only rock and dust to clear out, until eventually the air cyclers stopped working. It was only a matter of months before the dust and debris managed to make its way through the conduits down here.

Neither I, nor anyone else, could live here much longer unless something changed.

I rounded the corner to our corridor. A thin man in a Diboni uniform stood outside the door. My shoulders tensed. He was one of the soldiers from the lift earlier today, with the Nacaen volunteer who'd given me coffee.

"What do you want?" I demanded.

His eyes narrowed. "I have a message for Sheya Lehem."

The hairs on the back of my neck pricked. There was

no one else in the corridor, and Vance was out of earshot. All the other doors to cubbyholes were closed.

He held out a comm drive to me. I accepted it carefully, as if it were a knife.

"Watch yourself," he said as he walked away.

"What does that mean?"

He glanced over his shoulder. "We take care of our own. One Dibon."

"One Dibon means all of us," I shouted back, quoting from the campaign during the war: "Refugee, immigrant, and native-born."

The soldier turned around to face me. "Nice sentiment from a time when we still had a planet. How long will that last? How much longer will we rely on the mercy of the Ramaens and their emergency supplies? We have to take care of *ourselves*."

I glanced down at the comm drive for Sheya in my palm, frowning. Did he know she was Ramaen? He saw my badge and last name; he knew I'd married a Nacaen. Was he warning me, or *threatening* me?

When I looked up, he was gone.

But my vision caught the air ducts above me. All the things our leaders had planned for: war, evacuations, meteors. They planned for how we survive the impact, but not for the aftermath.

Not for this.

3

Sheya had already retrieved the dinner rations when I arrived, so I passed her the comm drive and set the table. She inserted the drive into her tablet, placing the speaker in her ear. I portioned out our dinner: protein "steaks" (blocks of calories in vaguely appealing shapes), canned vegetables, and lemon packets to flavor our water. I stirred them in, remembering similar packets handed out for soldiers to use with our canteens. Piss-water, we called it.

Sheya wiped her eyes as I set the plate in front of her, tearing the speaker from her ear.

"What is it?"

"My mom," she replied, handing the tablet to me. An image of Sheya's mother filled the screen, standing before the green gardens of a biosphere estate back in the Ramaen system that covered half a moon. Domes with gardens spread underneath, artificial lights to mimic sunlight. Compared to our dark, cramped bunkers, the moon gardens shone like gems, mini paradises, only a system away.

"She wants me to go home to Ramaen. I can't." She glanced over at Mara, rocking in her corner.

I jumped as Mara spoke. "Eli, we never should've left home."

"Mara." I rushed to her side. "Eli's not here."

"Max? We should've gone home when the war was over."

My heart caught in my throat. I hadn't allowed myself to cry, not even at the mass memorial service afterward. I wasn't ready to let go. Not yet.

"Mara, Max is gone. Chip is gone."

Stroking her arm, I tried soothing her as she wailed, but the grief I'd tried to keep down spilled out in my own tears. When Max and I married, I wanted to raise a family and he wanted to start a farm. I wanted the life taken from me when my brother and sister died. When my parents disowned me.

Now Max and Chip were gone, and all my dreams in dust. I couldn't pretend any longer.

"I want to go home," my mother-in-law blurted out, like a tired child. "I want to go home, to live and die there."

A sob escaped my lips. Tears I had dammed up flowed free.

Sheya knelt, her own face streaming with tears. "If you want to go home, Mara, I'll go with you."

I gaped. I'd not expected Sheya to concede so easily. The Nacaen Group was far away, across the arms of our spiral galaxy, part of the Outer Systems. Wild space.

The older widow narrowed her eyes. "How? We have nothing. God stole it from us, leaving us empty."

Sheya reached for Mara's hand. "I can ask my parents for help."

"No," I contested, but my sister-in-law caught my eye, a look that told me I didn't want to reckon with her.

It was me who had to let go. It was too dangerous to stay here. If Sheya was willing to sacrifice a chance to return to her family for Mara, I could do the right thing and let go of what was holding me back. Sheya shouldn't have to commit to anything beyond what she had. She'd lost as much as I had, and I needed to give up my own selfishness.

But fear clutched my heart like a hand squeezing tight. Dibon and the Noma System were part of the migration from the cradle of civilization, close to where the arms spread from the bulge of our galaxy.

Mara was from part of the outermost reaches of humanity, people who had crossed nebulas and survived stars collapsing in the Outer Systems. But unlike me, she had a home to return to.

"No," I repeated, shoving my fears and holding out my hand to her. "I'll sell the farmland. I can get us passage. Besides, there's nothing left here for me." And the sooner we got out of here, the better.

Sheya nodded, her eyes full of water. "I'll go, too."

I RUBBED the corner of my eye, scrolling through corporate buyer requests, the feed lit up as soon as I posted the farm for sale. A volunteer at another station motioned for me to cut the sound, and I shut off the audio notifications.

I thought it'd be easy to let go.

Ten to fifteen years with uninhabitable atmo, plus the layers of meteor dust that would have to be cleared away before the land would be useable. Still, it was the land Max and I put our hearts into. I couldn't sell the soul of what we worked for, not for it to be stripped away. Mining companies offered cash wired within twenty-four hours, and I deleted hundreds of messages.

I went back to my volunteer work, spooling through the regular feed to transmit messages, but I couldn't read the words on the screen. They jumbled together, reminding me I was only delaying the inevitable. "I can't stay here." It was no longer post-war Dibon, or post-meteor Dibon. It was post-Max.

"I'm sorry," the volunteer to my right said. His temples were graying, hands rough and calloused on the comm screens. "Selling your home?"

"My farm."

"You're a vet?"

I nodded.

"Me too. Community development myself. Helped start three of the farming villages northwest of here."

"That's where I met my husband, at community development."

After the war, development leaders gave instructions on how to dispatch neutralizer to make the soil rich again. When Max entered, the room went silent. He was a Nacaen, a Twelve, a refugee. There was an empty seat next to me; I gazed at the boy with golden hair and deep blue eyes, motioning for him to take the chair. We learned how to neutralize the soil from toxins, plant grain such as corn, and I learned a handsome Nacaen could persuade me to become a farmer's wife and leave the military behind. Both of us young and in love and ready for everything to be new.

"Gotta be difficult, now, to sell it all off," the volunteer said, bringing me back to the moment, without Max.

"Hard to see that all we worked for—all we fought for—is now gone, and the only thing its good for is mining."

Technology made it possible to go from war-torn wasteland to productive farm within a few seasons— technology would help redevelop the meteor-demolished land within a minute amount of time on a universal scale. But it'd be someone else's work, not ours.

"Better to get out now," he said. "Get what you can, and if you're lucky, find someplace to go. The Ramaens are only gonna send help for so long before they withhold supplies to get what they want. Then the riots will start."

I frowned. "Why do you say that?"

"They got slapped with sanctions for selling us arms before the last war. They haven't forgotten. They want something."

My shoulder stiffened. I angled away from the volunteer, uncomfortable. My gaze landed in the middle of my screen, a message from a biodome agricultural firm located in the Ramaen system, interested in dome farming and soil revitalization.

When I returned to our cubbyhole, I didn't tell

Sheya the latest rumor, only that I'd accepted an offer on the farm.

————

"COULDN'T you just buy a ship for what these lowlifes are charging?" Sheya asked, as she deleted messages from our search, prices much higher than we could afford. We both signed up for comm hours while one of her friends stayed with Mara. Neither of us were comfortable leaving her home alone, but Sheya was going stir-crazy from being in the cubbyhole and I couldn't blame her.

"I could, but I wouldn't know how to fly the dusted thing. I flew Buzzards, not exactly known for cross-galaxy travel."

Kittiwake Fighters were their proper name, but everyone used the nickname. The sleek fighters were known for their sharp angles and for "buzzing" our enemies—drawing them to follow us into the atmosphere, and then we'd skim off, while the other ship burned up. Besides, what I could afford to buy wouldn't get us halfway across the galaxy, and it was too high of a learning curve for me to learn new instrumentation and technology on the fly.

I scrolled through texts and transcripts. Passing cargo and passenger ships reported whether they had space for passengers or carried any needed supplies—a custom during planetary crises. The Noma Council, the advisory organization for our planetary system, issued a decree that any ship with passenger holds had to offer space to Diboni evacuees leaving the system. I paused to rub my shoulder, missing the man who knew how to knead the muscles to get the kinks out.

"Check this one out, Ami," Sheya called. I scooted over to the screen. "Cargo ship, recycling transport—room for five passengers."

"Where is its destination?"

"Bara System," she replied. The Bara System neighbored the Nacaen Group in the Outer Systems. From Bara, we could get passage home for Mara.

"That's the one. Put us in." She entered our name and unit number for our quarters into the transport lottery. Passage was not guaranteed, and ships had first right of refusal, but Bara lay in the Outer Systems and would take almost a of travel. Most Diboni hoped to get to the Ramaen System or other close planetary groups. I offered a prayer to Mara's god.

We descended the ramp from the lift to our quarters, but Sheya paused halfway down. "What's going to happen after we get to Bara?"

Shrugging, I avoided her gaze. "I'm sure we'll find passage the rest of the way for Mara." I didn't want to commit to more than that. I said I'd go, and I meant it. For Max. But I couldn't see beyond the days before me, let alone a year. I couldn't imagine going to Max's home without him. I'd get his mother as close as I could, then I'd have to figure out my own life.

Sheya's hands rested on the railing, her brow furrowed.

I frowned. "Do you not want to go?"

My sister-in-law tilted her head, her eyes downcast. "I don't want to leave her. But I can't imagine moving so far away from my family, my home—"

A loud boom clapped through the stairwell. Both of us gripped the railing tight as dust rose around us.

It was happening again. The world was ending.

Sheya's breath came fast.

The lights stopped dancing, and there was no more shaking. "Sheya," I said, "it's okay. Whatever it was, it's passed—"

But it came from the wrong direction—from below.

I took off, leaving Sheya behind, running to our quarters. I pounded on the controls to open the door, where I found Mara rocking in her corner, Sheya's friend next to her. "What was that noise?"

I spun around, bumping my sister-in-law as I rushed out.

A security guard appeared at the end of the corridor. He raised his hand toward me. "Stop!"

I slipped around him. At once dust settled into my nose and throat and I coughed hard. Tearing my jacket off, I used it to cover my mouth, as doors to other cubbyholes opened.

The guard caught up to me. "Go back."

"No. I'm going with you." I held up my badge, tapping next to the veteran's seal. I pleaded with him through my eyes. I had to know what was going on.

Finally, he motioned for me to follow. "Stay behind me."

We made our way through the corridor as the dust cleared, emergency panels still flashing red warning lights along the way. The Dibon Military Guard was in position, in full contamination gear, but their guns were pointed down and they began to remove their masks.

In the light from the headlamps, I made out Vance in

a doorway, his hands raised. "It's just an accident. There's nothing to be alarmed about. Everyone, go back to your assigned quarters."

I waited with the security guard. I figured that with the full military guard here and Captain Vance, no one was going to try anything now, but I needed to know what happened. After several minutes, I removed my jacket, able to breathe again.

The medical examiner brushed past me.

"I can help," I called out, stepping forward, but Vance blocked the door.

"Nothing to see, Ami," he said, his eyes narrowing.

My brows drew together. Lying was against our culture, but even evading the truth was difficult for us to manage. I pushed by. He grabbed my arm, slowing me down, but it was too late.

The door was blown clean out of the frame. A severed arm lay at my feet. Bits of hair and skin were strewn around the room, along with broken furniture and ceiling panels. The medical examiner was bent over the torso of the individual. Bile rose in the back of my throat.

"Who is it?"

"You don't need to know," Vance said as he pushed me back out of the room. "Take her back," he said to the security guard.

"You know who did this."

The captain sighed, crossing his arms before looking me in the eye this time. "The door was completely sealed before it was blown out. Notice how much dust was in the air?"

"Pressure valve malfunction in the ventilation system?"

"Not a malfunction. Intentionally set."

"By whom?"

Vance motioned to the deceased. "People are getting desperate. Not everyone can find hope, being shut in down here and told to wait." He sighed, sliding his hand across his forehead. "Murder. Bombs. Suicide. This all must stop. I don't know how much longer our society can keep going like this, without a purpose greater than survival."

The security guard grabbed my arm, and this time I let him lead me away from the destruction and death.

Vance was right. This had to end.

I needed to get Sheya and Mara the hell off this dead rock.

4

I didn't sleep again that night, and when I was finally drowsy, the doorcomm sounded, a messenger sharing the news we'd won our passage aboard the cargo freighter. At my last rotation on comm, I'd logged on to Dibon's interweb and downloaded the pictures I'd saved: our wedding, Chip and Sheya's wedding, along with photos of my brother and sister. Pausing at the image of my family of origin, I recorded a brief video message.

"Hi, Mom, Dad...I'm leaving Dibon. I'm heading to the Bara System. I'm helping Mara, my mother-in-law, get home. I don't know what will happen after that. I thought you should know..."

I bit the corner of my lip, trying to think of what else to say to my estranged parents. "After all we've been through, I hope you might try to understand." I stopped the recording and saved it to a comm drive, handing it off to a volunteer to transmit. I couldn't leave without trying. I'd never be in the Near Side Systems again.

Wild space. The Outer Systems were settled around the same time the Near Side expanded from the Bylon Cluster when humanity took to space centuries ago, but with collapsing stars and expansive nebulas in the outer arm, civilization never seemed to take hold in the same way. Governments imploded, people continued to move and migrate.

But how was Dibon any different now that a meteor had destroyed our surface?

I returned to our quarters one last time to retrieve Mara and Sheya and the few possessions we had accumulated since the meteor. When I opened the door, Sheya was sitting at Mara's feet, Mara's hand on her shoulder.

"I can't ask you to go with me," Mara said, her hair wrapped in a scarf as many Nacaen women wore in public. "It's too far. I've made the journey once, I can return. It takes over a Diboni year to cross the Galactic Ocean."

Mara's gaze lifted to mine. "You should go back to your families, both of you."

"You can't go by yourself," I said.

Sheya reached for her hand. "It's dangerous. Besides, we made the decision to go together."

"I don't know what awaits when I return," Mara insisted. "There may be nothing left, even with the war over, it may be desolate."

"Nothing's as desolate as Dibon," I reminded her. "We're going with you." I swallowed the lump that threatened to form in my throat. "You're *our* family."

She didn't protest further.

I checked one final time to make sure I had everything important I wanted to take with me. I clipped the small drive with my wedding photos onto a chain, sliding my wedding ring next to it and my old military tags. I'd stopped wearing my ring when I helped in medical, soon after we moved into the bunkers. When I put it back on after assisting in surgery, it felt heavy, foreign. I couldn't wear it without the constant reminder that Max wasn't here anymore.

As I took in the cubbyhole bunker, our apartment for these many weeks, a knot grew in my stomach. My feet froze to the cold metal floor. I was born here on Dibon. My childhood, before the war, was happy. I met Max here.

But Max was gone, my brother and sister long dead, and there was nothing left for me. Only more violence and death. It wasn't until Sheya flipped off the lights that I broke free and left the cubbyhole, following my in-laws through the corridors until we arrived at the far east lift that led to the shuttle bay.

We rode to the lift to the end, where Vance waited for us. A large hanger closer to the surface, it had been converted from an underground holding area for the Buzzards his squad was flying on the day of the strike. I glanced around, but there wasn't a single militarized vessel. Instead, commercial transports and commandeered personal shuttles filled the large hanger. On the surface, our spaceports had comfortable waiting lounges for boarding, but I imagined those were wiped out now. Destroyed. Instead, we stood in line on a steel and concrete floor while soldiers shouted out names for transports under the hangar lights.

"Lehem, I thought I'd offer you one last chance,"

Vance said. "Promotion to lieutenant commander, your choice of post anywhere in Noma or Ramaen Systems."

I tried not to smile, but my mouth twitched up. During the war, Vance saved my life more than once. When I volunteered in comm, the daily stats reported the number of missing or dead from the meteor strike. With the rumors and murders, I knew they needed help —*he* needed help—to restore order and rebuild Dibon below ground. But I slapped him on the shoulder. "Nope. My military days are done."

He hung his head in disappointment, but a grin cracked the surface. "You are the best dusting pilot I've known, Lieutenant Lehem. You'll be missed."

I felt a tug inside me for the old days. Not the days of violence and death as a flight medic—but the early days of basic, and those last days, the war almost over, when we knew we were coming home.

My former commander pulled a comm drive from his back pocket. "This came for you today. Another vet who knew you were leaving let me know." He placed the drive in my open hand, and I stared at it.

Who would've sent me a message?

"You can access it on board," he continued. "These shuttles used to be the luxury first class cabins, remember?"

I snorted. The wealthy flew in these before the meteor, to high-class destinations across the system. Now they were used to travel to the bigger ships—I suppose it's one of the perks when your home planet is destroyed. No one from Dibon was rich anymore.

Vance put his hand on my shoulder, and I thought

he might try to persuade me again, but all that came out was, "Good luck, Ami."

"Gods be with you," I replied.

We thanked our security detail for keeping us safe the last few days, and a guard called out names. "Shuttle *Arnon* passengers, transporting to the cargo ship *Ashkelon*: Allen, Dariah. Allen, Victor. Lehem, Mara, and Lehem, Ami."

I waited for him to call Sheya's name, but he didn't look up from his console. "Show your identification and board."

"There must be some mistake," I said. "You didn't call Sheya Lehem."

"There is only room for four passengers," the guard stated.

"The transmission read five," I declared, trembling. "I saw the transmission myself and she copied it into the transport lottery."

"They took on another crew member and reduced it to four. Sorry." He turned to Sheya. "You are back in the lottery for the next ship."

Sheya turned to me. "Take care of her."

I stared at her, not understanding.

"Go with her. I'll be fine."

I shook my head. "No. You're going, you can't stay here!"

My sister-in-law pulled me aside, her voice hushed. "Go. My family has wanted me home for some time, only I didn't want to leave you and Mara. But I don't know if I can..." She paused, the tears threatening the corners of her eyes. "If I can survive being so far away from them. Let me do this."

I set my hands on her shoulders. "Sheya," I began, but I didn't know what else to say. Instead, I gathered her in my embrace.

Vance stepped closer as Sheya pulled away from my arms. "I don't mean to intrude, but we have a military transport to the Ramaen System leaving this evening. I can take a civilian, if she is next-of-kin to active military. All you have to do is rejoin us now—" he held up his hand to stop my protest "—and then I can grant you leave of absence for a year and discharge. It's just a matter of paperwork."

My hand flew to my heart. "Seriously, you'd do that for me?" I blinked back tears. Vance was a fine captain and a good friend, but this went above and beyond. I'd always looked up to him, and even now he was doing whatever he could to help me and my family.

"Yes. You know I hate to lose you, Ami, but you saved my butt more than once and I owe you one. Let me draw up the papers."

He pulled a tablet from his side, bringing up the files for the terms of service. I signed my name and military ID number, sliding to the next form.

"Full Term of Service?" I frowned. The form indicated nothing about discharge or the length of service, only an emergency leave of absence for up to one year.

"Just a formality," Vance said, scanning the room. "I can't give you a one-year term now on the same day as a one-year leave of absence, but I can give you an LOA now, and after thirty days I will change it to one year of service, so it ends when your leave ends. Then you'll be discharged. Indicate at the bottom who your next-of-kin contact is, and I'll make sure she gets home."

I hated signing my name, but I didn't see another choice to get us all out of here. Besides, in one year, I'd be far across the galaxy when my term was up, and this was just to get my sister-in-law home. I added Sheya Lehem as my next-of-kin and finished the paperwork. He scanned my retina to seal the documents, giving my sister-in-law the right to travel as a civilian on board a military vessel.

Mara had been silent the entire time. She took her daughter-in-law's hand in hers and kissed her on the cheek. "Go in peace."

Sheya smiled through tears. "Peace be with you. I love you."

I drew breath to speak, but Sheya brushed a curl from her face and started first. "You know, when I married Chip, I thought the farmer's life was charming, but I assumed we'd move on after a few months." She wiped her cheeks with her palm. "But then you kept inviting me over in the mornings, and I saw the simple life you and Max had, and I wanted that. You didn't want anything else, just the old worn-down farmhouse and the acres of grain. You were happy."

I breathed out hard, fighting the tears that threatened. "I told Max that Chip would turn your head and get you in the game, and you'd see all we'd dreamed together, all we fought for at the end of the war." I shrugged. "Now there's nothing, except us. But I'm glad you have family to go to."

"*You* are family," she insisted, pulling me into her arms one last time. "I'm so sorry, Ami."

"There's nothing for you to be sorry for," I said. "We'll be all right."

Sheya pulled back, smiling at me one last time, before picking up her bag. Without another glance, my sister-in-law followed the soldier accompanying Vance to a waiting area.

"We'll get her home," he assured me.

I opened my mouth, then swore. "Gods dammit, you always come to the rescue." I couldn't fight the tears any longer as I hugged my old friend. "Thank you."

Vance slapped my back. "Take care of yourself."

I held him tight until the guard by the shuttle tapped his stylus against the console, calling out, "Final boarding for the *Arnon* en route to the *Ashkelon*."

"If there's anything I could do..." I began but didn't know how to finish. I couldn't do anything now. It was time to close the chapter on my life that had shaped me but couldn't give me life any longer.

"One Dibon," he said.

"One Dibon." I saluted my former captain.

Without another look back, I grabbed my bag and took Mara's arm, leading her aboard the *Arnon*.

The shuttle held eight cushioned seats, four on either side, with comm stations and screens at each. The more luxurious shuttles contained private booths, but I guessed the *Arnon* was an officer's transport, based on the armored hull and minimal offerings inside. However, the seats were upholstered with soft leather, a glimpse at life before the ADS failure. I offered the empty window seat to Mara.

"Do you need anything?"

She shook her head before staring back out the window. The comm drive Vance had given me lay pressed in my hand, so I inserted the drive and picked up the earpiece, ignoring the other crew and passengers around us.

A chill shivered down my whole body as my mother's face appeared on the screen. There was no way they would've received my message yet, which meant they had tried to reach me.

On their own.

"Ami, we don't know if you are alive, but we've heard what happened on Dibon. Your father and I—we'd like to invite you to come live with us. I'm sorry we didn't accept you when you married. I hope you understand, it's not easy to see your only living child marry a Twelve..."

I yanked out the drive. I didn't need to hear the rest. Not her prejudices about Twelves and beliefs that refugees caused our problems. I didn't want to relive her hatred and rage directed at me, for marrying a Twelve after the conflict that killed her other children, even though Max and his family had fled from their own ash-dusted war.

A wrinkled hand rested on my shoulder. "Your mother?" Mara asked.

I wiped my face on my palm. "She wants me to come stay with her."

"Ami, look at me. I've lost my husband, my children," she said with stunning clarity, as if somehow the act of leaving had woken her. "Perhaps you and your mother can be mended—maybe you'd find happiness there."

I closed my eyes. "No. There's no happiness there."

The launch bay cleared, the engines firing up. The bay doors opened into the launch shaft, a lock system to protect the ventilation infrastructure below. The bunkers and launch shafts were built during the war to protect those below from attacks above—now, they protected the air ducts from the dirt and dust on the surface.

The shuttle lifted off, and Mara gripped the table. I placed my hand on her shoulder. "Easy. It's all right." I didn't know if she'd flown since they arrived at Dibon, her and the two boys ten years ago. All I knew was her husband perished on the way, and they arrived from Melas with nothing. Max went to work when he was thirteen in a feed supply factory until our war on Dibon began, and then they went into hiding, while renegade Diboni killed refugees.

The bay doors closed beneath us as we continued to rise in the shaft. The doors above cracked open, and the shuttle rocked from the blast of air. Mara gasped. I held her as the thrusters charged the draft.

When we rose above the shaft, my jaw dropped.

"Stardust and ashes."

Though I knew the surface was destroyed, in my head I still pictured blue sky, not yellow dust clouds. The sun wasn't visible—not even as a bright light. The planet's surface had become yellowish gray, littered with debris. Long streaks on the surface showed where the roads once existed, and some shells of tall buildings remained. But if I'd come to Dibon for the first time, I wouldn't have been able to tell if it had been months, or years, or if this planet was destroyed centuries ago, uninhabited and forlorn. The shuttle was pebbled by the debris, like an aluminum can kicked about the rocks.

Somewhere down there, under the rubble, was where Max and Chip died. "Where you go, I will go," I muttered from memory, the ancient wedding vows of the Nacaens. "Where you live, I will live. Where you die, I will die."

But I didn't die.

"I'm sorry," I whispered, to Max, to no one.

My mother-in-law gripped my hand, squeezing hard. "Your people will be my people," she breathed.

"Your God, my God," I answered.

5

The *Ashkelon* had seen better days. The cargo freighter had a large patch on the hull, indicating an attempted break-in at some point in its history. The shadowed blast marks from previous attacks didn't boost my confidence that we'd avoid trouble. Another ship docked at the port airlock—a supply runner with a battered sign reading *Jabbok* on its side. I had to stop searching for faults and flaws on our ship's outside, wondering how it would survive interstellar flight speed, as the *Arnon* prepared to dock with the ship.

The other passengers on board perked up, some of them new crew for the ship. The shuttle rocked as the docking arm from the *Ashkelon* attached. I gritted my teeth at the ear-piercing slide of metal. The pressure seal released, and the artificial gravity and life support on the shuttle adjusted to the cargo freighter—our home for the next eleven months.

When the hatch opened, a stocky, short little man

with light skin like Mara's and a long brown beard entered the shuttle. He gazed up at us from the aisle, his hands clasped behind him. "I'm Captain Titus," he bellowed, his voice much lower than I expected. "Welcome to the *Ashkelon*. Let's get the tour over with, shall we?"

We followed Titus off the *Arnon* into our temporary home. The tight passageways reminded me of military transports. As we shuffled along, memories flew into my mind from years ago, when I was heading up for zero-gravity flight training. Instead of Buzzards lining the flight decks, crates of scrap metal for recycling were tucked against the hull. Crew members from the supply ship slipped through the line, stacking crates on the other side.

"Umph." Someone bumped my shoulder. I rubbed it with my hand, annoyed at the lingering discomfort from when it dislocated.

"Sorry, ma'am."

I frowned as the man touched my arm. "Ma'am" was not a Near Side systems expression. But I'd heard Max say it before to a new neighbor.

"It's okay," I muttered, pulling away from him. He wore an eyepatch, and the left side of his scalp and the skin below his cheekbone were scarred. I tried not to stare. His skin tone was like Mara's pale complexion, but I couldn't tell if he was Nacaen, and I wasn't familiar with the other Outer Systems peoples.

"Everything all right here?" Captain Titus called back, as the line stopped.

"Sorry, Captain," the man called back. "We'll be finished soon." His eye flicked from me to Mara.

"You going across the galaxy?"

"Going home," Mara answered. I shot her a look. I'd hoped to leave trouble behind on Dibon, not bring it with us.

"I hope to get back there someday," he said to her, confirming he was from her home system.

I didn't realize how fast my heart was beating, nervous others would overhear. I didn't like her revealing that she was Nacaen, but of course Mara would recognize someone from her home. It must be comforting to hear familiar speech, having been on a foreign world for so long. Is that how it would be for me, if I went all the way to the Outer Systems? I'd be the foreigner, the refugee.

"Blessed journey, ma'am," he added, before turning away.

"Let's move along," Titus called.

We climbed a ladder from the cargo bay—no one mentioned anything about the accessibility on this ship in the earlier communications. I stepped behind Mara to make sure she didn't fall, and the captain himself stayed at the top of the hatch to help her. Once I climbed through, we followed Titus along another narrow passageway, until he stopped at a small door. An identical door stood opposite.

"Passengers, these are your quarters," he motioned with one hand. "Crew, you're on the other side. Make yourself at home and then come to the dining hall at the end of the corridor."

Mara stepped through the hatch first. I ducked, reminding myself I'd better remember life on military transports, or I'd have a sore head.

"Wait, didn't I pay for private accommodations?" a middle-aged man whined, fists on his hips. He had thin, dusty brown hair, his shiny scalp peeking through. He wasn't a passenger from Dibon, and I didn't recall seeing him on the transport ship, but here the man was, sharing our room.

"Those are the 'semi-private' accommodations you paid for," Titus said from the doorway. "Only four room-mates instead of twelve with the crew. Makes the line for the washroom much shorter."

The capsule room held three racks on either side, enough space to lie down and to store the few belong-ings we brought with us. A divider ran through the middle, with a sink and mirror on either side, and a small closet washroom, one side the toilet, the other the ion shower. Dark steel walls curved up to the ceiling where white track lights ran along either side of the divider.

Mara settled on the lowest rack near the floor. "Oh no, that's mine," the balding man sneered, throwing his bag onto the rack beside my mother-in-law's.

I glared down at him, for he was several centimeters shorter than me. "You're telling me you're going to take the bottom rack from an—"

"—It's fine," Mara interrupted. "I'll take the middle, it's only one step up."

"No." I grabbed him by the collar. The man's eyes went wide, cheeks flushed.

"Ami!" she spat. "That's enough. I'm fine."

I released him and he stumbled, half-falling onto his rack below. I tossed my bag to the top rack. The couple from Dibon claimed the other side, the rack on the bottom replaced with additional equipment. Storage space was at a premium. I retrieved Mara's bag and placed it on the middle rack, the man below squeezing himself against the wall, out of my reach.

I led my mother-in-law along the corridor to the dining hall, which, to my surprise, contained a large old wooden table and farm chairs, with smaller tables and benches pushed up to maximize the space . No wonder the captain didn't call it a galley, it was too homey, too pleasant to be a ship's galley.

Titus beckoned us to take a seat. "As you might've seen, the *Ashkelon* was formerly a military cargo vessel in Liphes sector, but I've tried to make it more comfortable. As hard as this journey will be, we are family aboard this ship. We eat our meals together and we work together, crew and passengers."

We took our places at the table, our bunkmate sitting as far from me as possible. A few crew members sat around us, with Titus at the head of the table. The couple from Dibon—Dariah and Victor—sat on the other side. They both sprouted the thick ebony hair, dark brown eyes and brown skin we Diboni were known for. Next to were two young men, Frederick and Felix, the former a crewmember from Dibon, the latter having a slight accent—from one of our neighboring Noma system planets, I assumed. I didn't catch the name of the other crew members. They appeared to be from all over the galaxy. I recognized the sharp accents of the Tygan System and women with the customary dark tattoos as of the Bylon Cluster; I couldn't tell the systems of origin for the others. Everyone spoke Galactic, but a few whispered in dialects I didn't know.

Those of us from Dibon tucked into the meal, not having eaten meat for weeks. It was saltier than I preferred, but tasty, and I was careful not to overdo it and make myself sick. I glanced at Mara while I chewed. She ate without being coaxed. The ground whatever from whatever planet with whatever seasoning mixed in was a sign our lives had changed.

While we ate, the freighter shifted as the shuttle detached. The movement was subtle, but startling. I needed to get used to it all over again.

"Welcome aboard, everyone," Captain Titus declared again, rising from his seat. "As you can tell, we're not a luxury ship. There's no free passage, even if you paid for it. On my ship, everyone has chores to do. Doesn't matter what planet you're from, or what system. Whether you were a refugee or held political office, on this ship we all work together. We'll be breaking system before morning shift to make our next cargo destination. Like all ships that originate outside of Noma, we run on Bylon Standard for measurement of time. You get used to it pretty quickly—I've never understood how Noma system planets add hours and days for rotations between planets. Much easier with the same number of days in a month.

"When we leave the Near Side to cross to the Outer Systems, there'll be weeks or months between refueling stations, even at interstellar flight speed, what we call IFS. If we end up low on fuel and our solars can't collect enough energy, we may have days of rationing, especially while in IFS."

Power rationing was a familiar term for us refugees, but would take on a new meaning in interstellar space.

Solars were only effective when traveling in a star system, so ships like the Ashkelon banked on them to save fuel while rock-hopping when there wasn't a refueling station, using their battery stores in deep space as a backup for life support.

Our middle-aged bunkmate grumbled under his breath. The captain leaned on the table, his palms digging into the edge. "What's your name?"

"Aaron Peters."

"Well, Aaron Peters, another mumble outta you, and we'll leave you at the next refueling station. The agreement to stay aboard is I give the orders and there's no complaining. You can do that when I'm shipping you out. Anyone else wanna be dropped off?"

I scanned the table. The couple from Dibon stared at their hands folded in their laps. The new crew gawked at each other, but the seasoned members smirked. This must be a common threat from Titus.

"Good. If we don't run into unmarked asteroid fields, collapsing stars, or worse—cartels, a Modes attack, or Stiner scum, it shouldn't be too bad. Those of you who are passengers have posted chore lists. Crew to stations when you're done eating."

"Sorry, Captain," someone called. I peeked up from my plate, startled to see the man with the eyepatch enter the room. He'd changed out of the supply ship uniform and now wore the dark brown jumpsuits I'd seen on other crew.

"That's all right, Perry. I imagined you had goodbyes to give." Titus gazed around the table. "Perry has signed on with us to Jordan Station. He'll be in cargo."

He took a seat next to the captain, seeming just as

hungry as the rest of us from Dibon. I studied his face. The scars were burn marks, and crow's feet lined near his uncovered eye, though his brown wavy hair had no grays as far as I could tell—he was maybe ten years older than me. His good eye caught mine and I averted my gaze, heat rising in my cheeks from embarrassment. I'd seen similar scars from rainfire during the war—but never on civilians. I avoided watching Perry for the rest of the meal. The war was over, and it did no good for me to dwell there.

After dinner, Mara and I reported to the kitchen for the first of our chores. She surprised me by helping with the dishes and cleaning the counters without complaint. I stared at her, puzzled. For all the time she lived with Max and me, the older woman never did anything to help, often staying in her room.

Mara eyed me as she pulled a plate from the ion washer. "You never asked me to help before."

I set a pan aside. "Max told me you needed to rest."

My mother-in-law huffed, rubbing the towel on the plate. "The boys always thought I was so fragile. I was sad, not broken."

I squatted to place the dried pans in the low drawer. "Max told me that you—that you—"

"Had a breakdown? Hmph. If, while fleeing your homeland during a war, your husband is killed and you have two young boys to smuggle aboard ships as you make your way across the galaxy, you'd break down as well."

The chef stared at us from the corner of the kitchen, so I shut my mouth and finished clearing away the dishes, then followed Mara back to our quarters. Aaron was already asleep in the bottom rack. I didn't know what chores Titus assigned him, or how he finish them so quickly.

Mara sat on her rack. "Can you find my hairbrush?" she asked, and I obliged, rummaging through her things in our shared locker space. I handed her the brush, and she combed through her fine, gray hair.

"What else did Max tell you about me?" she asked.

"He told me you had a sharp tongue, that whatever you said you meant it, but sometimes not in the tone I heard it." I fumbled in the locker for my night clothes. "But then you hardly spoke to me, anyway."

She grunted. "Max told me you liked to keep to yourself."

I didn't know how to respond to that.

Once she settled in, I walked back along the corridor to the ladders, taking my night clothes with me. Above me, the next level held the command deck, bridge crew and captain's quarters, off limits to passengers. Below lay the cargo area and docking station. Our deck held the dining hall, kitchen, passenger, and remaining crew quarters. Unless the captain assigned me to cargo for chores, the ship spaces I could access were limited.

Near the ladders was a small alcove with a curved viewscreen, giving me one last look at Dibon. I remembered the first time I saw this view, a fresh recruit with shiny flight pins. The white-tipped mountain ridges, the rippling emerald and amber continental masses, the sapphire oceans, ribbons of rivers and dark veins of old, ancient quartz mines. Even then, the atmosphere was clouded with the dark smoke of explosions, the orange glowing fields burning from rainfire.

Now, there was only chalky yellow dust. No oceans. Nothing resembling the life I knew on the surface. Beyond the arc of the planet lay our two moons, unscathed by the destruction on the planet's surface. Far beyond the moons, out of visual range, lay the asteroid belt, the source of all my pain.

The freighter shifted again, and the supply ship floated into view, firing its thrusters once it was away from the *Ashkelon*. In the distance, more ships arrived, but I knew few came to transport survivors. Most were mining trawlers and cargo haulers.

Voices echoed down the ladder shaft from the command deck. "Thanks for taking me on," Perry said.

"I'd usually say no to last-minute transfers, but your captain is an old friend, and he reminded me that I owed him one," Captain Titus replied. "Said you'd gotten into a bit of trouble."

I froze.

"Yeah, something best left behind. I need to get back home, take care of my family there."

"You're safe here," Titus said as he stepped off the ladder. "Oh, sorry, Mrs. Lehem—didn't mean to disturb you."

"I was just leaving." I stepped back from the viewscreen.

Titus sighed, running his hand over his beard. Perry stood behind him, his eyes on the viewscreen. "It's terrible, isn't it?" the captain lamented. "We heard the news, of course, on the voyage out from Bylon, but seeing it firsthand is something else." He took a step closer to me. "I'm sorry. This was your home."

"Yes." I chewed the inside of my cheek. "You know

my name?"

"'Course I do. It'll take me a while to memorize who everyone is, but I know a Diboni military vet when I see one."

I caught Perry's look of surprise.

Titus motioned to the approaching ships on the view screen. "Mining companies. The dust isn't even settled yet and they're here to make their money. Guess they figure since the surface isn't habitable, why wait."

I remembered my own hesitation to sell the farm only recently. "There's nothing to wait for." I left the viewscreen without another word, turning my back on Dibon.

When I returned to our new quarters, I changed, climbed into my rack, and removed the chain from my neck, inserting the drive into the side console. I swiped through images of Max from when we first met, through our wedding and early days of marriage. I lingered on a close-up of my husband. His sparkling sapphire eyes peeked through the blond locks covering his high forehead. I often swept them away from his face so I could gaze into those eyes, deep set like his mother's. He was laughing with wide cheeks, mouth open, eyes half closed. Touching the screen, I remembered what it was like to touch his face. I couldn't remember if he'd shaved that last morning. Were his cheeks smooth, or rough with stubble?

My own cheeks were damp. I swiped through the next few photos, us riding on tractors, Chip and Sheya's wedding. I stopped at the picture of Max, his hand on my belly. I never noticed how wide my smile can be when I'm happy. We'd announced to family and friends that we were pregnant, and then I miscarried. I fingered my wedding ring on the chain.

I climbed out of the rack, stumbling to the sink to wash my face. The dim lighting of the evening shift revealed a haggard woman I barely recognized in the mirror as I wiped my cheeks. A harder, leaner version of myself than I'd become used to. On the farm, I'd let go of regulations and restrictions, allowed a vision of myself that was freer, more easygoing, ready for marriage and children and farming. That vision was gone.

My hair would be a problem on the long voyage. The ion showers neutralized bacteria and obliterated toxins, but wouldn't do much to clean long hair, no matter the type. The last time I cut my hair short, I was a raw recruit. The med kit I'd stored in my footlocker had scissors. In clumps, my thick, ebony hair fell to the floor as I cut it within a couple centimeters of my skull. I scooped up the remnants, placing them in a spare bag for refuse I found under the sink, for human hair was a commodity on some planets and perhaps I could earn something from it.

Because everything Max and I worked for paid for this voyage, and now, there was nothing left over. I wasn't a flight medic anymore, but I wasn't the smiling woman in the old pictures anymore, either.

I didn't know who I was. I'd have to start over. But I didn't know how to begin—where to even go once I got Mara close to home. Everything I once had been—a sister, a soldier, a farmer, a wife—lay buried in the dust of Dibon.

I'd have to become something new.

6

Mara wailed in her sleep. "Max, your mom is crying. Max?"

I rolled over, but Max wasn't there. Instead, the cold, empty edge of the rack greeted me. But my mother-in-law continued to wail. I swung my legs over and jumped down. "Mara," I whispered, shaking her arm as she cried. "Mara, it's okay, you're on the ship."

"Quiet down, would ya?" Aaron sneered.

I bent over, glaring at him until he jerked the blanket over his head.

My mother-in-law stopped crying. I pulled the blanket to her shoulders, watching the clock on the wall. Thirty minutes until I needed to be in the cargo hold for today's assigned chores.

A month in Bylon Standard time had passed since we left Dibon, a little longer than the month I was used to. Though we adjusted to life on board, Mara often experienced nightmares—I assumed from when she escaped her home during their war. I didn't have them, but almost every morning I woke thinking Max was next to me or had left the bed for a moment. Then I remembered his absence. A stitch had grown in my chest, possibly from helping to move cargo during my chore rotations, but I associated the pain with the loss of Max. Those two months in the bunkers I'd tried to forget he had died, but now I woke every morning knowing it—an unwanted truth.

Captain Titus kept us busy with chores while we made frequent stops among the smaller planetary groups and star clusters. Mara was still working in the kitchen, but he'd switched me to cargo a few days before.

"Going down?" I asked Dariah, referring to the cargo hold as we left our quarters together.

"On kitchen duty. Victor has the cargo shift." She stopped at the ladder as I passed by her to head to the cargo hold. "I heard you're going to the Bara System. Aza Station?"

I hadn't spoken to anyone about our plans yet, except for Perry, the supply ship crew member who bumped into me. Sometimes I talked with Mara about it at mealtimes, but we kept to ourselves for the most part.

"Yeah," I replied, setting my hand on the ladder rung. I hadn't decided yet if I'd go the rest of the way to Melas, Mara's home world. It was a short trip from Aza, but the commitment weighed heavy.

"So are we," she answered. "You're a farmer?"

"Was. Along with..." I swallowed the rest.

"Sorry," Dariah acknowledged. Everyone on the ship knew we were widows from Mara's wailing. "We kept cattle on the eastern plains. I hear the Bara System is thriving now, and they have several moons with biodome farms. Victor's cousin moved out there after the war. You might find work there."

I shrugged. I didn't know what I'd do once we got to Aza, but I didn't want to farm again.

Dariah headed toward the kitchen but I remained on the rung for a moment. She was already focused on what she and Victor would do next. I couldn't get there, couldn't grasp the future yet. There was today. Then tomorrow.

When I arrived in cargo, I startled to see Frederick, a crewmember who joined us from Dibon, ordering Victor to move empty pallets out of the way. Fairly certain he wasn't quite eighteen, I wondered how he managed to scam Titus to get hired on, let alone run cargo. He probably had no choice but to lie, losing his entire family on Dibon.

"Where're you headed?" I asked, as Frederick retrained me on how to use the forklift. We restacked the cargo from our last stop near the edge of a planetary cluster. As soon as the words left my mouth, I bit my lip. Asking the same questions as Dariah. Our Diboni cultural norms taught us to ask about the other person, be honest and forthright when asked questions, show discretion on personal details. Give the other person no reason to distrust you. On board a ship with people from all over the Near Side Systems and I'm still a Diboni, through and through.

"Jordan Station." Frederick answered, pushing his glasses up his nose, then stacked another pallet to the top of the pile. His cropped black hair stood straight.

Victor loaded another stack of empty pallets. "That's the halfway point?" he asked Frederick, as I stepped out of my forklift to pull the lever, securing the top stack of pallets to the steel rings above as he showed me.

"Yeah. The dead planet."

I'd heard of Jordan Station when I was in the service —an orphan left behind in the galaxy's creation, a rock too cold to support life with no star nearby, but with a unique mineral supplying a recyclable power source for the station. For now, it remained the halfway point between the Near Side and the Outer Systems. Almost all intragalactic vessels stopped at Jordan Station, because there was nothing else and nowhere else.

Perry was also headed there. I'd seen him at mealtimes, but he didn't engage us much, and as it was, Mara and I kept to ourselves. He was supposed to be on shift today, but he'd caught a cold during our last stop, which is why Titus switched me to cargo.

"Why Jordan?" I couldn't imagine living in the middle of nowhere.

"Seems like the place for a lonely guy to go. I could've left Dibon as a passenger and waited my turn in the lottery, but there was a crew spot open, so I took it to start earning some money. Captain Titus told me we'd be stopping at Jordan Station, so I looked it up. It's good pay—very few want to stay there—so I figure I'll work a few years, save up, and then move to Oceanya and buy an island and live out my days there."

Victor chuckled. "Isn't that every businessman's dream these days? How long before Oceanya falls into the hands of the Stiners?"

I nodded, thinking of the plethora of other mercenary groups known for taking hostages on luxury liners, and kidnapping wealthy tourists at destination planets.

"Well, a guy can dream, can't he?" Frederick answered, and I chuckled. "What about you? When this is done, will you go back to Dibon, try to see it recover?"

"No." I stacked another tower of crates. "There's no hope there. I don't want to go through it all again, like we did after the war. I can't wait that long."

Victor agreed. "Dariah and I want a new life. There are a lot of biodome moons in Bara looking for workers."

Frederick shrugged. "Well, you could see if Jordan Station works out for you, and then come to Oceanya."

A smile drew across my face. "Sounds like a dream."

"Yeah, hoping I meet the right person there, settle down, you know? Start a family."

Victor grunted. "Aren't you a bit young to be thinking like that?"

He shrugged. "Not too young, when you've lost everyone."

I stopped, my hand resting on the controls. All of us from Dibon had lost everything. Why did I think losing Max was a special case? I coughed, clearing my throat and my mind as Victor took more empty pallets away. "I thought I saw you eyeing that guy—what's his name, Felix? The one who's always joking around."

"Is it that obvious?" Frederick stacked another crate, though I noticed it wobbled a bit. Frederick glanced at it, but the pallets held, so he moved on to the next stack.

"A little bit. But a word of advice..." I began, not wanting to treat him like a child, having had to grow up so fast with the destruction of our planet, but also knowing the young man might be naïve of other cultures, their attitudes and prejudices. "Find out where he's from first and see if he is watching other men the same way." The way Felix dressed, and his taupe skin made me think the crewmember might be from Kir or Jahaz, both in the Noma System—and our social cultures were similar.

Frederick smirked. "Probably right. But thanks for the tip."

"No problem." I couldn't remember the last time I talked like this with someone, about crushes and dating. Maybe when Sheya was engaged to Chip—those conversation topics seemed normal after the war, when we were in a hurry to get back to life. "Hope you find someone in Oceanya. Sounds like a wonderful place to retire."

He stepped off his forklift to pull the lever to secure the pallets as Victor returned. My mind wandered, thinking of where I'd end up. Where would I settle? Or would I ever settle again?

The pallet that wobbled earlier slipped. The steel ring didn't catch.

"Frederick!" I snapped out of my wondering.

He locked eyes on me, puzzled as I leaped from the forklift and he pushed his glasses back up his nose.

Victor shoved him out of the way, but the load collapsed, crushing Victor's skull into the floor.

7

Captain Titus called us into the cargo hold for the funeral. On Dibon we laid the dead out in the temples of the gods, in the caves from our ancestral settlements in the mountains. Our funeral rites were simple and did not require a priest. The *Ashkelon* was too far out to transport him without his body decaying before we reached the next station, so Victor's body would be laid in a waste tube. It felt wrong to leave his body in space this way. No temple, no resting place, only empty space.

I sat with Dariah for hours as she wailed in grief, then into the silence of mourning. Titus asked what we should do for Diboni funeral rites, so with Dariah's permission, I laid out Victor's body, palms up. Keeping busy was my way of coping, even by handling his body. On our planet, the deceased faced the setting sun, but in deep space, I chose the rear cargo hold for the rituals, and planned for the assembly to face that direction for the service. His head was shrouded with a veil as our custom, but also to hide the gruesome disfigurement of his crushed-in face. Though we'd had a mass funeral for all who perished on Dibon, it wasn't the same. No bodies were buried in our mountain temples. We were told that most of the entrances to the temples had caved in during the asteroid collision. Tending to Victor's body gave me a sense of purpose. It had been impossible to care for Max's body, but I could do this for Dariah.

"Can I help?"

I spun around as Perry approached. Titus had left to call the crew and passengers down to the cargo hold. I shook my head. "It's all ready."

"I'm sorry," he muttered.

I wrinkled my brow. "For what?"

He ran his fingers over his shorn scalp. "I should've been there. I'd been training Frederick, and I thought —" his voice cracked. "I thought he could handle it."

"It was an accident. I was right there, watching the crates and I saw them wobble." The guilt hung heavy in my chest. "How is he?"

"Terrible. He blames himself. Said Victor should've let the crates fall on him."

"Dusted ash. It wasn't his fault. It could've happened to any of us."

"No, I should've..." his voice dropped away.

Dariah entered the cargo hold, her face red from weeping. She stared at the makeshift coffin.

"Do you want to see him?" I asked her, my voice almost cracking. "His face is veiled."

She gave a slight nod, and I led her to the waste tube, the front compartment open. "I'd like to be alone for a moment."

"Of course."

Perry followed me away to a corner of the cargo bay. A chill came over me and I hugged my arms. "I should go talk to Frederick, before the service."

"I'll keep an eye on her," Perry said, understanding that I didn't want to leave Dariah completely alone. "He's at the alcove.

I thanked him, leaving the cargo hold and climbing the ladder to the level with our quarters and the viewscreen. Frederick was sitting on a chair, holding his head in his hands. I hesitated. I didn't know what to say to him, to assure him it wasn't his fault, that bad things sometimes happen.

I wondered how mothers told their children about the asteroid that wiped out our planet.

He didn't lift his eyes as I sat next to him. "You know it was an accident."

"I know. Perry said that, too. But it was an accident I caused."

"I didn't check, either," I retorted. "But if Victor hadn't rushed in—"

"—I might've been killed."

I sucked in a breath. I was too young when I joined the Dibon Military Force. Too young to pilot a Kittiwake and understand that every time I fired my weapons, I was killing another Diboni. Too young when I transferred to the mobile med stations. Frederick was too young for this kind of guilt, the kind you carry for the rest of your life.

"I was younger than you when I enlisted in the military. I had to make split-second decisions about targets when I flew Buzzards. Sometimes, at the last minute something felt off, but I fired anyway, because those were my orders." My stomach turned in knots. "Then, when I was a flight medic, I had to make split second decisions as the wounded were brought in, separating out those who could be saved from those who could not. It was impossible, sometimes, to make a right choice."

"How did you get over it?"

I shook my head. "You never really get do. You learn to live with it. We do our best to honor Victor's life by living. By caring for Dariah. By looking out for each other."

"She must hate me."

I sighed. "She's grieving. She's mad at the universe. But she's not mad at you."

He removed his glasses, wiping his nose with the back of his hand. "Because I'm a kid."

"No. Because you're Diboni. Because you know what it's like to lose everything."

The sound of doors opening and feet on the floor was our signal. "The service is about to start," I said, standing. I reached out a hand to his. "Come with me, and chant with us."

Frederick pushed his glasses back on and followed me down the ladder. The crew filed in, and we took our places. I stood beside Dariah, draping my arm over her shoulder as Perry zipped closed the body bag in the tube. Titus addressed the gathering, commending Victor's work on the *Ashkelon*, how it was a tragedy the whole crew would hold in their hearts. But I kept my eyes on Frederick. I understood survivor's guilt all too well.

When Titus finished, I sang the funeral chant to our

gods. Dariah trembled beside me, but I heard the faint refrain echoed by Frederick. Mara approached the casket, wearing her funeral veil and chanting in her own way. After a moment, I added my voice to the Mourner's Prayer of her people, for I heard her recite it every day since Max died. When Mara finished, she turned to Dariah, and set her hand on her shoulder. For a moment, the three of us were still, united by the losses of our husbands.

Titus dismissed the assembly, but I lingered with Dariah. She set her hand on her husband's makeshift casket. "I know we always bury them in the mountains, but it seems fitting to send Victor off into space. I don't believe the heavenly temples are real, you know, or that our gods live in the sky above Dibon." She turned to me. In the Diboni religion, one returns to the temple of their ancestors. "The mountain temples were all destroyed, anyway. Better to send him to the stars."

I didn't know what else to say, so I simply nodded. We stood back as Captain Titus himself shut the waste tube and locked it, saluting as two crew members wheeled it toward the airlock. I joined him in honoring Victor. When the airlock opened to space, even though I couldn't possibly feel anything on this side, something in me let go. There were no temples to bury our dead. In the grand scope of the universe, Victor's body would return to the stars. Max and Chip, buried underneath the dust from the asteroid collision, were now part of the same stardust of the universe. Dust returning to dust.

"Ami, stay for a moment," Titus asked as the crew members left.

I turned to Dariah, but she nodded. "You go. I'm worn out and just want to sleep."

I pursed my lips. I was worried for her. But Mara was in our quarters, and she would not be alone. "I'll see you at dinner."

The captain waited until Dariah had left the cargo hold. "Thank you. I know that couldn't have been easy for you."

I knotted my fingers. "To survive with Dariah, only to die once he left home. It's too much."

"I'd like you to consider becoming part of our crew. I know your destination is the Bara System, but you could stay on. You're a good strong worker. It's good pay and you'd get to see the edge of the galaxy. Your experience in the military, especially as a flight medic, would come in handy. Think about it," the captain added, touching my elbow. "I know you've got the rest of your service to finish out, unless you're able to be discharged."

My chest tightened. "I'm not in the service. I only re-upped temporarily to get my sister-in-law home."

Titus frowned. "That's strange. I thought your paperwork lists you as on a leave of absence for one year."

My palm went to my chest. "Oh. Yes. That will be up by the time we get to Aza, but my length of service is also one year, so I'll be discharged then. My commander couldn't process the term of service on the same day." I hadn't told Titus because I'd forgotten about it. The change wouldn't have gone through until after thirty days, and we were not often in range of a relay satellite for communications. Comms often got disrupted passing through stellar distortions and gas clouds, which we had just traveled through.

"All right. I'll check it out, but in the meantime, think about staying on with my crew."

I returned to my rack, as Titus excused me from the chore list for the rest of the day. Staring at the curved steel ceiling that formed our capsule room, I imagined the small curved tube that Victor floated in, out in dark, empty space.

I raised my hands, palms up, but no prayer came to mind. The gods were silent. As a child I was taught the gods lived in the sky, but the sky rained death on us. The sky opens into space, and it is nothing. Lonely bodies floating in tubes—like Victor, like me.

———

I ROSE AS usual the next morning for my chores, but instead of cargo the captain reassigned me back to kitchen duty. Titus perhaps thought he was being kind —I knew I must keep busy. I stayed with Dariah between meals. She told me about Victor—his childhood, how he had gone to university in Nebo to become an artist before the war. I shared about my childhood in Nebo, my brother and sister who were at the university when it was bombed. Mara sat near us, listening. I wondered how much of my childhood she knew from Max, because I didn't talk about it much once Max and I were married, and she moved in.

After dinner, I cleaned the kitchen along with Mara. Some of the crew remained in the dining hall as we finished. "Go on," I told my mother-in-law. "Check on Dariah. I'll finish up."

"Ami," she began, but she closed her mouth, and

gave a brief nod before leaving me alone. I wiped the counters and stacked the pans, meticulous in polishing the metal counters until they shone spotless.

Laughter echoed into the kitchen, and I leaned out the door. Four of the crew remained there, playing cards. I'd worked with them before, but never held any long conversations.

"Hey, Ami, come join us," Felix called out. His hazel eyes twinkled.

Cori scooted over on the bench. "Sit with me." The thin tanned brunette wore her signature white T-shirt, her coveralls folded over. Cori, like most of the crew, also cut her hair short for the ion showers.

I hesitated for a moment, but this was how the gods answered: they gave new friends. Like I was sixteen again, my first days in the motor pool.

"Deal me in, then," I responded, tossing the kitchen towel over my shoulder. As Felix dealt the cards, I remembered the conversation with Frederick, right before Victor's death. Felix's stringy brown hair fell past his cap, but he had a twinkle in his brown eyes. I could see why Frederick liked him; he had an easygoing manner. I glanced around the room. Frederick hadn't stayed after dinner, or I would have invited him to join us.

"You've played Flashjack before?" Leonard asked, scratching his golden-brown scalp as I sat on the bench. His head was shaved, and he sat next to the dealer, across from us.

"Is that the Kir version of Bumperjack?" I asked.

"Yup," Felix answered as he dealt three cards to me.

"What's the ante?"

"Not allowed to gamble, per Captain Titus," Bricks responded stiffly, from the other side of Cori. The big guy was taller than me, with large blue eyes and bleached hair.

"Yeah, but what are you playing for?"

Felix jutted his chin out, and Cori burst out laughing. "How come you didn't join us sooner, Pinion?" the card dealer asked.

Pinion: a wing, or if one came from Dibon or other planets of the Noma System, our term for a fighter pilot.

"That obvious, huh?"

"We ain't allowed to gamble, but we do play to get out of septic duty when the time comes," the bald man answered.

"I was a Pinion too, on Kir," Felix added. "Retired a couple years."

"Three." I held up three fingers—both for the years retired, and the cards I wanted.

"I'm sorry about Victor," the Pinion offered as he passed the cards to me. "Dusted luck, I guess."

I wanted to say thanks, but instead, I swallowed my response.

"Always hard to lose a passenger on board," Cori added. "Titus said the kid forgot to secure the last stack."

I stared at the cards in my hand, but I couldn't recall the suits or the numbers. All I could see was Frederick, laughing with him as the pallet wobbled. I should've warned him. I should've told him to restack it before attempting to secure the next one, even though I knew he saw it, too.

And Victor paid the price.

"Ami?" Felix asked.

I shook my head no, turning over my cards to fold. I didn't know if I held a good hand or not, I couldn't think. Even if Perry thought he should've been there, I *was* there, and it still happened. Victor died.

Frederick might be too young for survivor's guilt, but I sure as heck wasn't.

"She needs a drink," Bricks offered, and Cori reached over to pour liquid from an aluminum canteen into a mug.

"What is it?" I asked, sniffing, and my eyes watered. It had a pungent, smoky scent. The liquid was clear, but the edges had a rusted tinge. My stomach churned as I imagined what it would do to the insides of my digestive tract.

"Felix's magic potion," she offered with a wink. "Don't ask, just drink."

I tossed back the shot and my throat burned. Coughing, I wiped my wet eyes on the back of my hand.

"Thatta girl," Cori laughed, patting my back as Leonard poured himself a shot.

I hadn't had a drink in over a year. After our first year trying to get pregnant, and then the miscarriage, our doctor recommended a clean diet. She suggested I might have problems because of the war and the toxic chemicals that were used. Giving up all alcohol, I drank herbal tea every day. Max did the same.

But Max was gone, our dreams of children gone, and I needed an escape. Victor was only the most recent in the string of losses.

I drank shots of Felix's horrid drink and played lousy hands of cards for over an hour while my throat burned, and I numbed the pain. I didn't win. Bricks lost out on the last draw.

"You all been with Titus long?" I asked, changing the subject from the big man's long, drawn out complaining about being on septic duty.

"Yeah," Cori replied. "The pay is good despite the semi-dangerous cargo," she teased, a smile spreading in her full red lips.

Despite being buzzed, I caught on to her lure. "What kind of dangerous cargo? How in the universe is recycling dangerous?"

"You think that's all we ship?" Leonard asked.

"Gods dust-and-ashes, Leonard," my fellow pilot hissed, slapping his palm on the table.

"She was gonna figure it out anyway."

I lowered my voice. "So, we—the passengers—are here to make it seem a legitimate operation?" I leaned in closer. "What is it? Drugs? Weapons? Money?"

"People," Bricks responded. The others stared at him, his large frame looming over us. "What? It's not like she wouldn't figure it out. Titus already offered her a job."

Felix whistled. "That's a record. Old man doesn't trust easily."

I gulped. "Anyone right now?" I asked Bricks.

"Classified," the big man answered. "But in the past, they've had the look of your Mara."

"Captain doesn't let us know," the Pinion added.

Refugees. Dibon was the only planet in the Noma System that accepted refugees from the Nacaens. All the rest had barred refugees from the Twelve, and the Ramaens would only accept refugees from other worlds who could afford their exorbitant resettlement fees. Some ports wouldn't even allow ships who had refugees on board as passengers without proof they would be accepted at their destination, and when Dibon entered its civil war, there was nowhere to go.

Was the ship my mother-in-law and Max came on anything like this? And who were the refugees this time?

8

I rolled over to touch his shoulder, and found his space in the bed, empty. I remembered I was on a ship, not in our flattened home, and Max was dead. My head felt like a crate crushed in my skull.

Mara sat on the floor, holding her prayer book. As she prayed, I watched her through squinted eyes, the pressure deep in my temples.

A question that had been on my lips for weeks breached the surface. "Do you really believe there is only one God, Mara?"

She broke her prayer to glance at me, annoyed. I didn't mean to say it out loud, but once I did, I propped myself up on one elbow, staring down at her.

"There is but one God, Creator of the Universe, blessed is God's name."

"I was always taught each world had their own god, and sometimes other gods below them. Sometimes our gods are the same on other worlds, but with different names. Why would your God be the God of the universe? Why not Dibon's gods, or Kir's god, or..."

"But you do not believe in your gods, or any god."

Shivering, I drew the blanket over my body. "I wouldn't say that, I—"

"You didn't pray after Max died."

"Of course I did. I said the Mourner's Prayer with you."

"But you haven't recited it since, except at the funeral. You don't pray as the other Diboni do, every night."

She was right. I'd heard Dariah and Victor pray in the evening, and Dariah had continued, even with Victor dead.

I tore the blanket from my body, jumping down from the rack. "You don't know what I do, or what I believe."

"No, because you don't tell me."

I folded my arms across my chest. "Look who's talking. Or rather, look who didn't say anything for months. Years."

I slammed the door shut to the ion shower, unable to hear her retort. I yanked my clothes off, hitting the settings to cleanse me and wake me up, the pounding in my head turning to a dull ache. Two minutes later, I opened the door. She was gone. As I dressed, Aaron opened his sleeping rack by the floor while I pulled on my shirt.

"Sorry," he muttered, smirking as he saw me half-naked. I rolled my eyes, and almost stepped on his fingers.

"What's your problem?" the balding man demanded.

"What's with you? You've been an ash-head since we came on board!"

"And you've been wound up as tight as a jackscrew. Lighten up. The ship doesn't revolve around you and your feelings."

"Oh, go dust yourself."

I fled our capsule room, angry at Aaron, and still upset at Mara. Not wanting to see her in the kitchen yet, I lingered by the viewscreen near the ladders. I wasn't angry at my mother-in-law over our differences in theology, I just didn't know how to live with her. For the thousandth time, I wished Max was alive.

Perry climbed the ladder from cargo. "Are you okay?" His brow furrowed.

"I'm *fine*."

"You don't sound fine."

I threw my hands in the air. "We've just been cooped up too long, that's all."

He tilted his head, frowning. "Us? As in, the crew, or..."

"Never mind." I passed by him.

"Ami," he called. "I know it's none of my business, but if you want someone to talk to..." He cleared his throat. "I know you've been through a lot."

I drew in a breath. "Thanks."

I kept my eyes on him longer than I should—I didn't want him to think I was staring at his scars, but it was the softness, the kindness in his eye that almost broke me. Almost made me tell him about Max, my parents, all I had left behind on Dibon. How Frederick was the same age as I was when the war neared its end, having to live with what happened, and how I could never escape the war within. Of all the people on this ship, something in my gut said he'd listen, instead of judging like Mara.

"Passenger Lehem, Ami. Passenger Lehem, Ami, please report to a comm station," a voice called over the shipwide.

I pressed the blue button on the wall panel. "This is Ami Lehem."

"Captain Titus is overriding your chore list today and requests your presence on the bridge."

"I gotta—" I began, but Perry was already gone.

As I climbed up the ladder to the command deck, I shivered. We left the last refueling station two weeks ago, when we picked up the cargo that Frederick and I had stacked. Now, we traveled in the intragalactic space between the Near Side and Outer Systems, and to reserve power, the heat was cut back, and lighting reduced in the corridors.

When I entered the bridge, I blinked, making sure what I saw was real. The view screens showed nothing. Only darkness remained—the absence of light, the nothing that absorbs everything in interstellar space between star clusters. Clouds of gas and dust hung thick in this space, hiding starlight from view.

"Amazing, isn't it?" Titus remarked. I couldn't tear my gaze from the screens. "The Galactic Ocean."

"How long until we reach Jordan Station?" I asked, breaking my silence.

"Searching for Jordan Station is like looking for a coin you dropped in the sea," the captain answered, standing. "It's out there, but difficult to find. Signals get disrupted in that mess and ships sometimes veer way off course. It's about luck and hoping your calculations are correct when you begin to cross. Look out there," he motioned. "A whole lotta nothing. But far across there is the light of other stars. Taking in the factor of the speed of light, the spinning nature of our galaxy and the expansion of the universe and our interstellar flight speed, we make our best guess as to where that island is."

He gazed sideways at me, folding his arms across his chest. "There's a lot of distortion in there, too—no one can really say why, as you can't see much, but for the first billion kilometers or so, comms are useless. Once we're in far enough, we will latch on to old public comm transmissions and use them to map our way in IFS."

"How in the universe was it ever found to begin with?"

His brow furrowed. "No one can remember, but the myth is that a single family once traveled this part of the galaxy by themselves. Parents and grandparents and children, they were the lone survivors of a collapsing star and landed there. Rumor is they cloned themselves to survive. Now, they're the only place to stop on the way across the Galactic Ocean. The metal found inside the planet is unique. With the right pressure it releases energy, and the waste solidifies and renews its energy potential. That first ship was scrapped, and its parts used to make their synthetic food printers and power their oxygen cells."

Titus faced me. "Of course, that's just a story. We don't know. But it became a mining operation and an island in the middle of nowhere. To go around the Galactic Ocean takes years."

He motioned to the control panel. "I want you to learn the piloting controls as part of your chore rotation. Roger is our backup pilot, but he's been sick off and on. Gene here will instruct you on the basics."

Titus kept a minimal command deck crew: comm officer Natalie, Gene, one of the pilots, and the chief engineer who wasn't on the bridge now. Roger was on his sleep shift. They all wore the drab gray bridge crew uniforms. I'd met Natalie before, and she was busy at the comm station. Her hair appeared the color of the grain we grew back on Dibon, shaved close to her head, and her skin was even paler than Mara's.

Gene grabbed a second chair, pulling it over to the panel. He was at least twice my age, his dark hair streaked with gray. "You're a pilot?"

I didn't know whether to nod or shake my head. "I flew Kittiwake Fighters for Dibon."

The older pilot smirked. "Sounds like fun. Of course, an interstellar cargo ship is nothing like a fighter." Gene must've run into his fair share of hotheaded Pinions.

"I know." I shivered with the cold and the anticipation. I didn't want to blow this. I needed this change. Taking the chair next to his, I pointed to the crimson-colored gauge. "That's the power level?"

"No, that's the fuel cells. This is the power level." He pointed to the aquamarine instrument. I was certain it once had been a different shade of green but discolored over time. Along with the faded panel edges and rust spots, I spied burn marks from an old electrical fire and evidence of corrosion. The control panel needed to be replaced. Titus was a patch-and-go captain—I guessed it'd have to completely short out for him to consider installing a new one.

As Gene finished going over the panels, I had a hard time remembering and keeping it all straight. The gauges were in opposite spots on a Kittiwake and used opposite colors. Forward thrusters were the only thing that seemed the same.

I racked my brain for questions, trying not to sound as clueless as I felt. "Shields?"

"That's the job of the chief engineer," a stern voice called from behind me.

Spinning around, I lifted my eyes to the woman at the engineering station. "I'm sorry, I didn't catch your name?"

"Esmie," she responded. The engineer stood taller than me, almost two meters. Her gray hair was pulled back in a bun, uniform pressed, her light blue eyes stern. She commanded respect in her firm handshake. "Engineering station controls shields and all life support, as well as monitoring power levels."

"Weapons?" I asked.

Titus sighed. "We have proton rifles mounted, accessible at my chair. Originally this ship had decent firepower in the Liphes sector, but now that we're a commercial vessel, we get what we get according to Interplanetary Law."

"I saw the blast shadows, looks like you've taken combatant fire before."

The captain nodded. "Unfortunately, yes. I upgraded the shields after that. Also reinforced the hull, which you saw when you boarded."

Gene went over the pilot's controls again, this time

more patient as I asked questions, until he let me take the conn. "Watch your stabilizer," the older pilot warned. As I checked the gauge for ship's stability, the engine lurched.

I grabbed the control panel to steady myself, almost falling out of my chair. "Watch your thrusters!" the engineer shouted at me. My elbow caught the edge of the throttle, and there was a rush of sudden speed. Gene grabbed the thrusters, pulling the ship back.

"Gods dust it!" I swore.

How did I mess it up this bad? My first chance on the bridge, and I'd blown it.

Titus' hands drew over his face. He hadn't moved an inch, not even swayed from where he stood when I bumped the throttle. A burst of laughter escaped, his cheeks bright red. "You'll get the hang of it, I promise," the short man said between chuckles.

The pilot shook his head, but as I left the bridge, Esmie joined me at the hatch. "You know Gene did that on purpose."

"What?"

"The throttle—it's usually on automatic pilot. He must've connected the manual override when you weren't looking."

"Hazing?" I raised an eyebrow.

Her eyes gleamed. "You'll make it just fine."

9

"**N**ow that you're being trained for deck crew, you won't want to hang out with us cargo and engineering mutts," Felix teased.

"I had one day of training. Besides, I'm back on cargo rotation tomorrow." I swallowed the shot fast, my whole chest burning. No matter how many times I checked the chains, I would never feel safe working there again. But it had to be done. I didn't want special treatment. Titus had moved Dariah off cargo rotation permanently, which was fine by her. She'd returned to kitchen duty, often paired with Mara. Sometimes, hanging in the dining room, I'd catch a glimpse of them talking as one passed a dish to another. An ache grew in my chest. I didn't understand why Dariah could connect to Mara in a way I never could.

I scanned the dining hall. Perry never hung out with us, often arriving at mealtimes when we were leaving. I worried for him, that somehow the guilt of what happened to Victor was weighing on him more than me.

"Felix is just jealous," Cori said as she shuffled cards, bringing me back to the conversation. "He's been dying to get to know Natalie since she was hired on last season."

"Despite the fact she's told you she's ace and not interested in six different languages?" Leonard added. Frederick snorted his drink. I'd made sure he was invited to dinner with us. I slapped his back to help him recover, and also to reassure him. He still had a crush on Felix.

"Hey, a guy can dream," Felix teased, winking at Cori, but the short-haired girl was still laughing with Leonard. The pilot cleared his throat. "I said, 'hey, a guy—'"

A blaring alarm echoed throughout the room. Red lights flashed near the entrance hatch to the dining hall, and we all stood at once. "Alert stations. This is not a drill," Natalie's voice echoed, her voice as flat as all of her other announcements, calm, without emotion. "Repeat: this is not a drill. Alert stations."

The burning in my chest hardened as a lump in my throat. For a moment, I was back on the flight deck with Vance, klaxons blaring, waiting for my orders. I blinked, and I was on the *Ashkelon*. A passenger, not crew. Watching the others scramble from the dining hall, they headed to their assigned placements during emergencies, even Frederick. I had no assignment. Passengers were to return to quarters.

"Mara," I called, opening the door. She sat on her rack, legs dangling over the edge, eyes wide. "Mara, it's okay."

She trembled, but her eyes met mine as I took her

hands. I know the Dahan custom was not to hold hands in prayer, but it was on Dibon. Dariah joined us from the other side of our quarters, moving to sit beside Mara.

"Pray with me," Mara pleaded.

I bowed my head, chanting with her while the metal screeched along the hull, the proton rifles sliding into place, the ship preparing for defensive action. I don't know if prayers are answered, but the chanting gave me something to do, helped steady my heart that wanted to leap out of my chest. I became aware of another voice joining in, of Dariah's soft soprano. Mara must have taught her recently.

"This is the captain," Titus announced, interrupting our prayer. "Looks like we missed the action, but we're taking precautions."

"What does that mean?" Aaron asked. I hadn't noticed him when I came in, curled into a ball in the corner of his rack. Did he ever leave the room? He never seemed to be on any chore rotation with anyone.

"Probably came upon some space junk, maybe traces of explosive residue," I tried to assure him. "Hopefully, whoever started it has moved on." I didn't tell him that the proton rifles on the *Ashkelon* were at least twenty years old, and if it were the Modes, they'd hack the ship's ancient systems, take our targeting computers down, and we'd be a sitting duck. Instead, I rejoined Mara in her chanting.

After a few minutes, the alarm silenced, though the red lights still flashed. My mother-in-law raised her head, finishing the prayer. I squeezed her fingers. The tension from our conversation in the morning faded.

"Aaron, it's okay." I surprised myself in feeling pity for him.

"Lehem, come up to the bridge," Titus ordered over the comm. I frowned.

"Why you?" Aaron questioned.

"They started training me earlier today on bridge duties, maybe he wants me to learn something from this?"

"But it's over now, right?"

I shrugged. "I think so." But neither Titus nor Natalie had given the all-clear, only the sound of the alarm shut off. Fear crawled across my chest. *What was out there?*

When I left our quarters, there were no other crew in the corridors, they were still at alert stations. I climbed the ladder to the command deck, entering the bridge.

"Take a look at this," the captain motioned to an object on the viewscreen. I stepped closer, and my hand went to my heart as the image magnified.

The large, empty solar panels were like wings with all the feathers torn off. As the wreckage rotated, the panels on one side wrapped around the length of a white fuselage. The wings and tail stabilizers were missing, torn from its body, along with the cockpit. But I recognized the remains of the Kittiwake Fighter as if it were whole.

I gripped the console, my head swimming. This wasn't possible. This had to be a hallucination. Sweat gathered along my brow.

"That answers one question," Titus said. "But how

did it get out here, in the middle of nowhere, and what happened to the distress signal we followed?"

"It disappeared, Captain," Natalie responded, her voice steady, as if the sight of a ghost ship and satellite which caused the death of millions was just another ordinary day on the job. "I doubt the signal came from the fighter, it's too damaged. The unmanned satellite wouldn't have had a distress beacon. Sir, it came from somewhere else."

The debris rotated, still in motion in the vacuum of space, and the letters I knew were stamped on the rear of the satellite came into view.

ADS.

"Do we have comm connection right now?" I asked Titus.

"We're in the dead zone. And besides, this is the kind of thing you want to send on private, and there are no comm satellites until Jordan."

"Scanners are not showing any other ships, Captain," Esmie answered, her face grave. "If there was someone else, they disappeared without a trace. I can't find a drive signature."

"We weren't hearing things. Find out where that signal came from before we do anything." Titus hit the comm button next to his chair. "Crew, remain at alert stations for now."

"We should take it to Jordan with us," I said.

Titus frowned. "We don't know who or what did that. Nothing comes on board my ship that was involved in a planetary disaster."

"But we can't just leave it here."

The captain sighed. "We can tag it with a tracking

beacon. When we get to Jordan, you can send a message. But that's it. We're getting the hell outta here."

"But this is evidence—"

"Evidence that could incriminate me or my crew or any of us on here. I'm not touching it, not having it on my ship. That's an order."

Titus' words bounced in my brain. *Incriminate my crew or any of us on here.* Who?

Natalie motioned for me to take a seat at her station, where she uploaded the images. "You can record a message here and as soon as we're in range to encrypt it, I'll send it."

While Esmie launched the tracking beacon, I recorded my message.

"Captain Vance, I didn't expect to be contacting you, but we found this out in the Galactic Ocean. We've no idea how these remains traveled this far. If they were towed, we didn't find the other ship. There was a distress signal, but it stopped as we arrived, and we were unable to trace it. The captain of the *Ashkelon* didn't want to tamper with the evidence, so we've set a tracking beacon for you to find it."

My mind replayed every possible scenario. A thruster misfire launching a fighter patrol into the ADS. A suicidal pilot. An enemy combatant. If it was the latter, then who? In the middle of the Galactic Ocean, with no other ships around, no drive signatures—what happened to the distress call?

I bit my bottom lip before finishing the message. "By the way, on my paperwork, it says I'm in service but on LOA, and I just want to make sure the term of service was changed so I'll be discharged at the end. Lehem out."

———

ONCE WE WERE on our way, the captain cancelled the action alert. I went to check on Mara, but Perry was just returning to the crew quarters. "What was it?"

I sighed, scratching my arm. "You won't believe it, but the wreckage of an ADS satellite."

His eye opened wide. "From Dibon?"

I nodded.

"Are we salvaging it?"

"Captain doesn't want to have anything to do with the evidence, I guess. We left a tracking beacon."

Perry frowned. "Ami," his voice quiet as he scanned the hall. He leaned in closer to me. "When I was with the suppliers—we heard rumors about the Dibon military covering up the investigation—"

"I'm Dibon military, you know. Retired."

"I know, I'm just saying, we know how the Twelve always get blamed for things. They're trying to pin the incident on the refugees."

"Diboni don't lie," I insisted.

He rolled his eyes. "Covering up is a loophole for a people who don't lie."

I folded my arms. We might avoid the truth but outright lying was taboo in my culture. "It's not the military," I insisted. "They're still investigating, trying to get to the bottom of it. I heard enough rumors in the bunkers." I thought about my parents, who hated Nacaens and all foreigners. The stories I heard at comm. Those who blamed Ramaens. I thought of my sister-in-law, and hoped she was safe at home by now.

"We ought to bring the wreck on board."

"I agree, but Captain gave his order. Natalie has pictures. We're turning it over to the authorities when we get to Jordan."

"What authorities?"

Something in Perry's tone, the squint of his eye, twisted a knot in my stomach. He'd come on board to escape some trouble, right when the investigation was still being conducted on Dibon, right when rumors were flying and Nacaens were murdered and others arrested.

But Perry had worked for the supply ship. He hadn't come from the bunkers. He wasn't there.

"It's in Titus' hands," I said.

"Okay."

He didn't press for more, but I grabbed his arm as he turned to leave. "Don't say anything about this to anyone. It's terrible enough as it is, I don't want anyone speculating that it was an insider job, or Nacaens, or anyone. Let the truth come to be."

I stared into his good eye as I let go. Even though I counted Cori and the card-playing crew among my friends now, there was something about Perry that drew me to him. And that could be dangerous if he were hiding something.

10

We reached Jordan Station five months into our journey. Natalie began to track comm transmissions while Titus adjusted our course based on the signals, helping guide us to the island in the ocean. As comm traffic picked up, we slowed from interstellar flight speed, on occasion spying lights from passing freighters.

However, it wasn't until we were almost upon the planet—in the gravitational pull—that we saw it. The same fuel mined from the planet powered everything at Jordan, but with no star to light the surface, it lay in perpetual night. Metallic fuel lamps dotted the sphere, blinking through all the ships in orbit. We docked at an arm, a conduit ten centimeters thick, connected to supply ships and to lower orbit satellites, in an organization of connecting conduits to the planet's surface hundreds of miles below. Like becoming tangled in a spider's web in the middle of the night.

From the web, a resupply ship docked off the cargo

hold. "Here is the catalog of amenities," Titus announced, handing us all a tablet from the ship's concierge. I touched the screen and saw all the options available at Jordan Station's connecting ships in orbit—and the costs. Getting down to the surface of Jordan itself was more money than I had left over after booking Mara and I passage on the *Ashkelon*. I'd have to stick to the ships in orbit for lower prices.

"You know there's a resort casino on the surface? We can't gamble of course, but they have an artificial atmosphere with blue sky. Blue sky!" Cori repeated, then sighed. "I'd just love to sit at the pool sipping some amazing drink and looking up with sunglasses on."

"Yeah, but look at the cost," I pointed out. "No one has that kind of money."

"What about him?" she jerked her head toward Aaron.

"Maybe, but I doubt it." I couldn't imagine him having that much cash after paying for the journey. The self-absorbed passenger wouldn't be on the *Ashkelon* if he did.

In the web of docking conduits sat other ships, abandoned, or repurposed. Shops, spas, and bars—lots of bars and clubs. They were all listed on the tablet along with prices. My mouth watered at the idea of imported cheese and savory synthetic protein—even synthetic protein with new flavors appealed to my palate after five months.

"Take advantage of the down time; you've earned it. But all the ship rules apply: no fights, no gambling, no criminal activity. Jordan Station has its own security here and punishments are more severe than they are in the Interplanetary Alliance. Now, the resupply ship has showers with water. Who wants to go first?"

All hands—crew and passengers—raised.

Frederick approached, towing his bags. "Well, it's time for me to say goodbye. Gotta go find a job."

I opened my arms and Frederick squeezed me back. "Good luck to you."

He pulled away, smiling as he adjusted his glasses. "I'm just hoping I can make enough to get to Oceanya sooner rather than later. Then, I'll invite everyone from the *Ashkelon* for shore leave."

"Deal," I said, smiling back.

Right at that moment, Dariah approached. "Swift travels."

"May the temple welcome us all home when it is our time," he replied.

Frederick turned to Cori and Leonard to give his farewells. "Are you going off ship for a while?" I asked Dariah.

"I can't wait. You know, in the mornings when I wake up..."

"It's like he's still there," I finished for her. "Have you thought about going on another ship?"

She shook her head. "I'm okay. It's not the ship, it's everything we lost and left behind. I'm going to continue to the Bara system on the *Ashkelon*. Victor's cousin is expecting us. I'm sending her a message if they can get a comm signal through. But right now, I'm gonna get a real shower since Titus is waving me through. Because one thing that is this ship's fault is not having a proper shower."

We both laughed. It was so good to laugh, to hear

the lightness in her voice. A tone I had missed in my own for a long time. Titus motioned to Dariah, and she followed Frederick through the airlock off ship.

Cori elbowed me. "Looks like your friend is really going."

At first, I thought she still meant Frederick, but I followed her gaze, finding Perry chatting with Titus while the rest planned their shore leave. His bag was slung over his shoulder.

I frowned. "You're leaving?"

Perry raised his brows. "Yeah. I only signed on as extra cargo crew to get here."

I nodded, hugging my elbows. Somehow, I thought he might decide to go on to Aza—or even go on to the Nacaen Group and help get Mara the rest of the way home. I hadn't told her yet that I thought of staying on with Captain Titus. At the very least, I'd hoped maybe Perry and I would get to spend some time together on shore leave, as there wasn't much privacy aboard the *Ashkelon*. My doubts about him had faded since the encounter of the wreckage. He'd been kind, helpful to Mara in the kitchen, and even joined Cori and me for cards a few times, when the other guys weren't there.

"I have some business to take care of here," he added. "I hope you have a good rest of your journey."

"We're going to be here for a few days—surely you could join us for a drink?" I asked, my heart beating a little faster. I meant to say *me*, but the word wouldn't come out. An image of Max flashed in my head, and I swallowed hard.

It didn't seem that long ago, but it was half the galaxy away.

"I doubt I'll have time," he said, shifting his gaze.

Though I still didn't know him as well as I knew Cori and the others, I opened my arms and hugged him, saying "Blessed journey," the Nacaen farewell. My feelings of mistrust earlier in the voyage now seemed misguided. He'd been reaching out as a friend, and I'd missed the chance.

His hand came around my back, holding me. Surprised, I found he didn't smell like the rest of the cargo crew from dust and metallic grime—more like sweet grass, a scent I'd missed. "Blessed journey," he whispered back as he let go. I gazed after him as he left the ship. Perhaps it was for the best to say goodbye now. My heart wasn't in the right place.

I made my way back over to Cori to make plans for our shore leave, but after, when I found Mara, she shook her head. "Don't go," she begged. "Stay here. I don't like this place."

"Why?" The likelihood she'd passed through here when she escaped to Dibon had crossed my mind.

"It's dangerous." Her eyes locked on mine. "There are thieves, bounty hunters, murderers—all sorts of people looking to take advantage of simple passengers."

"I'm former military," I reminded her. "I do know how to take care of myself!"

"I know you do..." Her voice trailed off. I longed to get off the ship after five months, but I couldn't leave her alone.

Captain Titus motioned for me to go. "I'll keep an eye on her. I don't leave the ship. Ever."

"What about the message to Dibon?"

"It's already sent," Natalie said, her bag in hand,

ready for shore leave like the rest. "Might take more than a day or two to relay across the ocean."

I glanced at Mara one more time, but Titus waved me off. "Go let loose, Ami. You need it."

Letting loose for me meant ten minutes in a shower using recycled water and old-fashioned soap. I emerged refreshed, reborn. From the supply ship, I boarded a transport to the communications hub, where I scanned the newsfeeds. Besides news from the initial impact, there was no more information. I couldn't find anything about Dibon's surface destruction. I found one headline on the Nacaen Group, that tensions had broken out again among Rebels on Nidos. The major story was on a truce declared between Airysa and the Tygan Systems, a war going on for decades. Dibon was old news now, forgotten.

I left the comm hub, distressed at the lack of information. For one moment, I thought about heading back to the *Ashkelon* and waiting until Vance's reply came through. But that might be days. Instead, to kill time, I explored the nearby decommissioned ships in our part of the web, each one offering different services. One hawked wares from around the galaxy for exorbitant prices. Another ran a spa. I spotted Leonard in line to receive a massage, but I needed to save what resources I could for the end of my journey, to make sure Mara got home.

When I rounded the corner in the connecting tube between a decommissioned passenger transport and old cruise liner, the flashing hologram signs of the luxuries available on Jordan hung shadows on me like a veil.

I ran into Bricks and Felix at the bar on a nearby

vessel, where they were on their fourth or fifth round. Shore leave routine was familiar to me—soldiers getting drunk and spending what they'd earned on passing pleasures. A stage lay to one side of the room where Cori listened to some old crooner, but I joined the guys, pulling up a stool and ordering Ramaen whiskey. I stopped drinking Felix's concoction when my urine changed color, but here they presented a bottle with the Ramaen seal.

"There she is," my fellow Pinion said. "Any news from Dibon?"

I shook my head. "Natalie sent the message, but it might take days."

"Do you think it was an inside job?"

Staring at the empty shot glass in front of Felix, I wasn't sure how to answer. "I don't want to believe that. Seeing the wreckage..." I trailed off. I didn't want to think about it right now. It was in Vance's hands.

"What made you retire?" he asked, changing the subject.

I shrugged. "I was done with war, done with fighting." And I met Max and fell in love, but that was our story, and it didn't belong to anyone else.

"You know there were two regiments from Kir that came to Dibon to fight against the Renegades?"

"I remember. Were you part of them?"

"Nah. I served on base at Kir. But I knew some guys who did." Felix threw back his shot.

Bricks came back from the bar with our drinks. "Here's to halfway to the other side," he offered, raising his glass, and we toasted.

"So, what's your plan, when this is over?" Bricks asked me, as Felix belched.

"Getting to the Bara System, then helping Mara get to the Nacaen Group."

The big man's eyes grew wide. "Ah, the Twelve. You know their story?"

"What's with them? They're always involved in some war or skirmish, every time I hear about them," Felix asked.

I tossed back the shot. The whiskey went down smooth, unlike Felix's horrible potion. "The Twelve were from another system, long ago, with twelve planets, but they were enslaved by Pyga."

The Pinion jerked his head back. "Like, the Pyga of all the horror stories my brothers told me?"

Bricks laughed as I chuckled. "I know, I didn't believe it at first, but Max told me the story—"

"Who's Max?" Felix asked.

I choked. Though we were half a galaxy away and many months since the ADS failure, my mind still slipped at times, forgetting Max wasn't here.

"Max is—Max was my husband. He died on Dibon. Anyway," I continued, not wanting to dwell on him, or what happened, or the fact we'd been shipmates for five months and I hadn't mentioned him. "Pyga enslaved them for a hundred years. Then an orphan was adopted by the Pyga lord, and when the orphan rose to power he turned against the regime."

"Biggest dusting rebellion ever," Bricks added.

"The legend is there was one ship from each original planet that escaped after the rebellion, and they crossed through the Red Nebula right before the star collapsed.

Supposedly it wiped out all Pyga's forces and their lord, utterly destroying them. Rumor is the whole system went down with the Red Nebula."

"Stardust and ashes," Felix muttered, throwing back another shot.

"Anyway, the escape ships, the Twelve—they settled the Nacaen Group. But then infighting broke out between them. They're all different peoples, different nations—I don't know the names of them all, only the three on Melas—Dahan, Sim'ee, and Jamin. They've been trying to live as a system without a warlord like the Stiners or a proper alliance." Dibon had its own government but aligned with Kir and the other Noma planets to form the Noma Council, and after our war, there was more talk of joining with the Ramaen System.

"It's more like how the old Bara Republic was run with the religious courts—they will have a judge appointed to rule but the priests have influence. They will have a generation or two of good leadership, then a civil war. It's strange. They all believe in the same God, all their priests are of the same religion though there are planetary differences. They all speak Galactic Language, but they are at war with each other often, when they're not at war with other systems. The Rebels formed I think twenty years ago or so." They were the ones responsible for Mara and her sons becoming refugees, but I still didn't understand why. Max told me that the Jamin extremists had tried to wipe out Dahan, but they had fled before the worst of it.

"What's their deal—the Rebels?" Felix asked.

"They are extremists within the nations that don't want a unified system. Afraid it will compromise their

individual national values, although I heard they sometimes made alliances with other systems for weapons.
So instead, they fight each other."

"And you want to go there?" my pilot friend screwed
his face up in disgust.

"Not at all," I admitted. "But I've a promise to keep,
at least to find her a way there. Besides, Melas' war is
over now."

"You know, you could get her there, then rejoin us.
The captain would be glad to hire you," Bricks
suggested.

"I know," I acknowledged, studying my fingernails.
Titus' offer lingered in the back of my mind, but I wasn't
ready.

"Well, we've got a few months yet," the big man
added, raising his hand to get the bartender's attention.

"I'm sorry," Felix said. "I'm guessing your husband
—"

"Yeah," I cut him off. "Let's not talk about it."

"Okay."

I'd almost talked about Max with Perry. An ache
spread inside my chest. Even though we hadn't shared
much, I'd felt close to the other Nacaen on board the
ship, and he was gone.

When Bricks returned with another drink, I took it
from his hand, swallowed it, and handed him back the
empty. The big man rolled his eyes. "Guess I'll get two
this time."

"If you don't want to join the *Ashkelon*," Felix added
after Bricks went back to the bar, "I've got a financial
deal coming through. May be heading out on my own.
Could use a fellow Pinion."

My ears perked up. "What kind of deal?"

Felix grinned. "Not one hundred percent sure yet. May involve collecting information on the whereabouts of certain persons—"

"You mean bounty hunting." I folded my arms across my chest.

"I didn't say it, you did. But I hear a lot of people come to disappear here at Jordan, take on a new life. I can see why," he added, leaning to one side to gaze past me. I glanced over my shoulder at the scantily clad women entering the bar.

"Would Titus let you out of your contract now?" I asked, turning back to the former pilot.

Felix frowned. "The captain still owes me for the last contract. Managed to pay Frederick and Perry their full amount but most of us were only paid partially. Titus said we'll get everything we're owed once we get to Aza, so I gotta wait until the next big payload comes before I go. But anyway, this wouldn't be a bad place to have to come back to."

I shrugged. "I'll think about it." But a shiver traveled down my spine. I didn't mind deep space as much as I minded being above a planet with no star. No daylight. Nothing around for billions of kilometers. No way would I want to stay for a long time on Jordan.

Bricks waved. I turned, spying Leonard enter the bar, and to my surprise, Dariah followed. "Looky who I found."

"So, this is where everyone got off to?" Dariah called. Somehow, I'd interpreted that she'd want alone time. She'd never hung out with the rest of the cargo crew as I had on a regular basis.

"I looked for you after the showers," I told her, "but didn't see you."

"I went and sent my message to Victor's cousin. But now that I've had a shower, and a good meal, I think I would like to get drunk."

I raised an eyebrow. "Oh really? We should call Cori over here for this."

When the music stopped, Cori made her way to us as the drinks arrived at our table.

Dariah picked up her shot glass first. "To Victor."

"To Victor," Cori repeated, throwing her arm around my shoulder as we all drank to his memory.

Dariah ordered another round at last call, and the others discussed going to the strip ship, but that wasn't my scene and I'd had enough. Even though Felix and Bricks were older than me, I felt years their elder. The pleasures offered on the other ships were hollow, temporary thrills. Besides, I had Mara to look after. It was probably better if I slept off these rounds at home.

"Ready to head back?" I asked Dariah and Cori, while the guys headed out.

"The night is young!" Cori whined. "Come with me. There's another bar two ships over that's still open."

"I'm game," Dariah replied. I started to shake my head, realizing I'd already had too much as that movement made me a bit dizzy. "I'm gonna head back."

I waited for the next single-passenger transport pods maneuvering the congested orbit of Jordan Station. I hadn't drunk this much since the night after Victor died, and the gravity was a lower percentage on the transport pods, making me queasy by the time I docked with the *Ashkelon*.

I stumbled out of the pod from the docking hatch. When I entered the cargo bay, my head smashed against the metal wall.

Stars surrounded my peripheral vision, pain shooting along my jawbone and nose. Something warm and sticky dribbled into my mouth. Turning, I made out a figure in front of me as her fist collided with my face. I dropped to the floor, new pain bursting into my eye socket. As the attacker stood over me, I twisted my legs around hers to bring her down. Third instinct of a soldier—immobilize your attacker.

When she rose, I lunged, slamming her back to the floor. I found the knife in her belt. The attacker squirmed under me, but I pinned her with my thighs, my knees digging into the woman's shoulders. Grabbing her brown hair, I held the knife to her neck. "Who are you?"

The masked woman didn't answer. Through one eye, I could make out between her shirt sleeve and glove the shade of her tawny skin. The attacker could be from any number of planetary groups. But the jagged tattoo on the back of her neck gave her away as a Stiner.

Titus' heavy footsteps came down the hall, but I dared not turn away. "Guess I need to post security," the captain said as he entered the cargo bay, huffing. "I thought Jordan did better security checks than this. Can you hold her for a moment?"

"Sure," I replied as she wriggled underneath me. I squeezed harder with my thighs to keep her down, but my stomach lurched. "I have to warn you, I might puke on her."

Titus chuckled. "You seem pretty sober to me, Ami."

He touched the blue panel on the wall for the comm link. "Security."

She thrust her arm to break my grip, but I knocked my head against her, jarring her, and kept the knife near her throat.

"Most likely the knife is poisoned," Titus cautioned.

"I know."

In less than two minutes, Jordan security boarded the ship, arresting the woman. They pulled her mask off, but I still had no idea who she was, beside guessing her origin as a Stiner. One of the guards handed me some gauze from his med kit for my nose. I touched my face gently. My eye was swollen, but I could see, the blurriness clearing from the periphery. The guard questioned me for a moment, but when they scanned my retina, my Diboni military papers appeared on their tablet, stating I was a lieutenant commander. They saluted me and moved on to their prisoner.

I narrowed my eyes. It took a minute to register, but the papers had the wrong rank. I was a lieutenant, not a lieutenant commander. Maybe Vance mixed something up when he re-commissioned me for Sheya's transport. Or perhaps it was his way of honoring me before my discharge. It would be like him to do that.

When I swiveled back to Titus, I was startled to see Aaron coming from the corridor. "What do you think she was doing here?" I asked the captain, ignoring my roommate.

However, Aaron folded his arms, frowning. "Looking for me."

"*You?*"

The balding man continued to keep his eyes down,

and I noticed worry lines for the first time. "I was a refugee there on Dibon, like your mother-in-law."

"Are you from the Nacaen Group?"

Aaron shook his head, lifting his eyes to mine. "From Paren. I lied that I was Nacaen."

I gawked. Paren was a planet. *Was.* Destroyed during a botched mining expedition by outside corporations, causing a volcanic rupture, rendering the planet uninhabitable. I remembered my parents talking about it, years ago. Anyone who survived received an enormous payout—which meant if one originated from Paren, they were a wealthy survivor. Which made them a favorite target for kidnapping and ransom.

Felix had mentioned before that Titus sometimes smuggled refugees. I assumed that meant people traveling through without proper documentation, not people with big pockets.

He then bowed to me, an unfamiliar custom. "You saved me."

I was trying to save my own life. "Why did she attack me?"

A shout from the guards caused me to spin around. The two struggled to keep hold, but the Stiner slumped over in their arms. I rushed to their side. The crushed remains of a deathroot capsule lay in her palm.

"Don't touch that," I warned them.

"We didn't even see her take it!"

"Deathroot doesn't have to be ingested." I'd seen too many Diboni Renegades take their own life in the last war. "You crush it in your hand, and it's absorbed into the skin. Takes a few minutes longer that way, but it's still lethal."

"Mother-dust-and-ashes."

Turning back to Aaron, I folded my arms. "You know who sent her, then?"

He shrugged. "Possibly someone I offended before."

I remembered how he took the bunk from Mara on our first day. "Not hard to figure out why you would've offended someone."

"Ami," Titus said, turning my attention back. "You need to get your injuries looked at."

The security detail called over for a med team while they hauled away the body. "Any idea who she is?"

The guard who attended me first shook his head. "Stiners like her erase all traces of their identity except their tattoo, and unless you know who their warlord is, you'll never find out who they are."

"I have a hunch. I moved to Dibon years ago after the destruction of Paren through Stiner territory, paid someone off to get me there, but they claim I didn't pay them what was agreed upon." He gave a sheepish glance to Titus, then to me. "I spent a little at some of the shops. Someone may have noticed. Someone who has been waiting for me to come back this way since Dibon's surface was destroyed."

"Why you ash-dusted—"

"Let's let these two finish their job," Titus interrupted, motioning to the guards who were still listening. "And as much as we've longed to see other people and eat better food and take showers, Aaron, I'm confining you to the ship. I doubt she is the only one looking for you."

W hen I tried to open my eyes the next morning, one was swollen shut. I stayed in bed most of the day. Mara changed out the ice pack, saying little, and I slept when I could. So much for shore leave.

Two days later, the skin around my eye was purple and yellow, and my nose back to its normal size. "I told you it was dangerous here," Mara said, an eyebrow raised. Just like Max used to look at me sometimes.

"Yeah, I remember."

"I think you'll mend, though." She finished applying ointment on my cheek.

"Thank you. For taking care of me."

She smiled. Not a full smile the way Max would, but the corners of her lips turned slightly.

I rejoined the crew in the dining hall for dinner. Titus announced our leave was cut short and we were shipping out the next day. I held out hope a message would arrive from Vance, but when I checked with Natalie, nothing had come through.

"I got a message from Victor's cousin, Iza," Dariah said, picking at her food across the table from me. "She looks so much like him, even sounds like him. Of course, she still wants me to come. I just didn't think about how difficult it would be around his family, the memories that we share."

"It was hard around Mara at first," I admitted, remembering how she looked at me earlier. "But she's so different, for the most part."

Dariah finished her meal and Titus took her place. Bricks sat down next to me. "You don't look half-bad for having survived a Stiner attack," the big man said.

I grunted. One side of my face still was sore when I chewed. "Hoping I heal up enough to enjoy one last meal on-station before we shove off." I motioned to Titus. "I saw you have Jordan Station security guards down in the cargo hold."

"I never liked it here. Too many people come here to hide. Too many end up with a knife in their back. Better to be safe. Even if it takes a chunk out of our profits."

As soon as Titus left the table, Bricks leaned over to me. "Is it true you saved Aaron's life?"

I shrugged, stirring my soup to cool it. These were the last vegetables I'd eat that tasted like vegetables for a while. "Yeah, but only because the attacker thought I was his personal guard or something and attacked me first."

"What would someone want with him?" Bricks pondered out loud, stroking his goatee.

"You told me you've taken a lot of refugees."

Leonard scooted over to sit across from me. "Yeah, but Aaron isn't our normal refugee. He's got money still —I saw him buying something off the resupply ship."

"So? I saw you in line for a massage. Felix and Bricks here probably spent way more than that on liquor."

Bricks snorted.

"Whatever he bought cost a lot more; they brought in a secondary banker to verify the credit transfer."

I frowned. It didn't look good for Aaron to be flaunting wealth, especially if a Stiner warlord was after him. He'd admitted as much to Titus and me earlier.

"He thinks he's more important than the rest of us. You know that he doesn't do any chores as a passenger? Must've paid Titus well. Might be time to teach him a lesson," Bricks threatened, stretching his arms and cracking his knuckles.

I remembered how Aaron acted when he realized he wouldn't get private quarters as a paying passenger. Bricks was right about Aaron being arrogant, but I didn't like the direction this was going. "Don't."

They both stared at me. The big man dropped his voice low. "Why? What is he to you?"

I closed my eyes, the dull ache now throbbing in my temples. "Nothing. I can't stand him." The last was true. "But there's no need for violence just because you don't like him."

I picked up my tray from the table, no longer hungry. I'd never felt uneasy around them, but this was a side I hadn't seen before, and it left me cold.

After I left the dining hall, Esmie caught me in the corridor outside my quarters. "Captain wants you on deck." Her voice was low.

I pursed my lips. Titus hadn't used the comm to call me, so he didn't want others to know. I followed Esmie up the ladder.

"What is it?" I asked as the hatch opened. The bridge was empty, save for the comm officer and the captain. Titus motioned to Natalie, who put the message on the viewscreen.

"This message is for Ami Lehem," Vance said, standing in full uniform. "We've received your message. Command has further questions regarding the evidence you sent. Ami, they're ordering you to return to Dibon—"

"*What?*" I grabbed the pilot's chair to steady myself.

"Stay where you are at Jordan. Don't trust anyone. I'll send someone for you, to keep you safe. Stand by for further instructions."

The screen went dark. "Is that all?"

Natalie nodded. "It came encrypted for you—"

"But I insisted on seeing it," Titus finished, turning to me. "Sorry, but it's my ship. What are you gonna do?"

Knees weak, I fell into the chair. "They must think I know more." My heart pounded in my chest. "But I'm on leave and will be discharged at the end. There's *no* way they can call me back to active now. He *told* me I'd be discharged." The idea of rejoining the military, of going all the way back to that tomb of bunkers—made me want to throw up. "I can't go back."

"Then it's settled. Natalie, inform the crew we're shipping out immediately, as soon as everyone's confirmed on board."

"Sir."

"And we need to kick the security out—though

they're not part of the Interplanetary Alliance Police, they will serve warrants if there's a reward."

I breathed out, trying to calm my body. Besides a warrant, the conversation with Felix about bounty hunters crossed my mind. Vance said not to trust anyone. *They've ordered you back*. Not him. He was sending someone to keep me safe—maybe he would hide me instead. He was fighting for me in this. "I need to reply to the message."

Titus raised his eyebrows. "Are you sure?"

"Yes."

Natalie recorded my message.

"Captain Vance. I sent you all the evidence we found. I can't add anything to the investigation." I paused the message, unsure what to say next. There was no way I would stay behind and leave Mara. We had a good jump on them, months ahead on IFS. My best chance was to hide on my own, if Command was trying to pin it on me.

I pressed the record button again. "I know this doesn't answer any questions, but it's all I have. I know you're trying to help, but I'm not coming back when my leave is over and service is done. One Dibon."

As Natalie sent the message, I bit my lip. Vance hadn't answered my question about my discharge—maybe something was mixed up and it wasn't straightened out yet. I trusted him with my life, but what if—*what if*—the ADS failure had been an inside job?

It meant all of us could be at risk—and the evidence might disappear.

"Do we still have the images and tracking info of the wreckage?"

"Of course," Natalie answered.

"It needs to be encrypted."

She let out a heavy breath. "How do you think I send all of our messages?" She switched screens to outgoing messages. "Where to?"

"The Ramaen System."

I sent a copy of the feed from the wreckage to Sheya. "We should delete the rest from the ship's computer."

The comm officer crossed her arms. "The data is sufficiently encrypted."

I raised my hands. "Hey, I'm not questioning your ability—"

"Ami's right," Titus interjected. "As I said, I don't want anything on board having to do with the ADS destruction, and right now I have a bad feeling about it. Dump the files."

Natalie sighed. "All right, Captain."

Titus motioned for me to follow him, leading me to the weapon's locker in his quarters. "Don't get me wrong, I trust my crew, just not with guns." He punched in the code, opened the door and handed me a pistol. The weapon lay cold and heavy in my hands—I hadn't held one since the war. I checked to make sure the safety was on. "Come with me."

My heart raced, my palms sweating as I carried the pistol. I followed the captain, holding it down at my side as we made our way to the airlock. Felix and Cori had just come on board, both drunk. The security guards were still posted at the door. "Heya, Ami," Cori called out, her cheeks red.

"Glad you're back."

"What's the ruuush?" Felix slurred.

Titus ignored him, and Cori pulled Felix along, her brows raised. I tucked the pistol behind me in my waistband, while Titus strode up to the security guards. My heart threatened to break out from my chest, unsure of the captain's plan.

"Hey guys, things have changed," Titus said. "We're shipping out, so your contract's been cancelled."

The guard closer to me frowned. "I didn't get a notice."

Titus pulled a credit chip from his pocket. "When's your shift up, anyway? Two, three hours? I'm the captain, I'm the one who hired you. Go enjoy the rest of your shift on us. We're pulling up early."

The other guard shrugged. "If they refuse service, we still get paid, so no skin off our back."

That was too easy. I raised an eyebrow at Titus while the guards exited through the hatch.

"Natalie's jamming the transmissions here. We've probably got a few minutes, at least. If there's no warrant for you, we might have longer. Guessing by how long it took for that message to get to you, and that they didn't know what they were looking for until you sent it, I'm assuming they didn't issue a notice for you until then. It'll still take time to process with Jordan's security—they'll also need payment from Dibon, and there would need to be a reward for the warrant."

"So, you didn't need me to get rid of the guards, after all."

Titus raised his weapon, barrel pointed up. "No, now we're security."

I pulled mine. "Who's left that we're waiting for?".

Most of the other crewmembers stayed on the ship overnight to avoid the expensive hotel fees.

The captain raised an eyebrow, punching the button near the hatch. "Natalie, did our message go through?"

"Affirmative, Captain."

"Then we're just waiting for one."

I furrowed my brow. "Who?"

The light above the airlock flashed. The captain didn't answer my question but motioned for me to be in position. I gripped the pistol tighter, sweat gathering on the back of my neck.

When the hatch opened, I gasped. "Perry?"

The scarred crewmember wasn't wearing his eyepatch anymore. A small flap of skin partially covered his left eye. He looked different with his burn marks exposed, similar scars to what I'd seen in the war. I thought they were more recent when I first met him, but now I could see they'd healed a long time ago. The patch must've been partially prosthetic to hide and distort the extent of his injuries.

"Natalie's message got to you," Titus said as the hatch closed, and he lowered his gun.

"Yeah." He gave me a quick glance before turning back to Titus. "The captain of the *Tigris* delayed departure suddenly."

"That's what I thought might happen. We're having our own bit of trouble. Welcome back."

"What's going on?" I asked, lowering my weapon.

Perry hesitated, frowning. My eyes narrowed.

"Come on," Titus urged. "Ami, you're not the only one trying to avoid Near Side authorities." He hit the comm button. "Gene, everyone's on board. Let's detach and go."

"What—" I began, but Perry interrupted me, his eyes wide.

"What happened to you?"

I'd forgotten my own injuries from the attack. "Stiner."

"There'll be time to catch up later," Titus said. "For now, let's shove off."

I tried to wrap my head around what happened. Cori had told me they smuggled refugees, but if Jordan was crawling with bounty hunters as Felix had mentioned, it wasn't safe. No wonder Titus said he didn't like it there.

"I'll take that back, Ami, if you don't mind." The captain motioned to the weapon in my hand. I handed it over, glad to be rid of it. I wiped my palms on my thighs. "If anyone asks, Perry was re-signed two days ago, during your recovery. The bridge crew will back up your story." He jerked his head to Perry. "Go join the crew at launch stations. Ami, all passengers should be in their quarters."

I locked eyes with Perry for a moment. I didn't like Titus asking me to lie to the other crew and passengers —it was one thing to be silent rather than have the truth used in a way that was harmful, but outright lying was against my people's teachings, against the scrolls of the priests. A knot twisted in my gut. This wasn't right. Everyone knew Mara was a refugee returning home. All Diboni were now in essence refugees. Even though I didn't know all of Aaron's story, I knew now that he had to hide who he was to survive. Now I was being asked to trust Perry—who'd said goodbye, and now suddenly was back, right when everything was going to stardust— and lie for him, who had trouble with Near Side authorities.

What if he wasn't with the supply ship? What if he had been on Dibon?

I shook the thoughts from my head as I left Perry behind. Titus had gotten us this far. I had no choice but to trust his judgment now.

When I arrived in our quarters, Dariah was reading on her tablet. Mara was in the restroom. I spied Aaron in his rack. I almost warned him about Bricks and Leonard, but he rolled over to avoid me. Even after the attempt on his life, he was still annoying.

"We are leaving the station?" Mara asked when she opened the door, as the ship's thrusters kicked in.

"Yes." I didn't tell her about the message from Vance, or that Perry had come back unexpectedly. I didn't need to worry her.

"Good. I'm glad we're leaving." She touched my face, still tender.

"Same here."

I began to climb into my own rack, my heart returning to its normal rhythm, when Natalie's voice called on the comm. "Lehem, report to the bridge."

I gulped, fear crawling along my spine. "On my way." I set my hand on Mara's. "I'll be back soon."

———————

I RACED up the ladder to the command deck. "What's going on?"

"We're being tailed," Titus said without looking at me.

Esmie pulled up the aft scanners on the viewscreen. "It's not Jordan security."

"Stiners?" I asked, spotting the two small, teardrop-shaped pods gaining on us out of the web.

Titus nodded. "If Dibon has sent notice, Jordan is still processing." He didn't mention Aaron's situation. I wondered if the bridge crew knew the full story of the Stiner attack or Aaron's true background. "We can't fire on them without bringing Jordan security on us, and we can't go to IFS until we're at a safe distance. As a former fighter pilot, I'm hoping you have some ideas."

I'd only flown against my own people, but what I knew of Stiners meant someone was paying well enough to keep on us, even after losing one of their own. Someone desperate to get Aaron, but without attracting the authorities. The pods trailed through the station traffic.

"Their technology is more advanced than this ship. The Galactic Ocean will distort their scanners, but I'm guessing they'll be able to compensate for that. Could we mask our drive exhaust?"

"It's possible," Esmie confirmed, "but if they follow us as we enter, even if we change the configuration of our drive plume, they could still catch us."

"What if we change course and speed at random intervals?"

"You mean on manual?" Roger asked, and I nodded. He raised an eyebrow at Titus.

"Let's give it a shot. Esmie, let us know when we're clear to go to IFS. Ami, you drive."

Roger slid over and let me take the controls while he fiddled with something underneath the console, switching over to manual. My heart raced. Gene's words from when he trained me threatened to assault my confidence, but Titus hadn't called for him—he'd paged me, and I had to do this.

"We're clear of Jordan," Esmie said, and I punched the controls before Titus said, "Go."

"Natalie, open the shipwide." The sound system crackled as I kicked up speed. "Brace yourselves, we've got a bumpy ride ahead."

The ship lurched and pulled as I shifted speeds, following Esmie's course suggestions as *Ashkelon's* artificial gravity tried to keep balance with her thrust. "Scanners are a mess behind us, Captain," she informed him. "I can't tell if they're following us or not."

"I've got an idea," Titus said. "Natalie, call Perry."

I concentrated on following Esmie's instructions but couldn't help listening in on Titus' conversation. "Perry, got anything we can jettison?"

"You'll have some unhappy clients in Aza, but we can afford to lose a few containers."

"Do it. Ami, slow us down."

I slowed the ship to half of our IFS speed while the airlock opened. Seconds later, the ship rocked.

"On screen," Titus called, and Esmie brought up the aft scanners. Though the space around us was clouded, right off the ship were the splintered remains of a cargo container and a Stiner pod.

"No sign of the other ship, Captain," Esmie stated. "From breaks in the distortion, it looks like we lost that ship a few turns back."

"Get us to IFS. Good work, everyone."

I shoved back from the controls, my hands sticky with sweat. Roger scooted back into position. "No matter what Gene says, you can fly anytime you want to, Pinion."

"No thanks," I said, my voice shaking. "I'd rather go back to being a passenger now."

12

"What was with the eyepatch?" I asked Perry before tossing back my shot. Cori had purchased a bottle from the Jordan distillery, and it wasn't bad. Better than Felix's stuff.

Perry drank his shot and sighed. "Didn't want to be recognized."

"Why?" I rested my chin on my palm. "What's your story?"

His brows drew together. "Let's just say a face like mine is recognizable."

Though no one else sat in earshot—Cori and Felix were at the far table playing cards and Dariah and Leonard were chatting at another table nearby—Perry still acted like people were suspicious of him. The crew had bought his story he'd re-signed with Titus, and he claimed his eye was now healed. But I knew, from being a flight medic, that those burn scars were old. I couldn't tell if he could see out of the eye or not.

I poured another shot. "You're Nacaen, like Mara. We

all know that. Are you also from Melas?"

He nodded. "Same nation, Dahan."

"Did you leave Melas during the war?"

"No, only after. We've been rebuilding the last few years, since the war was over. My family, that is."

"Not you?"

He shook his head. "I did what I could, but we needed aid from outside—and no one will help the Nacaen Group. Bara will trade with us but that's about it."

"I've never understood that. I mean, on Dibon, there was a lot of misunderstanding about who was responsible for the beginning of our war, and a lot of blame was placed on Nacaen refugees. Outside of Dibon, though, I don't understand it."

"When does it make sense, except to the people oppressing you?"

He had a point. "The Noma System is known for being militaristic, mainly us and Kir—and the Ramaens in the past called us savage. Yet they were the ones who supplied our arms."

Perry set his elbows on the table. "I did some diplomatic work in the Ramaen System, seeing if they'd listen to a small, devastated Outer Systems planetary group. Heck, even just help our one small world with their resources."

I poured him another shot. "No luck?"

Perry sighed, running his fingers over his hair. He hadn't cut it since before Jordan, and I noticed the beginnings of curls. "Turns out, there was a brush-up with some Jamin extremists from Melas. I'm out of that line of work now. Just want to get home."

"Back to your family?"

He hesitated, catching his bottom lip under his teeth. "Yeah," he offered after a moment. "You got family? Besides Mara?"

The question caught me off guard. There I was, being a good Diboni and asking questions, but now he reciprocated. "No. Not anymore."

"I'm sorry."

An awkward silence fell between us, while Cori's light voice carried across the room. *Why did she have to leave us alone?* I wasn't good at this.

"You're heading to Melas, I take it?"

I folded my arms, leaning on the table. "No. Once we get to Aza, I've got a job offer with Titus, but I'll see what happens there."

"Oh. I thought...With Mara as your family—"

"—So, you did diplomatic work? What were you, an ambassador, or negotiator?" I cringed as the words left my mouth, interrupting him. Evading my own answers. It was almost as bad as lying. Why couldn't I just tell him the full truth? Why couldn't I just tell him I'd been married to a wonderful Nacaen man, he'd been killed when our planet was destroyed, and I'm still grieving him, but *I like your company and I'd like to be friends?*

He let out a sound—not so much a sigh, more like a swallowed curse. "Let's just say what I used to be is in the past." He picked up the shot glass, turned it over, then set it back down. "I think I'm going to call it a night." Perry got up from the table.

Cori slid up next to me. "Girl, if you're gonna flirt with him, you gotta get better at your game."

———

I LOCKED the forklift into position. Besides saying hi, Perry seemed to be avoiding me. A knot grew in my stomach. I'd pushed too far in our conversation, and I didn't know why. Maybe we both were too awkward, and didn't fit in, not even with each other. I wanted to get to know him, but I also didn't know anything about him, why he'd been in the Near Side systems, why he hid his past—and I wrestled with why I couldn't open up to him, either.

I stepped down from the forklift, removing my gloves as Felix and Cori took their break and leaned against empty crates. Loneliness began to weigh on me. I'd gone from living with my family, to bunking with my fellow soldiers, to being attached to my squadron after completing flight training, and later to be a medic, to marrying Max right after the war. Though Mara was family, it wasn't the same. I'd avoided Bricks and Leonard since Jordan Station, but even among Felix and Cori, I didn't quite belong. Dariah and I only talked about what we'd lost, not what we were looking forward to. A hollow space grew in my chest.

I needed more than a friend to play cards with and drink shots.

I scanned the cargo bay while I drank from my canteen. Perry wasn't on shift this time. Bricks and Leonard were going over inventory lists when I spied Aaron. I almost choked on my water. He was wearing a jumpsuit and carrying a tablet.

Felix told some deplorable dirty joke which sent Cori busting a gut. I was slow to recognize my own laughter for the first time in a long time. It wasn't until she subsided that I noticed Aaron was no longer in the room, and neither were Bricks and Leonard.

I finished stacking the crates, double-checking the bolts to the ceiling—I hated the chore since Victor died —then slipped out the door. Voices echoed as I crept down the corridor, and I stopped when I recognized Titus', sharp and clear above me.

"You need to watch yourself!"

Aaron swore. "I dusting am! What do you think I was doing there?"

"Your stuff hasn't been touched. I made sure of it, so you didn't need to make a scene by being there."

"No one paid attention to me."

Their voices dropped. I moved closer to the ladder.

"You shouldn't have left the ship at Jordan." Titus said something I couldn't make out but sounded like *no one should have*. "Our comm is secure."

"But not as powerful. I was able to establish a direct connection this time."

"And?"

"*The queen* said to stay the course."

"How do we know they won't find us?"

"Stiners don't like the Twelve," Aaron said. "It's highly unlikely they'll come after us as we near the Bara System—that system trades with Nacaens."

"They tried to kidnap you at Jordan and followed us after. That mercenary killed herself rather than go back empty-handed."

"I don't know how they would know I was on the *Ashkelon*. I made sure that my documents showed me on another ship."

Titus' voice stung with anger. "Someone knew you were on board and knew your real identity. Remember the first day out from Dibon? I made sure no one knew who you really were, while at the same time warning you to do your part on this ship. Then you went and flaunted your wealth on Jordan. You've continued to make people not like you. Someone may be working for the Stiners—or worse, the Modes."

I swallowed hard. Titus must have had a run-in with the Modes at some point, hence all the safeguards to take the controls off network. From what I could tell, all signs pointed to the Stiners, and like Aaron, I had a difficult time believing they would've followed us beyond Jordan. If they wanted to capture Aaron and steal his wealth, it would be easier to track him down once we docked on the other side. However, the knowledge that Titus was nervous about one of his crew sent a chill down my spine. Until Jordan, I'd thought I was safe. Bricks and Leonard wanting to teach Aaron a lesson was bad enough. Titus believed we were all still in danger if someone was after Aaron.

"I already paid the Stiner lord what he was owed for the voyage to Dibon. He blames me for the trouble he had when the Ramaens seized his ship. But it was years ago. Not my problem."

"It is all our problem if that's why the Stiners followed us. Someone might have tipped him off. Some of the crew saw you at Jordan making large purchases."

"I had to buy the Queen a gift for when I arrive! It's rude to come empty-handed, but I lost everything on Dibon. Thank goodness my accounts were all off-world. Living in cramped quarters with other passengers was not what I expected when you agreed to take me on, and a few simple pleasures for the rest of the voyage were a necessity."

"And put a target on your back and let everyone know you're not a regular passenger like the rest. I let the chores slide because of the generous matching offer from the Queen of Etho for your safe arrival. But you've alienated yourself."

I'd heard of Etho, a cluster of stars, mineral-rich dwarf planets, and a handful of life-bearing worlds, though I'd never known anyone who had been there. Etho was a matriarchal, matrilineal society, ruled by an unbroken line of queens spanning centuries, according to their history. In the Near Side Systems, we all believed humanity began in the Bylon cluster, but I'd been told in the Outer Systems some believed Etho was the birthplace of humanity.

Titus continued. "It wouldn't hurt for you to try to make allies among the crew, or at least the other passengers, you know."

"That's not my style."

The captain huffed, his heavy footsteps echoing away. I hurried back down the corridor, running right into Bricks.

"Watch yourself," the big man warned as he brushed by me, and I knew that wasn't about me running into him. Bricks climbed up the ladder, and the chill in my spine spread into a shudder.

I waited a moment before climbing the ladder, following Aaron into our room, where Mara was asleep in her rack. Dariah was out on dinner prep.

"What does the Queen of Etho want with you?" I

demanded, my voice low, trying not to wake my mother-in-law.

His eyes flicked wide in anger. "What do you do, spy on people?"

"Bricks and Leonard are after you."

"How do you know?"

"They told me they wanted to teach you a lesson." I folded my arms across my chest. Arrogance would get him killed.

Aaron rolled his eyes. "Thanks for the information."

"I'll help you, but you have to tell me what's going on."

He threw his hands in the air, then stared me in the eye. "I have a financial arrangement with Etho's royal family, that almost fell apart because my departure from the Noma system was delayed. I couldn't find a transport willing to not ask questions. Etho is not far from the Bara system. Titus agreed to get me there because the Queen of Etho is doubling his payment."

"What were you doing on Dibon?"

"I never told anyone else I was from Paren after the Interplanetary Alliance Court awarded all survivors settlements. I lied and said I was Nacaen, so the only place I could go was Dibon. But too many Paren survivors ended up out the airlock by the very crews they contracted to get them home. Some made to the Ramaens because they could afford Ramaen resettlement fees. I didn't think it was fair to have to pay so much. Since Dibon's surface was destroyed, I had to find another system and people who understand the comforts of life the way I do, without costing an arm and a leg."

I crossed my arms. "You need to get to Bara without someone throwing you out the airlock—"

"Get me safe to Bara. Keep me safe on this ship in case our paranoid captain is right, or at least ease his fears. I'll pay you, ten thousand a day, to be my personal guard."

Stardust, that was a lot of money. I kept my face neutral. "That's a fair deal, but I have the chores here and Mara to care for."

"Titus will let you out, and I already live here with you. You keep her safe enough since she's a Twelve—no one's even tried to mess with her."

I pinched the bridge of my nose. "They will figure out pretty quick I'm your bodyguard if I'm not doing chores."

"Not if Titus makes you an assistant-on-deck," he said, folding his arms across his chest.

"Huh?"

"He mentioned he already trained you to be a third pilot in case something happens."

I set my hands on my hips. "How does that help you?"

"Titus decided he needs to assign me chores on the bridge, so I'll be nearby."

Aaron crawled into his rack, as I stared at him in disbelief. I didn't want to be a bodyguard, but the honor of being asked to be assistant-on-deck, and not having to go back to cargo, outweighed my reservations. And the money would be more than enough to get Mara home from Aza, and help me start over somewhere new.

13

I reported to the bridge for my first full day of duty, and Gene handed me a spare uniform. The drab gray shirt was baggy in the middle, but the trousers fit well. As assistant-on-deck, I filled in for anyone who needed a break. I learned the comm system from Natalie, which was antiquated compared to the station on Dibon, but easy enough to figure out. Titus was right—because of the outdated ways one selected channels and the locking configuration, the encryption was hard to break. He might be old-fashioned in outfitting the ship, but the captain had his reasons.

When I sat in Gene's chair, I reached underneath the control console, finding the small panel with my fingers. The smaller cable capped off was input, the larger output. With skill, one could uncap them with one hand and plug in for manual control—what Gene must've done the day he hazed me, and what Roger did quickly when we evaded the Stiners. Every console on the bridge had a way to be taken offline from the ship's networked computer and run manually. Titus knew he wouldn't have to explain it to me. He trusted me to figure it out.

The engineering monitors seemed standard—the monitors had been upgraded more recently than the other control consoles, showing fuel conservation and radiation levels on the hull. The scanning monitors for debris and asteroids were in working order, and every system underwent a manual check daily.

"Think you could handle this every day?" Gene asked, pretending to nod off at the controls.

I shrugged. "If the cook keeps the coffee on, I can manage."

After the first day, I was bored on the bridge. Gene's gesture made even more sense over the following monotonous, tedious days. Aaron stayed there, and despite working for him, I still didn't like him. Half the time he cozied up near Natalie, who didn't seem pleased the arrogant passenger chose her to hang around.

When I did chores with the rest of the crew, I accomplished something. I had friends. Now, I never saw Felix and Cori anymore except at the evening meal. Leonard and Bricks still sat with us sometimes, but the wedge of doubt forced our conversations into casual chats about work and Felix's dirty jokes. Perry joined us but seemed more open to Cori than me. My life hung in limbo, in the nothingness between Jordan Station and the Outer Systems, the thrill of being on the command deck having long slipped away.

Weeks passed into months. I began to think Aaron was as paranoid as Titus, despite the encounter with the mercenary at Jordan. Bricks and Leonard didn't seem to be provoked by him any longer, and there was no other threat on board. The captain seemed more annoyed than anyone, but he didn't let on what was bothering him, and I didn't press.

———

"I HARDLY SEE YOU ANYMORE," Mara whispered to me one evening as she turned in.

"What do you mean? I'm here when you wake, and when we go to sleep, and I see you at meals—there's not many places to go on this ship."

The older widow folded back her blankets and sighed. Turning to me with her sad gray eyes—a little brighter and bluer, and they'd be reminiscent of Max's —she grabbed my hand, her bony fingers pressing into my palm.

"Don't leave me."

"What are you talking about?" I tugged my hand away, shaking it out. "We're on a gods-dusted ship in the middle of the Galactic Ocean, how am I gonna leave you?"

Her brows drew together. "Don't shut me out."

"Shut *you* out? You've shut me out since Max and I got married!"

"I never shut you out," she insisted, her voice stern. "I might not have had much to say, but I didn't shut you out. I grieved because of what we'd lost. Our traditions, our culture. Max and Chip both spent their adolescence on Dibon and I felt them slipping away, becoming more Diboni and less Nacaen. It was never about you." She sighed. "It was about me. What I'd lost.

But I was always there. You just walked away, every time."

Her words slapped me in the face, waking me up. I'd just assumed for all these years she hadn't liked me. And a small part of me understood. I'd been focused too damn long on my own losses.

"You're making plans," she continued. "Joining the crew, leaving me in the Bara System. If you're going to leave me, why didn't you let me go when I left Dibon? I told you to go back to your family. You could've gone anywhere."

My cheeks burned; jaw clenched. "Anywhere? For gods' sake Mara, I've no family left. Nothing. Max was my world, my rock, and he's gone. You're all I have that connects me to him!"

I stormed out of our quarters, stopping to lean against the wall next to our door. It wasn't right for me to lose my temper. And I shouldn't have walked away, because I did exactly what she said I did, what I always do: run away from my feelings.

A moment later, the door opened with Aaron on the other side. He yawned, then frowned. "Where are you going?"

"Out."

"Aren't you on the clock?"

"I'm taking the night off. Besides, you're fine."

I wandered the corridors, restless, angry at Mara, frustrated at Max for leaving me alone with her. Descending the ladder to the lower level, I shivered in the cooler circulated air. I found Cori at the side viewscreen panel, staring into the darkness.

"Want to go for a walk?" she asked, and my anger

rolled off with my laughter. It was a joke the short-haired girl started, about going for a walk along the fifty meters or so we could to the cargo hold, then up to the command deck, then back down to the dining hall. We all took advantage of the fitness room near the cargo hold, to use for thirty minutes during prescheduled times, but otherwise, this was our exercise.

There was one spot, at the end of the corridor from the captain's quarters, where the hull curved in a large clear viewscreen, larger than the one on the lower deck. There were two metal folding chairs there, often occupied by whoever happened to be on break, but they were empty. We raced to dive into the chairs, laughing as I almost stumbled into the viewscreen.

The stars seemed to glow brighter, though I knew it was an illusion of traveling at IFS, as we approached the edge of the nothing-ness with the gas clouds behind us. "Where is Bara?" I asked.

"Over there, the star cluster that looks like an hourglass?" I nodded as Cori pointed. "About two more months, maybe? That's to Aza, deep in the system. And it depends on if we get any calls for pickup. Regular calls will come through again as we get closer to the edge of the ocean."

The short-haired brunette leaned into me, resting on my shoulder, and I rested my chin on the crown of her head. We'd hung out a lot when we worked in cargo, but I didn't see her much these days.

"How's it going with Perry?" she asked.

"Terrible. I think I scared him away."

"Hm. He's definitely been more lost in thought, you know? Not paying attention when we're talking to him."

"You see him a lot?" I asked.

"We've been on the same cargo shift. Are things cushy up on the bridge?"

"Boring. So boring."

Cori laughed, and her laugh was a song that rang in my chest. Her laugh always ricocheted around the cargo bay. I'd missed it up on the bridge. "Yeah, well, cargo ain't a peach. I'm the only girl down there now."

"Sorry about that. I don't think Dariah will ever go back to chores there, either."

A loud, popping sound erupted, slapping the walls around us. The blast shuddered along the hall, knocking Cori out of her seat. Heat and air rushed along my bare arms. I grabbed her hand, yanking her up. My heart quickened as we ran toward the bridge, but a slow fear crept over me. Titus thrust the door open from his quarters, pistol in hand, his uniform shirt unbuttoned. With his eyes locked on mine, the captain tossed me his weapon.

"Go."

I rushed toward the bridge, but he yelled behind me, "No, go down! I've got this!" Spinning around, I raced back toward the ladder. Mara. Aaron. Titus handed Cori another pistol as I shimmied down to the crew and passenger quarters, my heart in my throat.

I found Bricks banging on my door, carrying a large stingshot—an electric stunner—and he had a lock-melter fastened on the door keypad. I raised the pistol to eye level, finger on the trigger.

"Drop your weapon."

He didn't take his eyes off the door as he slammed against it. "This isn't about you, Ami."

"Drop it," I repeated through gritted teeth.

The ship seemed to sway, though the artificial gravity still worked. We must've dropped out of IFS.

Bricks stole a glance at me. "Stay out of this, or I swear I'll kill you if you get in my way!"

The lockmelter hissed, disintegrating the keypad.

"Bricks. This is your last chance. Put the stingshot down."

He shoved the door open.

I pulled the trigger.

The force from the bullet leaving the pistol vibrated through my forearms, my shoulders bracing against the recoil. The large man with bleached hair slumped to the floor as Mara shrieked, blood splattering against the doorframe, along with bits of Brick's jaw and skin. The lower left side of his face was gone.

I couldn't lower the pistol in my hands. Aaron pried the stingshot from Brick's fingers, then he set his hand on my wrist. I breathed hard and fast.

I killed someone. I'd killed someone I knew.

The entire time I was a pilot, I fired weapons from a Buzzard, but never saw death from my own hand, only torpedoes resulting in explosions. I saw bodies like Bricks on my table as a flight medic, as I decided whether to triage them or to administer pain medication to ease their death.

I'd never pulled the trigger on someone right in front of me, someone I knew, and watched life fly from their eyes as their body hit the floor.

Why hadn't I tried to fight him, tried to get the stunner away from him?

The shock wove through my arms, and I lowered them, my fingers still tight on the grip.

"Mara?" I managed to call out.

"I'm here." Her wide eyes betrayed her fear.

Dariah emerged from the other side of the wall, her jaw agape. "What happened?"

"Bricks was after Aaron. You all stay here. Aaron, if anyone comes through the door, shoot them. Don't ask questions."

I handed my weapon to Dariah, only because I remembered her telling me she'd fired one before. "Same to you."

"What about you?" she asked.

"I'll find something." I didn't know if I could shoot again, but I wanted Mara protected. And Aaron. Something in me knew that Dariah understood the drive to stay alive right now.

"Where are you going?" my mother-in-law demanded.

"Back up to the command deck. Titus and Cori were securing the area."

I left before they could ask another word, and Aaron shut the door behind me. Leaning against the wall for a moment, I attempted to calm my breathing.

I killed him. I killed Bricks, and he only carried a stingshot. The big guy couldn't have killed Aaron with it. He wouldn't have killed me with it. But I shot him without hesitation.

Across from me, shouts were muffled from the door. The keypad for the crew quarters had been melted. I banged my palm on the door.

"Ami?" Perry's muffled voice came across.

"Perry!"

"We're locked in."

Another popping sound echoed down the ladder shaft.

"Get down and stay safe!"

I raced to the ladder. Titus needed me. Climbing two rungs at a time, I slid against the wall near the entrance to the bridge.

"This is mutiny," Titus' voice quivered.

"This is payback. You still owe me for the last contract."

Felix?

"And you know good and well payment is waiting for you in Bara, I confirmed it. I kept you on despite the bad report from your captain on Kir."

Felix scoffed. "None of that matters now. The Stiners pay a lot more than you, and the Modes will pay even more for that Paren scum you're transporting. And besides, I've got someone interested in your special passenger."

"No. You can't hand them over."

Them? Sweat poured across my brow.

"It's too late, they're already on their way."

"Stop, Felix. Stop this all now, and I'll let you off at the next station, with your full payment. Haven't you killed enough people already?"

"This is your fault, Titus. You told us all that taking on refugees would be our big break, that this trip would pay out our contracts and then some. But even at Jordan, you couldn't pay us and then you pulled the plug on our leave time. You owed us."

"I owed *you*. Everyone else understood these are

hard times in this part of the galaxy. No one else questioned their payment being delayed. But now you will pay. This was my family. Gene. Natalie. Cori was like a daughter to me."

"Cori was useless."

I bit my bottom lip to keep from crying. Sweet, laughing, loving Cori, was dead.

"Why you ash-dusted—"

A single shot rang, and I shuddered. Titus' body crashed to the floor. My chest ached. I was the only one left—the other regular crew were either dead, detained, or in on it with Felix.

Rage flashed over me at the betrayal. But rage would get me killed.

I breathed. In, out. One, two, three.

Shifting to get a better view, I spotted Felix at the controls, back to the door. His pistol lay on the console. There were bodies and blood strewn across the bridge, but I didn't focus my eyes on them. I didn't want to look for Cori or Titus. Instead, I spotted the captain's pistol on the floor.

But to my right, movement caught my eye. There was a hand, a subtle movement of a finger.

Cori. She was still alive.

If I went to her, Felix would kill me. I prayed to the gods that she hung in there, just a little longer. I turned back to the weapon. I bent low, in case my reflection appeared on the monitors, and in one stride held Titus' pistol in my hands.

Felix spun around. My hand trembled as I pointed the weapon at him. "Stop."

The former Pinion laughed, his hands up. My skin

crawled from the callous gleam in his eye. "I've nothing against you, you know, even if you are a Twelve-lover. I hate the Twelves but doesn't everyone? Aaron is rich. We could split his worth between us."

"No."

Felix lowered his hands. "The Modes are already hacking in. I sent them our coordinates and they have the codes. You're a sitting duck. Kill me and they'll still be here to take this old dustbucket, and you."

His right hand grazed the handle of his holstered weapon, but before he could raise it, I spied his reflection on the monitor behind him.

I sprayed his brains on it.

Seconds, maybe minutes passed before I lowered my arms, the force of firing dissipated. There was a body in front of me, someone who was once my friend.

There wasn't time to contemplate how much money it took for Felix to betray us. I rushed to Cori's side. Blood had spread along her rib cage. Her hands covered her wound.

"Get us out of here," she breathed.

The proximity alarm tore my attention from her—a ship was approaching. I shoved Felix's body from the control panel. The nav system was locked, and even a few minutes out of IFS made our capture imminent. I dove underneath, finding the pull-away panel. Gene had made it seem easy when he hazed me, but I assumed the pilot must be among the bodies on the floor. I popped the caps and connected the wires to the outlet.

When I stood, the aquamarine gauge for the power level had turned deep green. The ship was old, but Titus knew what he was doing by keeping the old control console: ease of manual control in case the computers were compromised.

I found the coordinates Felix set in, a combination I didn't recognize—to intercept the Modes ship. I started to reset the coordinates for Aza Station but stopped after the first three numbers. They would know we were headed there. I had to get us somewhere closer—much, much closer—and pray we weren't boarded, because I didn't know if I could survive killing again.

Racing to Natalie's console—I didn't see her body nearby—I searched the viewscreens. The list of rendezvous points for recycling was on her comm log. The closest one was Balec—at the edge of the Bara System. I jumped back to the conn. I heard Cori nearby, shifting herself to her side. "Hang in there," I coaxed. "Is Balec safe?"

"Yes," she squeaked. "Anywhere is safer than here."

As I programmed in the coordinates, the lights went out. Emergency power tried to kick in, but my whole body rose as red lights flickered, systems sputtering out, artificial gravity disengaged. I gripped the control console.

The Modes. They were already hacking the ship's computers.

I knew engineering could be reprogrammed, but I still didn't know how. I couldn't get us away without getting the engines under manual control.

Someone clamored behind me. I swiveled, holding on to the panel. Esmie floated through the doorway. I breathed out hard, not realizing I had held it in. Her hair floated around her as she gripped a metal support beam above.

"You know how to override navigation?" she asked.

"Yes, but I've no power, no scanners, nothing!" Panic seeped through my veins as I watched Cori rise from the floor. She managed to wrench her arm around a metal conduit, keeping herself as steady as possible.

"Gods know why Titus didn't trust me to know how to override navs, but I always knew there was a way. Where is he?"

My eyes dropped to the floor, then shifted away. I didn't want to see his face.

The engineer shuddered, tears forming as blobs on her cheeks.

"Esmie," I snapped, my voice sharp. "We've got to get out of here, you've got to get the systems up and running. Cori's bleeding and we have no gravity. The Modes are almost here."

She pushed off from the beam to the engineering panel. "It's completely offline."

"You have to reprogram from my console."

The tall engineer pushed over and began punching combinations into the keypad. The lights returned, and we dropped to the floor. I leaped back to my feet, pushing the thrusters as far as I could, and the ship lurched. I surged us forward at full IFS until the scanners showed the proximity clear.

When I spun around to Esmie, she was cradling Titus' head in her lap.

14

The smell of blood lingered on the bridge, though it had been scrubbed several days before. Surprising me, Aaron and Dariah volunteered to clean the command deck after the bodies were removed. I never thought Aaron would deign to do menial labor, but without hesitation, he went to the bridge and didn't leave until the job was finished. "I owe them that," he said to me. "Only Titus and you knew the truth of who I was. I don't know how Felix knew, but the others—they risked their lives for me. And I can never repay that debt."

I touched his arm. "None of us can repay them." Along with Titus, Natalie and Gene lay among the dead.

"After you left," Roger told me later, "Perry and I tore the bunks apart, managed to jam a rod into the door and get it open. We heard Dariah shouting from the passenger side, but Aaron wouldn't open the door."

"I told him not to."

"Turned out Perry had a weapon hidden in his bunk—"

"Wait—*what*?"

"Yeah. He told me Titus knew about it. We went to cargo and found Leonard there, hiding behind some crates. He wouldn't say anything at first, but Perry—well, he roughed him up and managed to get Leonard to say he knew Felix was plotting something against Titus. We found two others in the dining hall with weapons. When the lights went out, we took them down. Two others surrendered."

Meanwhile, Esmie had been in Titus' quarters. When the systems went offline, she defied his order and came to help. I hadn't known they were lovers.

"They're assembled," Roger said. "You okay?"

I stood, straightening out my drab gray uniform. "Yeah." It was the only lie I could tell. I hated that question, asked after every death I'd experienced. I'd never be okay. But I was okay enough to press on. "I need to visit Cori first."

"She's gone down. Dariah helped her down the ladder."

"Dammit. She's supposed to be resting." The bullet had grazed her ribcage, missing all organs but I'd still been scared she'd bleed out when we had no gravity. We'd set her up in the bridge crew quarters to recover.

Roger walked with me to the cargo hold, where the remaining mutineers were imprisoned for the journey to Balec. The local authorities would place them on trial according to interplanetary law since the station remained dually aligned with the Interplanetary Alliance. The stricter courts of the Bara System might've taken our evidence and executed them without a trial.

Cori sat nearby. Her eyes were ice, staring at Leonard and the two others from the cargo deck crew who had betrayed us. The remaining crew constructed a makeshift holding cell from scrap containers chained together. Leonard stood among the prisoners. Brown fuzz on his scalp had grown back in patches, and his wrists bore deep red lines from being tied.

My former friend pleaded with me. "I'm telling the truth. I'll take truth serum if I have to. I swear I knew nothing—Felix didn't tell me anything."

I glared at him. Truth serum in the Interplanetary Alliance was only allowable in court. "You wanted to help Bricks teach Aaron a lesson."

"Because he was so smug, like he was better than all of us. It was going to be a joke, nothing more. I swear again, by the gods of all the Near Side Systems, I knew nothing about their dusted plan." He bit his bottom lip, trembling. "Cori, I'm so sorry. I never meant for you to get hurt—I never meant for any of this to happen."

Cori's brow twitched and her lip quivered. Her eyes met mine, cold with rage.

Part of me wanted to believe him. Leonard always seemed to be the one following along in that group, not a leader. But when Bricks locked the crew in the cargo hold, Leonard hadn't stopped him, didn't try to fight him. For that, I couldn't forgive him, even if his crime was only cowardice.

"You will stand trial, with the others, on Balec."

I chanted the Diboni prayers over Titus, Gene, and Natalie. Dariah joined me in the recitation. When Mara chanted the Nacaen chant over Bricks and Felix, I couldn't join her. There was no honor in what they'd done, nothing redeemable of their lives. My mother-in-law believed in death we were all the same, enemies and friends no more, but I don't know what happens when we die. Like Dariah, I wasn't sure I believed in the temples of our gods anymore. Death is an emptiness, like the ocean we crossed.

Turning to Esmie, I hoped she would speak, but she shook her head. Though the engineer was now in command by rank, the captain's lover had fallen apart, unable and unwilling to serve in that capacity.

Clearing my throat, I set my shoulders back, and began. "Captain Titus was a fair man, a good captain. He commanded respect and treated everyone with equality and dignity." I recited almost word for word what Vance said when his commanding officer was killed during our war.

"Captain Titus did not care where you came from, or who you were beforehand. He gave everyone a fair chance, encouraging all to do their best."

I thought of Felix, how Titus had taken him on despite his bad report. Perhaps it was his weak point, being too generous, too merciful. I stole a look at Perry, but his gaze was on Titus' body. Titus had also trusted him, even allowed him to have a weapon on board.

I spoke briefly of Gene and Natalie. Roger added a few words, having worked with them longer. Then Roger turned to Titus' casket. "There was no finer captain of a ship to serve under, civilian or crew. To the stars, beyond the edge of the galaxy into the vast universe, we commit the body of Captain Titus."

I saluted his casket, thumb a hair from my forehead, and the crew responded by standing at attention. Even Leonard bowed his head in respect, and I spied Aaron, hand over his heart, bowing.

The bodies were sent through the airlock into space, except for Titus. I gave room for Esmie to have a moment alone with him.

Roger helped Cori to her feet. When her eyes met mine, they brimmed with tears. "You know how many times I hung out with that bastard, drinking and playing cards?" She shook her head. "I never knew Felix. I thought I did, but I had no idea he'd sell us out."

"None of us did."

I remembered how Frederick, long ago on that fateful day when Victor died, revealed he had a crush on Felix. It was good he wasn't here for this. I stole a glance at Dariah, who had gone to Esmie. Another death, another widow.

Dariah turned to me, giving a nod that Esmie was ready. I moved to stand on the other side of the casket, saluting once again as the tube was sent into the airlock.

When the cargo hold cleared out, I lingered. Long ago I had thought our lives had changed when we boarded the *Ashkelon*. I remember thinking Mara and I had left death and destruction behind. Instead, it had continued to follow, stalking like prey, striking when I least expected it. But every time, it missed *me*. Victor. The Stiner that attacked. Natalie, Gene, and Titus. Death was close, raking at me with its claws. These wounds were nothing compared to the lives lost, to the pain of Dariah and Esmie, and the rest of the crew that survived the mutiny.

PERRY WAS WAITING by the ladder when I returned. "Ami, I'm—"

"I want you to hand over your weapon," I commanded.

He frowned, his brows drawing together, but he acquiesced, removing it from his waistband underneath his shirt and placing it in my palm. "If I didn't have it things might have been worse."

"Why did Titus let you keep this?"

Perry let out a deep breath. "Titus didn't know everything about me, but he knew enough. My family has a lot of influence on Melas. That's why I went to the Ramaens, and I went alone to not attract attention. I wore the eyepatch so that other Melas nationals wouldn't recognize me. It's the truth. At Jordan, I was switching identities and papers to avoid anyone tracking me, but Natalie sent me a message about the Stiner attack. There was a chance they weren't after Aaron, but perhaps me. Right when Natalie messaged me, the captain of the *Tigris* suddenly announced that departure was delayed. I immediately messaged Natalie back that I would accept Titus' offer to continue on with the *Ashkelon*."

"But you worked cargo this whole time."

"Because of the crisis on Dibon, all passenger space was required to be used for the evacuation of Diboni residents, per the Noma Council decree."

I turned the weapon over in my hand. The image of Felix flashed in my mind, me pulling the trigger. I pushed it back at Perry. I didn't want it. He'd never been a threat on board, no matter what secrets he kept. "Take it, then. If Titus trusted you, then so do I."

He placed it back under his shirt, and I climbed the ladder.

"Ami," he called, his hands on the rungs. I glanced down at him—from this angle, with his eyes wide, I could see his left eye from under the flap of skin. He had soft, brown irises. "My name is Bo. Bo Perez. Perry was just the name to get me back home—along with the eyepatch."

"Why are you telling me now?"

"Because you deserve to have the truth. After all we've—*you've*—been through."

His lips curved, a soft smile, and though everything weighed on me, my lips curved slightly. "All right, Bo."

───────

WHEN I ARRIVED at our quarters, Mara reached out and grabbed my hand, pulling me to sit on her rack with her.

"What is it?"

She reached for my face, surprising me with her tender touch. "I killed someone, once."

My back stiffened. "What?"

Mara closed her eyes, folding her hands in her lap. "Max never told you what happened—how Eli died?"

I shook my head. "He only said that he was killed on the way to Dibon."

She opened her eyes, staring at her hands. "We were at Jordan Station. No one would take Nacaen passengers because only Dibon would accept them, and the Noma System sanctions were starting to be imposed on cargo traveling through. My husband didn't like the captain of the ship who had smuggled us, was paranoid he was going to abandon us, so Eli met another pilot to try to work out passage. Only someone overheard, or the captain had someone come after us—I don't know. We were in our quarters on the ship. Someone banged on the door, and Eli told me to hide the boys in the closet. He had a gun in there, but he didn't take it. Instead, my husband opened the door, argued, and," Mara swallowed hard, "the man killed him. I told the boys to close their eyes and cover their ears, as I watched the whole thing through the vent in the closet door. I grabbed Eli's gun, and when the man started to leave, I opened the door and shot him."

I gasped. "How'd you escape?"

"I turned back to the boys and told them that they had to promise to keep their eyes closed, but they needed to trust me. I picked up Chip, grabbed Max by the hand, and ran. I never stopped to check if Eli was still breathing. I found a different ship, lied about our names, and got us to the Noma System and Dibon."

She tilted her head, gazing at me with her sad eyes, before taking my hands in hers. "We can only trust each other. I know you were in the military, and you had your squadron who had your back. But this isn't the military. This isn't Dibon. You cannot regret what you've done. I've lived with regret all these years, wondering if I left Eli alive at Jordan, abandoning him to some worse fate. But thinking like that doesn't help anyone. Don't regret doing what you had to do. You saved us."

I wiped my eyes with the back of my hand. "Do you still regret going to Dibon?"

"No. That wasn't fair for me to say, after Max and Chip died. For all I've lost, I have you. And you have me."

I pulled her into my arms, holding her close. She didn't absolve me of Felix and Bricks' death alone: she absolved me of Max and Chip. There was no way I would leave her now. She was now my mother, and I would go with her, and make a new home together.

15

W hen Balec's comm station came into range, Esmie and I sent our reports and video feed of the mutiny. Balec authorities from the Interplanetary Alliance Police escorted us into dock and boarded first, confiscating all the ship's data. They didn't allow anyone to disembark. I knew the IAP needed to do their job and complete their investigation, but all I wanted was to get off the dusted ship.

"You didn't know Felix Jerim before this voyage?" the IAP detective asked.

"No. I only came on board as a passenger at Dibon with my mother-in-law, didn't know anyone else on board before."

The detective raised an eyebrow. "Your report is thorough, and the video evidence is all there. Just a few more questions. It looks like there was a data dump during the ship's stay at Jordan Station."

I folded my hands. "Yes. We sent a transmission back to Dibon and deleted it afterward."

"Why?"

"The captain didn't feel it was important enough to keep, once it was sent." I didn't mention the second copy I'd sent to Sheya. Diboni may not lie, but sometimes we didn't reveal everything.

"We don't get many passengers coming all the way from the Near Side Systems into Balec. Most of your planet's survivors resettled in nearby systems. Why were you on this ship?"

"As I already told you," I said, as calm as I could, after almost two hours of questions, "I'm helping my mother-in-law go home." I wondered if he'd ask the same questions of Perry—Bo.

"I'm just trying to figure out how an active-duty Diboni flight medic is now across the galaxy from their homeworld."

I gripped the armrests of the captain's chair, narrowing my eyes. "I'm not active-duty."

He held up his hand. "I'm not here to arrest AWOL soldiers from other systems. We're only trying to find out who contracted Felix to go after the *Ashkelon*. It takes so long for things to update across the galaxy, I'm sure it's a mistake."

I relaxed, breathing out through my teeth. "I'm not AWOL. At the time of my passenger reservation I was active, but on leave of absence. My term of service is up."

The Interplanetary Alliance Police detective shrugged, swiping back over his tablet. "Discharge hasn't come across yet, but not unusual with comm delays." He tilted his head. "Perry Samson. What do you know of him?"

"Not much." I leaned forward, elbows on my knees.

"He joined us from a supply ship—the *Jabbok*—when we left Dibon." All true.

"He's listed as crew until Jordan Station, but his crew file wasn't updated."

"He was supposed to be on another ship, but it didn't work out."

"Why?"

I rolled my eyes. "Why don't you ask him?" Inside, my stomach turned over.

"Says here he's from Nidos. Hear that planet's a mess right now."

Nidos? He told me he was from Melas. My heart sank. It might be part of his cover. Or he might have lied to me.

"That's a shame."

"One final question," the detective said, setting down his tablet. "Aaron Peters. He says you work for him?"

I shrugged, then folded my arms across my chest. "He's a refugee from Paren, though his papers say he's Nacaen. But you know how that goes. He hired me to be a personal bodyguard."

"Why did he hire you?"

"There was an attack by a Stiner at Jordan—someone after Aaron. It's in our report. He hired me after that."

The detective's eyes lit up. "Then that gives us our motive. We found personal comm transmissions between Felix and the Modes. Most likely hired the Stiners as well. We suspect he'd been planning the kidnapping since Jordan Station. Must've intercepted the message from the Queen of Etho."

"What?"

Aaron entered the bridge with two other IAP officers. "Titus didn't want me sending my message to her from Jordan. I didn't like how the captain treated me there and I looked at booking passage elsewhere, but the queen, you see, helped pay for my voyage—"

"She told you to 'stay the course.' I overheard the conversation."

He avoided my gaze. "I thought you might've. I had to contact her to ask her for more money."

"I thought she was doubling *your* payment."

"I had to have her cover the rest of the payment, as I wasn't able to pay Titus the rest of my portion until we got to Jordan, and then, money was tied up."

My eyes widened. I remembered how much money Aaron spent at Jordan, which caught Brick's attention. The "necessary items" he bought. Probably went to the casino ships as well and lost it all.

Dusted ash. The *formerly* rich passenger couldn't pay me for the bodyguard job, either. "You don't have the money."

"No, no—I'll pay you. I promise. It's just my money is tied up for now, until the wedding."

"*Wedding?* Holy stardust, you're marrying into the royal family?" I bet the Queen had no idea he'd wasted all his Paren settlement already. "And let me guess, you told her your money is tied up?"

Aaron blushed. "I still have some accounts I haven't accessed yet. But yes. Etho's monarchy doesn't marry for status, as other planets and systems do. They marry for wealth and...fertility. I'll be the queen's fourth husband, although she's divorced one, so technically, I'll be the third."

Not just the royal family, but the Queen herself. I shook my head. I couldn't imagine how that relationship would go, and how he would talk himself into her still marrying him once she discovered most of his money was gone. Whatever gift he bought on Jordan, it had better be worth it. It might've been what convinced Felix to sell us all out and cost us our bridge crew. Titus. Natalie. Gene.

"This was the best way to secure a future. Surviving two planetary destructions in my lifetime is enough. I need to settle down. The queen's delegation will arrive and escort me the remainder of my journey."

"Mr. Peters," the taller IAP guard interrupted. "We are taking you into protective custody until the delegation arrives from Etho. Time to go."

Aaron looked me in the eyes, his full of regret. "I'll find a way to pay you back, Ami. I will. I owe you my life." He nodded to the guard, and they escorted him off the bridge.

The detective raised his eyebrow. "You're free to go. Thanks for your help."

I stood, relieved it was over, but I stopped at the door. "What's going to happen to Leonard?"

"He'll stand trial."

"Can I speak to him?"

The detective shrugged. "They might've taken him off already."

I rushed down the ladders to the cargo hold. The three prisoners were still there as the Interplanetary Alliance Police removed the makeshift cell.

Leonard stood near the front, and above the shouts from the officers, he called my name. An IAP guard blocked my path. "We're removing prisoners. Crew and passengers need to remain out of the way."

"The detective told me I could talk to him."

I don't know if it's how I stood, or that he knew I was acting as captain, but the guard relented and let me come close to Leonard, whose hands remained tied in front.

His eyes flew open wide, pleading with me. "I told you the truth, I didn't know. I'm so sorry. I thought they only wanted to teach Aaron a lesson."

But he did nothing to stop them, not even when Bricks banged on the door of my quarters.

I stepped back as the guards took hold of the other two prisoners. "Ami," Leonard said, one more time, but I left him with nothing. I had no words for the one who betrayed my friends, who let Titus, Gene, and Natalie become casualties.

After retrieving my belongings from our room, I headed back to the cargo bay with the remaining crew and passengers. Once the authorities finished, Esmie paid Roger and the others the remainder of their salaries.

Cori turned to me. "I've got to go. My brother is meeting me here on Balec, I got word his ship arrived during our questioning." She threw her arms around me.

Even though we were at the end of this journey, for some reason it hadn't hit me that I'd be saying goodbye to Cori. There was so much I wanted to say to her. How much I loved her laugh and missed it now. How much I enjoyed her company.

I squeezed her back, mindful of her healing wound. "Blessed journey."

As I let go of Cori, Dariah hugged Mara. "Blessed journey, Mara. Thank you for all you have done for me. Both of you."

"I'm glad you are returning to your kin," Mara said, grasping Dariah's hands when she pulled back. "May his memory continue to live in you."

I hugged Dariah, and she followed Cori off the ship.

I turned to Esmie, frowning. "Where's Perry?"

The last IAP officer glanced through his tablet. "Perry Samson disembarked already."

"What?" *He didn't even say goodbye?* "Did he say where he was headed?"

The officer shrugged. "Said he didn't need help rebooking passage to Nidos."

An ache settled in my chest. How could Perry leave without saying goodbye, after all that happened? He'd even trusted me with his real name, Bo Perez, but didn't trust me enough to tell me what his plans were. Maybe he was in more trouble than he let on, though the IAP officers didn't seem as interested in him as they had been with Aaron and me.

There was a chance I'd see him again. Nidos lay in the Nacaen group—if he hadn't lied about going there. After sharing who he was, I thought we were finally opening up to each other. For him to just go with no word, it was another loss on this journey of losses.

The IAP officer left us alone, and Esmie, Mara, and I were all who remained.

"What will you do now?" I asked the engineer, turning my thoughts away from Bo Perez.

"Sell the ship. I can't stay. Titus never told me who was on board, what we were doing. I wish he'd never gotten involved at all."

"I understand." None of the crew wanted to stay on. I couldn't shake the feeling the captain would be sad if he overheard our conversation. Titus said once that he never left the ship. Most likely the *Ashkelon* would end up as scrap.

"Here." Esmie offered me a credit chip. "It's not all you deserve, but hopefully it will get you both to Aza."

"We're not going to Aza." I glanced at Mara, having made my decision after the mutiny. "I'm going with her to Melas."

My mother-in-law hissed. I remembered her caution about not trusting others, but this was Esmie.

"The Twelve?"

I nodded. I refused to leave Mara alone. Not after all she'd been through to bring Max to me.

"Be careful," the tall engineer warned. "They aren't under the Interplanetary Alliance. I know Aza isn't, either, but the Bara System doesn't have the same kind of struggles the Nacaen Group has."

Mara's eyes narrowed, her brows drawn together. I knew she hated the assumptions made of her people. I also knew from Max the challenges that faced his home system were real.

Smiling at my crewmate, I assured her. "I know. We'll be fine." I hugged her. Esmie nodded to Mara, and we gathered our bags. I took one last look at the cargo bay of the *Ashkelon*, the place that had first held our hope, and then so much sorrow.

———

A SMALL, blue-green orb, Balec lay outside the shadow
of a gas giant. Smaller than Dibon, the tiny world
supported a tropical environment across its surface. The
Bara System stretched far and wide, containing twenty-
some planets and countless moons with settlements
under biodomes, holding as much ethnic and cultural
diversity within its system as most of the Near Side
Systems combined. Balec Station, in orbit above the
globe, was cluttered with foot traffic, being the only port
dually aligned with the Interplanetary Alliance.

Pilots and travel agents shuffled us from one desk to
another, trying to find a ship headed to the Nacaen
Group. I kept scanning the crowd for Perry—Bo—but
there were so many people I could miss him, even if he
was still around. The passengers, diplomats and other
crew passing us wore strange clothing, with elaborate
colors and headpieces and robes, accessories that
seemed excessive and useless to me. Diboni attire was
neutral earth-tones, made for practical wear. I'd thrown
my uniform in the ship's recycler before we left, going
back to wearing my Diboni-style, button-down cream-
colored shirt and brown pants.

I overheard strange tongues alongside the Galactic
Language. The variations in accent of our common
language were slight, almost unnoticeable in the Near
Side Systems, but now I caught a sharp consonant, a
rolled R, a hissed pronunciation, and many words I
didn't know at all. I found myself staring at the people
with silver tattoos which shimmered in the light. I
couldn't tell if they were permanent or temporary. I

appreciated their beauty much more than the jagged tattoos of Stiner mercenaries.

"The Twelve?" one pilot asked, as if she didn't hear me the first time, jerking my attention back to the task at hand: finding a way to Melas. The pilot stood even shorter than Titus, and thinner. Under her dark pilot's cap peeked auburn curls, and brown freckles dotted her cheeks. "I heard Nidos is in civil war again, the Tali and the Hessan fighting each other."

I tapped my fingernails on the desk as I handed her our travel records. In most systems, every world was a single nation. Ones without a united government were viewed as barbaric. Bo said his family was influential on Melas—maybe he left to help on Nidos. Or he had a reason to lie to IAP officers after a mutiny investigation.

"I won't go to Nidos, but I can get you to Melas," she offered, after scanning our records.

"Good, 'cause that's where we're going."

"How soon do you want to depart? I've room for two on my ship tonight. It's not a direct flight—I've got stops to make on some of Balec's moons—but we should be there in about six weeks."

"Tonight would be perfect."

"You don't want to get down to the surface?" she asked, her eyes peering up at me, unbelieving. "Haven't you been traveling for a while? I know a pilot going next week, if you want to wait."

"No. We'd rather go on now," I insisted, though the temptation of fresh air and water made it difficult to resist.

"Home," Mara breathed. I noticed her face no longer bore the hard lines of anger, the bitterness she carried for so long. Somehow, although we traveled far, faced death and danger, she softened as we got closer.

The pilot entered her vessel's information into our travel documents. "I leave at twenty-two hundred."

Mara and I had little left over after paying for this voyage, but we ate our dinner at the refectory, splurging to dine on real meat and vegetables once again. Balec cuisine offered a variety of fish, and my mouth watered, wanting to try it all. I settled on scallops in butter sauce. I remembered an officer in my unit long ago talking about the seafood from Oceanya, the same planet where Frederick wanted to retire. I smiled for the first time since the mutiny. I'd almost forgotten Frederick. I hoped that his dream to move to Oceanya would be fulfilled. I was glad he missed everything that happened after Jordan. He'd experienced enough loss.

I used the table's vid screen to scan the news feeds. Gasping in surprise, I tapped the screen—a top story was on Dibon. "The Noma Council has confirmed the recovery of debris found in the interstellar expanse between the Near Side Systems and the Outer Systems. Admiral Donovan of the Diboni Military Force offered this statement:

"'We received a transmission months ago with coordinates for a tracking beacon. The debris has now been turned over to Dibon for further investigation into the failure of the ADS. All signs point to a systems failure—'"

"No," I said out loud. "They're lying." A Buzzard rammed into an ADS satellite and they called it a *systems failure*?

"What is it?" Mara asked, carrying her dessert, her brow furrowed with concern.

I bit my bottom lip. "It's news from Dibon. The Noma Council analyzed the evidence we found before Jordan, but still believe it's a system failure." I'd no way of knowing if Sheya got my message, or if it was intercepted.

As we finished our meal, a Balec security officer—not IAP—approached our table.

"Ma'am, are you Lieutenant Commander Lehem?"

I froze. I hadn't heard the term "ma'am" since Perry —Bo—first used it, back when we left Dibon. We were in the Outer Systems now, and it was a common term here. But fear overcame my confusion.

"This came for you," he said, handing me a comm drive. The officer walked away before I could say anything. I held the drive in my hand, my heart thumping hard. Mara didn't seem to notice my expression, excusing herself to use the restroom. I dug my earpiece from my bag and inserted the drive into the table screen. A cold chill spread across my chest as Vance appeared.

"Lehem. I'm telling you as your friend, you need to set the record straight." His voice was low, his eyes narrowed, sweat beads on his brow. "I've gone through your recording and images over and over, but we can find no evidence of a distress beacon. Based on the data you sent, showing no other drive signatures, no signals of other ships—" he leaned in closer to the camera, his voice barely above a whisper—"Word is coming out the evidence was on board your ship all along, that somehow you were involved."

I covered my mouth with my hand to keep from crying out. This was impossible. How could anyone think I'd have anything to do with the destruction of our homeworld?

"I know this isn't true. Ami, I'm trying to help you," my former captain pleaded, his voice trembling. "I've sent this message to intercept the *Ashkelon* in the Bara system. When you get to Aza, stay there and contact me. I want you to be safe." He scanned the room before speaking into the screen again. "We'll get you back, tell the truth, and get this sorted out."

I yanked the drive from the comm screen. This couldn't be happening. Not now. Not after surviving the Galactic Ocean. I couldn't go back. If Command lied about what happened and wanted to pin this on someone, better for me to disappear. No better place to disappear than a war-torn world with limited comm systems and infrastructure.

I jumped at the touch on my shoulder.

"What is it?" Mara asked. I hadn't noticed her returning to the table.

I breathed out hard. "Nothing." Everything ached inside as I lied to her, but we were so close to Melas. I would not worry her further. Are you ready to go?"

"Yes."

"Then let's go home."

16

"There's no one left?" Mara asked, trembling.

I stared out over the bowl-shaped land before me. I'd witnessed the terror of rainfire, and horrors caused by disintegrator rifles, but I never saw a weapon do this. Nuclear weapons were banned centuries ago, biological warfare made illegal. Then again, so was disintegrator technology by the Interplanetary Alliance, and Bricks managed to use a lockmelter on the door to our quarters.

But we were not in the Alliance anymore, we had arrived in the Outer Systems, beyond Balec. Wild space, where the Interplanetary Alliance did not hold among the Twelve.

What once was the city of Ephra lay in the rubble of the crater blast. I imagined many of Dibon's cities were like this after the meteor shower. However, the atmosphere of Melas was clear, the early morning sky a pale lavender streaked with cirrus clouds. I breathed deep, the air crisp and clean despite the destruction.

Above us hung Horeb, the ringed, cream-colored gas giant of the planetary group, with several more of its moons barely visible.

The thin, tanned woman who brought us here shook her head. "Everyone we knew has fled or died. Deborah buried the last of her sons, and she left for Chaldea a year ago. Our old classmate was the last from the city." She brushed her silver hair from her face as the breeze picked up. When we arrived on the surface yesterday, Anna—the only person who responded to Mara's message—met us when the ship landed and took us in for the night. Our comm transmissions since we left Balec were spotty from the stellar disruptions.

The crater stretched several kilometers wide. We stood on the ridge, a good sixteen meters above the ground behind us, and sixty above the ground in front of us. Beyond the edge of the crater I could make out destroyed buildings and what were once roads. The major difference between here and the meteor strike on Dibon, besides the clean atmosphere, was this happened to be a calculated attack. The nearby village where Anna met us suffered less damage.

"We shouldn't have come here," Mara muttered, the river of tears unstoppable. I placed my hand on her shoulder, but she shrugged away. "What is left for us here? God brought us all this way, and for nothing."

Anna grasped her friend's hand. "No. There's still life." She motioned to the green fuzz growing nearby, the promise of grasslands to come, in the middle of the obliterated city.

I pressed my hands on my lower back as we walked to the truck. My muscle tone had weakened, and my joints ached from almost a year of artificial gravity that was slightly lower than Melas, but I knew my body would readjust, with so much more space to move than a cramped freighter.

Anna drove us back to her village, away from Ephra as the sun rose higher. I smoothed out my tunic. Because Melas was warmer than Dibon, here they wore light trousers and longer shirts laced in the front. Many workers donned scarves or hats during the day.

Mara's friend was right. As we drove down the road, I watched from people sawing wood and hauling stones. Life had returned to this war-torn land. Most everyone I spied from the window were Dahan like Anna and Mara —pale skin turned tan in this season, but now and then I saw some of the Sim'ee, with darker tones like my own. However, their hair grew thinner, lying flat. The Jamin hair tended to be thick and dark like mine, but their skin shone brighter, flecked with gold.

The Dahan, Sim'ee, and Jamin peoples made up Melas, three different nations of the Twelve. We were on Dahan land, but now there was peace, and the peoples lived and worked together here.

"Where are the children?" I asked, not seeing any young ones from the window.

"We didn't have many children who survived the war here," Anna replied. "Most families were like Mara's and left. We've lost almost an entire generation, either killed by the war, or being raised on a foreign world."

I shifted my gaze away from the window. As much as I grieved for my miscarriage and inability to have children, the loss experienced here was beyond what I imagined. I glanced at my mother-in-law, recognizing her own painful decision to leave here with Eli for a better life. Children were the first to be transported off Dibon, the first few days after the meteor. Entire planets lost generations as refugees.

Anna helped us to find housing on the outskirts, where the settlement expanded into a new city. "They are calling this city Ephra now, but who knows, it may change names again."

"Everything has changed so much, I don't recognize it," Mara muttered.

Our new two-room house on the outskirts wasn't much bigger than the bunker we lived in back on Dibon. The kitchen area contained a small table and two chairs, a sink and stove, and a small corner cupboard. The bedroom held two beds, a shower and toilet in a corner closet. The floors were constructed of wide boards from the tall, thick conifers growing near here. Anna swept the floors for us and shared some food. Otherwise, the house was bare. "I know it isn't much, but until you can afford something more, you can at least stay here until you're on your feet."

"Where can I find work?" I asked.

"You recently worked on a cargo ship, right? There are some freighter transports that come through here."

"No. I need something that keeps me close to home."

"We've lots of folks after the war trying to farm again, maybe you could get a job helping in the fields."

Mara snickered. "My daughter-in-law knows more about farming than those knuckleheads back from war. She could probably teach them what they're doing wrong."

Heat rushed into my cheeks, and my chest swelled with my mother-in-law's praise.

"All the farm managers meet in the village square before dawn to hire day laborers for the fields," Anna told me as she poured the tea. "There are other jobs available, but if you're unknown, you're less likely to get hired in a reputable establishment. Make sure whoever hires you pays in credit chips from the Outer Systems Regulated Bank—the OSRB is the only legitimate bank tied to other systems. Otherwise, you're likely to be paid in currency that will be no good for most business."

"Where was Eli's farm?" I asked Mara.

"On the north side of Ephra—the old city." She closed her eyes. "I don't want to see it."

Our friend gazed at me sideways. "Among the Nacaen peoples, if you owned land once, your family owns it forever. The deed is passed down through the family. If you leave, the land goes to the next-of-kin. If no next-of-kin can be found, then it's sold. However, since you're back, you can claim it. Although, from the destruction on the north side, you'd be digging out ordnance and blasted rock from the war."

"I don't want it, even if its farmable," Mara admitted. "It was taken from us by Dahan leadership, remember? We'd already moved into the city so they could park their tanks and missile launchers on Eli's farm. When the bombing raids began," she shuddered, "that's when Eli said it was time to leave. No, I don't want that farm again."

I woke well before dawn, preparing breakfast for my mother-in-law, as she'd eaten little the day before. The new tunic I'd purchased was light beige with red embroidery and red laces across the chest near the neck, and I tied a soft blue scarf around my scalp. Though I hadn't thought of Max first thing in the morning for a long time now, when I made my lunch for the day, I remembered how he stopped to pick up his lunch—after we found out we weren't pregnant again. Did I tell him I loved him? I couldn't remember. That was over a year ago.

The village-turned-city contained new constructions and propped up walls that weren't demolished by bombs. More houses stood there, but also restaurants and hotels and saloons. I spied people stumbling out of the latter in the early dawn, the reek of liquor and body odor spilling into the air. Though it was still dark, the sky was only beginning to turn from black to navy, others were setting up shop, selling everything from recycled metal to baked goods. I was tempted by a root bread, which I remembered Max making once, but I didn't have any money—the last of our credits went to renting our tiny house and buying clothes for Mara and me.

Near the village square day laborers drew near, a haggard gathering. Some wore sidearms strapped to their belts, which made me uneasy. Postwar Dibon was a more structured society. Plans were in place for reconstruction, teams ready to instruct on cultivation, and communities planned with purpose. The Diboni culture taught us to value working and living together. There, I never worried, for I held a place of honor as a veteran.

Here I was a nobody. I had no desire to carry a weapon and, dusted ash, I did not want my first wages going to purchasing one after all we went through. Killing Bricks, then Felix—I couldn't do it again.

A few transport trucks parked as dawn broke, ready to hire workers for the fields outside the city, but I eyed holsters on their hips and the probable knives hidden in their pantlegs and I kept walking. I wasn't interested in working for armed guards, even if they were for my protection.

A truck pulled in, kicking up dust as it spun around. A couple of men leaped from the back and several workers stood, so I stepped closer. "Listen up," one of the men called out. "We're looking for day laborers about twenty klicks south of here. The pay is forty thousand."

Everyone gasped, including me. Forty thousand was a lot—what we would've made in a week on Dibon, if I understood the exchange rate correctly. "That's the day rate. But we won't guarantee any work beyond today. We're picky about who we invite back. The owner doesn't tolerate weapons of any kind. He doesn't care if you fought for Dahan, no weapons allowed."

Grumbles rippled among the crowd. Some of the armed workers walked away, but others stepped forward and removed their sidearms, handing them over to the man speaking.

I hesitated, until he called out to me. "You. Are you interested?"

"How do I know you're not going to take us all to a ravine somewhere and dump our bodies?"

The first man laughed, but the second took a step

out from the shadows, and I gasped. His hair was slightly longer than the last time I saw him, the brown curls tighter. The familiar scars on the left side of his face, from his scalp to his cheekbone, continued in a thin line down his chin.

"Ami?"

"Bo," I said, wanting to say his other name first. It had been less than two months, but it seemed like a lifetime ago since the *Ashkelon*. "You didn't say goodbye."

He stopped short.

"We're not gonna hurt you," the other man called out. "I promise, we're just farm boys with a farm to run. And besides, you've the look of someone who knows how to defend herself. You're not from here."

I didn't answer him, keeping my eyes on Bo.

"Dan, give us a minute," Bo called back, before turning to me again. "I'm sorry—"

"Why?"

"I honestly didn't expect to see you again, and when the IAP officers grilled you for longer than usual, I got nervous."

My eyes narrowed.

"I thought you were going to Aza. What are you doing here, anyway?"

"I came with Mara. Decided to stick with family."

Bo pursed his lips. "I should've offered to help. But now, you're here—"

"And I need work. So, if you'll excuse me, I'll go find someone else to hire me."

"Hey—"

"No." I pointed right at him. "You lied to me, too many times."

He rolled his eyes, one hand stuffed in his pocket. "Okay, I get it. Here. You don't have to work for me, you can leave." He tossed a chip cartridge in the air, which I caught one-handed, never taking my eyes off him until it landed in my palm.

I flipped over the cartridge and saw the financial chip still intact, marked 40K.

"Why?" I asked, referring to the cartridge.

"Because I want to help."

"I don't need *your* help."

"Fine. I don't have time to wait, anyway." The other workers were already on the truck and Dan was calling for Bo.

I stared at the truck until it started to pull away with the crew for the day. I *did* need a job, and there wasn't anyone else I knew on this damn moon besides Mara and Anna.

"Wait!" I called out, running. Bo grinned, but he didn't make the driver stop. I ran faster, pumping my arms and legs, and reached the truck right as his hand reached out to grab mine, pulling me up.

"Now, I've already paid you for the day, you realize," he said, as I caught my breath. "Don't expect to get paid again just because you worked."

"Got it."

"I'm just joking, Ami."

"It's not funny."

Bo studied me for a moment before turning to talk to Dan. I needed the job, but if I got a chance with him alone, I'd let him know how it felt to survive a mutiny and feel like the only person you could trust could just walked out of your life.

The other laborers chatted on the way, but I watched the scenery. The construction faded into the landscape of tall conifer trees and rolling fields. We mainly had evergreens on Dibon, but I'd seen images of trees like these from other planets. I searched for familiar crops, but here they grew wheat and barley native to Melas. Max told me about his father's barley fields—the fields the tanks had overrun. I tried not to think about Perry—Bo, but I stole a glance. Fury burned in my bones. He was here, from the same region, same *city* as Mara, and had never told me.

After a half-hour, the truck pulled through a large gate. Fences and walls around the large farm protected the crops from vandalism and theft. Guards were posted at the gate, which caused me to sit up tall, but I didn't see any visible weapons. I knew they were there, though, and I had to accept the fields would be guarded on the outside. Still, I saw no security inside when we rolled to a stop, near a large farmhouse with several barns at the end of the drive.

"Welcome to Lehem Farm," an older man announced, walking from the barns. I stumbled, but no one paid attention. *Lehem*, like my name, like Max's name. Mara never mentioned any extended family. I scanned the gathered crowd of workers for Bo but didn't see him. He'd known my name was Lehem.

The older farmer wore his long white hair tied back; his fair skin weathered from years of sun. A scar ran along his left arm all the way to top of his hand, visible beyond the rolled-up sleeves of his tunic.

"Here are the rules: No violence. Any outbreak of violence and you'll be escorted out, with no pay. None of our neighbors will hire you, either. We don't tolerate it. Take your revolutionary ideas elsewhere. No harassing, no lazing about. Do your fair share, we'll feed you and pay you. If we like you, we'll invite you back. Show up tomorrow and every day on time or early and do your work, and you might earn a room in the bunkhouse. We've got seasoned workers here along with you greenies, they'll help show you the ropes."

I followed some new workers over to the fields. A petite woman with white hair addressed us. "You'll gather the grain the machines leave behind. Thousands of years of technology and we haven't perfected this, so there's always work to be had. If the stalk is damaged or blighted, we've got a burn pile over there. If you need a break, take one. If you didn't bring water, there's a hose over there running from the well. Toilets are back by the bunkhouse." Her teal eyes fell on me. "Work as long and as hard as you can, but don't dehydrate and faint on me."

Falling into line, I gathered the grain, separating out the damaged and blistered crop. There were patches where most of the grain had sizzled in the heat, where they didn't bother to reap. I crouched, touching the soil. Dehydration didn't cause this—the soil was missing certain nutrients. Other patches seemed fine, but whatever treatment they used for the soil had not mixed in well. It was hard to make out in the bright sun, but it might be rainfire ash. *If so, wouldn't they have spread neutralizer?*

A shadow covered my path, but I didn't move. "Enjoy getting your hands dirty?" he said from behind me.

I recognized Bo's voice as I stood, brushing the dirt off my hands. "Just looking at it."

"Why?"

I scowled turning to him. "I don't know, it's interesting to me."

He sighed, stepping closer to me. "I owe you more than an apology. I owe you the truth."

I folded my arms across my chest. "All right, I'm all ears."

"Not everyone knew I went to the Ramaen system. Most thought I was just working for the family in Bara. The war here was much longer than Dibon's, and the divisions on our planets run deep."

"I just need to know why you left without saying goodbye."

He nodded. "After Titus told me about the Stiner attack, I got worried they might be after me. And then he told me that Dibon had sent you a message—"

"He told you?"

Bo stepped back, as if he realized he gave too much away. "Yeah. I didn't want to be anywhere near the *Ashkelon* if Diboni authorities were involved. Knowing the Ramaens would be interested if there was sabotage involved with Dibon's ADS—they got hit with severe sanctions after exporting weapons for your war—I figured I'd better stay away, with my connections to Ramaen diplomats."

My heart pounded in my chest. "I sent a copy of the evidence to my sister-in-law. She's Ramaen."

"Does the Diboni military know that?"

I shook my head.

Relief flowed over Bo's face. "If she sent it to her government, then they'll handle it."

I considered what he said. I hadn't thought Sheya

was at risk, and now Bo had put doubts in my head about her safety. But I was across the galaxy from her, without reliable comms.

"I left as soon as I could under my alias, in case someone had bribed IAP looking for me. I tried to find you, but they were still questioning you, and I didn't want to get you involved in my troubles. I didn't know you'd changed your plans and were coming here."

I wasn't, until the mutiny. Until Mara told me all she'd been through, and how awful and similar our lives have been.

He tilted his head, his lips turning up. "I'm glad to see you again."

My anger dissipated. For all the people on this side of the galaxy, except for Mara and Anna, he was the only one I knew who was still alive.

A voice called to Bo—the woman who had met us when we got off the truck. Other workers drew closer. "I know you want to know more—why I traveled there to begin with—and I *will* tell you, another time."

"All right."

He chatted with the woman, then left the field. I'd meant to ask him about the farm's name, but all the other questions about him took precedent.

I worked all day. The knots in my stomach from earlier faded as curiosity took over. I kept finding patterns in the soil showing decay and over-mineralization. Someone had tried to correct this, but much of the harvest on this side of the field was damaged.

When the sun set, the white-haired woman gathered us together near the bunkhouse, next to a small stand of tall trees with needle-like foliage. There were small stands of thin, papery trees, old boundaries of farms from years past that survived the war, amid the fields.

A strange man, wearing a tan religious robe, slipped into the stand of the tall needle trees. I glimpsed him for only a second before I lost him among the trees, but he gazed in our direction, right at me. I'd never seen a priest outside the Noma System before.

The old woman addressed us, drawing my attention back to her: "Y'all did fine work. The truck will be waiting for you to take you back into town, but there's more work tomorrow if you want it. I have your pay."

The overseer handed each laborer a chip cartridge. When she came to me, I shook my head. "No, I already received my pay."

The white-haired woman squinted, studying me. "How is that?"

"The manager—Bo—paid me this morning, because I was skeptical about coming here."

She chuckled, then lifted my hand and put the chip in my palm. "Take it anyway. You deserve it."

My cheeks flushed. The last thing I wanted was for the other workers to be jealous. "No, please, I didn't—"

"—Take it," the overseer repeated, and walked away.

I rushed off the truck to make it through the city, knowing I carried eighty thousand and in that moment, I wished I had a gun because I carried *eighty thousand* and could be an easy target. However, no one else knew I carried the money, and the women who were in the field didn't follow me. I made it back to our little house and shut the door, sliding the bolt.

"How was it today?" Mara asked me. She sat at the dining room table, her hair combed out, parted along the middle, and wearing a soft green dress wrapped around her—another fashion from this system. For the first time in years, she seemed more alert, more alive.

Despite Ephra being a crater, I knew coming home was the right move. Max's mother didn't lose her family here—this was the last place they were together.

"Good. I found work at a farm—and Bo—Perry—he's the manager there!"

"Oh, that's wonderful! He was such a nice man on our voyage. I'm sorry I didn't get to say goodbye to him."

"He didn't tell us who he was, or where he was from. And the name of the farm—it's *Lehem* Farm."

"That is strange," Mara pondered, frowning. "I was told all our kin were killed. I didn't remember anyone of Eli's immediate family in this part of the continent."

"Maybe the name of the farm stuck?" I asked, untying the scarf from my head, scratching the back of my neck. I stopped cutting my hair right before we got to Balec, and it now brushed my shoulders when loose.

"Maybe. I'll ask Anna what she knows. Did you meet the owners?"

"There was an old man with a scar that ran down his arm, with long white hair, but I didn't hear his name, and an older woman who helped us in the field, but I don't know if she was an owner or only an overseer." For that matter, I didn't know if Bo was related. He mentioned he had family here.

My mother-in-law set her elbows on the table. "I wish I knew more of Eli's family; it could be some of them still live here."

"I made good money today," I announced, tossing a 40K cartridge on the table. "I've another one, too."

"*Eighty thousand?* My goodness, Ami, you must be careful on the streets with that kind of money!"

"I know. I was careful. Remember who you're talking to," I assured her with a wink, though I was the one who bolted the door after I came home.

"I know, but still—carrying that much can be dangerous!"

"Deposit it then."

Mara pulled out her wallet—a small device with a screen assigned to her when we set up our account at the OSRB after we landed—and inserted the cartridge. "Why did they give you so much?"

I shrugged. "Bo gave me forty thousand at the beginning of the day—I think as a peace offering, for all we went through. When the woman paid me at the end, I told her I was paid already, but she insisted I keep it."

"There," my mother-in-law remarked, putting the wallet away. "I hope you go back tomorrow, then."

"They don't allow weapons at Lehem Farm, and I prefer that."

"Well, that's good, and having Bo there is a bit of luck, for once." Mara set root bread on the table that she baked, and my mouth watered. "I know this place is so different. Dibon was a good home. I know I didn't appreciate it when I was there, but your people had infrastructure in place—military, medical, community planners. When we arrived, we were resettled immediately. When the civil war broke out, your government kept us safe. And when the war was over, your community planners informed Max and Chip of opportunities to be involved in farming. Even with the threat of meteor strikes, there were underground bunkers. Everything was thought out, and when the unexpected happened, your people improvised."

I tore off a piece of root bread and slathered it with olive oil, from the trees in Anna's yard. "Dibon is older, you know," I reminded her. "We joined the other planets in our system to form the Council and we've had a hundred years more of living on the same planet in the same system than Nacaens have, which is why we have one nation, one people, one planet: One Dibon."

And one massive cover-up, when it came our home's destruction. I hadn't thought of it for a while, and I didn't want to believe it, but a part of me worried Bo was right, after Vance's message. Seeing Bo brought it all back. I shivered at the thought.

"We're still babies at this, in many ways," Mara said. "It's a wild place, here. We go round and round in circles, fighting our own so we won't go to war, destroying ourselves."

"Maybe this time will be different?"

"Indeed. Anyway, tomorrow—ask about the farm's name, will you?"

17

T he older woman's name was Rachel, I learned as I got off the truck for my second day at Lehem Farm. I didn't have an opportunity to ask her about the farm's history, as she didn't stay with us long. There were a few new greenies working with us, as some of yesterday's workers didn't come back. "Take their pay, spend most of it on the first night and wake up with a hangover after the workday has started," the white-haired woman complained.

We finished clearing the portion we worked on the day before, completing it by noon. The farm provided lunch, I discovered, so I helped myself to the hearty bread and cheese offered in the bunkhouse. This bread was made from several different grains, and as I tore off a piece, I breathed in its warm, delicious scent.

"Y'all have a choice this afternoon," Rachel informed us, "to move on to another field or help with maintenance on the machinery, wherever you think your skills might lie."

To my surprise, I was the only woman who stayed to help with the machinery. Back on Dibon there were many women steelworkers. I learned on machines as a child, but once we were a couple, Max and I learned to repair farm equipment together.

Cleaning a large tilling machine, I noticed gray soil on the lower blades. I bent lower, brushing some of it with my gloved hand into a cup.

"Playing with dirt again?"

I didn't look at him, though Bo stood close behind me. "There's something wrong with the soil. See what the lower blades are churning up?" I spun around, shoving the cup forward.

He peered into it and shrugged. "Yeah, most of the fields are full of it. Ash left over from rainfire during the last war."

"It's not ordinary ash."

"How can you tell?"

I sighed, lifting my gaze and searching his brown eyes. He seemed to genuinely want to know. "I was a farmer after our war, along with my husband."

"Oh." His eyes grew wide.

I hadn't talked about Max with him. I'd barely mentioned my husband on the voyage at all, but it had been over a year now since his death. "Max was Mara's oldest son. We were married for two years."

"Did he die when—"

"Yeah. Along with his brother. We bought an old farmhouse and several acres after the war." I wiped the sweat off my brow with my glove. "Our government retrained many of us to be farmers or teachers, to offer community support. Because that's what our people do, what our government does, what our military is about— we are one planet, one people."

"Ami," he began, but I ignored him.

"So, while you can come in and tell me all your conspiracy theories about my people, I know *my* people. And I know *your* people. We helped save the lives of thousands of your refugees, even though there were Twelve Rebels among them. We didn't let the Renegades win with their ideology, but that all of us who live on Dibon are one people—refugee, immigrant, and native born. One Dibon."

I went back to my work, cleaning all the blades, inspecting the gears. Bo left me alone, but I saw him watching me at the entrance to the barn. I don't know why I was so defensive, or so angry. Even Vance seemed to be warning me there was a cover-up. I didn't want any part of it. I wanted to leave that behind.

I shifted gears back to the dirt on the blades. I'd seen the aftermath of rainfire—the land Max and I farmed was loaded with ash. We spent the first year of our marriage adding neutralizer, bonding with the ash to change the PH levels, and then tilled with the soil underneath for even distribution.

Strains of neutralizer streaked through the ash. A gray film stuck to the edge of the cup, but I observed darker swirls in the soil. Either something else was added to try to neutralize the soil and it didn't work all the way through, or this was not the remnant of rainfire.

———

RACHEL WASN'T THERE in the evening to dole out our pay, so Bo came to each of us with our money. He slipped two cartridges into my hand. When I opened my mouth to protest, he glared at me. I didn't know why he paid me so much, after the way I spoke to him.

The sun had been down for a half hour when the truck dropped us off back at the town square. No one else walked my direction. The streets with vendors I passed in the mornings were now dark and empty, the noise of the saloons fading. I walked a few blocks, but the hairs on my neck pricked. Something wasn't right. I stopped. A footstep echoed behind, faint.

I dove down a side street, swerving down an alleyway, but they managed to keep up, gaining on me. I carried *eighty thousand*. Footsteps and heartbeats sped up.

My heart crawled up my throat. I didn't want a confrontation. I had no weapon to protect myself. I could run, scream, but I didn't know where help was, or if any would come.

I could offer them the money. Leave it behind and run for my life.

But we needed this. Mara deserved better than this. I was Diboni military, and I would not be taken.

There were two—one heavier-footed than the other. A shadow in the starlight caught the corner of my eye. One breathed out hard—a woman taller and larger than me. The other, a man, had quicker steps.

A hand descended on my arm. I spun around, jamming my knuckles into his nose. The crunch of cartilage reverberated through my arm as he fell back, blood spurting from his face. Pain rang through my fingers with the contact. The woman's arm came around my neck to put me in a choke hold, a ring on her finger scratching my cheek. I stomped on her foot, then dropped to my knees, throwing her over my shoulder.

The man with the broken nose came at me again as I stood, thrusting my elbow in his face. With my other hand I grabbed his shoulder, yanking him toward me and kneeing him in the groin. Spinning as the woman raised a handgun, I rushed her, twisting her arm. She fired, missing me and hitting the other. I body-slammed her to the ground, kicking the weapon away.

She lay there, moaning, but didn't rise. Keeping one eye on her, I bent over the first attacker, blood pumping from the gunshot wound in his chest. His eyes were glazed, his mouth open. I shook out my hand, still smarting from striking his nose. I pressed his hand to his chest but there was no use—his heart was in pieces. Dropping his hand, my fingers grazed his neck, catching the silver chain he wore—a chain just like mine. My cheek stung from the scratch below my eye as I squinted in the starlight; his dog tags poked from underneath his shirt.

I jerked my head as the woman stirred and attempted to raise her head but fell back to the dirt. I raised the tags to where I could read.

Ensign. Amman, Kede.

Dibon Military Force.

The tags slipped through my fingers as my mind raced. What was another Diboni doing on Melas?

I swallowed hard, trying to quiet my heart as it struggled to escape my chest. There were no other sounds beyond a moan now and then from the woman. I yanked the tags off the dead man. Removing my scarf, I used it to pick up her weapon, careful not to get my prints on it.

Creeping over to the woman, I searched her body with one hand as her eyes rolled to the back of her head. She still breathed. There was no identification on her.

Stardust and ashes. The dead Diboni soldier with his dog tags removed disturbed me enough—leaving the woman alive scared me.

The woman had a rich, gold complexion—she was not from here, nor was she from Dibon. She was either hired, or this was just a robbery, with a former Diboni soldier who by chance landed on the same world as me.

But nothing was ever simple. This must be a Diboni hire. Illegal, off the books, but an attempt on my life. I stood there, uncertain of what to do. I couldn't let her live.

I couldn't kill her.

An engine roared in the distance. I ejected the handgun's magazine and placed both in my bag, along with the dog tags, wrapping my scarf around them all. The glow of headlights near the alleyway gave me the signal to run.

My chest pounded as I noticed every shadow, every movement, my muscles taut with fear, until I reached the front step.

Dusted ash. I *should've* killed her. Too late now.

"What happened?" Mara asked, alarmed, as I entered our home. I'd already forgotten I was scratched and bruised, my knuckles bloodied and sore. Sliding the bolt behind me, I fell back against the door.

My voice shook as I spoke. "I was attacked. I fought them off and they didn't follow me. I'm home now, and I'll be okay." I handed her both credit cartridges.

"Don't go tomorrow. It's too dangerous. We'll have to figure something else out." Her hands closed on mine.

"We've gotta eat."

"Ami, please," she croaked out, falling into a chair. "I can't lose you."

Moving to her side, I knelt so I could see her face to face. "I'm fine. Really. I'll go wash up and we'll eat supper." I couldn't let her know how terrified I was. I didn't want her having any regrets about returning to Melas, or me continuing the journey with her. "I'm okay."

As I washed my hands and face, I thought about what would happen to Mara if I wasn't here. Sheya wouldn't have survived half of what we went through if I'd stayed.

But was it safe here for us? Surely it was a coincidence that a Diboni soldier happened to be all the way in wild space, in the Nacaen Group. On Melas. In Ephra.

We hadn't been here long enough. Not for someone to be searching for me here. I leaned my head against the mirror, the scrape below my eye stinging from the water, but the realization there was little chance Command had sent someone after me that soon brought on a wave of fresh tears, the tightness easing in my chest. It must be a coincidence. A random attack. Even if they knew Mara was from Melas, they thought I was going to Aza.

They didn't know anything until I was at Jordan, and they couldn't have arrived that quickly across the galaxy.

I shuddered, thinking how close I'd come to death tonight, if it wasn't for my training in the Diboni military.

However, before we went to bed, I promised Mara I'd find work elsewhere.

18

T
hough I woke early, I stayed in bed, long after the truck would've left. I put the kettle on and prepared breakfast, started the wash, and swept the floor all before the sun rose.

"What will you do?" Mara asked me.

Sipping my coffee across from her, I shrugged. "I don't know. I suppose tomorrow I'll go look for something else."

Her brow furrowed. "The money was good there."

"Are you saying you want me to go back?"

My mother-in-law reached across the table as I set my cup down, taking my hands in hers. "No. I don't want you to risk your life for me."

But I knew she was still curious—as I was—how Lehem Farm got its name. I never got to ask. I didn't want to see Bo, not like this. All his Diboni conspiracy theories would be confirmed.

I'm not ready to face that.

The morning wore on. After glancing through my

wedding photos once again, I remembered I still had the drive with the message from my mother. I'd never finished watching it, all those months ago when I left Dibon. Pulling it from the drawer, I inserted it into the console.

"Ami. We don't know if you are alive, but we've heard what happened on Dibon. Your father and I—we'd like to invite you to come live with us. I'm sorry we didn't accept you when you married. I hope you understand, it's not easy to see your only living child marry a Twelve, when your other two children..." She stopped to wipe her eyes with the tissue in her hand. "But we were quick to judge, and for that, I'm so sorry. I wish I could've known your husband Max.

"I know we've no right to ask this, but please forgive us. Please consider coming and living with us. Let us be a family again."

My father entered the screen. They both sprouted the same dark hair as me, but my father had an olive complexion—his grandfather immigrated from another system, but I didn't recall where. My parents' eyes were soft, their expressions conveying sincerity. In text at the bottom of the screen scrolled their contact information and location in the Ramaen System.

I unplugged the drive and held my head in my hands. It was too late—but at that moment, I missed them. What would my life be like if we'd reconciled?

Shoving the drive into the drawer in the bedroom, where I kept my wedding ring, my fingers graced the barrel of the handgun. I'd stashed it there last night. I didn't know what to do with it.

The knock at the door whipped my attention back. I

wiped my eyes—I didn't realize I was crying—and took it with me, sliding the magazine into place. However, when I peeked through the peephole, the first thing I noticed were the scars on his face. I let out the breath I'd held, setting the weapon aside and throwing my scarf over it before unfastening the bolt and opening the door.

"What are you doing here?"

"I came to see how you're doing," Bo replied, his voice soft, eyes full of concern.

"How'd you find me?"

He shrugged. "I asked around."

"What do you mean?" I folded my arms across my chest.

Bo reached up—I jerked my face back. "Sorry," he mumbled, pulling his hand away, "but that scratch below your eye—"

"Oh, that. Yeah." It looked a lot worse than it felt today.

"I got worried when you didn't show up—worried I'd really said something...anyway, two others didn't show up this morning, and we heard rumors they were involved in a fight and attempted robbery."

My palm went to my chest. "They worked for you?"

Bo stuffed his hands in his pockets. "Yeah. I didn't hire them; they were hired on earlier this season when I was away."

Confirming my suspicion that the attacker couldn't be a spy for Dibon. I swallowed hard. "I didn't kill him. I mean, I did, but she was going to shoot me—"

"Ami," he said, his eyes traveling down to the bruises on my arm where my sleeve was rolled up. "There are no police here. They worked for us on the farm—we handle what happens with the farm and its workers. No one is blaming you."

"Did she—did she—"

He set one hand on his hip. "Beat up pretty good, but she'll live. When she's well enough she'll stand trial."

"Trial?" I frowned. "I thought you said—"

"No police, but we have a court system," Bo clarified. "Made up of elders and our judge who makes decisions here on Dahan land. It's how we do things." He shifted his feet. "I'm sorry this happened to you. And I'm sorry for what I said yesterday. Take as long as you need, but you're welcome to your job if you still want it."

My lips twitched, but I suppressed my smile. "Thanks, I'll think about it."

"I hope you will. I want your opinion on something."

"On what?" I leaned against the doorframe.

"Soil neutralizer."

"Oh, so you recognize I know something about ash and soil now?" I cocked my head to the side, no longer holding back my smirk.

"Yes, and I need your help."

"Who's there?" Mara called. She'd been resting in the bedroom.

I leaned in from the doorway. "It's Bo."

"Bo!" my mother-in-law said, embracing him. My eyes flew open wide at her show of affection. "It's so good to see you. I'm so glad you came by."

"Thanks, ma'am, but I ought to be getting back." He managed to remove himself from her arms. "I hope to see you soon," he said to me.

I waved as he walked out the door, and I closed and bolted it behind him.

"Did he offer you your job back?" Mara asked.

"Yeah. I told him I'd think about it."

"Good, good," she encouraged, patting my arm.

———

I DIDN'T RETURN until the end of the week. As much as I thought I was fine, I had nightmares of the attack after Bo's visit, and thought twice about those farms with armed guards. In my nightmares, the attackers were Felix and Bricks.

Nonetheless, Lehem Farm treated me well the first two days, paying me double without reason. Over time, I could afford to buy a larger home for Mara with the money I made there. But something else drew me there. The name. The mystery in the soil.

When Bo spotted me in the crowd after several days, his lips curved up for a second in acknowledgement. After I climbed into the truck, he sat next to me.

"When we get there, go to the maintenance shed."

"More machinery for me to clean?"

He didn't answer.

When we arrived, I followed him and a few others to the maintenance shed and got to work changing fluids out of an older model tractor. Right when I finished, Bo stood by the door, waiting for me. "Come this way," he whispered, and my eyes narrowed.

He led me from the maintenance shed to a smaller building nearby. "Here, put these on," he told me, handing me a yellow jumpsuit and gloves. Bo pulled his own on over his clothes, before handing me a protective mask and opening the inner door.

Inside lay rows of tables with lights hanging above. Each table held vials of dirt and ash. A few tables had samples spread out under the light.

"Analyzing the soil?"

"Determining the toxicity," Bo acknowledged, his voice muffled through the mask.

"If you're this worried here, shouldn't we be wearing these suits out there?" I questioned, pointing to the door.

"Nothing comes up on our regular screening outside, it's only in here when we test with neutralizer that we've been able to find anything. The suits and masks are merely a precaution."

"Why did you bring me here?"

"You know about this stuff," he admitted. "I know about soil nutrients for planting, and we all know how to neutralize rainfire ash, but we've run into problems with some of the crop dying, and even when we till and replant and add more minerals, it still happens. We thought perhaps an infestation, but there're no bugs. If it's the soil, why isn't neutralizer working?"

Turning away from him, I walked over to the table where the ash lay spread out and peered over it. I knew it was different, but it was hard explaining how. "It doesn't look like the rainfire ash I've seen."

"Was rainfire used during your war?"

I scanned his soft brown eyes. "Yeah. Mostly by the Renegades, but..." I let my voice trail off. I still didn't want to admit out loud some of the things we'd done to ourselves.

Bo stood there for a moment, seeming unsure of what to say.

I moved on. "Neutralizer effectively neutralizes all toxins left from rainfire and reduces the acidity. It also bonds with the dirt to form nutrients, which is why it's so effective. The genius who invented it makes a fortune every time a war ends. Within a year, the soil is so rich you can plant almost anything."

"Right, but why isn't it working here—you think this isn't rainfire ash?"

"No. Some of it is, which is why in patches you've got barley growing rapidly. But there is something mixed in —another form of neutralizer I've seen poorer communities try to use with little effect for rainfire—when it encountered the regular neutralizer, it's leaving those gray traces there." But I pointed to what puzzled me. "Then there is this light film, and the dark brittle ash."

"What kind of ash is it then?"

"I don't know."

"Would you be willing to help me find out?" he asked, setting his elbows on the table across from me.

I shrugged. "It'd be helpful for me to see more of it. I'm not an expert, but I'm guessing the experts weren't able to help."

"No. They said we had a bad batch of neutralizer, but we tried a different source and got the same results."

"I can go back out to the fields and collect more."

Bo grabbed my arm from across the table. "If you do, be discreet about it."

"Why?"

"I don't want anyone else knowing." He let go of my arm.

"Who? Rachel, or Big Boss?" What the workers out in the field called the old man.

"No, they know what I'm doing. He's Jonah, by the way."

"Then why the secrecy?"

Bo removed his mask and stood from the table, the overhead light hanging in my line of sight. "We're some of the biggest supporters of Dahan's claim for leadership and governance. But there are some Jamin neighbors who continue to stir up trouble. We have peace with most of them, but there are a few we don't."

He pointed to his side, and I understood. He'd been carrying a sidearm all along. While they didn't allow weapons and violence, I wouldn't be surprised if Rachel carried one too.

"It's also why I was in the Ramaen System," he added. "I was there to speak for Dahan—not for the Jamin, or the Sim'ee, who also share this world."

"I take it that's controversial?"

He laughed out loud. "You could say that. But if word got out I'd been to the Ramaen System as a diplomat—hell, even as a tourist—it could jeopardize some of the negotiating. That's why I didn't tell you much while traveling. Now that I'm back, there's been more time since the peace accords, and it's different. They know I didn't come back with Ramaen weapons at least, which is what they'd be afraid of."

"How did you end up at Dibon?"

"Really by accident. Apparently, there was a Perry Samson, a Dahan man, who had been a refugee years ago who had a contract to work for a supply run between Ramaen and the Noma Systems, and I just happened to stumble through after he died. It was the perfect alias."

"How did he die?"

Bo looked away for a moment. "He was on Dibon."

I gulped. The real Perry Samson had died just like my husband.

When he finished showing me around the lab, we peeled off our suits, and I headed back to the field. "Remember, don't tell anyone what you're doing," Bo said, before he went back to the machine shed.

Out in the field, I paid careful attention to the blighted and stunted grain. I helped collect the good stalks left behind, to not attract suspicion, while I studied the soil underneath. Next time I needed to make sure I had equipment for samples, but I could tell by sight that beyond the edge of the good grain the soil was poor. The dark, brittleness of it puzzled me. I hadn't seen anything like it on Dibon. Digging with my toe, I discovered the same scene underneath, the brittle ash mixed in with soil.

"Hey! What are you doing?"

A laborer yelled from across the field at me. I scanned the field. The rest of the workers were far ahead. How long had I gazed at the dirt?

"Nothing," I called as he ran over. "Something stuck to my shoe."

The worker wore a wide-brimmed hat. I recognized him as the man with Bo on the truck the first day. His thick black hair cut just above his dark brown eyes, and his rolled shirt sleeves revealed golden-flecked arms. I caught up to the others.

"You're the one from Dibon, aren't you?" Dan said as

I passed him. "Wasn't your planet scorched by your own people?"

The muscles in my arms tensed, my fists clenched.

"Your Renegades murdered our refugees. Hundreds of Jamin went to your planet and died. Why should we take any of your kind here?"

I gritted my teeth. The Diboni Renegades thought that way when we erupted in war. They blamed the refugees, specifically because there were Jamin among them.

Spinning around, I got my face right in his. "The murder of the refugees was repulsive. It caused our war. My brother and sister were killed in the beginning, and everyone blamed the refugees. But those of us who lived through it want nothing but peace—"

"*Peace?* Your kind was here before, stirring up war with your weapons."

My eyes narrowed. "I've no idea what you're talking about."

"Diboni are all the same. Liars, who wash their hands when it's over."

I squared to fight.

"That's enough!" I kept one eye on the antagonizing man while Bo rushed toward us. "Dan, I've got it from here."

The man in the wide-brimmed hat smirked, stepping away as Bo grabbed my arm. I yanked it away. "Don't touch me." My fists were still clenched, ready to strike.

"Sorry," he muttered. "Just come over here for a moment."

I followed him a short distance. "Steer clear of Dan. His entire family fled from here, only to be killed."

"Guess it doesn't matter I'm married into the Dahan." My rage neared its boiling point.

"I'm just warning you. Keep to yourself, don't make enemies."

"He came at me. He needs to keep to himself." I spat on the ground. "And I don't need your help."

Bo raised his eyebrows, his left eye twitching under the flap of skin that shielded it most of the time. "You're right, you don't. But you don't need another fight."

I tugged the sleeve on my tunic, covering bruises that still smarted. I bit my bottom lip, frustrated because I wanted to hit something, and angry he was right.

"Take some time to cool off, and steer clear of the Jamin workers here, for now."

Bo left me without another word, alone in the field.

———

WHEN IT CAME time for our usual wages, Rachel handed out our pay, and like before, she paid me double. I opened my mouth, but the white-haired woman shook her head.

"It's not about the money," I insisted, "I need to ask you a question."

"What's that?"

"The name of the farm: *Lehem*. That's my name, by marriage. Ami Lehem."

Rachel's brow wrinkled. "Well, that's interesting. Jonah bought the farm through a family member, they were related to the Lehems, I think."

"My father-in-law was Eli, one of the refugees."

The old woman frowned. "The names aren't familiar to me. I'll ask Jonah later."

"Thank you. I don't mean to pry; I'm only now learning more about my in-laws' family."

She gave a quick smile before moving on to the next worker.

On the truck, I stared across at Bo, who chatted with the overseers. My temper had cooled from this afternoon, and while I still stewed at the encounter with Dan, my anger with Bo dissipated. When the truck pulled into the center, he jumped off and started walking with me. He didn't ask, but I was glad for the company.

When we were out of earshot from the others, I asked him the question that nagged at me. "Why are you paying me so much?"

"What do you mean?"

"You offered me money the first day, without doing anything. Then you've paid me double each day I've worked for you. Why?"

"You work hard, and you're determined." That wasn't the answer I assumed—I'd expected pity for the voyage on the *Ashkelon*, for all we'd been through on the ship. My heart skipped. He admired my work. "The first day I wasn't sure what you found in the soil, but by the second day I knew you'd figured out something was wrong. We need help, if this farm is gonna succeed."

I kept my eyes on the street ahead. He needed me. But it was more than that—Rachel and Jonah were generous, too. "You pay much more than any of the other farms. Why?"

"Faithfulness to the community means loyalty. People need a living wage. Before the last revolution, the philosophy was to keep people hungry, so they knew where their food came from. Those leaders are all dead. This time, those of us who have land and power are using it to provide and build up."

"But still, most of the people can't afford to own."

"With any luck, that'll change," he said, his hands in his pockets. The bulge of the gun was barely visible under his coat. "Paying people forty thousand a day means once they've paid their bills and taken care of their families, they can still save up. If we can figure out the problem with the soil, we can begin to lease out some of the land for tenants to work to own." Bo glanced at me. "There's no reason for us to own that much land. Besides, Jonah and Rachel are getting up there and I know they don't want to manage it forever. If there's going to be a future here, it can't be a version of the past. It must be something different."

We turned down the street leading away from new Ephra, toward the settlements at the edge near the old village, where I lived with Mara. "Besides all you've been through, you cared for your mother-in-law, even leaving everything you know behind to get her here." He looked at me, his expression thoughtful. "That kind of loyalty among us isn't forgotten."

My heart soared for a moment, but memories flooded in. Titus. Gene. Natalie. All dead.

"What happened to your husband? I mean—how did you survive?"

I tugged on my bag, slipping from my shoulder. "By the time the alarms went off and we figured out it wasn't a normal dust storm, we had five minutes to get below ground." It didn't pain me as much to talk about it anymore, but grief always lurks, never fading completely. "He and his brother were out in the field, and I couldn't contact them. I barely had enough time to get Mara and Sheya—my sister-in-law—into the bunkers."

"My parents were killed," Bo blurted out, and I stopped as he faced me. "Transport shuttle crash."

"I'm sorry." All my wariness around him eroded. I guess for him, no longer on his mission, he was free to tell me who he really was. Warmth spread through my chest—a deep appreciation, compassion. "How old were you?"

"Seventeen. I came to live with my aunt and uncle—Rachel and Jonah—and they bought this farm at the end of the revolution, to start over."

"You said you stayed during the war."

He tilted his head. "We went to the mountains west of here for most of it, where some others fled. We weren't in Ephra when the bombs dropped."

We continued walking to the house in silence. I wanted to ask him about his scars, but I didn't. It didn't matter. He'd revealed enough of his pain for me to know him better. For me to trust him more.

As I reached my door, Bo gave a half-smile. "I'll see you tomorrow?"

"Yes. I'll stay on."

"Great. If you want to, you can get a room in the bunkhouse. We have separate quarters there. I'll see if your mother-in-law can stay, too."

"That's kind of you, but we have this, and I'm not

sure how much more moving she can take." I didn't want to live in tight quarters with others again. Though Aaron and I parted in peace, I still remembered what an awful jerk he was.

"Well, goodnight then." Bo waved, turning to walk back.

I leaned against the doorway for a minute, watching as his figure faded into the shadows. A million thoughts raced through my mind—of Max and Chip, of a boy losing his parents in a shuttle crash, not much older than when I lost my brother and sister. Of all the losses notched on our hearts, and yet somehow, we soldiered on, becoming strong again.

When I entered the house, Mara set root bread, vegetables and cheese on the table. "Someone walked you home?"

"Yes. Bo." I bolted the door behind me.

"Anna tells me Bo is the nephew of Rachel and Jonah, and that Jonah may be a distant cousin of Eli's."

I dropped my bag to the floor. "I asked Rachel today about the farm, but she said the Lehems were all dead, and Jonah bought the farm through a family member related to the Lehems."

"The Lehems they knew are dead," Mara confirmed. "They may not know who you are, yet, or that your husband was Max Lehem." She picked up a plate and began to serve the vegetables. "I need to learn how closely Eli and Jonah were related to the man whose farm they bought. It could be the farm was supposed to stay within the Lehem family, which would mean under our laws, it'd be yours."

I froze.

"Keep this to yourself for now. We don't know much, and if it comes to light that the property was to fall to Eli..."

Her voice dropped off. I understood. I was a foreigner, a Diboni, with claims on their land. "We must consider this matter carefully."

19

Mara didn't press the issue about ownership, and I pushed the subject away from my thoughts as the days blended into weeks. I wasn't interested in getting involved in a legal matter in a foreign system. When the autumn rains passed, a clear newsfeed came in from Bara. I spent an entire evening going through the feed, but there were no messages for me, no news from Dibon, nothing new from the Noma Council. Even the attack after my second day on the farm became a distant memory. Life started afresh.

The first harvest was over. Because Nacaen barley ripened fast, Rachel and Jonah planned on a two-harvest season. We tilled the soil, preparing for the next planting, so it would be ready to harvest by spring. Which didn't give me much time to figure out what happened to the soil.

They say you can't go back in time, but with Mara, the layers of bitterness and resentment peeled away, as if my mother-in-law was reborn, week by week, day by day. Her energy returned, and she sometimes went to help Anna, whether preparing the garden for winter or sewing blankets for those in need. The Dahan widow kept herself busy, and once in a while, she even laughed.

Sometimes, when I worked late, Bo would drive me home or lend me one of the farm trucks. We sought out each other's company during meals and break time. Over the weeks, our friendship had grown, slow and casual. Our conversations still centered on the soil, the harvest and crop rotation, but there was an ease between us. Sometimes, we even talked about the *Ashkelon*, and Dariah and Esmie, Cori and Roger and the others, even Frederick, whom we left behind on Jordan. It was easier now, after over a year, to talk about Max. Even when I couldn't speak of it, Bo knew my own losses, and I knew the man must've experienced something horrific to carry those scars.

While I analyzed some of the soil samples, comparing to others Bo managed to retrieve from some neighboring farms, he asked me, "What was your husband like?"

I glanced at him for a moment, both our faces covered in masks, before peering back into the magnifying glass. "Kind. Thoughtful. Always optimistic." I thought of all the negative pregnancy tests after our miscarriage. "Why do you ask?"

He shrugged. "Curious, I guess. Wondering if you perhaps find me kind or thoughtful."

I snorted. Soil samples blew across the glass. "Rule number one: if you want to flirt with a widow, don't bring up her dead husband."

He pulled his mask off and ran his fingers through his hair. "That obvious, huh?"

I blushed, hoping the mask hid my face well enough. "Yes, but I'll let you give it another try." It was about dusting time. I was in no rush, but curious why he took so long, after all we'd been through.

"Dinner, tonight? Away from the farm?"

I raised an eyebrow, my lips curving up. "All right."

There had been casual touches in the lab, the brush of his fingers on my hand when we peered at the same soil sample, or the way Bo would touch my arm and say, "Good night," when he dropped me off at home some evenings. I caught him watching me more than once, averting his eyes, but I noticed. I liked the attention.

With Max, things happened fast—we were both young, eager to start a new life and family after the war. Bo, however, took his time, tried to be deliberate, and at times, fumbled. I enjoyed the journey. For me, there was no rush in this new life.

However, my stomach fluttered as I climbed into the truck with Bo. The other laborers prepared to head out for the evening, going to the saloons, but he drove me to the crater near what had once been Ephra, the rim of the blast zone.

The rush of new love was both familiar and foreign as time passed. Bo and I grew into our friendship, deepened by our mutual respect and silent understanding of previous pain. Even though I'd been married, the old nerves took hold, as I smoothed my hair down more than once.

"This is your idea of a date?" I asked, raising an

eyebrow, as I waved out over the crater where the city had been obliterated.

"I'm not good at romance," Bo admitted as he set a woven blanket on the ground. "It's harder to do this when half your face is burned."

I winced. I could only imagine how hard it was to put himself out there. No wonder he'd taken it slow.

"What happened?" I'd wanted to ask him some time ago, but I became used to his face, forgetting it was that different. It was simply his face.

"Rainfire," he said, sitting on the blanket, confirming my suspicions. I'd seen plenty of rainfire burns during my days as a flight medic. "We were running, fleeing the raid. Rachel told me to get into the truck. I was eighteen then. Thought I was faster than the fighters and went back for something."

"What in the universe would make you go back?"

Bo hesitated, avoiding my eye. "My dog."

"Your dog?" I repeated in amusement, sitting next to him.

"Yeah, a big old sheepdog named Fluffy."

I laughed at the name, knowing I should be horrified, as this was the story of how he lost part of his face.

"Fluffy was everything. I saved him. The dog was singed, I was burned badly, but I got that blasted son-of-a-bitch into the truck in time."

I learned that "blasted" meant the same as "dusted" on Dibon and the Near Side Systems. "Do you still have Fluffy?"

"No, he died, but at a good old age, not because of the war."

The sky draped like a deep purple curtain around us after sunset. I still startled when I gazed up and saw different star patterns than what I remembered. The next nearest moon floated above us, half full, bright against the night sky, and Horeb, the gas giant at its zenith.

Bo brought a basket with the six-grain bread they often made at the farm, some cheese and fruit, and water. "Unfortunately, the ale we brewed last time didn't turn out well, and no one has been able to grow grapes post-war, so I figured we would stick with water rather than Jonah's moonshine."

There was something sweet about not having alcohol on our first date, no crutch to help get over our nerves. Which both pleased me and made me a little timid.

"So why here?" I asked, still curious why he chose the crater.

Bo shook his head, as if he didn't know the answer. "Something about this place. I know—I remember when this happened."

I guessed there were a lot of bones underneath the very dirt we sat on, and a chill ran down my back. My companion noticed, grabbing a small blanket he brought out of the truck and draped it over my shoulders. "Thank you."

"I also know this is a place that few go to. Too many bad memories. But for me, it is peaceful here."

"What kind of bomb did this?"

"Baratanium. Made in the Bara System, but the increased possibility of it blowing up during transit means few were used successfully, save for places like

here. At least the half-life is short, which is why we've
come back."

The purple night sky faded to black as we ate our
dinner. I regretted my earlier comment. Under the
canopy of stars, the crater seemed a beautiful amphithe-
ater. We sat close to each other as we finished our meal.

"When did you join the military?" he asked.

"Sixteen." I drank from the canteen.

Bo whistled. "That's young. Dahan militia have to be
eighteen."

"My brother and sister were killed." I swallowed
hard, but I wanted him to know the truth. "By Diboni
Renegades, but originally it was blamed on Twelve
Rebels."

I glanced at him, noting the rainfire scars running
down to his chin, but he didn't respond, simply listened,
his eyes on mine. "I enlisted right after their funerals.
Motor pool at first, but then I learned to fly Kittiwakes,
and later transitioned into a flight medic."

"Did you see much combat?"

I smoothed out my tunic over the top of my trousers.
"I don't want to talk about it." I hated remembering the
war. I hated remembering it almost as much as I hated
remembering what happened on the *Ashkelon*.

"Sorry."

"It's okay," I replied. Bo was trying, and I knew he
wanted to know more about me after all our secrets on
the ship, but I didn't know what he expected from this. I
tugged at my tunic again, nervous. I hadn't been
touched by someone else in so long my skin ached,
needing to be soothed.

"What about you?" I asked him. "Have you always

been a farm boy?"

"Farm boy?" Bo replied, raising an eyebrow and a smirk. He must've forgotten Dan had called them both that, my first day on the farm. "No. Before this, I was in the Dahan militia, fighting for our freedom."

I gasped. "You never told me that before."

He shrugged. "I didn't want you jumping to the conclusion I'd gone to the Ramaens for weapons. The less you knew about that, the less likely you were to tell someone I'd been in the Ramaen system. But that's all in the past now." He shifted his gaze from me. "We weren't like the Rebels—we had no interest in raiding other systems or seizing ships for the cause. I only went to the Ramaens for support for our leadership and aid for our people."

"Oh."

Talking wasn't getting me anywhere, so I turned toward him, folding my legs, leaning on one arm. I contemplated using my free hand to pull him closer to me but found his face already close to mine. We bumped noses. Giggling, I closed my eyes and let him kiss me, slow and soft. My mouth opened. He pressed one hand to my cheek. Gooseflesh ran along my arms as Bo kissed me again, electricity flowing through my blood.

Lights flashed, racing across the ground as we broke apart. Bo jumped to his feet, hand on his hip, ready to draw his gun. Instincts kicking in, I moved behind him, hoping we wouldn't have to fight.

My companion relaxed as a truck rounded the bend, and the driver came into view. "Jill, you scared me."

"Sorry, Bo," the driver apologized as she climbed out

—a tall, thin woman with long, copper-colored hair tied back at her neck. She was close to my age and height, and had a pistol strapped her thigh. "Rach sent me to find you. Some Jamin broke out in a brawl at supper, and she's clearing out the bunkhouse. Fired just about everyone."

"Blast it." He reached over, squeezing my hand. "I have to cut this short tonight."

I swallowed my disappointment, giving a slight smile. He glanced back at Jill. "Can you take her home?"

"Sure." The copper-haired woman started picking up the woven blanket and the rest of our food. Bo arched his eyebrows. "I'm sorry."

I tried to swallow my regret. I missed being with someone. "It's okay. I'll see you tomorrow."

"Tomorrow."

Bo got into his truck and peeled away.

Jill peered inside the canteen. "No moonshine or anything? Dude is not romantic at all."

I didn't know this woman, as I'd only seen her from a distance. I opened the passenger door and saw a disintegrator rifle half-hidden under the bench seat. "Mother-dust-and-ashes," I muttered.

"Get in," she ordered.

I hesitated, glancing at the direction Bo had gone, wishing he hadn't left me behind. But I didn't have a choice, if I didn't want to find my way home alone, in the dark. The memory of the attack was still too raw. I jumped in, slamming the door.

"Where do you live?" she asked.

"Not far—the outskirts."

The redhead put the truck in gear. "This happens

every so often. Dahan, Jamin, and Sim'ee, we all live here, but some Jamin are upset about the agreement for peace with Dahan so they bring up the last war every time. You know about that?"

I shrugged. "Somewhat."

"It was mostly Jamin dissidents who didn't want unification and formed the Rebels, though there were Rebels of every nation, including Dahan. Now Dahan has the upper hand. Rach and her generation want peace, but sometimes a good blaster will get people in line."

I rolled my eyes at her arrogance. "Or a disintegrator."

Jill's eyes flew wide open, and she slammed on the brakes. I hit the dashboard, my head banging against the cracked glass of the windshield. "How'd you know that's a disintegrator?"

I rubbed my forehead as she raised her pistol at me. "What?"

"How do you know that is a disintegrator?" she repeated in a harsh tone.

My heart pounded. I could try to open the door, but she'd shoot me before I got out.

"I've seen them before." I knew disintegrators because they were manufactured in the Ramaen System. Diboni Renegades used them in the war. I'd seen images of them. I'd never actually seen one up close, only the aftermath of their use. "They're illegal."

"Interplanetary law has little hold on us. We're the Twelve, the scum of the universe. No one cares about us."

I kept my eyes on her gun. My only way out was to

convince her I wasn't a threat. "I was married to a Nacaen refugee on Dibon, you know. Dahan."

"Blast." Jill put away her pistol and opened the glove box, pulling out some tissues and handing them to me. "Sorry," the redhead apologized. I pulled down the mirror from the visor, spotting the blood from a small scrape on my forehead. "I didn't know you were from Dibon. I thought you were Ramaen."

"Why does it matter?"

"Ramaens sent weapons in the past to the Jamin. Stole information from Dahan."

I wiped the blood from my forehead. But what Jill said didn't square with what Bo had told me.

"I'm suspicious of everyone," Jill said, putting the truck back in gear. She kept her eyes on the gravel road as we headed back to the outskirts. "Doesn't matter if you are Diboni and not Ramaen, I'm still going to keep my eye on you."

I didn't respond. All I could think about was how to turn the gun on her if she reached for it again.

"It would just be like a Ramaen to send someone to seduce Bo."

I didn't know what game Jill thought I was playing. Also, she didn't know the difference between Ramaen and Diboni? I gritted my teeth at her ignorance.

And *why* would someone be interested in getting to Bo now?

"I'm not Ramaen, I'm Diboni, I lost my whole family and came across the galaxy to get my Dahan mother-in-law home. That's it. I don't want anything else, from anyone."

Jill grunted, and drove in silence the last ten kilometers as I motioned toward the street, our house near the end. She pulled into the driveway and I got out without speaking, slamming the door. The redhead screeched the truck out the driveway before I entered the house.

"What happened?" Mara asked, her face grave as she reached up to touch my forehead.

"Just a cut."

My mother-in-law gave me a look—knowing I wasn't telling the full truth—as I sat at the table. I sighed, giving in. "Apparently, I've made someone jealous."

Mara's brows arched, her cheeks rose, and I knew I'd offered too much. Way too much.

"About Bo?"

I cradled my head in my hands. She patted my shoulder. "Be careful out there." My mother-in-law brushed a strand of hair out of the way. "I hoped you'd fall in love again."

I jerked my face. "Love? Oh no. This is more admiration, curiosity." *And lust.* Definitely lust and loneliness.

"And love doesn't start from there?"

I shrugged. "I don't know. He's got a lot of secrets to keep."

"As do you."

"What do you mean? I'm an open book."

"Except with your heart," Mara argued gently. "It's been over a year now, Ami. It's okay to open up again. Even if it doesn't last, give it a try."

I opened my mouth to retort but thought better of it. "I'm going to bed," I said to end the conversation, rising from the table. However, I squeezed her hand once before I left, warmed that she approved, had accepted it was time for me to move on.

20

Except for Dan, and a few other workers I recognized, everyone else was new in the morning. Bo gave them the same speech he gave the day I arrived, and most handed over their weapons. I sat away from him after I climbed aboard the truck, avoiding his gaze. When we arrived at the farm, I followed the workers into the field where they tilled the soil. I wanted to get some deeper samples.

Crouching over, I took the third sample that morning—a place where I could see a layer of filmy dark gray in the soil above the rainfire ash—when I sensed him stepping behind me. "Why are you avoiding me?"

I stood. "Because I don't want to get shot by your redheaded bodyguard."

Bo studied me, and recognition washed over his face, followed by frustration as his eyebrows came together. "Blast it, what did Jill say to you?"

I scanned the ground nearby, but no one stood

within earshot. "Said that she was wary of Ramaens or others seducing you. Why? Why would she say that?"

He stepped closer to me. "Remember on the *Ashkelon*, I'd just come back from some diplomatic work among the Ramaens? I'd had an encounter with Jamin extremists while in the Near Side systems. Let's just say some threats were made about finding my family. Even though I hid my identity, I could never be sure if Jamin extremists had gotten to the Ramaen officials first." He pointed at his face. I remembered how he wore an eyepatch, tried to hide some of his scars, kept to himself on board until the mutiny.

"And with Dibon having assistance from the Ramaens, there's a history there, too." I paused, glancing around again. "What about Dan?"

"He's not a threat, not to me. Just steer clear of him, and I'll tell Jill to keep away." He reached for my hand, and I extended it, feeling the roughness of his callouses against my own.

He squeezed my hand, and my expression softened in response. "I've got to go, but I'll see you after lunch," he promised.

I RETURNED to the lab after lunch and magnified the lens again, studying the patterns in the vials of soil and ash. One contained neutralized rainfire. The other held the filmy dark gray ash, and I recognized it as neutralizer that didn't mix. The ash didn't come from a wildfire, as far as I could tell, although I hadn't seen enough natural fires to know for certain.

Rainfire, like Baratanium bombs and disintegrators, was banned by most systems, but rainfire was easier to transport, and from what I understood, easy to make. Could some of the Baratanium fallout from the crater blast have mixed in with rainfire, rendering the neutralizer useless? And what about the other, weaker neutralizer I had found?

Someone knew what was here and tried to hide it.

I left the lab an hour later, as Bo hadn't shown up, and walked toward the bunkhouse to find him when I saw the priest entering the copse—the small stand of needle trees near the farm's center. Max had told me his people built stone altars among the trees. I'd seen the priest only once before, on my first day on the farm, but I'd no reason to enter then.

Curious, I followed him into the copse where the stone altar stood. Mara had lent me her leather-bound prayer book during our last month on the *Ashkelon*, but I still didn't know how the Nacaens worshiped. On Dibon, our ancient temples were built into the caverns in the mountains.

I sat on the ground in the center of the copse mimicking how Mara often prayed from the floor. The fragrance of the bark smelled familiar—similar to our cedars that grew on Dibon—but stronger here, the trees growing higher than what I remembered. They rose to form a natural canopy above me, their branches hanging several meters from the ground. Sunlight peaked through in diamonds and circles, squiggles lighting on the earth in front of me. I traced a line in the dirt, the soil there rich and dark, no sign of any contamination. Whatever happened out there, these trees weren't affected. This sanctuary survived the war.

"Do you have need to make an offering, child?"

I lifted my gaze, fixing my eyes on the priest. Crow's feet drew from the corners of his deep eyes, so blue they were almost violet, his short gray hair standing on end. His skin appeared darker than most Dahan, like the needle trees around us, but he bore no other features of the Sim'ee or Jamin, as far as I could tell. The priest wore a long tan robe, his jaw square and patched with stubble.

"No. I needed space to think."

"Then I will leave you," he replied. But when I pulled the scarf from my hair and face, the robed man stopped. "You're the Diboni who traveled with Mara."

I narrowed my eyes. "Yes."

He crouched, peering right into me. "You're a widow."

Swallowing hard, I didn't reply. I tore my gaze away from him to the dirt.

"You're still young. You'll marry again."

I jerked back from him, standing. "What business is it of yours? You don't know me."

"I know you've carried children but have borne none. I know you dream of your children at night."

He stood, never taking his eyes off me. My mouth was dry, my fingers knotted in frustration and fear. I had dreamed of children, running through the fields, but I never spoke of it. Not since I imagined children in the field when Max left, that fateful day.

His lips quivered. "In your blood is our future. I will not live to see it, nor will you. But I promise you, your child will be blessed, and their children and children's children. They will unite us all."

I ran from the copse while my whole body shook in tremors. I ran until I reached the far side of the bunkhouse—where I rushed right into Bo, who grabbed me by the arms.

"Ami? What is it? What happened?"

Trembling, I shook my head. He let go, standing close to me. "What happened?" he asked again, drawing his hand to my face, his fingers behind my ear, his palm on my cheek. His tender manner, the gentleness of his touch, freed me from the emotional lockdown I'd been in for so long. I collapsed into him, unable to control my tears. Bo cradled my head, his other arm wrapping around me.

I didn't see the barns, but instead the golden fields of Dibon. My chin rested on Max's shoulder, but I couldn't cry because I must be strong and hold on to Max's promise that next time it would happen. Next month we'd be pregnant. Golden-haired children would soon play in the fields.

I blinked, and I was on Melas, next to the barns, weeping for my children who were no more.

21

"What'd he say to you?"

Bo gave me a cup of water. My body had calmed, my vision cleared. I sat at a table in the bunkhouse dining hall, the rest of the laborers back at work.

"The priest knew who I was, but he knew things he couldn't."

"Like what?" He sat across from me.

I glared at him.

"Sorry, it's none of my business."

Shaking my head, I let out a deep breath. I hadn't meant to direct my anger at him. "He knew I had a miscarriage."

"I'm sorry," he repeated, his hands clasped, elbows resting on knees. "Phin is—hard to explain. He's been a priest for a long time, and our doctor, too, but he hid in the mountains during the war—not in the bunkers with the rest of us, but by himself—and he doesn't really know how to talk to people."

"He said things—things he couldn't know, but he did." I stared at the cup in my hands, parsing out the words in my head. "He predicted things about my future."

"Phin saw a lot of horrible things during the war, one of the reasons he doesn't say much, but when he does it usually isn't good. He claims to have visions, but they sound more like ramblings. He'll listen to your prayers and take your offerings, but I wouldn't put much stock in what he says."

I remembered why I needed to find him when I went into the copse. "I have to show you something."

"Are you sure it can't wait?"

"I'm fine," I retorted, and regretted saying it that way. I didn't mean to snap at him. It wasn't his fault Phin set me on edge. "Sorry."

"Totally okay."

Bo followed me back to the lab, where after we suited up, I showed him the gray filmy ash I found. I explained my suspicions about the Baratanium being used here.

He arched an eyebrow. "If Baratanium was used here, there'd be a crater."

"You don't think it could be fallout from the one in Ephra, mixed with another neutralizer to try to reduce radiation?"

"We found no Baratanium residue traces when we came here. It clears out fast, anyway, which is why rebel groups continue to use it. Conquerors can resettle much faster."

I frowned. "I'm fairly certain this is the residue from

some sort of weapon. What else was used here during the war?"

"Only Baratanium and rainfire were used on the large scale. Otherwise your regular assortment of small arms, short-range missiles, grenades and the like."

"From Bara, or from other systems as well?"

"Do you want to see?"

I stood straight, almost hitting the overhead lamp with my head. "Are you still stockpiling?"

Bo tilted his head. "We keep a small arsenal," he said, somewhat sheepish.

"What do you mean?"

"Ami, I'm the leader of the Dahan militia."

I didn't blink. I didn't move. Inside, my mind raced a thousand different ways.

"I know I told you I was part of it during the last war, but I still am—we've moved below the radar, trying to build a coalition. We're opposed to the Rebels and their actions to keep unification from happening. We want Melas to be a unified world, and hopefully, someday, a unified Nacaen republic, across all moons and planets."

"But you have weapons."

"We have to. Some we collected in disarming Rebels; others in case we got attacked by a ground invasion. We don't have many fighter ships at all—the Sim'ee do—so we have some antiaircraft defenses. It's not much. It's a last resort." He leaned across the table. "I'm not looking for a fight, Ami. The Dahan are trying to prevent one."

I pulled my mask off. As much as I wanted to turn away from anything that might drag me back toward war, I needed to find an answer to the problem in the soil. "Show me."

After we removed our suits, he led me away from the barns across a section of land I hadn't traveled before. The crop growing here was blighted, but still standing. "When we first bought the farm, the first season we spent digging out all the mortar shells and remnants from the war. We tested for Baratanium at the time, along with deathroot."

I nodded in acknowledgement. Deathroot, the poison the Stiner at Jordan Station used, came from a ravenous weed with white flowers. It wasn't indigenous here, or on Dibon, either, but easily transferred and planted, and within its stem the deadly poison. When evil takes root, there is no stopping the creativity of weaponry hell bent on destroying the enemy, even when it destroys you. Most likely, those who dropped the Baratanium bomb that wiped out Ephra also died from the blast, or from the fallout. Others kept deathroot pills handy to take their own life if captured.

We neared the edge of the farm along the high fence, where three fruit trees stood. Beyond the fruit trees lay a pile of overturned dirt—tree stumps and weeds, along with decomposing roots and soil. I noticed the neutralized rainfire ash, but none of the gray film I found earlier. The tall grasses growing here were healthy. We skirted the pile, until we were out of sight of the barns and fields. Bo found a stringy branch among the upturned weeds and pulled on it.

A crack formed in the dirt pile, opening like the teeth of a giant soil monster, ready to swallow us. As the door lowered and widened, the smooth concrete inside became visible. Bo offered me a hand to step over the metal teeth, and after we climbed inside, he pressed a button to shut the door behind us. Lights flickered on in domino effect, and I descended the steep slope inside the bunker, not letting go of his hand until the floor became level again.

On the walls hung racks of guns and ammunition. "This is what we have, what we were able to store up after Ephra was destroyed."

"But Dahan emerged in power?"

"It's a loose alliance right now. We have peace, but until we can unite the system, we have to be ready."

Unite. Phin, the priest, spoke that word to me, about my children. One who would unite them. A shiver crept over me. I shook the thoughts from my head.

Instead, I focused on the variety of weapons. I recognized sluggers—grenade launchers—and dartbombs. The rest were sniper rifles, pistols, and electric stingshots—designed not to kill but to paralyze. Bricks had one on the *Ashkelon*.

I'd killed him. I killed Felix.

I spied a Ramaen blaster—a high-impact assault weapon, with the capability to pierce most armor and steel, even on fighters. As much as I hated weapons, as much as I hated what they could do—I pulled the Ramaen blaster off the wall. I couldn't be afraid of them. I'd used them before, and I might have to again.

A spark of mischief ignited in me, wanting to shed the grief and anger I experienced earlier.

"I don't think anything here could cause the kind of contamination you're thinking of," Bo speculated, watching me hold the blaster. He motioned to the firing range—a long narrow corridor off the main room, with a buffered target area. "You want to shoot it?"

"Yes."

He tossed me a magazine from the wall, and I slapped it in, waiting for the double-click of blaster activation. "Now, be careful, the kickback is a bitch—"

I'd already raised the weapon, lined the scope and pulled the trigger. The familiar ricochet of the blaster through my shoulder and back was softened by my stance and years of experience. The entire inner circle of the target sucked inside itself—a smoking, gaping hole. The buffering of the target tunnel softened the explosion, but the blast would've sent body parts flying.

I lowered the blaster and grinned at the jaw-dropped militia leader. "You knew I was in the military on Dibon."

"But you were a flight medic! Didn't think they fired anything after basic."

He knew I'd killed Felix and Bricks, but he hadn't watched me do it. Plus, this was a much bigger gun. "Still combat trained. And I was a Pinion, flying Kittiwakes before that. We called them Buzzards."

"Jack of all trades?"

"No," I replied, shaking my head as I removed the remainder of the magazine from the blaster. My shoulder stung, but I held my head high. I enjoyed surprising and shocking him. "I got sick of seeing body parts everywhere." I handed the gun back to Bo. "You're right. I don't see anything here that could've caused the contamination."

I made my way back toward the entrance, hiding that I was rubbing my shoulder. But he grabbed my arm, spinning me around. "We didn't get to finish our date last night."

I raised my eyebrows. "After talking about violence and body parts, really?"

"No," Bo replied, his voice low. "After watching how strong, how precise you are."

I blushed, biting my bottom lip in nervousness. His hands caressed my arms, and I wrapped mine around him. Before, his embrace was comforting, gentle. In that moment, he became firm, steady, his muscles expanding and contracting beneath my hands, and my heart quickened, my stomach fluttering.

Bo's lips drew close, his breath on my mouth. Closing my eyes, I tasted his lips and tongue. I drew him in, feeling the brush of stubble from his chin on mine. He kissed me again, and I yearned for him, aching to be touched because oh, it had been so long!

Bo pressed his body against mine, chest against my chest, thighs tight against my own. My hands traveled up his back as he held me tighter. I kissed him, firmer this time. We broke apart only to breathe—he was sweating through his shirt. I leaned back for a moment, grinning. He was nervous, but he was a good kisser.

We kept kissing until Bo pushed me backwards, toward an old desk. The smooth surface slid under my thighs as I scooted back. Smiling shyly, his eyes locking on mine, I tugged on the hem of his tunic until he pulled it over his head. I tore my gaze from his eyes to admire the muscles cresting down his body, his hard abdomen. Burn scars ran up his left pectoral muscle to his shoulder. He unclasped his belt and removed his holster, placing both on the desk nearby.

I grabbed his hand and jerked him back to me, gently grazing the scars on his chest with my fingertips.

His heart beat fast under my palm. My fingers traveled up the scars to his cheek, and I gazed right into the eye which had the flap of skin hanging over, excited to touch him, honored to share this intimacy. Though I knew he could see out that eye, it was like seeing him for the first time. I breathed in his scent, an intoxicating mixture of sweet grain and grass and sweat.

Bo tilted my face, his mouth finding mine again. I wrapped my arms around his neck, and his strong arms tightened around my body. His mouth traveled along my jawbone, and a moan escaped from deep inside me as he tickled the sensitive spot below my ear, his hands moving to slip under my shirt. My hands tangled in his curly hair as I arched back, his fingers leaving my sides to the laces of my tunic. His lips traveled along my collarbone.

It'd been so long since I felt—anything, other than grief.

He pulled his head back, hands moving to my arms, fingertips grazing my bare skin. Our breath came fast and hard, and Bo leaned in, pressing his forehead against mine. I reached for his trousers, but he stopped my hands.

"Are you on prevention?" he asked, leaning back to look me in the eye.

I shook my head. I hadn't been on it since before Max and I got married.

He breathed out in a huff. "I didn't bring anything. I wasn't expecting—this."

"We shouldn't worry. I wasn't able to conceive except for the miscarriage, and I probably won't be able to, ever."

Bo raised an eyebrow. "You don't know that, and we don't need to risk it."

I raised an eyebrow back. "There are other things I can do for you, you know."

He laughed, pressing a finger to my lips. "No, not now. Not yet." Bo's thumb grazed my earlobe.

"Why not?"

"Because" he said huskily, his arms wrapping back around me, "I don't know if I could watch you go home."

After a few more long kisses, he pulled away, strapping his weapon back on and pulling on his shirt. I laced my tunic, and followed him out the bunker, satisfied for now, a bounce in my step. The sun hung much lower than I expected as we headed back toward the barns.

He stopped, while we were still out of earshot from others. "I've got a meeting tonight. Dahan leadership."

"Okay," I replied, unsure of what else to say, both to his revelation about his role, and as to what had just happened in the bunker between us.

"You can take my truck home instead." He handed me his keys. I wanted to lean in, to kiss him, but there were other workers not far off, so instead his hand lingered on mine a second longer than normal before we parted. Bo wasn't ready for this to be public knowledge yet, and I understood. Nonetheless, I was giddy with memories of those rippling ab muscles and his kisses as he walked away.

My warm feeling faded. I had no desire to get involved in the ongoing struggles of this world. Whatever this was, between Bo and I, it wouldn't last if he stockpiled weapons. I was done with war, done with violence. Firing the blaster reminded me I hated war so much. I hated the smell of blood and decay, body parts and rotting corpses. A vision of the *Ashkelon's* command deck flew to the front of my mind, Gene and Natalie, Titus and Cori strewn across the floor, me pushing Felix's bloody remains off the control panel. I glanced at Bo again and imagined a mine exploding as he walked away, sending him to kingdom come. No, I wanted no part of that. It was too early to tell where we might go, and too late to go back to being just friends. We'd entered dangerous territory.

22

I finished at the lab. Right as the distant sun dipped below the horizon, I saw a black transport car in the driveway of our small house as I drove in. Who would be visiting at this hour? And from where? Alarmed, I hurried inside, stopping short when I saw Vance.

His hair was still cut short in regulation, but he wore a tan button-down shirt and dark brown slacks—the dress of Diboni civilians. Except for the clothing, the captain appeared as he had at the launch bay over a year ago.

"Hey, Ami," Vance greeted me.

I remained frozen in the doorway.

"Is that how you greet an old friend?"

He opened his arms, and the fond memories rushed in from the old days. He wasn't here in uniform, and he was here alone. After a moment, I hugged him fiercely, slapping his back.

"My gods, I never thought I'd see you again!" I

answered, breaking loose from fear and falling back into trusting my former commander. We slipped into our old way of speech, taking our gods names in vain as you do in the gods-dusted Dibon Military Force. "What the mother-dusted-ash are you doing here?"

"Came to see you. Took me a while to find you, as for some reason I thought you were going to the Bara System."

I stepped back, uncertain. I shot a look at Mara, who stood smiling as she put away dishes. "We were. We did, I mean. Just didn't make it to Aza."

Vance chuckled. "I know, I heard when I got to Aza. Trouble is the local pilots don't always file their passenger manifests. Guess it's not required in the Outer Systems." He accepted a seat at the table. "I heard what you two went through, and it's no wonder you left Balec when you did. When I finally got there, they'd recently convicted one of the three involved in the mutiny. I forget his name—Lawrence?"

"Leonard." Sorrow drew across my face as I sat down, because I didn't want to believe Leonard was guilty. "What was his sentence, do you know?"

"Life in the Bara mines."

I grimaced. "I thought the Interplanetary Alliance Court would put him in prison."

Vance shrugged. "Prisons are overcrowded, apparently. Bara System is taking in almost all Outer Systems sentencing now."

"I'll leave you two to speak," my mother-in-law offered, excusing herself to the bedroom.

A shadow of fear fell on me. What if my message to

Sheya had been intercepted? What if she'd never left Dibon?

"Sheya made it home, didn't she?"

Vance smiled, placing his hand on top of mine. "Of course." He slid a comm drive across the table from me. "She recorded this and asked me to transmit it to you, but I decided to bring it myself. We've had relative peace in the Ramaen System, where I'm stationed now."

"What? Why? What happened to the rest of our unit on Dibon?"

The captain's expression drooped. "You didn't hear?"

I shook my head.

"Baratanium bombs, a few months ago. Most of the bunkers collapsed."

The shock took a moment to set in. I closed my eyes, trying to shut myself off from the grief welling in me. The rest of our neighbors, gone. The other veterans I knew, gone.

Everyone left. Gone.

My whole body trembled. Vance set his hand on my arm as the wave of loss overwhelmed me again. At least Sheya was safe. I felt guilty for thinking it.

"Who?" I whispered, demanding to know.

Vance leaned closer. "After you left, the remaining Nacaen refugees banded together, demanding to be included in decisions, in leadership. We tried to protect them from being murdered, and they turned on us. Just like the dusted Rebels at the beginning of the war."

"No." I clenched my fists. "I knew those people. The ones left after the war wanted peace." Like Max.

The captain continued, not hearing me. "We now

know they dismantled the ADS, attacked the patrol unit, and purposefully blasted an asteroid into orbit."

I shook my head again, tears streaming down my face. "But I thought you agreed with me—the ADS couldn't have been the work of the refugees?"

Vance handed me a tissue. "I thought so at first, but after we arrested one of the refugees, she confessed."

I knew our own interrogation methods, and I raised an eyebrow. False confessions were much easier to produce. "You have proof?"

He frowned, and his brows drew together. "The images *you* sent. That was the proof we needed."

"A Buzzard fuselage imbedded in the remains of an ADS satellite. How in the world could it be the work of Nacaens? They don't have ships, never had a flight division—"

"Never had an organized military," Vance countered. "But their Rebels are precise and deadly."

I couldn't believe the accusations. "But what about the distress beacon?"

"There's no other record of a distress beacon, only the *Ashkelon's* memo. Even other ships flying through that sector of the Galactic Ocean have no record of this."

"The *Ashkelon* went on alert, but the captain assumed the ship was long gone."

"All we know is somehow, you found it. It took a while to convince Command that you weren't involved."

"How could I, you saw—"

"I know, Ami. I did everything I could to tell them there was no way you'd do this. But you married into a Dahan family, and suspicions arose. Along with your evidence, we have transmissions that originated from this world, from this continent." Vance drew a deep breath. "The last transmission came from near here, from what we believe is the headquarters of the Rebels."

My mouth dropped open. He knew Dahan's leadership was here. Somehow, he'd linked them together.

The dead Diboni soldier. The one I thought tried to rob me. Ice traveled down my spine. He'd been spying on Dahan. Even before the asteroid.

"It couldn't be them. Maybe Jamin dissidents, as they've had trouble with them, but not Dahan."

Vance squinted. "Ami, you're a good soldier. You're Diboni, and we need you. We have the refugee's confession. We need you to find out more information for us, find who is responsible for the murder of millions on Dibon, due to the ADS failure."

Fear spiked in my blood, as I realized what he was asking of me. "No, Vance. I'm not military any longer, remember? I'm done. I left."

The Diboni captain pulled a tablet from his bag. "You re-upped, *remember*? You signed a new term of service."

"And you promised I'd be discharged at the end of my leave!" I stood, my voice shaking. "That was only to get Sheya home safely!"

"Calm down. I know this is a shock, but your people need you. Your fellow soldiers need you. *I* need you. We need to find out who is at the head of the Dahan militia. Your sister-in-law's home could be their next target. You want to protect her, don't you?"

I slumped into the chair. This wasn't a warning, but a threat. I should've known my former captain was not my friend, but still working for Diboni Command, covering up the truth as an excuse. But for what? Why accuse the Nacaens, who had nothing?

Vance pushed the tablet across the table. "Here are your orders, Lieutenant Commander, and the information we need. For Dibon."

I stared at him. He couldn't be serious. There was no air force, no military, no government. The people would be defenseless. Even with the arsenal Bo had—

Bo. Vance didn't know who he was. He didn't know the Dahan leader had traveled on the *Ashkelon* with me, didn't know he'd been in our home system. Bo told me he'd gone to the Ramaen system as a diplomat for Dahan, but he never went to Dibon's surface, was not involved with the Rebels. Besides, there was no real government here, no infrastructure between the warring nations to pull off something like that.

Vance shifted in his seat, his hand setting on his pocket. He had a weapon. Nothing I could say would get me out of this right now. I needed time to think. I had to talk to Bo.

"For Dibon," I muttered, so used to responding to Vance that way, but with utter dejection in my voice.

He rose from the table and made to leave but hesitated with his hand on the doorknob. "Remember, Lieutenant Commander, the punishment for going AWOL."

I swallowed hard, avoiding his eyes.

"You are active duty, and I expect regular reports. My contact information is all there."

"Lieutenant Commander now," I replied, now recognizing why my military papers kept showing a different rank.

"That's right."

I scanned the table for anything—a dinner knife, a screwdriver, something I could use as a weapon, but I had nothing. The pistol sat in the drawer, in the room with Mara, and she wouldn't be fast enough.

Panic spread throughout my body and froze me to the chair. This couldn't be happening.

"Thank your mother-in-law for her hospitality," the captain added as he reached the door, and I knew it was too late. If I killed him, they would kill me, and Mara.

The tablet with my orders flashed in the dim light.

23

S till dark, I drove Bo's truck from the house, hoping to find him before he headed out to hire laborers for the day. I didn't know what to do about Vance. Maybe Bo knew a secret place to hide Mara and me.

When I arrived, Jill stood outside the lab, waiting. "If you're here for Bo, he had to go on a mission today. He told me you know now, about him."

I had to see him, to explain what Vance was hunting for. "When will he be back?"

"Not until late." The redheaded woman leaned against her truck, her hand on her hip—no, on her pistol. "Rach tells me your last name is Lehem, like the farm."

"What's it to you?" I snapped, exasperated. I needed Bo.

She glanced at her fingernails, one hand still near her pistol. "Rather odd that a Diboni refugee would travel all this way, only to coincidentally find the lair of the most powerful man on Melas happens to be of the same name."

I stepped back, raising my hands. I had no weapon to defend myself. She drew her pistol and aimed it at my face. "Why shouldn't I shoot you right now?"

"Because I'm not what you think I am."

"What's going on here?" a voice called out from the shadows. Rachel stepped between me and Jill. "What the hell do you think you're doing?" She snatched the weapon from Jill's hand. The redhead quickly let go, raising her palms.

"Mom, she's after Bo."

Rachel's eyes narrowed, staring at Jill. Even in the dim light, I could see similarities in facial features, Rachel's own long white hair tied low like her younger version. "You're too hotheaded for your own good. Go cool off. And if I ever catch you raising this at anyone on this farm again, I will have you thrown out."

"But Mom—"

"—No, I told you, we don't tolerate violence here. I don't care if you're my daughter, you follow the rules like everyone else!"

Jill's eyes threw darts in my direction, but the redheaded woman walked away, leaving Rachel holding her weapon. The older woman removed the magazine from the pistol, pointing the muzzle down.

I breathed out hard. "I didn't know she was your daughter."

"Yes. Stubborn as they come." She cocked an eyebrow. "You all right?"

"Not the first time I've had a gun in my face."

Rachel raised an eyebrow. "Come with me."

The older woman led me past the barns to the south, to where the farmhouse stood, a beacon in the darkness with all the downstairs lights on. As we passed the copse of the needle trees, I spied the priest, chanting some prayer. He watched me pass by. Over the breeze I heard his voice: "Childless one shall be mother of all." A chill traveled down my spine.

Bo's aunt noticed my reaction. "Pay him no mind. I've known Phin for years, much of what he says is religious nonsense. A lot of doomsday prophecies."

I followed Rachel up the steps to the wide wrap-around porch, where she held the door open for me. We entered the large, spacious kitchen, with double farm sinks, double ovens, and a large refrigerator. A long kitchen island contained stools underneath the granite overhang. Rachel motioned for me to pull over a seat. She held up Jill's pistol. "I'm gonna go put this away. Make yourself comfortable; there's tea in the kettle."

A rack of mugs hung on the wall between the countertop and the cupboards near the stove. I chose a blue stoneware mug and poured myself some tea. "Where's Bo?" I called out, hoping Rachel might be able to help me.

"Not sure—he said he won't be back until later, I think."

The farmhouse was at least four times the size of the house Max and I owned, with its narrow hallways and old window shutters. I remembered how Max and I planned to build out, after we expanded our family. I sipped my tea with my elbows on the counter as the older woman returned.

"Jill's upset because we learned some news yesterday, which will change things."

"What news?" My hands trembled, but Rachel didn't notice.

"I looked into the Lehems who owned this farm, after you told me your name. It turns out they're related, as we suspected, but Cale Lehem, the owner who died, was Eli Lehem's great-uncle. When Jonah purchased the farm, no next-of-kin were listed, but that was because Cale assumed when Eli died, his sons must also have died. So, the bank found Jonah as the closest living relative."

I placed the mug on the counter. "What does this mean?"

She eyed me sharply. "It means, having being married to Max Lehem, this farm belongs to you."

Her words became a jumbled mess in my head. I came here to find Bo, to warn him about Vance, and Rachel was telling me I inherited a farm. "That can't be. You paid for it, it's yours."

"The money would be credited back to us. While it may be chaos here on Melas, with a proper government still to be formed, our money is connected to the banks in Bara. We'll be fine. This farm is yours."

"But what about..."

Rachel waved me off. "I'm tired, Ami. This was a dream, after the war, to stop fighting and start planting. But it's much more than we can manage, and Jonah and I are only getting older."

"But what about Bo? And Jill?"

Rachel laughed. "That girl is no farmer. She's

hotheaded, just like many of the workers we hire. Bo is destined for more than this."

I wondered how much the older farmer knew about Bo's role in the militia, or how much she suspected I knew.

"If..." I began, thinking through my words, still not quite believing this large farm would come to me. "If I were to be the owner, wouldn't that cause more division? I'm Diboni, and some know of the slaughter of refugees that occurred on my planet." *Not to mention what is left of Dibon's military is going to start causing trouble here.*

"It might bring unity, especially if the right people stay on."

"How so?"

"You're not Nacaen. You married a refugee who left during our war with Rebels, aren't interested in politics, but are interested in peace."

Before I could respond, Rachel motioned toward the window. "Sun's coming up. I've got a chisel plow that needs the blades replaced in the barn."

"Do you need help?" I offered, wondering if it might be better to stick closer to her until Bo came back.

Rachel chuckled. "No, go to the lab. We don't have anyone else who can figure out the problems with the soil. I've got plenty of knuckleheads who can fix the plow."

I thanked Rachel for the tea and walked with her outside. The truck with the day's workers pulled up, scattering my fears about running into Jill alone. I still had to figure out what was going on with the soil.

I had to figure out how to tell Bo about Vance, and find a way through this.

BY MIDMORNING, Bo still hadn't showed up. I pushed my fears about Vance to the background while I gathered soil samples and analyzed them, comparing the samples to those taken from neighboring farms. I found more gray film, and some of the brittle ash from my first day on the farm, the ash so fine it seemed to disintegrate in my hands.

Disintegrate.

The weapon under the seat in Jill's truck. Parked right where she left it, and locked.

I hadn't seen the redhead since Rachel took the gun from her. Heading back to the shed, I found a screwdriver and stuffed it in my pocket. I walked to Jill's truck and waited until all the workers were out of sight before jamming it into the lock. With some finagling and brute force, I twisted the screwdriver until the door opened.

The disintegrator was still there, so I grabbed it and hid it behind my back, hoping to conceal it as best I could as I made my way into the lab.

I set the disintegrator on the table and suited up. Placing one of the soil buckets away from everything else, I powered up the weapon. I'd never used one before, but I knew how it worked. When the war ended, we learned about disposing of certain "special" weapons safely as part of our discharge process, including illegal weapons we were not supposed to have. The program was instituted by pressure from the Ramaen government, probably to make sure none of their weapons were still in our stores. The switch on the stock powered the molecular disintegrator. Two subatomic particles resided in separate cartridges, but combined once it was at full power, and the fuel channeled into the barrel where it converted into a beam that disintegrated matter. When the shooter aimed at a target, they fired at the head, and swiped down.

When the fuel cells charged, I picked up the rifle, placing the butt against my shoulder, and raised the weapon to aim. I squeezed the trigger, and the disintegrator fuel funneled into the barrel, concentrated, and blasted out a blazing orange beam.

The entire bucket appeared to collapse on itself, folding in from the tremendous heat. Tables upended and chairs slammed into walls, and I was thrown by the blast. Soil samples blew through the air. I slammed into an overturned table. Sliding along its length to the floor, pain shot up my spine.

The bucket was gone. Nothing was left of its contents, either. When I peeled myself from the busted table and crawled to my target, I couldn't find any trace —no residue, no ash, nothing. Collapsing to the floor in pain and exhaustion, dust from the flipped tables filled my throat.

I broke into a truck, stole an illegal weapon, and destroyed the soil lab, to disintegrate a bucket of dirt. For nothing.

The door to the lab flung open, and in the settling dust I made out Bo rushing toward me.

"Stop, put on a suit," I warned him, coughing, as anything in the air might be a contaminate. He ignored me, moving to my side.

"What the hell happened?"

"Disintegrator," I wheezed. He threw my arm around

his neck, but I pulled away, grimacing in pain. "No. Find me a magnifying lens."

His eyes blazed, I guessed, for both blowing up the lab and not accepting his help.

"Just do it!" I barked.

Bo searched the rubble and found an unbroken glass. "What were you blasting trying to do?"

"Research," I responded, taking deep breaths as he handed me the glass. Lying on my stomach, I placed the glass as close to the floor as I could.

"There it is! Look at this!"

"Ami," he said, his voice quieter. "Your back is all cut up."

"I don't care—come see!"

Bo crouched next to me, taking the lens from my hand. "The brittle ash."

"From a disintegrator rifle. This was only one soil bucket, but on a mass scale, and against people or livestock—"

"Ami," Bo interrupted. "We've got to get you help."

I pushed to my hands and knees and wobbled, clinging to him. My eyes flew open wide. Vance's threat. "I've got to tell you something," I began. I didn't know how I managed to make it that far, but I fumbled, my head fuzzy from pain.

"Infirmary first," he ordered as he lifted me, throwing my arm around his neck as we exited the lab.

Several other laborers gathered outside, along with the Jill. She stared at me with the same ferocity of the disintegrator.

Bo jerked his head at his cousin, and Jill addressed the crowd. "Everything's okay, you can go back to work," she lied. Murmurs waved among the workers, but they dispersed as we continued walking. But I didn't know how much further I could go.

Bo carried me to the infirmary by the bunkhouse. "Jill, help me," he growled. I didn't know she'd followed us. The redhead opened the back door to the infirmary, leading to a smaller chamber. No one else was in there, so why was Bo taking me to a private room?

I collapsed onto the bed, still coughing from the dust from the lab. My back burned with pain.

The man I kissed only the day before had gone cold, his eyes boring into me. "Where'd you get the disintegrator rifle?"

I locked my gaze on Jill—her eyes wide—and I understood. Bo didn't know she had it. This was my chance to get her on my side, and I needed allies. Especially with what I needed to tell him.

"I bought it on the black market, last night," I lied, avoiding his gaze. "I had a suspicion about the soil contamination."

"You bought an illegal rifle on the black market in Ephra." His voice was flat. He wasn't buying it.

"Yes."

"You told me you hate guns."

"Yes," I repeated, finding his eyes. There were two of him. The pain was upsetting my stomach, as was the lie.

"Stop it," Jill interrupted. "She needs to lie down." She moved forward and helped me adjust to my side. The malice had left her eyes.

Bo grabbed the medical kit from the wall. "You've a long gash on your back." He jerked his head toward Jill. "Go get Phin."

When his cousin left us alone, Bo sat on the bed next to me, but suspicion didn't leave his eyes. "Who'd you buy it from?"

"I don't know, some guy dealing near Kishon Street," I lied again.

"Why didn't you come to me?"

"I couldn't find you."

Bo opened the kit and retrieved sterile gauze strips and peroxide to clean my gash. "Turn over," he ordered, and I obeyed, rolling onto my stomach. I tensed as he touched the wound with the peroxide-soaked cloth. "If your theory is right, and the ash is from a disintegrator rifle—we're talking a massive scale disintegrator attack."

I winced as the wound stung.

"Even if it was a massive slaughter, this ash is found all over the fields. The scale of it doesn't support the theory."

"Unless there is some other weapon that uses disintegrator technology."

Bo stopped. I propped myself on one elbow though my back hurt like hell. He stared at me and I stared back at him. I couldn't understand his sudden disbelief, his distrust. Tears welled in the corner of my eyes. I had a high pain tolerance, but the doubt in his voice hurt worse.

Phin entered the room with Jill. "Clear out," he ordered. Jill obeyed, but Bo stood with his arms folded. The priest pointed at him. "That means you."

"No."

"Are you questioning my authority? Are you qualified to treat her?" Phin demanded, and I smirked, raising an eyebrow as I remembered the priest wasn't simply a healer—he was a doctor.

"She's a prisoner."

I shuddered with Bo's proclamation. Phin's eyes burned with frustration. "Whatever you call her, if you're gonna stay, you're gonna help stitch her up." Phin laid out the suture kit and prepared a syringe. He hesitated. "This will sting, but you know that."

I closed my eyes as he plunged the needle into my back to numb the area. The sliver of doubt Vance had planted—that the Rebels were headquartered here, that they had blown the bunkers and caused the ADS to fail—pricked in my heart. Even though he didn't seem to have the resources to do what Vance accused the Rebels of, Bo knew me well enough by now. He knew my history, who I married, how I'd come this far through all the trials on the *Ashkelon* to get Mara home. To call me a prisoner for firing one illegal weapon allowed that sliver to wedge deeper.

Phin directed Bo to collect gauze and tape from the cabinets as he stitched me up. He then covered the wound and examined the rest of me. I didn't appear to have broken anything, but my lower back was bruised, which made it hard for me to walk.

"Go get her a fresh shirt and some sheets," he commanded, and Bo left the room. Phin got right in my face. "In your blood is our future. Try not to get yourself killed."

"What do you mean?"

"You will lead us out of this madness into glory, or we all will perish. Your child will be Diboni and Dahan, Noma and Nacaen. The people have turned away from

God, and they insist on their own ways, on their own leader, but they choose violence every time."

My child. But I had no child, save the miscarriage. For the first time I saw Phin—I really saw him. More than a priest, he was a prophet.

A memory flew into my head. I was sitting in an ancient temple in the mountains, my brother and sister's bodies laid out for the crematory rite. Local priests officiated our funerals, but this time, the high prophet came. He knelt before me, wearing brilliant green and golden robes, and told me the gods were sad for me. There lived a god who called all people children, and this god would provide for me one day a new family.

The memory had faded, for my dreams of a family died with Max.

I closed my eyes. "A prophet once told me there is a god who calls all people children."

When I opened my eyes, Phin was staring at me. "This is our God, the One God, Creator of the Universe. This God has promised you a child, and will deliver, if you trust."

"How? How can I trust?" I thought of all my theological arguments with Mara, all my assumptions that the gods were silent and dead. Why now, with this prophet, was the doubter in me beginning to believe I'd come this far for a reason?

The disintegrator ash. The ADS failure. I had to find the truth.

Bo returned, and Phin gave me a sideways glance. "Trust the wise," the priest said, turning to face him. "She needs to rest. There's pain medicine in those vials for her to take, every four hours. Let her remain here."

Bo watched the priest leave the room, closing the door behind him. I swallowed the first round of pain relief and antibiotics. "Take it," Bo snapped as he handed me the clean shirt. I untied the laces on my tunic as he turned around.

"You almost saw me naked yesterday," I mentioned, pulling the torn decontamination suit and bloodied tunic from my body. I grimaced—the numbness was already wearing off and my entire back burned with pain.

"I know."

I attempted to pull the clean shirt over my head, but afraid of pulling out the stitches, I could barely raise my arms. "Can you help me?"

Bo sighed, turning around. He picked up the shirt and pulled it over my head, helping me push my arms through. He held my arm as I sat on the stool, then changed the bloodied sheets on the bed. Once he finished, I lay back down, and he sat at the edge of the bed.

"Why am I your prisoner?"

"You purchased an illegal weapon. I have to enforce the law."

I frowned. "I thought you said there's no police here?"

Bo clenched the mattress, his face red. "Generally, it would mean a trial with our judge and elders. But the punishment for having a disintegrator here is death."

I froze. What the hell was I protecting Jill for, then?

Bo took my hand, surprising me, his voice much softer. "I'm not gonna let that happen. I'm gonna find a way out of this for you, but right now, everyone on this farm knows something happened in the lab, and if word got out..." His teeth caught his lower lip. "Although it was an experiment, and even if it helps us solve the issues with the soil, you purchased and fired a banned weapon. Until I can figure a way out of this, I need you to stay here. I need you to be safe."

My sliver of doubt eased as the anger left his voice. I rubbed my thumb over his knuckles. Though he was harsh, it made sense. "Please tell Mara what happened, where I am. She'll be worried sick."

Vance had left for now, but what would happen when he came back? What if he used Mara to get to me?

Bo nodded. "I will."

"There's something more I need to tell you," I started, but the dizziness set in, the meds uncoiling in my veins. "I used to be a pilot..."

"I know, Ami. Get some rest."

"But..."

"Shhhh," the gentle, scarred man hushed as he leaned over, brushing his lips to mine.

24

I opened my eyes to darkness. For a moment I gasped, panicking. I was in the bunker, Max was dead, and Vance came to kill me.

"Hey," Bo called from across the darkened room, and I remembered. The blast. The infirmary.

"Did you get in touch with Mara?"

"Yes. I told her you were injured at work but you're okay, and that we're keeping you here overnight." He stepped closer, his silhouette appearing in the shadows.

"Is she all right?"

"Your mother-in-law's only concerned about you. She mentioned someone came by your house, someone you knew back from Dibon?"

I drew in a breath. "Yes. Vance, my old commander."

Bo stepped back. "What is it, Ami? Tell me everything."

"He wants me to find out who the leaders of the Dahan militia are."

He flicked on the light. I covered my eyes with my

hands, blinded. When my vision adjusted, I first noticed his eyes, glaring at me. But his hand wasn't on his weapon—it lay on the table. He'd slept on the floor.

"What did you tell him?"

"Nothing. He doesn't know where I work, who I work for."

"He might by now."

My head throbbed. "I'm trying to figure out how to save Mara, and you. He'll have her killed, or my sister-in-law, and there's nothing I can do to protect them." I rubbed my eyes, for they were filling with tears. "He claimed that Rebels from here, specifically in Dahan, were responsible for Dibon's destruction, for the ADS failure. The bunkers were bombed, after I left."

Bo sat on the edge of the mattress, placing his hand on my shoulder. "I know."

I jerked my arm away. "What do you mean *you know*?"

The militia leader sighed, drawing a hand over his face. "I received an intelligence report, a couple of months ago, that Dibon's bunkers were bombed. I wanted to tell you, but we're still trying to find out who was behind it. It wasn't anyone associated with the Dahan militia."

I tried to sit, but the pain spiked, overwhelming me. Bo put his hands to my shoulders, pushing me back. "You need to rest."

"Dust that."

He smiled, for the first time since I fired the disintegrator. "Listen. I still have connections in the Ramaen system—I'll work to get your sister-in-law and her family to safety. As for your orders, I think you should follow through on them."

"What?"

"Follow through. I'll give you information to feed to Vance."

"You want me to play double-agent?"

"Yes."

"But who—" I tossed my head back on the pillow. "Who is behind attacking Dibon? I can't believe Vance would make all that ash up. He's only following orders."

"Someone's lying to him. Or it might be Twelve Rebels after all, but not from Dahan. I assure you, it's not my people," Bo said, studying me. "Vance was your commander, and you trusted him."

"Yes. But once he threatened my family—"

Bo grasped my hand again. "Ami, you can trust me."

"How? You don't trust me, though I've told you the truth."

"You didn't tell me the truth about the disintegrator."

I swallowed hard, knowing he hadn't bought that story, but for now I didn't have a certain redhead trying to kill me, either.

Bo sank closer to me on the bed. "Look, I trust you. If you wanted to kill me, you could've done so in the bunker easily. You could've turned the blaster on me or any of the other weapons, including my own." I recalled how Bo placed it on the desk next to us while we kissed. "But you didn't. And you knew I was the leader of Dahan's militia when he asked." He tilted his head toward me. "I believe you. I've known you what, a year now? I know what you've been through. I need you to trust me. And I need you to do your part and lead on

Vance, and I'll make sure your family is safe, and that you are safe."

Bo pushed me over to the edge of the bed, lying next to me, his hand stroking my arm as he kissed me. My mind was a mess, but my body knew what it needed. I melted into him, letting his mouth take over as my stomach rippled with the pleasure of his touch. His fingers brushed my side where my tunic pulled up, his hands slipping under my shirt. I clutched his shoulder as Bo kissed me harder. I moaned as his fingers wandered, until he reached my lower back and pressed me closer. Crying out, I bit my bottom lip and pulled back, the wound still tender and bruises sore.

"I'm sorry," he whispered, his hand gliding over the curve of my hip to my thigh. Bo's kisses moved to my jaw and below my ear. I was still in pain, but I didn't want him to stop.

But he did. Bo pulled the blanket over us, and his nose touched mine, his breath in mine. "Rest," he ordered, gently.

———

PHIN ARRIVED IN THE MORNING, and Bo was already up, making sure I swallowed my pain meds and antibiotics. The priest changed the dressing on my stitches. My back was too sore to work in the fields, and Bo hadn't figured out how explain the disintegrator yet. He didn't ask me again where I got it before he left to continue the investigation on the lab.

I remained in the infirmary, sleeping through the

morning. Around midday, Jill entered the room, carrying a bowl of soup and some bread.

"Thank you," she offered, after setting the tray next to me. She brushed the ends of her copper locks off her shoulders. "I know you broke into my truck, and for whatever reason destroyed the soil lab, but you didn't rat me out."

"I was testing it. It looks like the soil contamination comes from the ash residue of a disintegrator. But Bo's right—the amount of it in the soil doesn't make sense."

"What do you think caused it then?"

"A much larger weapon that uses the same technology."

"Who would have that kind of weapon?" Jill asked, her arms folded. "The Jamin Rebels? Or others?"

"Possibly. I don't know. Sorry I broke into your truck."

She waved me off. "How come you didn't tell Bo I had it?"

I shrugged. "I figured he knew, until I realized he didn't. Then I assumed it was better to not piss you off anymore since you'd already threatened me once."

Jill laughed. "Sorry. I guess I'm prejudiced." She paused, studying me. "I mean it. I'm sorry I judged you."

I shook my head. "Forget it."

"Have you told Bo about the inheritance?"

"I still don't quite believe it. Rachel didn't show me anything official." I also hadn't thought of it since leaving the farmhouse.

"It'll be hard to give this place up."

My eyes narrowed. "What makes you think you'd have to leave?"

"Wouldn't you get rid of the girl who tried to kill you?"

I snorted, and then Jill laughed, too.

"That still leaves me in possession of a disintegrator," I mentioned, once I settled down.

Jill scratched her head. "I know. I got it from a Sim'ee leader."

"What'd you pay for it?"

"A lot." Jill bit her fingernails. "He told me he could get me more, too. I just wanted to have one in case the Jamin Rebels rose up again."

"Do you think you could arrange another sale?"

The redhead's eyes flew open wide. "Are you crazy?"

"Maybe. It's totally a long shot but I need to talk to someone who knows more about these weapons."

I had to find out if a mass disintegrator existed.

———

Bo RETURNED in the evening with dinner. "Cleaned up the lab—doesn't look like any contaminants spread." He sat on the stool across from me. "The disintegrator is in a lock box for now, until we can figure out how to dispose of it."

"What's gonna happen to me?"

"It looks like, so far, no one else knows it was a disintegrator. They think it was a lab experiment gone wrong. For now, you're in the clear."

"No longer your prisoner?"

"No longer my prisoner," he repeated with a smirk. "But don't do this again. Ami, next time, tell me before you plan to blow stuff up."

I rolled my eyes. "Okay.

Bo's own smile faded. "I'm serious. If anyone figured out this was a disintegrator, I'd be forced to hold a trial, and you'd be convicted. And I'd be expected to... handle it."

I raised my hands, flustered. "You're the leader, aren't you? Couldn't you explain it was necessary to figure out what happened here?"

His brows drew together, eyes narrowed. "I'm the leader, but that doesn't mean I can ignore the laws set by the elders." He crossed his arms. "Anyway, as long as it doesn't happen again, we don't have to worry about it."

I shied away, swallowing my guilt, but Bo caught my expression. "What'd you do?"

"Nothing." I didn't meet his eyes.

"Blast it, Ami, don't lie to me!"

Sighing, my gaze caught his. "I'm arranging to meet the dealer."

"Why?"

"Because I need to find out who manufactures the fuel, how they produce the weapons—and if it's possible to create a massive disintegrator weapon. Because that's what happened here. I'm sure of it."

Bo stared at the floor.

"You know I'm right."

"This isn't the way," he said, his voice much quieter. "You don't even know who you're dealing with."

"Do you?"

Bo clenched his fists. "I steer clear of banned weapons for a reason."

"Good. I have to find out if this is possible, if this is what happened—and then, why."

"I'm going with you."

Dusted ash. I was afraid he was this stubborn. "I don't think that's wise," I replied as calm as I could, though my stomach tied in knots.

"Why? Is your commanding officer involved in this?"

I folded my arms. Throwing that back in my face hit me hard. "I'm telling you the *truth*. I'm trying to figure out what happened here. To help *you*."

Bo stood, pacing the floor, running his fingers through his curly brown hair. "This can wait."

I rolled my eyes. "Just let me do this, then we'll figure out what the Diboni military is up to."

"So you can get yourself killed?"

"Don't be the overdramatic, overprotective boyfriend type."

He scoffed. "I didn't think we'd gotten that far."

"Listen, I don't know yet if it's going to happen. I'm waiting to hear back."

"When you do, tell me," he demanded, slamming the door on his way out.

Max was so different from Bo. When we fought, my husband would try to rationalize with me, pace the floor, and if he was still angry, he'd go bang on some tool in the barn, then come back inside. All the anger would be gone, we'd apologize to each other and make love. I don't remember him ever blowing up at me. But then again, I didn't have any reason to keep secrets from him.

My only purpose since Max died was to keep Mara alive. But now, too many people had died, for no reason. There *must* be a reason. I had to find out what happened here.

Jill came to see me after I finished eating. "Bo said you should go home tonight. I'm to drive you."

He's still angry. Not like Max at all. "Did he tell you why he's mad at me?"

"Yeah. But you're right not to tell him. Not only would I be in trouble, but these guys will absolutely kill him if they know who he is. They don't know who I am."

"Is it arranged then?"

Jill nodded. "Yep. Tomorrow night, an hour after sunset."

"Who all needs to be there?"

"Just you and me."

I tapped my fingers on my empty dinner tray. "How much do they want?"

"They don't tell you; you have to come ready to negotiate."

I didn't know if I had enough money. I'd saved everything I'd made so far except for the first couple of weeks, which I used to secure our small house for the foreseeable future. But I feared it wasn't enough.

I needed to find out what they wanted to know. Information goes much further than money.

Jill drove me home. My back was still bruised, but I walked with less stiffness to the door. Mara greeted me with a fierce hug, and though it hurt, I held her for a long time.

"Did Vance come by again?"

She shook her head no, and I breathed out deep in relief. I hoped he'd left the for now. After assuring her I was all right, that it was simply an accident, I found the comm drive Vance gave me with Sheya's message.

Unsure of what might be there, I waited until Mara left the room to play it.

"Hi Mara, hi Ami, it's me. I made it home." My sister-in-law appeared much as she did the last time I saw her. Perfect black ringlets framed her face, and she wore a bright colored blouse as they did in the Ramaen System —their fashion was all about brilliant color. Behind her, a beautiful artificial sky blazed bright blue, projected inside the biodome estate her family lived in. "I hope you're both doing well. My family is good. I hope to hear from you soon, how your travels went, and where you're living. Miss you."

Sheya didn't know what we'd lived through when she recorded the message. She didn't mention the message I'd sent her, which meant she'd given this to Vance before then. I cradled my head in my palms, thankful Sheya was okay, but I also knew anything could've happened to her after this. It might take months for a transmission to get through. But seeing her again, even on a recording, gave me a small assurance she was all right, that Vance hadn't harmed her, yet.

I watched the recording again, making sure I didn't miss a signal, but she didn't indicate that she'd seen my other message or that Vance was forcing her to make it sound like everything was fine.

I set the comm drive aside to give to Mara later and picked up the tablet Vance left, scanning my retina to unlock it and read my orders.

"To discover, by any means possible, the leader of the Dahan militia. Determine strength of militia, weapons capabilities, and report all details to commanding officer (Captain Vance). Report all other dissident movements, including Jamin, Sim'ee, and others associated with the Twelve Rebels on Melas."

I tossed the tablet onto my bed. There was nothing there I could use to bargain with the arms dealer. I couldn't use what I knew of Bo and the Dahan militia, which wasn't much anyway except for the one arsenal bunker.

But I did know a Diboni officer was in the vicinity, coming from the Ramaen System, with access to Ramaen technology. Maybe I could use this information not only to bargain with, but to set Vance up.

25

I didn't see Bo at all the next day. The stiffness lessened in my back, so I helped finish tilling the soil. The next planting would start soon. I wore a coat over my tunic to stave off the chill, as the winds had shifted, sweeping down from the hills. Melas was warmer than Dibon, with a mild winter, but the winds were cold.

When we finished, I waited behind the bunkhouse until after nightfall. Jill drove her truck around back, stopping next to me. She leaned to push the broken door open.

"Where's Bo?" I asked.

"He's with the Jamin leadership today. They're trying to broker an alliance."

"Oh." I half-hoped to see him, half-glad he wasn't there to interrupt what we were doing. Climbing in, I shut the broken door carefully. "That for me?" I motioned to a pistol in a thigh holster on the bench seat.

"Yeah. Don't need to steal one from me this time."

I hesitated.

Jill gave me a sideways glance. "Better put it on now, in case we're ambushed."

She was right—I just hated the idea I might have to use it. I strapped the holster on my right thigh. There wasn't another way. Whether I liked it or not, I was a warrior again. But for whose side?

Jill drove north along a dirt road northeast from the farm, out to the gravel pits thirty kilometers away. The other truck had already arrived, much earlier than we planned. There were no other lights around.

"That's him," she acknowledged as we pulled up, turning the lights off on her truck. Four men stepped out from their vehicle, also armed. The one in front wore his long, dark black hair tied in a low ponytail. He sported a dark curled moustache and bushy eyebrows that almost came together. I couldn't tell what nation he belonged to for certain, though he could've been Jamin.

I spoke first. "You have the disintegrator?"

"What do you have for me?" the moustache man demanded. He chewed on a toothpick.

"Information."

He chuckled. "No money, sweetheart, no guns."

"I have information you may want, and I only want information about the...gun."

"What sort of information?" the moustache man asked. I couldn't tell if he was intrigued or annoyed. The toothpick clicked the inside of his teeth.

"There's a Diboni military officer here. He wants to assassinate Dahan leadership."

Jill's eyes flew to me. I didn't look back, keeping my focus on the four armed men in front of us.

The man with the moustache narrowed his eyes. "Diboni, you say? What do the Diboni have to do with Dahan, or Melas?"

"He's got access to Ramaen weapons and technology, he just came from there."

His eyebrows lifted. "Ah, Ramaen, you say?" He tossed the toothpick aside. His manner of speech was different from the other Jamin I heard on a regular basis.

"What I need to know is where you get these weapons, how they're made, and if it's possible to make a large-scale disintegrator."

The other three men stepped closer. Jill and I both dropped our hands to our weapons.

"What you are asking—why?"

I swallowed hard. "I need to know if this kind of weapon is possible, and if it was used here before."

The tall man in the back, with skin as dark as mine, stepped to the front. "You want to know about the Rupture Device?" He pronounced his consonants sharper—an accent I hadn't heard before or associated with other Nacaens.

"Rupture Device?" I repeated.

He tilted his head, frowning. "The large disintegrator."

"Who made it?"

"We don't know. It was sold to us, to use in our last stand when Dahan rose up."

"Against Dahan?"

"Against ourselves."

I blinked, not following. "You don't mean—"

"—Only way to escape without imprisonment or

torture. They believed Melas would be cursed by their death."

"How do you know this?"

"I am Sebuj, from the remnant that fled to the south. We make disintegrators now."

Sebuj, not Sim'ee. I'd never heard of them before.

"Pay us," the moustache man interrupted.

"I gave you information—"

"No," the tall Sebuj protested. The snap of his pistol leaving its holster spurred us into action, with everyone drawing their weapons, one of the men holding a rifle. Jill trained hers on the moustache man and I aimed at the Sebuj, but they were four against us two. "Money. Now."

Dusted ash. I'd have to arrange a meetup with Vance. They didn't trust me enough.

"I can give you five hundred thousand."

"Two million," the moustache man countered.

I scoffed. "I don't have that much."

"She does," the Sebuj replied, jerking his head toward my companion. "She did last time."

Without shifting my aim, I half-turned and shot Jill a look, incredulous. "You gave them *two million*?"

"What can I say, I really wanted one," she answered, her voice quivering.

"One million. That's all I can get you," I insisted. I'd clearly underestimated exchange rates for illegal weapons.

"Two million, or two dead women," the man with the long hair sneered, his lips curving up into his moustache.

"What if I can pass on more information from the Diboni? Would that be worth anything?"

The moustache man held his fist up, signaling the other three to stand down. "You're saying you'd be our informant?"

"Yes." I lowered my weapon slightly, though Jill kept hers on the moustache man.

He stroked his beard. "That may be worth two million, for now."

I didn't have long to worry about how to be a triple agent. An engine roared over the rise from the southwest, and the tall Sebuj turned his head. I kicked gravel into his eyes and lunged, knocking his gun from his hand. I twisted his arm, using him as a shield while I fired at one of the other men, striking him in the shoulder. Jill fired at the moustache man as he ran toward the truck. I trained my weapon on the man with the rifle, right as the vehicle that interrupted us drove between me and the dealers' truck, blocking my shot.

Dan and Bo in a farm truck. I cursed.

Right as their vehicle stopped, the man with the rifle fired at Jill, and she went down with a cry. I shoved the Sebuj man away, getting around Dan's truck to fire at the man who shot Jill, aiming right at his head. He dropped to the ground. The moustache man reached the driver's seat, with the man I first shot barely making it to the passenger side.

Dan and Bo jumped out of their vehicle, guns drawn. The engine of the dealer's truck sputtered, then turned over. The Sebuj on the ground reached for his gun, but I kicked it out of reach. He scrambled to his feet away from me.

Dan reached the body of the man who shot Jill. The truck with our arms dealers spun their tires as the Sebuj man climbed into the bed, and they sped west out of the gravel pits.

"I need help!" Bo shouted. I rushed to Jill's side, where Bo was kneeling next to her head. She screamed as I moved her arm. Dusted ash—the man that shot her used a blast-shot rifle, ripping the skin and sinews to shreds. I threw off my coat, breathing fast as I tore a strip of fabric from my tunic, tying a tourniquet at her shoulder.

"They're gone," Dan said as he jogged over, stopping short at the sight of us on the ground with Jill. I tore another section from my tunic, leaving my stomach bare as I wrapped the strip around her arm to hold the skin together.

"Help her up," I ordered, and Bo obeyed, careful with her injured arm. Dan had the door open on their vehicle, his gun pointed to the ground, a vein pulsing in his forehead. I glared back at him. If he hadn't driven in front of me, Jill wouldn't have been shot.

"Take her to Phin," Bo said to Dan, and I hugged my bare stomach, my heart galloping in my chest as Dan helped Jill into his truck and shut the door. Dan raced off back toward the farm. I glanced at the body of the man I'd shot. Like Felix.

"Tell me one reason why I shouldn't have you locked up," Bo yelled at me, startling me with his reaction. My own anger was burning up the fuse since he arrived, and it exploded.

"Because if it wasn't for you, Jill wouldn't have been shot! We had this mother-ash-dusting situation under control, until you had to be the 'hero' and dusting save the day or whatever it is you're trying to do!"

Bo got right in my face, and I stared back at him.

"You didn't have to drag Jill into this!" he shouted. "Blast it, you should've brought me!"

He'd forgotten who I was—a soldier. "I couldn't bring you because they would've dusting killed you right away!"

He scoffed. "Don't act like you were doing this to protect me."

"I'm not acting." Once my fuse exploded, it fizzled. I was done with being angry. I was tired, I ached all over, and I worried as hell about his cousin.

Bo broke away, walking over to Jill's truck. "Unless you want to be left out here by yourself to get killed, I suggest you get in."

"If you want to know what happened at the farm, I suggest you *listen*." I tore the magazine out of the pistol I carried, jumped in the truck and slammed the door.

Bo glared at me as he turned the ignition but didn't reply, shifting the truck into gear to follow after Dan.

Counting to ten to clear my head, I breathed out hard. I had to get through to him. "You heard of the Sebuj before?"

He didn't answer me, but I saw recognition in his face.

"The Sebuj people killed themselves in a mass suicide using something called a Rupture Device. Apparently, they used to live here, and the ash we've found is left over from their last stand. Someone tried to cover this up with a form of neutralizer I hadn't seen before, and it's mixed in from the plows, but it's why the grains are blighted, why there are patches where nothing will grow." I paused, swallowing hard. "They cursed the ground with their very lives."

The stubborn militia leader didn't respond, his anger still burning in his silence. I stared out the window. There were no lights out there, no settlements, only the stars.

"When did Dahan take the land from the Sebuj?" I asked.

"They didn't," he finally answered, still not looking at me. "The Jamin took it from the Sebuj. We were always told they surrendered themselves, but it was right after that when the last war started."

Dan was Jamin, and Jill was with him.

"Do you trust Dan?"

"Of course," the militia leader spat back.

"Bo, I'm serious. How well do you know him? How much would Jamin leadership want to cover up what we know?"

His eyes lost their blaze, instead growing wide into worry. He sped up as we flew over the dirt road back, past Ephra to Lehem Farm.

I breathed out in relief when I spotted the truck next to the infirmary. We rushed inside, finding Phin already working on Jill's arm, Dan standing nearby. I stood near the doorway, folding my arms across my chest, as Bo reached his cousin's side.

The doctor stretched the wounded arm under the light. "I need help getting all the blast-shot out."

Bo moved closer, but Phin motioned for me. "Gloves are over there along with sterile tweezers. Everyone else out."

Dan cleared his throat. "Is she going to be..."

"She'll keep her arm if we do this quickly."

He turned, swinging the door out of the infirmary so hard it hit the wall.

I glanced at Bo, but he didn't lift his gaze until Jill squeaked out, "Bo, don't be mad at her. It was me."

"What?"

"It was me that had the disintegrator. I had it in my truck. She's covering for me."

"That's enough!" Phin slammed his hand on the metal tray. "Clear out. Now."

Bo left us alone. I put on gloves and a mask as Phin plunged a needle into her neck, sedating her. I got to work picking the shot out of Jill's shredded arm.

"You'll do a better job if you don't allow your anger to interfere," Phin said.

I adjusted the tweezers. He was right, I was still angry, at Bo and Dan. And at myself, for getting set up in the first place.

"What do you know of the Sebuj?" I asked Phin, changing the subject.

He paused, the shot plinking in the pan, echoing in the sterile room. "The Dahan, Jamin, and Sim'ee have been here on Melas for two hundred years. But there were people here before us. They lived in this planetary group for thousands of years, and some still call themselves Nacaen, because that was the name of the system. Our people adopted the name but never the unity. The Sebuj were here first, then lived among us."

"They killed themselves to avoid imprisonment and torture."

The priest stood abruptly, turning away. I frowned,

wondering what I'd done to offend him, as I continued to work on Jill's arm.

"There's much we've forgotten, on purpose. We've erased their story and told only our own, twisting the truth to excuse our responsibility." Tears rolled down Phin's cheek.

"What is it?" I dared to ask.

"Before our last war began, most of the Sebuj disappeared." The doctor's eyes found mine. "I knew a Sebuj girl, a long time ago. She disappeared, too."

I paused from my work, touching Phin's shoulder, tears in my own eyes. He'd caused me pain before with his words, and now I'd done the same.

When I finished cleaning out the shreds of Jill's arm, he began stitching inside the muscle. The skin was too damaged, so we used a synthetic graft machine, creating new arm skin for her.

"I've never done this before," I admitted to Phin as the sleek, synthetic skin emerged from the machine. It smelled like burned rubber.

"I'll show you." Phin placed the new skin around her arm and used the graft machine to help seal it on. Her skin became crimson and deep blue and purple with bruising, swelling twice the size it was before, but it was better than leaving her arm in shreds. He gave her two rounds of antibiotic injections, and we bandaged the arm.

"She'll need anti-rejection drugs every four hours, along with the antibiotics. I'll stay with her tonight," the doctor assured me.

"Why are you a priest, and not a full-time doctor?" I asked.

"I'm a doctor because people keep hurting each other and need healing. Same reason I'm a priest." He cocked his head. "Same reason you are you—a flight medic and a farmer."

He was a strange man, but his words didn't bother me anymore. Probably because they weren't directed at my future or pointing out my barrenness, but also because I saw him in a different light now, scarred like the rest of us, on the inside. Scarred by the lies we tell ourselves and the stories we create so we can live with who we are, and what has been done to us.

What we've done to others.

It was still dark when I left the infirmary. Bo was outside, apparently waiting for me the whole time. I stared at him, wanting him to break first. I might've been wrong about Dan, but he was wrong about me.

Hugging my arms across my bare stomach, I shivered. I'd left my coat on the ground back at the gravel pit, and my tunic was ripped and stained with blood from saving Jill's arm. He could've at least thanked me for saving his cousin's life—or asked if I was all right.

"Dan went back for the body," he finally said, breaking the silence.

"You still don't trust me," I accused.

"I don't know what to think, Ami."

"I'm sorry Jill got hurt, but it wouldn't have happened if you let us be."

"You were outnumbered—"

"—I had it under control. I've done this before, and Jill has done this before." I stepped closer and pointed my finger at his chest. "You were the one who had to jump in."

Bo shoved my hand aside. "She's my cousin. I had to protect her. And I still don't know about you..."

My eyes flew open. "You can't trust me. You've known me all this time, you know what I've been through. All I've done since I came to your farm is try to figure out what's wrong with the soil, what happened here, how to fix it—and you don't trust me." Tears stung the corner of my eyes. "I told you the truth about Vance and Dibon, everything except this, and only because it wouldn't work if you were involved."

He shrunk back from me, away from my hurt. I wanted Bo to hold me, to tell me it wasn't true, to tell me he cared too dusting much.

"You should go," the militia leader muttered.

I opened my mouth, but clamped it shut. His mind was made up.

I spun away from him, from the farm that bore my name, from any future that might have held hope.

26

I'd left the pistol Jill lent me back in the infirmary. At the gate, the guards were reluctant to let me go out alone—it was cold, dark, in the middle of the night, but I insisted, walking the last part home to the outskirts. I'd been afraid since that time I was attacked, but not tonight. All my fear had drained with my anger.

Mara was asleep. I went to the shower, shedding my torn and bloodied clothes, tossing them in a recycling bag so she wouldn't see later, and crept to my bed. Retrieving the tablet from the drawer, I reviewed the orders again from Vance. I needed to find a way to get Mara and I out, away from here. I didn't know when he might come back. But how could I make Mara move from her home, after all we went through to get here?

"You need to tell her," Max said, shaking my shoulder. "Tell her what's going on."

"I can't," I told my husband. "She's been through too much."

"You need to go to work now." He shook my shoulder again, and I shot up in bed, eyes open.

It was Mara shaking my shoulder. "Won't you be late for work?"

"I came home pretty late last night," I yawned. From the light in the window, it was already midmorning at least. "What is it?"

"Vance is here."

I curled back, the fear slamming me like a weight in the chest. "You let him in?"

"Of course." She frowned. "Everything okay?"

"Yes," I said, flashing a quick smile, knotting my fingers behind my back. "I'll be out in a minute."

I waited until Mara left to retrieve the handgun I'd kept since I was attacked. I slid the magazine into place, and tucked it inside my belt at my back, hidden under my tunic.

My commanding officer greeted me with a hug, as if he hadn't threatened me the last time we spoke. "How's my favorite Pinion doing?"

"Unemployed right now."

"Oh?"

"Yeah." I glanced over my shoulder as Mara closed the door to the bedroom, giving us privacy.

"Do you have any news for me?" he asked, sitting at the table.

I scratched my arm. I needed to give him something, but not the whole truth—to buy some time. "I've been digging into the history of the farm I was working at. What do you know about the Sebuj?"

"The Sebuj," he repeated, without surprise. "What do they have to do with anything?"

I sat at the table with him. "I don't know, but last night I learned they were here before the Dahan, and something happened to them. Maybe it's a long shot, but it seems like there was a cover-up here. Maybe it's linked to what happened on Dibon?"

The captain considered. "How can I help?"

This was the old Vance, and there was a part of me that longed for what we had on Dibon. I looked up to him, and we relied on each other, trusting each other. But those days were dust.

I folded my hands. "I don't need help. I just need more time."

Vance leaned back, his expression dubious.

I sat up straight. "I can infiltrate the leadership. Most work on the farms around here. They're getting ready for another planting, and I know why the soil is contaminated. They need me."

"Good. Keep making yourself indispensable. Remember who you're loyal to."

"One Dibon," I replied, the familiar soldier chant etched in my mind.

"One Dibon." Vance patted me on the shoulder and stood, walking to the door.

I had the handgun. I should've shot him. He walked right out the door; confident I'd never shoot.

"You seem upset," Mara said, and I jumped. I hadn't noticed her come to the door.

"I'm tired." I stood, my hand moving to the weapon stuffed in my belt, making sure it was secure. "I have to go find a new job today."

"Why?"

"I got fired last night. It's a long story." I hated lying

—it betrayed the values I was raised with. Finding her eyes, I breathed out hard. "I had a falling out with the manager." That was true, enough.

"Let me speak to Rachel."

I furrowed my brow. "How do you know her?"

"Anna introduced us. Let me speak with her," she pleaded with me. "I'm sure you can get your job back. Besides, the farm really is yours."

"I don't want it, Mara." I folded my arms across my chest. "Jill—Rachel's daughter—was hurt last night. It's my fault."

She drew closer to me. "I'm sure it's not your fault."

I pursed my lips. I'd promised I'd never let her down. But a lot of promises would be broken soon.

———

I MISSED the early calls for labor the next morning. It rained on my way to the village center, so I bought a wide-brimmed hat from a street vendor. I contemplated some of the nearby farms still open for day laborers— the Lehem farm truck was long gone with their workers —but I spied the firearms the others carried and was too nervous. Which ones were Jamin ready to join the Twelve Rebels? Who would attack me in the fields? Bo, Rachel and Jonah saw to it that the Lehem farm was safe.

But safety was not an option.

Instead, I found a hotel owner hiring, and I scrubbed toilets and sinks, cleaned floors and made beds all day. At the end of the day, he paid me five thousand. I clenched the cartridge until it made a red imprint on my palm.

"You can earn more, you know," he told me, motioning to the women entering the rear of the establishment, with painted faces and skirts of many colors.

"No."

Back on Dibon, I knew sex workers, and plenty of my fellow Pinions visited the brothels. When we began rebuilding after the war, some went that route because it was guaranteed money, the only business to survive war and destruction.

"Clean the cellar rooms and you can go."

"Do I have a job tomorrow?"

"I'll see if I'm as generous tomorrow."

Hanging above the entryway to the basement, a sign read *The Threshing Floor*. A large, dark space spread underneath the hotel containing tables, a bar, and a dance floor, but down the narrow dark corridors lay the cellar rooms. They were not the bright rooms above with their posh furnishings and embroidered towels. These were dark, with no windows. The rooms contained beds, but also heavy locks on the doors requiring security keys from the inside. They locked women in those rooms. I didn't finish cleaning. I flew up the stairs and out the door—

—and bumped into Bo.

I'd forgotten my new hat, and it was raining hard.

"What are you doing here?" he demanded of me, his strong hands gripping my shoulders. The rain poured behind him, past the door's overhang.

I narrowed my eyes. "Working." I broke free from his grasp, stepping back. "What are you doing here?"

He spat on the ground. "I didn't think you were that type of girl."

My anger erupted in a slap across his face. I stormed away into the rain, not caring it soaked my hair and clothes, surprised I struck him, furious at his assumption. I rounded the corner and broke into a run, fueled by anger and pain.

"Ami!" he called out behind me. I ran until I was out of breath, my hair and coat drenched. I needed to steer clear of him, in case Vance was around, watching me—and yet, I wanted to be with Bo so badly.

My chest ached. I leaned against a metal piling, left over from some bombed-out building, panting as he caught up to me.

"Ami, I'm sorry." His wet hair hung over his eyes.

"You keep saying that. You keep apologizing, but then hurt me more."

"I knew you weren't there for that."

My eyes narrowed. "Yeah, but you were."

His voice was stern. "I was there on business, not for pleasure, if that makes a difference."

"The owner is a creep." I shivered. "I cleaned the rooms for him, then he sent me down to the cellar. They keep women locked up there."

"I know. Some of those women are spies for us." Bo hesitated, then stepped closer to me. "I didn't want to hurt you."

"Yes, you did. The way you said it, the way you looked at me, with such hate."

"I don't hate you," Bo pleaded. "I can't get you out of my mind."

I stared at him, wide-eyed. "You need to. You need to keep away from me."

"Why?" He stood so close his breath warmed my cheeks.

"Vance is coming. He won't stop until I turn you over to him."

"I can help you."

"No—you want to shut me in, lock me up. You still don't trust me."

"How could I when you lied to me about the disintegrator, and the meet up with Jill?"

"I had to! Jill told me you would've stopped it, and we needed it to find out what happened!"

Bo's eyes dared me to touch him, to kiss him.

"Don't," I whispered, his lips a centimeter from mine. He stared at my mouth, but he didn't move any closer. "I'm leaving."

But I couldn't leave—my feet froze to the ground. I gazed into his eyes, his face scarred, like his heart—and mine.

I grabbed his coat, pulling him against me, kissing him hard. The man with the face I knew so well pushed me against the piling, his hand tangled in my wet hair, and I wanted him. I didn't care that it was raining, I wanted more of this, and no complications. I clawed at his shirt as he tightened his embrace. Lightning flashed in the hills nearby.

Then I pushed him back and walked away in the rain. Bo swore, calling my name, but he didn't come after me again.

———

I FOUND a new job working for a neighbor, cleaning and doing minor repairs on their machinery. Days passed, but Vance didn't return. I didn't know what to tell him when he did.

Mara didn't understand when I pleaded with her to move, maybe to another part of Melas. "Why would we move? This is our home. And Lehem Farm should be yours. Why haven't you talked with Jonah and Rachel about it?"

"I can't. I can't come take what is theirs."

"The bank will repay them, and there's other land they can buy. But this rightfully belongs to you."

"I don't want it."

"But it's Eli's birthright—Max's birthright—and therefore, yours. Why would you deny this?"

"Why do you keep on this?" I threw my hands in the air. "You didn't even know about it when you lived here before. Eli never farmed this land, only his ancestors. Besides, I'm not a farmer. They fired me."

"Eli's family farmed this land for generations. I keep on this because you're denying Max's rights," she said through gritted teeth. "You're denying my rights as his mother, because of your hurt feelings."

My mother-in-law huffed out of the room, the most anger I'd seen from her in a long time. The guilt seeped in, weighing on my shoulders. There were much worse things happening, but I couldn't worry her. "Mara," I called, following her to the bedroom. "I'm sorry. I'll think about it, okay?"

She sat on a chair by the window, staring out, much like she did at the old farmhouse on Dibon. I followed her gaze out through a gap in the buildings and thin trees. The crater of old Ephra lay in view.

"I shouldn't have said that. It's not about me, or Max. It's about you." She shifted her gaze to me. "What I said to Anna when we arrived on Melas, I meant it. Max may have had some childhood memories from our farm here, but when he met you, all he could talk about was this smart Diboni girl he met at the community development farming class and how much he was learning from you. Not from the instructor, but you. He believed in you. You have the ability to run a farm like Lehem farm, and I believe that despite all that has happened, this is for you. This is yours, *if* you want it."

I blinked back tears.

"But I shouldn't be pressuring you this way," she said. "I know what it's like to have to start over, again and again. But I'm not you."

"You're not pressuring me, Mara. It's just...something I have to work out." That was the truth. I had to figure out how to stop Vance, and how to repair everything with Bo.

Something Mara mentioned before stuck in my mind. "You said Eli's family farmed this continent for decades. There were a people here called the Sebuj..."

She frowned.

"What happened to them?"

"The Sebuj were here when the Twelve migrated to this world. When Dahan came, they settled here after negotiating with the Sebuj. Jamin also negotiated, but there were always tensions. When the last war started, I heard the Sebuj killed themselves. We were already on our way to Dibon when it happened."

"Was Lehem Farm area part of the negotiated area with Dahan, or Jamin?"

"It went back and forth. Eli's family and mine are Dahan, of course, but some of our relatives intermarried. Cale must've still been alive then, though Eli never introduced us."

"Did any of them leave as refugees like you, with the first wave?"

Mara shrugged. "I don't think so."

A thread caught in my mind, and I followed it. What if the Sebuj didn't kill themselves, but were killed? By Jamin—or Dahan? The Sebuj arms seller said someone sold them the Rupture Device. That technology originated in the Ramaen System—who also supplied the Dibon Military Force.

What if the Rupture Device was still around? What if Vance *was* searching for it?

WHEN MY COMMANDING officer arrived the next morning, I knew what to say to him.

"What have you learned?" he asked.

"Much. I think I'm close to the leadership now."

Vance smiled. "What do you know?"

Drawing in a deep breath, I hesitated for a moment. I hoped the truth I told him was enough to lead him off, and not betray Bo and Jill. "The Lehem Farm, which is run by a prominent Dahan family, is where the militia networks. I worked there until recently, but I believe I have a way to take control of the farm." None of that was a lie.

"Good!"

My eyes narrowed. "I need to ask you again—what do you know about the Sebuj?"

"Nothing," he said, shifting his eyes away for a moment, the end of the word dropping off. Enough for me to doubt. "Why? Are they allies of the Dahan?"

"No, but most of them were killed by a Rupture Device."

Vance's eyebrow twitched. "Are you certain?"

"You've heard of it?"

"Yes."

I had to bide my time, not pry too much, but I was certain of the connection now.

Setting my hands on the table, I continued. "I was working on the Lehem Farm to discover why the soil was contaminated, and I figured out that a mass death occurred there during the war. How would they have gotten their hands on a Rupture Device?"

"Maybe it wasn't that, but the Baratanium blast instead." Vance averted his gaze, and he *knew* I noticed.

"I know what I saw, what contaminated the soil."

The captain's eyes narrowed, turning back to me. "What are you saying?"

I leaned forward. "It means someone sold a Rupture Device to people here, and it may have ignited the war. We use Ramaen technology. We had training on how to dispose of weapons we might come across after the war was over, including disintegrators, though we were never supposed to use them. They were banned before our war, but they might have been in use before then. Our involvement here might have led to what happened on Dibon, and I have to know if it's true."

Vance stood, staring me down. "Lieutenant Commander, you are under orders. Whatever your personal feelings are about what happened on our planet, we need to stop these people from doing this again. We need to stop the Dahan militia from controlling Melas and the Twelve."

"Personal feelings?" I stood, staring back. "Isn't that what this is all about? Isn't that why you're here, because they attacked us? How is it any different if we were the ones who started the conflict here?"

The captain didn't answer me. Instead, he lifted his sidearm out of its holster. I thought for a split second about jabbing my elbow to his nose, attempting to disarm him, but he set it on the table. "This is for you. You are to gain control of the Lehem farm immediately, and you are to kill the leader of the Dahan militia as soon as you find them." His eyes narrowed, as his mouth curved up, a sinister grin. "Our *last* remaining Albatross carrier—the *Tristan*—will be in orbit in thirty hours, and our Buzzards ready to attack."

I swallowed hard. Our flight division—my *former* flight division—was coming here, to engage a people without air defense.

"We have help from a Jamin informant. We will cripple the Dahan so they cannot rise again. *You* have your orders."

Vance started to leave, but he placed his hand on my shoulder. "I'm sorry. Your husband was a good man. But whatever we do, we are trained to put our personal feelings aside and assist our own people. One Dibon."

"One Dibon," I managed to squeak out.

I'd half a mind to shoot him in the back as he walked

away, but I recognized our conversation was probably recorded. We were under surveillance in this house, probably since he'd first arrived.

Though I imagined killing him, I couldn't bring myself to do it. I hated him for it.

But there was another way. A plan began to take shape, a plan that would not only save me and Mara, but Bo, Jill, and everyone else.

The hardest part would be getting Bo to trust me.

I stuffed Vance's sidearm in a cupboard to hide it for now, then entered the bedroom. "Mara, you're right. Let's go sign the paperwork and claim the farm."

27

Mara called Rachel and Jonah, told them the decision was made, and I filed for Max's birthright to the farm. We met at the Outer Systems Regulated Bank near the center square. Bo didn't come with them. Jonah wouldn't even look at me. I knew he never expected this, and though this was my right within their laws, I knew the old farmer saw me as the foreigner taking advantage of them.

After several security measures, including a quick DNA test, the OSRB officials confirmed my identity, that I was indeed Max Lehem's widow, who was the son of Eli, the son of Seth, the nephew of Cale.

Once all the contracts were signed, the bank remitted Jonah's initial payment on the farm. The fields were now mine, but there were also fines and taxes to be paid, which meant—if I lived long enough—I needed to get the farm productive as soon as possible.

Which meant I needed to get the contaminant out of the soil.

Which meant I had to find the Rupture Device and find a way to reverse the effects. There must be a way to neutralize it. Whoever tried before had failed.

But first, I needed to get my mother-in-law to safety. Then I needed to save Bo. Because the Dibon Military Force was almost here, and none of the rest mattered until we stopped them.

Jill waited outside while we finished the transaction, her arm bound in a sling. Jonah thrust open the doors from the bank, heading toward her, but I called them both over, along with Rachel and Mara.

"You need to know I don't intend to take the farm from you. I only did this to protect you. All of you."

"What?" Rachel asked, her brow furrowed.

"I don't have time to explain, but your lives are in danger. I need to know—do the bunkers in the mountains still exist? Are they intact?"

"Yes, but—"

"I need you to take Mara there, until we send for you. There's someone from my past who's threatening her life and will stop at nothing to get what they want."

My mother-in-law stared at me, stunned.

"I'll take her," Jill began, but I cut her off.

"No, I need your help here." I turned to Jonah and Rachel. "Please take her to safety and stay there."

Jonah set his hands on his hips. "I don't understand."

"I know this is sudden," I said, rushing the words out. "We've known for some time the farm belonged to my deceased husband, but I'm doing this now to not attract suspicion."

"Suspicion of what?" the old farmer demanded.

The injured redhead glanced at her father. "Dad, I'll explain later. Trust Ami, she's got this."

Mara opened her mouth to speak, but I took her hands. "I'll be fine."

"Be careful, my daughter."

Tears stung my eyes as I held her close. I pulled from my bag the handgun I took from my attackers. "This is for you. I know you never wanted to use one again—neither do I, but we can't be sure. Go. Be safe."

She stuffed it in her bag.

I gazed back to Jonah. "Anyone else on the farm—get them to the mountains."

Turning to Jill as the three elders loaded into Jonah's truck, I bit my lip before speaking. "I need to know right now if you trust Dan, completely and absolutely."

She cocked her head. "Yes."

"I need you to tell him the Diboni remnant is preparing to attack—they're almost here. And they have inside help from Jamin dissidents."

Jill's jaw dropped open.

"Lastly, I need you to tell me where Bo is."

"I don't know for sure. I think the Dahan militia leaders are meeting tonight."

"At the hotel?"

Jill raised her eyebrows. "The club downstairs, *The Threshing Floor*. They won't let you in, though."

"I've got to see him. If I don't, they'll kill him."

"I can try to get him a message—"

"No. It might be intercepted by Jamin spies." I put my hand on her shoulder, knowing what I must do. "I need to go back to my house first to get a few things, then you'll have to drop me off near the inn. Then head directly to Dan's and tell him what's going on."

———

I HADN'T WORN a dress in years. Jill tilted her head and raised an eyebrow as I climbed in. "I never thought I'd see you like this."

"Shut up and drive." I wore the weapon Vance gave me strapped to my thigh, under the long dress. I'd found an old garment of Mara's, removed the seams, and cut into the slinky emerald fabric. I could stitch wounds together—I could sew clothes. Two bands of cloth criss-crossed my body to barely cover my breasts, clasping around my neck. The ends were sewed into the skirt, slit up the non-weapon-bearing side. I painted my eyes and lips with thick color, and I twisted my hair in ringlets, something I hadn't done since my wedding day.

"This is close enough," I told her, as we approached Ephra's main drag.

Jill rested her hands on the steering wheel. "He and I grew up together, he's more like my brother than cousin. Once his face was burned—there was no one. He shut himself off from the idea of love, until you came along."

I understood all too well.

"He cares about you, Ami. And he thinks he's keeping you safe by staying angry at you."

"I pushed him away, last time." Because I wanted to keep him safe, too. "But if he meets with leaders of the other nations here, they must at least think that he... frequents..." My voice trailed off.

Jill tilted her head, frowning.

"One more thing," I added. "When you go back and help evacuate the farm, tell Phin to stay. We'll need him."

"He'll want to help, anyway. Good luck."

After I climbed out of the truck, Jill drove off in the direction of the farm. Taking a deep breath, various eyes stared at me as I made my way to the back entrance of the inn. I hoped there'd be more Sim'ee girls, or otherwise I'd stand out among the Dahan and Jamin. Except for my thicker hair and darker eyes, I could pass as Sim'ee, and in the dark cellar no one should notice.

I descended the stairs to *The Threshing Floor*. Two guards stood at the entrance to the corridor. When the owner sent me there before, it was empty. I didn't know there'd be security.

"No one's allowed down here, without an escort," the shorter one said gruffly.

"But I am an escort," I replied, my fingers tangled in front of me.

The larger Dahan guard grunted. "Who sent for you?"

I wracked my brain. Bo wouldn't use his real name here, most likely, but his face was recognizable.

"Samson paid for me."

One of the guards raised an eyebrow, but then jerked his chin. "Follow me."

I followed the guard through the corridor, sweat gathering across my forehead. The rows of doors in the dim light caused me to shudder. The air hung thick, veiled with pipe smoke, the smell of body odor and sex piercing my nostrils. Loud music blared over the speakers. Bodies entwined along the hallway, grinding to the rhythm of the bass shaking the walls. I gulped, praying for the courage to do what I had to do.

The corridor ended in the large windowless room, dimly lit. People were dancing—Dahan, a few Sim'ee, and several Jamin. One of them might be the informant for Vance, trying to find Bo. I had to play my part well, but a lump grew in my throat. This could go horribly wrong if I messed up.

Several guards surrounded a table in one corner, and I spied Bo's face, his scars identifying him even in the smoky light. Four other men sat at the table. At least two of them were Sim'ee. Lights danced off the empty shot glasses.

The large Dahan guard shouted, "Perry Samson! This one claims you paid for her?"

Bo rose, his companions following suit. The sound of guns pulled from their holsters echoed around the room as the music stopped, and at least a dozen weapons were trained on me. I stared into his eyes. Bo blinked, his mouth opening and closing quickly. "Yes, yes I did," he answered, his voice low.

The men at the table stared at him in shock. "Well, the lion is on the loose!" one shouted, eyeing me up and down. Another whistled. "Did you get one for me too, Perry, or are you sharing her?"

My heart threatened to beat out of my chest, so I stole a shot from the table. The Bara gin slid down my throat. I stepped carefully over to Bo, placing my hand on his shoulder, straddling his lap. He swallowed hard as I draped my arms around him, the smell of liquor lingered on his breath. His eyes never left mine, though his hand traveled up my thigh, searching for a weapon.

Stopping his hand with mine, right below where the weapon was strapped to my thigh, hidden under the folds of my skirt, I licked my lips. "Do you want to start here, or go someplace a little more private?" I teased, moving one finger down his shoulder to his chest, where I knew his scars lay.

"Private," he whispered, and I stood, not letting go of his hand.

Bo led me away from them, past the writhing bodies in the hallway, to one of the empty rooms. He jerked me inside and slammed the door shut, throwing two deadbolts and keying a number into an electronic lock. No one could get in, but it also meant I couldn't escape.

The brief moment of relief I had when he followed my lead now passed into fear.

"What the hell are you doing here?" Bo demanded, his eyes burning.

"Vance wants you dead."

"We've been through this, Ami."

"It's different now. The remnant of the Dibon Military Force will be in orbit within hours. They've got an Albatross carrier with Buzzards ready to strike. I was given direct orders to assassinate the leader of Dahan, and they're going to assault Lehem Farm."

Bo folded his arms across his chest. "We scan all communications that manage to get through and have some of the best codebreakers working for us. We've heard none of this."

I lifted my skirt, showing him the gun strapped to my thigh. "Recognize that? Ramaen issued officer's pistol."

"How do they know it's me?" he accused, his hands dropping to his sides. His eyes bore the fury of betrayal.

"They don't know you're the target—at least, I don't think they do yet, but I was ordered to find out. They're coming to invade, and there are Jamin resistance fighters —Rebels—helping him. Probably in this club."

Bo threw his hands in the air. "Not this again. Dan is—"

"I'm not talking about Dan. There are others, and they're looking to side with the Diboni remnant and retake Melas for themselves. They may even have more Ramaen weapons now, which would be very, very bad." I caught my breath, talking so fast. "I don't think the Sebuj killed themselves. I think they were killed so Dahan or Jamin or whoever was in charge at the time could take the land, and the technology came from the Ramaen System."

"How do you know all this?"

"Because some of the Sebuj survived. One of them was there the night Jill and I made the arms deal."

Bo paced the room, staring at the floor. "Why didn't you tell me this before?"

"Because I didn't know until that night, and you wouldn't listen to me." I breathed out hard, frustrated I couldn't get through to him. "I didn't want any of this. I only came here to get Mara home. Then I saw the soil contamination, and I couldn't let it go—I had to find out what caused it."

He glared at me, and I sat on the bed, away from him. "It wasn't until after that—after our date—that Vance, my commanding officer, found me, and only yesterday that he gave me the order. If I could have gotten Mara to safety, I would've killed him right there, but I don't know who his spies are, who's working for him."

"How can I trust that you're not lying?"

I reached under my skirt, removing the weapon, and held it out to him. "You can shoot me with it."

Bo scoffed. I caught his gaze, locking onto his eyes. "No, seriously. If you do, then the farm goes back to your family."

"What are you talking about?"

"It turns out my husband Max was a closer relative than Jonah and it should've come down to him. Lehem is my husband's family name, and there are no remaining Lehem's. I didn't know until Mara found out. I went and signed the papers with Jonah and Rachel today to claim it so Vance would think I was serious, but if I'm dead, it reverts back to the closest relative. If you shoot me, it goes back—Mara won't want it without me."

I laid the pistol on the bed and stared at my hands. My skirt lay bunched up my thigh, my legs revealed. He stood away from me, as if unsure of what to do next.

"How do I know you don't have any other weapons?" Bo asked, his eyes searching mine.

I stood to face him. Inside I trembled, but as calm as I could, I reached around my neck and untied the straps holding the dress, letting it fall, exposing my breasts. Unclasping the fasteners on the side of my skirt, I allowed the whole dress to drop away, leaving me bare as I tugged off my shoes.

He gulped. "Get dressed."

"No. I want you to see me." The cool air from the vents circled around us. My heart thumped hard in my chest. I longed for him to believe me, to trust me, to know I never wanted any harm to come to him.

"Ami, this isn't the time—"

"It's never a good time."

He swallowed again. "Put your clothes back on."

"No. You take yours off."

Jill was right all along—I had come to seduce Bo. But only to get him to trust me.

He stared at me, and I refused to move. The militia leader shook his head, then retrieved the pistol from the bed, and I flinched. But he placed it on the small table near the bed. Then he removed his own pistol, unclasped his belt, and stood right in front of me. His eyes traveled down my body. I breathed out hard.

Bo removed his tunic, slipped out of his trousers and shoes, and now it was my turn to gulp, out of nervousness, out of anticipation. He revealed it all—his strength and his scars, sculpted thighs, taut muscles—every part of him.

All of him, all of me, exposed and open and vulnerable. There was nothing more to hide, nothing more to cover up.

"Do you trust me now?" he asked.

"Do you trust me?" I repeated back.

We stood there for seconds, waiting for the other to move.

I closed my eyes.

He kissed me roughly, his hands on my cheeks. I crushed myself against him, feeling his skin against mine, chest to chest, thigh to thigh. My arms wrapped around him, and his around my waist. Nothing else mattered in that moment. My fear was overcome by my need for him.

Bo kissed me again, biting my lower lip in eagerness, as my fingernails dug into his shoulder blades. My mind buzzed, senses overflowing with the smell and taste of him, the sound of his heart pounding against mine. His hands slid over my buttocks to the back of my thighs, lifting me up as I leaned against him, wrapping my legs around his strong body, before we tumbled onto the bed.

———

AFTERWARD, as our breathing slowed, he held me against him, our legs entwined. "What happens now?" Bo asked, desperate.

I propped myself up on one elbow, my fingertips tracing the edge of his scars, down his face to his shoulder and chest. His fingers weaved into my hair, forcing my gaze into his. My lover's urgency made it plain—there was no time for second-guessing intentions or sorting out feelings. Vance's ship would be here, and Bo put his trust in me to get us out.

"We fight back."

28

Bo snuck me out of the inn before the sun rose. We had to be careful we weren't spotted together, in case Vance had spies there. Adrenaline fed off the threat of danger in my blood. I stayed hidden under a blanket in his truck until we entered through the gate to the empty farmhouse, Rachel and Jonah long gone to the mountains. Bo found me a change of clothes—an old tunic and pair of trousers, while I found a pair of boots in a storage closet—and he handed me back the gun Vance had given me. "Best to be safe and carry it, so it looks like you're still carrying out your mission."

Then we woke Phin and went to the copse.

"Are you sure about this?" Bo asked.

"Yes. This way, you'll be my next of kin, should anything happen."

The sky tinted a deep purple, the gas giant Horeb a long, thin crescent slip above us as we stood before the stone altar in the copse, with Phin as our witness. I clasped Bo's hands in mine, and recited the vows I once spoke to Max, the same I promised to Mara, and now, I made to him. "Where you go, I will go. Where you live, I will live. Where you die, I will die. Your people will be my people. Your God, my God."

Bo repeated the words back to me, and Phin declared us married before their God. I had no ring for my new husband, but he brought one for me—Bo had retrieved his mother's ring when he got me clothes—and he slid it onto my left hand. Though it had been over a year since I stopped wearing Max's ring, the weight felt comforting, familiar.

Phin scanned our retinas, entering them into a tablet also containing our marriage license to make it official. As soon as he was out of earshot, I whispered to Bo. "The farm is now legally yours. I wanted to make sure there's no doubt of my intentions here."

My new husband ignored the last. "It's yours, too, don't forget. I share," he teased.

"But if something happens to me—"

"I'm not going to let anything happen to you."

The sky lightened, daybreak fast approaching as the golden disk of the sun peeked above the horizon. We didn't have much time.

"Is the arsenal bunker the only one you have?" I asked as we headed back to the bunkhouse, where Jill was to meet us.

"No."

"How many do you have?"

"Arsenal bunkers? Three. Bunkers to hide in? Twenty-seven."

"Twenty-seven? We might actually stand a chance. Any anti-aircraft defense?"

"Sluggers and blasters."

I gazed at him sideways as we hurried to the bunkhouse. "Hoped you'd have a little more as a militia."

Bo kept his mouth shut.

Jill and Dan arrived, along with other Dahan and a few Jamin and Sim'ee workers I recognized. "We've evacuated almost everyone from Ephra to the mountains," the redhead informed me. "I'll get Phin on the last transport out."

I gazed around at the small militia left, including the injured Jill, but we needed her. "Time to arm up."

Bo led us to the nearest arsenal bunker, where we strapped on bulletproof chest guards and the stockpiled lightweight armor. In addition to the weapon Vance gave me, now in a proper tactical holster, I added another pistol to my belt and enough ammunition to for a few reloads each. Bo handed me a Ramaen blaster. I strapped it to my back, along with several magazines of incendiary rounds, and wrapped a comm link around my ear.

I never wanted to fight in a war again. But violence stalked me across the galaxy, through Jordan Station and the Galactic Ocean. Every time, I'd been the one to react, to reluctantly take up arms. This time, I would face it, and not alone.

"Listen up," I began. Though I'd never led a squadron before, this was now my squad, and I had to exert authority right now if we were going to survive this. "The enemy will be flying Buzzards—Kittiwakes—

and they're tough birds to take down. Exhaust fuel port is the way to get them. If you hit their weapons, you might disable them, but they're loaded with Ramaen blaster technology much more powerful than this." I slapped the barrel of the blaster Bo gave me. "We're going to be outgunned by the fighters. But they're not expecting us to be ready for them."

One of the workers drew close. "What about the Jamin working with them?"

"We'll be ready to turn on those traitors," Dan announced, glancing at me. I trusted Jill and Bo, but the Jamin's gaze made me uneasy.

"How many Buzzards?" a militia member asked.

"I can't say for sure, but the average Albatross carrier holds up to a dozen."

We scattered out among the barns, watching the skies, and waited. The distant sun rose to its zenith, the much closer gas giant dipping near the horizon. A flock of giant birdlike creatures —something like herons, I guessed from their silhouette, but they grew larger here on Melas—flew by in formation. Otherwise, the farm was still.

The time when Vance reported they'd arrive in orbit passed, and still we waited. Bo asked me if maybe I got the information wrong, but I shrugged him off.

It's when I heard the faint rumble of engines that I knew Vance hadn't divulged the full plan to me. He hadn't sent the Buzzards yet. I scurried up a ladder on the side of a barn, leaning over the peeked roof, and sawdust clouds rising along the roads to the farm.

"Stardust and ashes!"

The Jamin Rebels were coming to take us. And we sent everyone away, preparing to take out twelve fighters —not a thousand Rebels of the Twelve.

I rushed down the ladder. "What are the weak spots in the fence?"

Bo considered. "The two side gates are easiest to break through. But the main gate, without our guards, will fall quickly."

I called out over the comm link, "Everyone, head to the gates. Make sure you have at least a Ramaen blaster or grenade launcher at each gate. When the Buzzards get here, they will be aiming for the fence."

We scrambled. I headed to the main gate with Bo, knowing the likelihood of us surviving had shrunk a thousand-fold. Near the main gate stood a half-built grain silo. The top was capped off with boards because of the recent rains, creating a platform. One side of the curved wall construction was a meter higher. It would do. We climbed the ladder and took our positions.

I raised the blaster as the first vehicle rolled into view, firing as soon as I had it in my scope. The engine exploded, launching its passengers and driver as the blast shook through my shoulder. But behind it came three more. I aimed at the closest, hitting the right front tire. The vehicle spun, flipping on its side. Two men managed to get out and run with their weapons. Bo took them down while the sniper with us shot the driver of another.

We fired at four other vehicles, and then I whipped my head around at the all-too-familiar whistle of Buzzards. "Go," said Bo. The other vehicles would drive toward the giant holes in the fence the Buzzards were about to create if we didn't stop them.

"I need some cover!" I shouted, aiming at the first Buzzard passing through. The pilot hit the ground near us with rapid fire from proton rifles. I knew even with a Ramaen blaster I wouldn't do much damage hitting him in the front where the armor was strongest—we needed to wait for him to pass by. Bo fired anyway, striking near the hatch, barely making a dent. But as the Buzzard passed, I aimed right for the fuel exhaust and fired. The fighter erupted into flames, striking the ground and exploding.

A thud rocked the platform behind me. Our sniper went down, his chest armor splintering from a blaster hit fired by the Jamin. Ducking behind the raised side of the silo, I took shelter as Jamin rebels fired on us from an armored vehicle. I hated to waste my blaster on them, but I took two deep breaths, rose, and took out the vehicle with one blast. Bo checked on the wounded man, but I knew from one glance he was beyond help. Readying myself for the next Buzzard, I fired a blast at the nose. The Kittiwake fighter lurched, but the pilot righted the bird as it flew by. I fired again, striking the wing.

The broken fighter darted in a spiral, flying right into the bunkhouse and shattering it like a house made of toothpicks, with large fireballs blasting through the walls. I huddled back down behind the silo wall. Getting those people away from the farm was the right thing to do.

"He's dead," Bo announced, his hand leaving our sniper's body. One of the armored vehicles attempted to ram the gate. They'd been expecting the Buzzards to give them a wider hole to get through.

I fired at the front vehicle. The explosion of its engine pushed it back into the next. Bo fired and gunned down the Jamin who managed to get out of the second vehicle. Another man climbed up to take the place of our downed sniper, and fired on the truck behind that one as I took aim at the third Buzzard coming our way.

But that Kittiwake didn't attack. The fighter looped in front of us, flashing its underbelly, taunting me. I aimed for the exhaust port and fired, but the blast disintegrated right off the engines.

I lowered my gun, recognizing a circle of gray ash near its stabilizer, the remnant of the blast that should've caused much more damage. A familiar barrel-shape mounted on its underside swiveled its aim.

"Mother-duster. That thing has a disintegrator armed on it."

"What?" Bo shouted.

"Get down!" I yelled, pushing him off the platform as I jumped. The militia fighter on the platform with us was too slow. Glancing back, I witnessed the remains of the silo disintegrate into the thin film of ash.

That's when it hit me the Rupture Device was much larger than the disintegrator weapons being used on us right now. Whatever it was that killed the Sebuj here was neither a handheld weapon nor mounted to a fighter. It was much, much bigger.

The Buzzard neared for another loop. I grabbed Bo's hand and ran, heading for the nearest bunker. Heart pounding, we pumped our legs toward the opening in the ground. The shadow of the fighter chased us as we both leaped, hitting the sloped steel of the bunker hard. We rolled, Bo on top of me, and I cried out in pain—my shoulder separated. I lost the grip on my blaster. The whistle of the Buzzard passed. We were only safe until the Jamin Rebels on the ground found us.

My Ramaen blaster lay half in view at the entrance to the bunker. Bo reached to retrieve it, right as the Buzzard's whistle neared again. "No—"

The blaster, along with his arm, disintegrated before my eyes. One moment, he grasped the gun. The next, there was no gun, and Bo had no lower arm.

He screamed, his arm a severed mess right below the elbow. My mouth opened, but no sound could escape the silent panic seeping over me. Spots filled my vision.

Seconds later, two other Dahan militia fighters jumped into our bunker, and stared in horror at Bo. "Is there a med kit?" I cried out, shaking myself out of shock. I couldn't afford to pass out now.

One of the militia fighters grabbed the med kit from the wall. I held my useless arm against me. "Tie a tourniquet," I ordered. "If there is anesthesia give it to him right away."

"No," Bo shouted, but the Dahan militia man restrained him while the woman plunged the needle in his neck. My husband—my new husband of a few hours —slumped over, his eyes rolling to the back of his head. The man finished tying the tourniquet at the shoulder.

"Wrap his arm as best as you can," I commanded, my voice quivering, my vision clearing despite my fright. The woman wrapped as much gauze as she could find in the kit around the stub of his arm, red seeping through to the surface.

"Is there any way to escape?"

The two looked at each other. "There's a passageway, under the farmhouse," the woman divulged. Where Bo must've went all those nights, for those meetings with Dahan leadership. Out the tunnel to Ephra.

"You two are gonna carry Bo, get him out of here. Get him to the mountains. He needs to see Phin."

"How?"

"I'll cover for you, if you pop my shoulder back in." I searched the med kit and found pain pills. Popping four in my mouth, I dry swallowed, while using my good arm to move my injured arm in position.

"Do it," I ordered to the one who tied the tourniquet. He grabbed my arm below the elbow, and feeling on the back of my shoulder, popped it in.

"Mother-blast it," I blurted out in pain. It still hurt but I could move it. I reached for my blaster, and remembered it was gone. The two pistols were all I had left. I'd expected to use them on pilots—they wouldn't do anything against a Buzzard.

But the one who popped my arm back in had a blaster on his back. "Give me your weapon," I ordered. He handed it over, and I swapped in a fresh magazine and waited for the familiar double-click.

I counted to steady my heart. One. Two. Three. "Let's go."

Rising from the bunker, I took off running and fired at the Buzzard coming at us. I hit the wing, and the pilot jerked the controls, overcompensating, sending the fighter into spin. Firing again, I hit the fuel exhaust. The

Kittiwake drove to the ground, exploding in front of us. We ran past the downed fighter toward the farmhouse.

I spun around, ready to fire at the next Buzzard, but the armored vehicles had managed to bust through the fence and were coming our way instead. "Go!" I yelled at the Dahan fighters, and they moved past me, carrying Bo. They entered the farmhouse ahead of me at the side door while I stopped to head off the trucks heading our direction. I fired, managing to blow up two, while the roaring grew behind me.

The Buzzard with the disintegrator aimed at the farmhouse. The walls and what was left of the roof caved in. The building collapsed, a house of cards falling in on itself. Flames overtook the demolished walls.

I remembered the heat from the weapon I fired in the lab. Bo and the others could not have survived it.

More armored vehicles approached, but I was out of breath. I scanned the farm and didn't see any of our Dahan militia left. They'd either found places to hide, or they were dead.

Though I still had a few more rounds left for the blaster, and the two other pistols with me, I tossed my weapons to the ground and placed my hands on the back of my head in surrender. There was no other way out. My arm blazed with pain.

The vehicles circled me, and Jamin rebels aimed their weapons. I lay prone on the ground, and again placed my hands behind my head, face into the dirt. A buzzard landed—the one with the disintegrator—and I waited a long time before I spied Vance's boots in front of me.

"Rise, Lieutenant Commander," he told me. I lifted my face, peering up at the captain, who knelt and held out his hand. In disbelief, I took it, and stood with him. "You've done well. Lehem Farm is ours, and soon, the Dahan leadership will be dead."

29

I didn't understand as Vance led me to one of the barns still standing. I spotted gaping holes in the fence while I covered my mouth and nose, the air choking and half the farm burning. Smoke billowed from piles of rubble—most of the barns destroyed, now smoldering lumber. I didn't see any other prisoners or survivors.

We entered an undamaged barn, and my former captain faced me. But he stayed silent. I held my injured arm against me, the pain excruciating. My heart stuck in my throat. I'd no way of knowing if Bo made it out alive.

"Why don't you kill me now?" I asked, breaking the deafening silence.

"Because you know where he is."

"Who?"

"Don't play dumb with me. I know the reason you couldn't fulfill the mission is that somehow you ended up protecting the leader."

I shrugged my good shoulder.

"Last time I saw him, he was running to the farmhouse."

"You're lying to me," Vance accused, staring into my eyes.

"You tell me." I stared back, not blinking. For it was true—the last time I saw Bo, he was carried inside.

"Then he's dead."

"Yes. Your mission's complete," I snarled.

The captain laughed. "I don't understand you, Lehem. Your own planet was destroyed by these people."

"You're lying. It wasn't Dahan."

His eyes didn't move, he didn't even blink. Bo told me they didn't know who bombed Dibon's bunkers, but he was working to find out. I blew out air between my teeth. "What are you gonna do now?"

"With the help of the Jamin here, we're going to take control of Melas. From here, *we* will crush the Twelve and restore peace."

"The Jamin are with Dahan. Only the Jamin dissidents are part of the Twelve Rebels," I insisted. "You're siding with the wrong people."

"The Dahan militia, those who claim to be forming a government here—*they* are the Rebels." He smirked, tilting his head. "Didn't you know that?"

I stood motionless.

"There'll be no more Rebels destroying our homes, stealing our resources and causing fear in the galaxy. Together, we can take Melas and begin to set things right."

I thought he was talking about the Jamin united with him, but he held out his hand.

"Together?" I asked in disbelief.

"Of course. You were always my favorite pilot." He placed his hand on my good shoulder. "You were loyal to your husband's family, and I can't blame you for that. And according to the laws here, this land is now yours, correct?"

I didn't know for certain how Vance knew, but I suspected I was right about my home being bugged. Maybe I was spotted in the hotel, after all. If I didn't show my hope that Bo was still alive, I could also hope he didn't know about my marriage.

Maybe I could play this out, for Bo's sake.

I nodded. "It's mine."

"I told you I have a Buzzard all ready for you. Don't you want to see it?"

"Yes," I acknowledged, and I did want to see it, especially if it carried the disintegrator weapon.

"Then come with me."

There was no Buzzard outside, I noted as I followed him—only a shuttle transport to get off-world. I stopped mid-step. Vance folded his arms across his chest.

"I'll make this easy for you, Lehem. Join us and take revenge for Dibon. Help us to restore peace. Or side with the Rebels, and we'll carry out your sentence now."

The guards nearby raised their rifles. Vance had it wrong about who the Rebels were, but there was no choice for me to make. I followed him.

"The *Tristan* is in orbit with the new Buzzards on board."

"Are they all armed with disintegrators now?"

"Some. I had that one personally designed."

"Disintegrators are still illegal."

The captain didn't acknowledge my statement. I opened my mouth to speak, but clamped it shut.

Because before me, with the Jamin rebels, stood Dan.

Vance grinned. "I believe you've met our other operative."

I bore daggers into Dan's eyes. I'd known I needed to watch my back with him. His face was stone, expressionless, except for his eyes, revealing triumph.

He knew the raid was coming.

My fists clenched. "You dusting bastard, you set us up!" I lunged for him, but Vance grabbed my injured arm and I went down screaming, subdued like a sheep led to slaughter. One of the guards shoved their gun in my face, but the captain released me, waving the guard off.

"Ami, the fight is over. You're on the winning side now. One Dibon."

Moving to my knees, I struggled in pain, choking back my own cries. I hoped I might be able to get Dan alone, as I thought of all the ways I'd hurt him for betraying Bo. There were a thousand things I'd shout at him before I watched him die, slowly.

Vance extended a hand once again, and I took it, following him away from Dan to the transport shuttle. If Bo was still alive, I only hoped he understood what I was doing.

———

ABOARD THE *TRISTAN*, I expected to be led to a holding cell. Instead, the guards led me to officer's quarters, assigning me a stack of dark blue flight uniforms. I buttoned the collar up tight, though my arm still hurt, and managed to pin the three bars overlayed with the silver star for my rank as lieutenant commander. I slicked my hair back into a bun—regulation would have me cut it short, but there was nothing regular about this. Vance hadn't mentioned the ring on my finger, but it appeared similar to the band Max had given me. I kept it on regardless.

I didn't understand what my old captain was doing. He acted as if I was one of the crew, save for the guards who followed me. I should've been in the brig. Others saluted me, even with armed guards escorting me. My stomach roiled in disgust.

Similar to the vessel I served on years ago, the *Tristan* had room for twelve Kittiwake fighters. Albatross carriers were usually called up for specific missions, to hunt and destroy an enemy target. Smaller than warships, with stealth technology, they could slip in and out of orbit without detection from most regular surveillance.

After stopping at the infirmary, where medics examined my shoulder and administered pain meds, I reported to the flight deck where six Buzzards were ready. "We will begin patrolling the skies of the northern continent, where Dahan is centered in power," Vance announced. "The other two continents are mainly Sim'ee, some Jamin, and other members of the Twelve. We will deal with them once Dahan is under our control."

"When is my shift?" I asked, falling into my role.

Vance put his hand on my shoulder. I used to love that gesture. Now, I wanted to take his hand, twist it as I jabbed the pressure points, and shove his head into my knee.

But I showed no emotion.

"Not yet. I need you here. Walk with me."

I followed alongside the captain. "These are the Gull 7's, what we had transitioned to before the meteor strike. Standard proton rifles underneath the wings, but new proton bomb cannons underneath the fuselage," he said, motioning to the long barrel on the Buzzard's belly. When the landing gear was retracted, the cannon had full range of rotation. The footsteps of the two guards echoed behind me, reminding me not to try anything, confirming Vance was no fool—he didn't blindly trust me.

"We've only built two cannons with disintegrator technology," Vance added.

"I asked you before—isn't it illegal?"

He glared at me. "If we don't use it, they may use it against us, when they fire up the Rupture Device again."

"What do you mean?"

"I have confirmed that a Rupture Device was purchased from the Ramaens before the last war— before disintegrators were outlawed. It was sold to the Twelve Rebels—that much I know."

"And used against the Sebuj."

"It was sold to a Nacaen arms dealer. They thought if they had control of a weapon of that power, others would fall in line."

I still didn't buy it was Dahan, but I played along. "Through fear."

"Through fear," Vance repeated. "A man named Sal was their leader then, and he fought for Dahan independence. The leader used the device to clear the land of 'undesirables.'"

"The Sebuj didn't kill themselves, then." I remembered what Phin said, about the stories we tell because the truth is too hard.

"They lost track of what happened to the device after it was sold, and then they were banned and Ramaens stopped making them. But our operatives have been searching for it, and that's when I came across the name Sal Perez, the leader of Dahan. He was killed during the war. And now, his son Bo is also dead."

I stopped in my tracks. Bo? His father can't be responsible for the slaughter of thousands. He told me his parents died in a shuttle crash.

Vance paused, facing me. "Lieutenant Commander, what is it?"

"Nothing. I didn't know that."

"Most likely, the Rupture Device was in his possession all along."

I shook my head. "No. Bo didn't know the land was contaminated from a Rupture Device, had no idea one was used."

Vance raised an eyebrow. "You're certain of that, certain you knew him that well? Tell me, did the leader of the Dahan militia ever tell you his father was the former leader while you seduced him?"

I'd given myself away, but I didn't care anymore. My captain could kill me or imprison me, but instead, he tore off the veil, exposing Bo's unfinished stories, weakening my trust. Tearing me down from the inside.

"Did he tell you about the Dahan transmissions, or deny them? The transcripts are all here," Vance said, handing me a tablet. "They were in contact with Rebels in our bunkers all along."

I scanned the tablet Vance gave me. The transmissions record, with the latest at the top, did come from Ephra, but Jamin dissidents also lived there. There were coordinates, names I didn't recognize, short messages. "This doesn't prove anything..."

Except the earliest transmissions. They weren't from Ephra, or even from Melas. Dated over a year ago, from Dibon:

Contact has been arrested. It's gone too far.

--There's no other way?

Negative. The order is given.

--There's got to be another way. Let me come down--

Negative. We will take as many out with us as we can.

--The Lion is going back to the den.

Godspeed, Lion.

--Give them hell.

ORIGIN OF TRANSMISSION: MOAB BASE

RECIPIENT TRANSMISSION: *JABBOK* (IN ORBIT OF DIBON, DOCKING WITH *ASHKELON*).

Dated the day we left Dibon.

Not even two nights ago, they'd called him the Lion at the inn.

Bo knew I was a Diboni soldier, knew they were after me. He told me he'd received a transmission, knowing the bunkers were bombed. But he made it sound like it was only a few months ago, and not from the orbit of Dibon. Had he escaped from the bunkers the day we did? Did he use me to cover his escape, then use me to figure out how to reverse the soil contamination?

I knew what Vance was doing, and I knew why it worked, because Bo Perez kept too many secrets.

Swallowing my doubt, I shoved it down on the surface, but inside everything that held me to the militia leader unraveled. I married Bo, promised to love him. Did I? Did he love me? When I seduced him, to make him see he could trust me, was he playing me the whole time?

"And Dan Hilo?"

Vance smiled. "We weren't able to infiltrate the leadership until we found a Jamin willing to leak us information, around the same time I finally tracked you down. We didn't inform either of you, to keep our situation uncompromised."

The captain started walking again, and I followed. "We're keeping him on the ground for now, to help us find where the leadership has gone. Much of the land has bunkers they could be hiding in."

"Yes, there were twenty-seven bunkers on the farm alone." They would've secured the farm by now and discovered that anyway. I only hoped the others were able to get out, but I wanted Vance to feel I didn't hide anything from him. I had to play my part now, if I could bring any good out of this. If Bo hadn't been lying to me the whole time.

"I'm suspicious of where they've gone. The southern hills are a likely hiding spot. We'll begin our reconnaissance mission tomorrow."

Either Vance didn't know about the bunkers in the western mountains, or he was lying to get me to divulge more. Dan had to have known—unless Jill didn't disclose it to him. I had to hold on to the hope that Mara and the others were safe for now. Until I could figure my way out of this.

"I'll expect you to report to me every morning, Lieutenant Commander, for daily briefing," he said, stopping in front of my quarters. "Well done today." Vance set his hand on my shoulder again, squeezing gently. "I know this is difficult, and I don't blame you for being caught up with the Dahan rebels. I can't imagine being torn, between loyalty to your married family, and to your people." He let go as the guard opened my door and motioned for me to enter.

Vance was playing me, manipulating me, but he didn't trust me. Yet his words carried a weight I couldn't shake, a truth that had been bubbling beneath the surface the entire time I'd known Bo.

As soon as the door closed behind me, I lost it. Bo had withheld information, avoided the truth. The mother-duster lied. I'd risked my life for him, gone to him and confessed my orders, slept with him. Married him. Still, he hadn't told me about his father, about the Rupture Device. For all I knew, the militia leader might be dead now, unable to answer me.

He wanted me to play double agent. Bo had used me all along.

I cried out, swearing at the gods, throwing whatever I could find against the wall—chairs, a canteen, the mother-dusting uniforms I'd been issued, the tablet with all the incriminating evidence. I yanked Bo's ring off my finger and threw it across the room, sinking to the floor, broken.

Vance had me.

30

Time slipped away. I had no instrument to mark the passage of days. Except for being marched into Vance's quarters each morning for the daily briefing, I was confined to my own quarters, sparse with a rack on the side furthest from the door, a closet and shelves on one side with two chairs, and a small sink, recycler, and private head and shower on the other, a perk of being an officer. My nights were filled with terrible dreams, of the Buzzards finding the western bunkers and disintegrating everyone I loved into ash. I'd retrieved the ring on my own. I didn't know what to think about Bo, but I started twisting the ring on my finger, muttering the prayers Mara once did in the bunker long ago. "Blessed is the one beyond blessing." Turn the ring. "Blessed is the one beyond song."

I refused to eat for a few days, and everything became fuzzy. On the fifth day, when I failed to show up for the morning briefing, Vance barged into my quarters. "I'm not leaving until you eat something."

I backed against the closet door as the guards came in. But instead of apprehending me, they wheeled in a cart of eggs, fruit and bread. The smell overwhelmed and suddenly I was ravenous. Vance motioned to the small table that unfolded from the shelves. "Mind if I join you?"

The guard pulled the table down and set out the food. My mouth watered.

"Or I can eat this delicious breakfast and have you taken to medical and force nutrients with an I.V." he said.

What good was a hunger strike if they would just force me to eat anyway?

I sat, not looking at Vance as I scarfed down the meal.

"Don't make yourself sick," he warned, and I paused only to brush a crumb from my cheek as I took a fourth roll.

When I finished, the guards cleared the table and Vance followed behind them.

A few minutes later I pulled down the recycling hatch and threw up.

There was no hope. Everything drained me. But after that I ate normally, and I slept.

I didn't know how many days passed—at least another week, maybe longer—until one morning the guards were no longer posted. When I left my quarters, other soldiers saluted as if I'd always been an officer. Wandering the ship, I traveled the length of the corridor through the officer quarters to the crew quarters, a path I remembered from years ago. Above me was the command deck. Below was the med bay, life support systems, and to the rear of the entire ship, the flight deck. The guards only stopped me from going to the command deck or flight deck, which was standard protocol if you weren't scheduled. I tried the weapons locker, but he hadn't given me the code.

The longer I stayed on the ship, the easier it was to slip into my old habits. At times in the morning, I'd wait for the daily briefing and expect to be assigned to some mission before I remembered I'd surrendered. But there wasn't anything I could do. Even if I gained access to a weapon, it wouldn't get me far. Vance counted on it.

I had to play the game to survive.

"Lieutenant Commander," a man called out, running along the corridor. "Captain Vance needs you."

I turned on my heel without question to Vance's conference room, adjacent to his quarters. When I entered his room, I stopped short. Dan sat at the table in the Dibon-issued uniform. He kept his gaze on the captain. I took my seat at the table.

"Sergeant Hilo. You have a report for us?"

I bit my bottom lip to keep from saying something foul to the Jamin spy.

"Yes. Jill Zerah, a leader of the Dahan militia, is dead. I found her with the remaining fighters. We shot them. I used my methods to get information from her before strangling her."

A cold chill spread over me.

"Excellent," the captain said. "You've discovered where the bunkers are?"

"The western mountains of the continent."

I couldn't keep my eyes away any longer. Staring at Dan while he gave his report nonchalantly, I devised

schemes in which I stole a weapon from an officer to
shoot him, knowing there was no way I could pull it off,
at least right now. I gritted my teeth. He killed the
woman he once helped rescue, when the arms deal
went down for the disintegrator. Betraying their hiding
place. Betraying Mara, in front of me.

"Lehem," Vance called, jerking my attention back
to the captain. "You're on reconnaissance for tomorrow. I'll be flying with you. Meet me at fourteen
hundred."

"Sir," I acknowledged, betraying no hope in my
expression.

The captain dismissed us. But when I rose from my
chair, a wave of nausea swept over me. Were the gravity
controls fluctuating? No one else seemed to notice. Just
nerves, then.

I made my way back to my quarters when my legs
wobbled. I grabbed the railing on the side of the corridor. The walls were bending, my legs turning to jelly. I
made it to my room and lay down. Something was off. I
closed my eyes for only a moment.

My comm link in the room beeped. "Lieutenant
Commander Lehem, report to the captain immediately."

I stood. The vertigo was gone—I'd fallen asleep.
Straightening out my uniform, I left my quarters.

As I turned the corner along the shaft, I spied Dan,
alone. The Jamin glared at me as I approached. I kept
my focus on the hallway ahead before I threw my weight
into him, shoving him against the wall. "Is he alive? Tell
me, or I'll kill you."

Dan laughed, pushing me back. I had no weapon

but my hands. "You're lucky to be alive, Vance's pet. If it were up to me, you'd be dead already."

The Jamin betrayer shoved me hard with his shoulder, then walked away.

Stewing with anger, I continued to the captain's conference room. Vance was alone with his tablet on the table. He stood when I entered.

Vance frowned. "Soldier, you were scheduled to meet me fifteen minutes ago. Do I need to post guards at your room again?"

My anger faded, remembering how nauseated I was earlier.

"I felt dizzy, sir. I apologize, I fell asleep. That will not happen again."

He wrinkled his brow. "Report to medical."

"Sir," I acknowledged, but turning to leave, the vertigo came back. Vance caught my arm as I almost fell over. His eyes widened in concern. "Go directly there."

"Yes, sir."

I took the lift to the med bay a deck below, though the nausea seemed to pass the moment I left Vance's conference room. The moment I entered, I knew something was wrong. There were no medics attending in the front examination room, they were all behind the glass in the surgical suite, suited up. Two injured soldiers lay on the tables. I leaned against the counter, watching through the glass. I remembered too many times when I was assisting the surgeon. Despite this being an enemy ship, despite my unwilling participation, I still wanted to help. I was still a medic. But I feared the nausea returning.

"Sim'ee fighters are starting to launch a counterattack on our reconnaissance. Didn't expect they had the capability," a medical assistant said, her voice coming over the speaker into the examination room.

"Wait until we launch disintegrators on them. It'll stop quick," the surgeon replied.

"Ahem," I cleared my throat. "Lieutenant Commander Lehem."

"Commander Alton," the surgeon answered. "What's your business here?"

"I was ordered here by Captain Vance. I had a bout of vertigo."

"You're going to have to wait, Lieutenant Commander."

"I used to be a flight medic—you can check my records. If you tell me where the standard blood meters are, I can run the diagnostics myself."

The surgeon cocked her head in disbelief, but I shrugged and continued. "Either you can stop what you're doing to follow the captain's orders, or you can let me help you by giving me the dusted test. I'll file the results right here where you can see. I'm supposed to fly tomorrow."

"To your left, third cabinet from the corner," the surgeon responded before moving to the next patient in the suite.

I opened the cabinet and found blood meter kits and some bandages. I sat at the stool near the counter and tore open the sterile package, popping the cap off and jabbing the meter on the inside of my arm. The light on the meter flashed that it was working, then turned a solid green when finished. I pulled it off, setting the cap back on and bandaged my arm, and removed the blood reader card from the meter.

The cardiac alarm went off. "Dusted ash!" Commander Alton cursed, as the medical assistants turned their attention to the patient in distress. I almost jumped from the stool, but I knew there was nothing I could do.

I inserted the card into the reader on the counter while Alton stabilized the patient. If I didn't get a clear pass on the diagnostics, I wasn't going to be able to fly tomorrow, either. Not that I wanted to fly reconnaissance, but I wanted to know everything I could about Vance's mission to find the Rupture device. To stop him, if I could.

The test analysis popped up on the screen. My blood draw showed no disease or common illness. Instead, it showed elevated human chorionic gonadotropin levels.

"Mother-dusting-ash," I whispered, as I read the test results again.

I was pregnant.

I yanked the blood card out while the medics were distracted. How long had it been? The days blended into one another. Spots filled my vision as I tried to remember. I sat on the stool, leaning against the computer and waited for my vision to clear. I couldn't faint now. The computer station wasn't locked, the database open. I took a deep breath as the spots faded, finding my file with the updated HCG level information.

The words PREGNANT: APPROXIMATELY FOUR WEEKS GESTATION appeared in the diagnostics. I deleted the results, and manually entered MELAS VIRUS:

UNKNOWN into the medical records. That would cover anything from the common cold to something as severe as the Noma Flu, and put me under simple observation. I could explain away the vertigo as a cold affecting my ears.

If they had time to actually read it. I spied the medics still assisting the cardiac patient, as I tucked the blood card into my uniform pocket.

Walking away from medical, I straightened my uniform, shoving the panic deep. I rounded the corner and almost bumped into Vance. "Everything all right?" he asked.

"Yes, I'm fine," I lied. "Took a blood draw, possible cold, that's it. But really, I feel fine now."

The captain set his hand on my arm. "As it is, take the rest of the evening off. See me at o-four-hundred on the flight deck."

"Sir," I acknowledged, maintaining my composure, my face expressionless. He released me, accepting my lie as the standard "I'm-fine-I'm-not-sick" denial soldiers often delivered before a mission.

When I returned to my quarters, I crawled onto the bed and hugged my knees.

Pregnant? Not possible.

Though I wasn't on prevention, Max and I'd only conceived once in our two years together. We'd made it to twelve weeks before I bore cramps that became contractions, my hope fleeing my body along with the blood. I didn't imagine it would be possible again, without help, and the doctor hadn't given me much hope with a post-war body exposed to toxic elements.

I shook in spasms. I felt as if I was tightly squeezed, pushed inside a tube in which I couldn't breathe. Like

Victor, zipped into the body bag and shoved inside the waste tube, into the nothingness of space. But death was not an option.

The Buzzards. This might be my only chance. Not only for a child, but to escape this ship.

To find Bo and make him give me the truth.

I lifted up a prayer to Mara's God, for if they were the God of the Universe, they must hear my prayer, my plea, my desperation.

31

S uited up and ready at two minutes to four, I
entered the flight deck with no nausea or dizziness. I carried the helmet under my arm, having
been issued my gear last night. I hadn't worn a flight suit
since before I met Max, but it felt so familiar, going
through the routine of making sure everything was
fitted and fastened.

"You're going to like your Buzzard," Vance told me as
he led me to a Kittiwake Gull 7 on the far end, though
this one had no cannon mounted below. I climbed the
ladder to the cockpit.

Frowning, I scratched my ear. Nothing seemed
different from the last time I flew a few years ago.
Updated onboard computer, slicker controls, but I
couldn't see what the captain was getting at.

"Check the drop-down on the right."

I narrowed my eyes, finding a small tab, revealing a
toggle control. Glancing at Vance, I wrinkled my brow,
because I imagined a disintegrator on a ship would need

to charge and fire in a similar way as the handheld weapon.

He chuckled. "You think I'd give you one of the birds with the disintegrator ray? No, this is much better. You'll switch to this screen," he instructed, flipping my onboard computer on, pressing a lower button. A targeting screen opened for a bombing run.

My jaw dropped.

"That's the kind of response I expected."

"What is this?" I asked, not recognizing the weapons display.

"Disintegrator bombs. You fire them, they drop, but they don't detonate until you press the button."

"The Rupture Device," I breathed.

"In a smaller version. We tested one out over the Sim'ee continent yesterday."

I bit my lip, trying not to think about innocent Sim'ee disintegrating into ash. "But this is what was sold to the Rebels?"

"A large disintegrator device, yes. These bombs are more stable to transport."

"Who sold it?" I asked.

Vance's brow furrowed. "The Rupture Device? I don't know. I'd guess a rogue Ramaen agent. They were selling arms back in those days to any side they could."

I remembered Jill mistaking me for Ramaen at first.

"How do they work?"

"Like how all disintegrator technology works: there is a fuel cell wired to the trigger—which is what explodes. The other side has the two subatomic particles contained in cartridges which, when combined, cause the chain reaction that disintegrates all matter, breaking down quickly so all that's left is a residue, once the reaction is complete."

"What stops it?"

"Nothing stops it. That's why it was banned." Vance called out to the others who reported for duty. "Load up."

I spied Dan climbing on a ladder into a Buzzard.

"And Lehem, we're not on reconnaissance today. We're wiping out the Dahan militia."

I FLEW on Vance's right flank as we left the atmosphere, entering the deep blue sky of Melas. Part of me felt the familiar thrill of the engine rumble through the cockpit, the way the fighter felt like an extension of my body as we turned, the way I felt five, six years ago. Part of me wanted to bank hard, take out another Buzzard or two, or see if I could detonate a bomb and take out the fleet. But I also knew this might be the only chance I had to escape.

It wasn't because I was pregnant. When I surrendered to Vance, to save the others—something inside me had come alive, hell bent on surviving. And the need to know the truth. Not the truth Vance believed in, but the truth of what really happened, at the farm, and on Dibon. What happened to the Rupture device.

The five other Buzzards in our formation banked over the open ocean, toward the coastal hills of the northern continent. I followed Vance, sweeping near the rolling folds of earth, where the Dahan farms lay. Craters and rubble dotted the landscape where the cities stood during the former war, followed by parceled farmland reclaimed from the destruction. We skirted to the south of Ephra. I scanned the northern horizon, but we were too far away to see the damage from the attack on Lehem Farm. A small ridge rose between us and the Western Mountains. I didn't know where the bunkers lay hidden, and I'd no idea what their defense might be once we engaged.

If that happened, then I'd take out as many Buzzards as I could.

"K-3, do you hear me?" Vance called to me over the comm link embedded in my helmet. My control display showed his craft and the other four Buzzards on the mission.

"Yes, K-1, got you."

"Be prepared to take the lead on our strike against the first bunker."

"Copy that, K-1."

Take the lead, so he could fire on me from behind if I tried to pull anything.

I was still trying to figure out how not to deploy my disintegrator bombs against Dahan when the warning alarm inside my Buzzard went off.

"Incoming!"

I rolled, and a surface-to-air missile flew between me and my wingman. The next missile struck the Buzzard behind me.

We broke formation as another barrage of missiles launched at us, antiaircraft fire pelting the hulls of our fighters from the ridge not marked in our briefing as containing armaments. Another Buzzard went down.

The Dahan militia knew we were coming.

"Turn back! Repeat, head back."

"Lehem, return to the *Tristan*, now," Vance ordered. I didn't have to glance at the console to know his targeting computer was locked on me.

A Buzzard exploded on my left, the fuselage spinning right into me, sending me into a roll. Trying to correct my trajectory I pulled back, but the damage to my wing made it impossible to right myself.

I was headed for the ground fast, with disintegrator munitions on board.

"Eject, K-3, Eject!" Vance yelled.

I hit the eject button as soon as I rolled skyward. The cockpit swung open, launching me high into the sky.

I pulled the parachute and it unfolded, jerking upward and catching the air. My craft spiraled to the surface, darting right inside a narrow chasm in the hills. A flash half-blinded me, and I shielded my face from the intense heat. Another Kittiwake must've been struck. More ammunition launched from the ground, aimed at the Buzzards now retreating.

"K-3, I can't see you!" Vance yelled over my comm link. "Did K-3 eject?"

"Yes," K-6 called out. "But I don't see her now."

I didn't respond. This might be my only shot.

"K-4 also shot down." Dan's fighter. Black smoke rolled out of the chasm where my Buzzard had disappeared. "K-4, do you copy?"

There was no response.

"K-3's tracking signal is on—find her!" the captain yelled over the comm.

I ignored the rest of the chatter when I hit the ground in the hills, hard in the ejector seat. After a moment, when I caught my breath, I stood. Nothing felt broken. I unhooked myself and removed the straps from the seat and the parachute. Pulling my helmet off, I found the tracker, and ripped it out of the helmet along with the comm link. I tossed them down, then smashed both with a large rock. Dahan's antiaircraft missiles continued to fire in the ridge above me.

My blue flight suit would stand out against the gray and tan rocks, unless I went in the shadows. Vance should've expected an attack. Years ago, he would've prepped us for possible scenarios. The old captain wasn't thinking things through. This belief that Dahan must be destroyed had overtaken the rational, calm demeanor I'd known him for.

I found a cleft in the rocks and climbed inside, huddling as far as I could. The whistle of a Buzzard swooped by, and I squeezed, tucking my head. The ground vibrated in a rhythmic fashion from the proton fire, and the fighter passed, away from me.

A long time passed before I realized the air was silent. The sun hung lower in the sky. The echoes of antiaircraft weaponry firing had long faded, the Buzzards gone.

I pulled myself out of the cleft and dizziness over-whelmed me. I tasted bile and threw up over a rock, wiping my mouth with my glove. Pilots carried only six ounces of water in their suit—the ejected seat contained a larger canteen. If I went back for it, I'd either be rescued by the Buzzards, or captured by Dahan, unless Bo was with them—if he was alive.

If I were going to survive in this wilderness, I'd need more water. "Dusted ash." I started climbing.

But as I crested the ridge, the smoldering outline of my parachute, from where the Buzzard fired, was all that remained of my ejected seat. So much for treating me like an officer.

I frowned. My Buzzard, when it hit the ground, should've disintegrated. The weapons on board should've gone off with that amount of force, disintegrating everything around it with the bombs. The burning parachute remains shouldn't be here. I shouldn't be here.

The only explanation was that my Kittiwake somehow managed to crash-land without impacting the weaponry. Nonetheless, I couldn't go find it. Vance either had it now, or it crashed out in the open, too exposed. I needed to get off the ridge and toward the mountains, without getting caught, and find Bo. And if not Bo, then Mara.

I descended the ridge carefully, but my dizziness subsided. When I reached the bottom, I relieved myself behind a boulder, spotting blood in my urine. Damn. I drank a swallow of my water.

The sun lowered as I trudged on, crossing the barren valley of rock and dust between the ridge and the mountains. Stunted trees rose from the rubble. This was once a fertile valley, destroyed in the last war. Above me, as I approached the mountains, I spotted the telltale signs of armaments hidden in the rock. Cuts made too evenly, dark residue of after-blast.

I neared the base of the mountain when a sharp voice said from behind me, "Hold it right there." I stopped, putting my hands up.

32

S trong hands patted me down from behind, taking the pistol along with the knife from my boot. The figure stepped out from behind me, and I leaned back, surprised to see Dan's face. "Always knew you couldn't be trusted," he told me.

"You're probably right. But whose side are you on?"

Dan cocked his head. "Are you still trying to pull off being in love with Bo? Because that ship has sailed."

"He's alive?" I couldn't help but smile, though the Jamin dissident pointed his weapon right at my head.

His eyes squinted. "Are you telling me you didn't go running back to Vance the moment you had the chance?"

"What are you talking about?" I asked, thinking about how to distract him so I could disarm him.

"Vance has done nothing but try to get you back since he tracked you down here. He was determined, no matter the cost, and didn't care if you committed treason in his view."

"Who are you with?"

"The Jamin allied with the Dahan militia to bring peace. I've worked for Bo for a long time and warned him against you—"

I knocked the pistol from his hand and pulled him over my shoulder. Dan twisted my arm—the same shoulder that had been separated twice now—and it hurt like a mother-duster. I yelped in pain as I tried to break free from his grip, shifting to flip him over my body—but the Jamin spy overpowered me to the ground. He managed to reach the pistol, placing the barrel right at my temple.

"I should've done this when I first met you. Jill's too trusting, still convinced you're on Bo's side."

The redheaded gunslinger was alive. Thank God.

"I'm pregnant," I blurted out, desperate.

"What?"

"I'm pregnant with Bo's child. Get me to a med station and I'll prove it to you."

Dan gritted his teeth, pressing the gun harder into my temple. "Blast it, you're lying."

I closed my eyes. "Kill me and get it over then. I'm tired and ready to throw up." The metallic taste of blood lingered on my tongue.

The Jamin swore under his breath, something I couldn't quite make out. The pressure was gone, the barrel removed from my temple. When I opened my eyes, Dan still held the pistol trained on me. "You'd better not be lying, because I will shoot you, first in the belly so I can watch you squirm in pain. Get up," he ordered.

I rose to my knees, vomiting again in the dirt. Bo's

supposed friend didn't bother to help me as I stood. My lip bled, and I had a gash on my arm cut straight through my uniform, but Dan spun me around, barrel of the weapon in my back. "Go."

We walked along the mountain's base for almost an hour, until a shaft opened in the side of the rock. The camouflaged door opened, and four guns aimed at me. My Jamin captor urged me forward, the door closing behind us.

Out from the shadows, I spotted him, the scars on his face, his curly hair having grown out a bit. My lips quivered, tears forming at the corners of my eyes. I choked as I spied his arm. His shirt sleeve was rolled up above his elbow, and a prosthetic arm of shiny, silvery metal fitted below. The scars on his face were as I remembered, the relief in his eyes apparent.

"Thank God you're alive," he breathed.

"Stay back, Bo," Dan ordered, but the Dahan leader ignored him, rushing to my side. I stepped back, uncertain.

"You okay?"

I didn't know what to think or feel. The weight of his ring hung on my hand, my belly turning with illness and with life. All the lies he told hanging between us, like the veil of death.

I pushed through the veil, collapsing in his arms. For now, I needed Bo, desperate despite all the secrets he kept. I tucked my head into his shoulder, breathing in deep his scent, wetting his shirt with my tears as sobs of relief overtook my body. His arms crossed over my back.

"Take her to the medics," Dan ordered, motioning to the guards at the door.

"Are you hurt?" Bo lifted my chin to look into his eyes.

I shook my head and wiped my face, though my wounded arm throbbed with pain. "No, I need to show you something." I held back, searching the room. "Is Mara here?"

"She's with the other civilians, along with Rachel and Jonah. I'll take you there soon." Bo motioned to Dan. "You can stand down now."

"Not until we get to medical. I don't trust her."

"Well I do, and my word ought to be good enough."

Dan lowered his weapon but followed us all the way to the med station.

As we entered, I approached the medic. "Administer a blood meter with a DNA match file," The medic waited for affirmation from Bo, then prepared the meter. "He needs one, too," I added.

"Why?" Bo asked, frowning.

"You'll see."

Our blood samples were ready as soon as the medic bandaged my arm, and I rinsed my mouth out. I showed him the analysis, side by side. My HCG levels were still rising, and despite the blood in my urine earlier, I wasn't miscarrying yet. "This is me," I said, pointing to my blood test, "And that's yours..." and then I pointed to the third, which showed the HCG levels and our DNA match file, though still early, "And this is the match for the baby."

His eyes remained blank for a moment before widening. "Holy stardust!" he exclaimed, wrapping me in his embrace.

I glared at Dan, my head against my husband's shoulder. "Does that satisfy you?"

He eyed me shrewdly for a moment, before leaving us alone.

Bo led me away from the guards and the gathered crowd. We headed along a corridor to a small room on the left.

He closed the door behind us, throwing his arms around me again, squeezing tight. I rested against him, his heart beating next to mine. The pain in my arm faded into the background. For a few minutes, I let him hold me, as he stroked my back and kissed my forehead, his lips lingering, pressed against me. Even if we'd barely spoken the words on the day we married, I knew.

He loved me, and I loved him, and despite the doubts and misgivings Vance drilled into my head, it was enough for the moment.

I pulled back to touch his prosthetic hand, studying it, so different from the hand I had known. The silvery material felt like skin, but harder, thicker. I lifted my gaze to his, setting my hand on his scarred cheek. What he had gone through, losing not only his hand, but losing me.

"I'm so sorry it took me so long to get back to you."

He laughed. "I'm so glad to have you back." He kissed my palm. "I wanted to come after you so badly, but they only released me last week with the prosthetic."

I frowned. "You knew, all along, about Dan?"

Bo pulled back, nodding. "Dan was spying on you for some time. He didn't trust you."

"He went to Vance?"

"Yes. Dan and I have worked together for a long

time. I told him Vance had found you, but he was determined to prove you were a spy. I knew you weren't, after the *Ashkelon*. Still, you kept things from me, like the arms deal. I had Dan find your captain and feed him information that was true enough, but hoped to throw him off track, so we could figure out how to get you away safe. But we didn't know about the attack planned on the farm until you came to me that night. When it became clear we weren't going to make it, Dan played the other side."

"I surrendered, because I didn't know how else to buy time, and I hoped you all had gotten out before the farmhouse disintegrated."

Bo's lips curved up. "I never gave up hope. I knew you didn't betray me, not after...everything."

He brushed a stray hair out of my face. Even his light touch caused my stomach to stir in anticipation, in longing, but also regret. My love bore no doubts about my loyalty. I'd allowed Vance to corrupt me, fill me with apprehension and misgivings and fear.

"Dan was able to get a transmission to us that there was a plan to attack today, but we didn't know you for certain you'd be part of it."

"You lost your arm," I muttered. A sign of his sacrifice, for me.

"I'm alive. And you're alive. And...our baby is alive."

Bo cupped my face with his hands and kissed me, slow and gentle, and all I wanted was to melt into him, to remain with him forever. I slid my hands around his waist, yearning for more, to push away my doubts and to lose myself in him.

But he broke away. "There are clothes and a shower here. Then we'll go see Mara."

———

AFTER I SHOWERED, we found my mother-in-law among the other civilians. She embraced me fiercely. "My daughter, I thought I'd lost you."

I held her tight. "So did I."

"What did that ash-duster do to you?"

I laughed at Mara swearing for the first time. "He manipulated me, tried to get me to believe his twisted view of Twelve Rebels." I didn't want to worry her too much about what I'd been through, she'd been through enough lifetimes of loss and now I was back. "I think he believes I'm still one of them, that somehow I will always be..."

Then I remembered what Vance insisted before, about the ADS failure, the bombing of the bunkers on Dibon after we left. The transmission from just before Bo arrived on the *Ashkelon*. That Bo's father bought the Rupture Device.

"What is it?" Mara asked, concerned.

"Just, something I need to talk to Bo about," I said, but I glanced at Bo, wondering if I'd ever have the courage to ask him if his own people destroyed my home world. If they were behind Max's death. And if his father was indeed behind the destruction of the Sebuj, and the war that caused my mother-in-law and her family to leave here in the first place.

For the time being, the need to belong overcame my longing for the absolute truth.

"I'm just glad to see you," I replied, hugging her again.

I left Mara, walking with Bo back to the main control room where Dan and the other leaders waited. Jill ran from across the crowd, squeezing me in her embrace. Her arm was discolored, but no longer swollen or in a sling. "I told Dan you were with us," she said. I caught the Jamin's look, his arms folded across his chest. It was impossible now to believe the worst about each other, but I wasn't sure he'd ever completely trust me.

Bo addressed the militia. "We know they'll be planning another attack soon. Though most of our battery arsenal is south of us, which is what brought the Buzzards down—" he shot me a glance, "they can probably guess where we are. As far as they know, both Dan and Ami are dead, but we can't be sure."

"We have the loaded gun," the Jamin leader responded. I furrowed my brow, puzzled. "Your Buzzard," he spat the words out. "I flew into your flight path, ejecting right before self-destructing mine, so they thought yours was destroyed."

"It survived? I wondered why it didn't disintegrate itself and everything within miles."

"After you ejected, autopilot righted itself enough to crash without damaging the launch tubes. The anti-aircraft fire was too heavy for them to come back for it. We were lucky," Dan finished, hands on his hips. "Captain Vance gave you the only one with disintegrator bombs."

Vance no longer had me. Mara was safe, and Bo was safe. But I didn't doubt for a second the Diboni captain wouldn't try for the Kittiwake or for me again.

"We've got bigger problems," Bo said, pulling up the Nacaen System chart on the screen. "There's another ship approaching the system. We caught wind of it less than a day ago."

"What kind of ship?" I asked.

Dan's eyes narrowed. "Ramaen hunter-class, the *Astarte*. Vance told us it was en route."

My heart raced. "He didn't tell me that." Hunters had been out of service for years, when the Ramaen system agreed to the Interplanetary Alliance regulations on destructive weapons and disarmed. Vance must've found one out of salvage. Hunters were designed to enter atmo and often carried weapons capable of wiping out entire cities. They also had the capacity for carrying smaller craft, possibly up to sixteen Diboni Kittiwakes.

Either bombs or cannons alone could take us out and cause other Nacaen worlds to surrender.

"He called for an emergency briefing the evening before—you were confined to quarters."

When I learned I was pregnant.

"We don't have much time to waste," Bo interrupted. "This ship probably has larger disintegrator cannons and more Kittiwakes. We've held them off so far but Jill, get on the comm to the Sim'ee, see if they will come to our aid. We've only transport shuttles and one Sim'ee Sparrowing. And now the Buzzard."

"No other flyers?"

The militia leader shook his head. "Post-war we've been rebuilding mainly as a ground force."

Bo dismissed the militia to move to action stations. I started to follow Dan, but Bo caught my wrist.

"You're staying here."

"What are you talking about?"

"You're staying here," he repeated, his voice sharp. "You're not risking your life—or our baby's life—again."

I jerked free from his grip. "You don't get to tell me what to do."

Two guards moved to block the door. "You can't be serious," I muttered. I wouldn't be treated like a prisoner again. Ever.

"Leave us," he ordered, and the guards, along with everyone else, cleared out. He folded his arms across his chest. We were standing off, once again.

"You have to let me go," I insisted. "No one else can fly that thing."

"Dan will. There's no need for you to go."

"He doesn't understand the technology, I do. Dust it, I've been studying this for months!"

"I don't care, I—"

"No. You can't keep doing this to me," I asserted, tears stinging my eyes. "You can't keep acting like you know better than me, that you're protecting me—you're not respecting me or my authority and experience."

"But you're—"

"Pregnant? I was pregnant on the *Tristan*. I was pregnant when I ejected from a Buzzard, managed to land, survive, and get back here to you. I want this baby to survive more than anyone." I choked, trying not to break down. "But you can't keep doing this to me, or this won't work."

Bo gaped, and I continued. "If you and I are gonna make it, despite everything else happening out there, you've got to stop trying to protect me when I know what I'm doing. You've got to stop shutting me in." I ran my fingers through my hair. The spring inside me wound tight suddenly freed, my voice rising. "You've got to stop keeping things from me and tell me the truth. I know I withheld things from you, but I came clean with everything, told you everything I know. I've given up everything of who I was, left behind everything I know to come to Melas to choose this life. I made a promise to Max and Mara, and now I've made those vows to you, and you need to uphold your part. I've come this far, uncovered this much, and I'm not stopping now. I'm the one who knows the Rupture Device was a disintegrator weapon that contaminated this land to wipe out the Sebuj. That's why all the crop was blighted and decayed. And I know it was sold to the Rebels but your..."

An image popped into my head—the blighted stalks we removed. The first day on the farm we pulled out all the decaying and stunted crop, piling it to burn. But in places where it stayed, like the field near the arsenal bunker, the decaying stalks must have released enough nutrients to break down the disintegrator ash. That's why there were no traces of the gray film there, or the brittle aftermath. Removing the blighted grains kept the disintegrator ash from neutralizing. Where the grain had been allowed to decompose naturally, the soil's PH balance returned.

I'd thought it odd when I noticed there was no disintegrator ash, in the soil by the arsenal. Because the decomposing stalks neutralized it already.

"I think I know how to stop it," I finished, my voice soft.

"What are you talking about?"

"The disintegrator ash—I know how to neutralize it now."

Bo scoffed. "How are we going to stop Buzzards with disintegrator rays?"

Captain Titus on the *Ashkelon* gave me the answer, long ago on my journey here. When technology can be used against you, take it apart. Manual override—take back control.

"With neutralized bombs. Do you have the disintegrator that Jill bought?"

He hesitated for a moment. "Yes. It was taken with some of the militia who left first. I didn't want it used or taken from us."

I let out a breath. "I think we can reverse the process and make a weapon that can block the disintegrators. We have to go back to the farm."

"Ami, that's impossible. They will be attacking us again at any time. Who knows if more ships will have joined them in orbit?"

"Then you must call upon the Sim'ee and all Jamin —and while you're at it, others of the Twelve. It's time they know you need help. They've got to buy us some time."

"I don't want you to go," Bo pleaded.

I gazed at the man I'd fallen in love with, piece by piece, and how much of him was taken by violence: his skin by the rainfire, his arm by the disintegrator beam. The scarred man couldn't lose another piece. Not the baby. Not me again.

"I know. But more than ever, I need you to trust me on this."

"I do," he admitted. "I do trust you."

33

We worked through the night to repair the Buzzard, replacing the chair with one from a Sparrowing, a small fighter made in the Bara System that the Sim'ee nation often used, and the Dahan milita had managed to secure one. I worked on the engine while another mechanic repaired the wing.

When I finished engine repairs, I left the hanger bay to find Mara, but she wasn't in her quarters. I made my way back to the control room and found her with Rachel. A comm technician motioned to her. "We're on the universal channel. Go ahead."

"This is Mara Lehem, of the Dahan Nation," she began. I choked, welling up as my once silent mother-in-law addressed the entire system. "I was a refugee from our last war. I lost my husband Eli as we fled. My sons and I found welcome on Dibon in the Noma System, where they both married. When Dibon's surface was destroyed by the asteroid, Ami Lehem, a

Diboni military veteran, risked her life to get me home, to get me back to Melas.

"Melas is at risk of being destroyed again. The remnant of the Dibon Military Force orbiting our world does not represent the people of Dibon, just as the Rebels do not represent the people of the Nacaen Group. We are different nations, but we all believe in the One God. We survived the Red Nebula and were led here, to our new home. By God, we can't let that be taken from us. It's time to come together. Jamin and Sim'ee, we share Melas. Don't let an outside faction divide and destroy us. We beg you, come to our aid!

"To our siblings on Richo, Nidos, and Samar—if you receive this message, we need your help. The Diboni separatists have a Ramaen hunter en route to our system. Do not think for a moment they will let you be. They blame us for what happened to them. They want to destroy any chance for unity among us. They will come after all worlds in this system, once they are done with Melas. We need your help. In the name of our God and your God, the One, help us." When she finished, I pulled her into my arms, tears streaming down my cheeks to her shoulders. "I love you, Mara."

"I love you, Ami."

We waited, as the comm technician played Mara's message again.

"They have to respond," Rachel said, leaning over the technician's shoulder.

"Give it some time, it can take a few minutes to cross—"

"Dahan, this is the Sachar. Send us coordinates on secure channel." I breathed out in relief, as other nations in the Nacaen group responded. By the time I said goodbye to Mara and Rachel, the Hessan and Tali of Nidos, who'd been at war with each other, agreed to send ships to intercept. The Sim'ee nation on the southern continent confirmed that their Sparrowings would head into orbit, to buy us some time for what we needed to do.

———

AT DAWN, with minimal sleep, I flew out of the mountains back toward the plains, to Ephra. The fighter rattled a bit, with the hasty repairs. Dan flew the Sparrowing. Jill accompanied Bo in the transport shuttle, with the disintegrator weapon she'd purchased from the arms dealers on board.

When Lehem farm came into view, I gasped. The fence was torn down. The farmhouse was destroyed, along with the bunkhouse, and most of the barns. But the lab—and surprisingly the copse—still stood, with a few other buildings. A field that was at rest, sitting out this harvest, stood intact with minimal damage. Some of the blighted crop waved in the wind.

I landed near the lab. Dan set down behind me in the Sparrowing, and Jill and Bo landed on the other side of the lab. Bo rounded the corner with Jill following, carrying the disintegrator weapon.

I pulled my helmet off. "Bring it inside." We had no time to waste. If the Sim'ee Sparrowing pilots were delayed, the Ramaen *Astarte* might be on its way, targeting Dahan's survivors with its cannons. I glanced once more at the sky before heading inside.

The lab had been put back together after my incident with the disintegrator, surviving the Buzzard assault. Most of the soil samples were gone, but Bo managed to gather new ones before the farm was attacked. Jill set the weapon down on the center table.

"Get some of the soil with the disintegrated ash," I ordered. Bo brought me a sample from a nearby table.

"Dan and Jill—gather as much of the blighted crop as you can, from the roots."

"With what?"

"There's a shovel and scythe in the tool shed. Use that for now."

Dan threw his hands in the air, but he obeyed, and the redhead followed. Bo's eyes were full of concern.

"What are you doing?"

"Hopefully not killing us."

I knew from our discharge training how we were supposed to dismantle these types of weapons. The first thing was to remove the power cell so that there was no accidental power up and discharge, so I found the release and removed it from the stock. From there, I could see the two separate cartridges where the particles resided, encased in aerogel, behind the barrel.

My forehead dripped with sweat.

"Ami, you shouldn't be doing this. The baby—"

"I know," I interrupted. "But we've got to try, for the baby and for all of us."

When Dan and Jill entered, I jerked my head, motioning for them to come over to the table. I peered over what they brought me—the long roots of the blighted crop which had begun to decompose. "Break up the roots, smash it with your hands." They tore off the roots, using their bare hands to smash the moldy, decomposing plant. A wave of nausea flowed over me, but I ignored it. "Add it to the soil."

When they added the crushed plants to the gray soil, the gray ash bonded to the decomposed root. It clumped together, then crumbled, some of it turning to a rich brown.

I breathed out in relief. "It worked."

"What worked?" Jill asked.

"You see?" I used my finger to divide the new soil from the old ash. "Chemicals are released naturally when plants decompose, and our crops are all genetically modified to grow on different worlds and to enrich the soil when they die. Neutralizer breaks down rainfire chemicals, but this wasn't rainfire—it was ash from a disintegrator weapon. It killed the crop and stopped decomposition in the soil. The soil was tilled, neutralizer spread—but in certain parts of the farm, the concentration of ash killed them, making that field unusable without decomposition. Now," I pointed to the new soil, "with decomposing plants introduced, the chemicals already released bonded with the disintegrator ash and truly neutralized it. We're going to test this theory in the weapon."

"How?" Dan asked.

"These particle cartridges—we're going to add the soil, then put the rifle back together and see if it still disintegrates. If my theory is right, this is going to stop the disintegration process right in the chamber of the weapon."

"What if you're wrong?" Jill asked.

I swallowed hard. "It could be that nothing happens. Or it could be something bad."

I held the weapon, barrel pointing down and away from us, and pricked open a cartridge. "Pour in some of the neutralized soil," I told Bo.

He cupped the dirt in his non-prosthetic hand, funneling it into the cartridge. I closed that side, then picked open the other, having Bo add the soil. Acrid fumes arose. I worried about inhaling, but I couldn't do anything about it now.

"Everyone stand back," I said, as I picked up the power cell.

"No," Bo said, grabbing my wrist. "Let me do it."

I opened my mouth to protest but Dan set his hand on Bo's shoulder. "Let me do it. You're still recovering," he said, then turned to me, "and you're pregnant."

A look passed between us. Whatever animosity we might still hold, we were on the same team for now. Dan took the weapon from my hand and the fuel cell. Bo, Jill, and I all stepped back to the door.

"Get behind some cover," Dan growled. Jill and Bo turned over a table and we all crouched behind it, as Dan slid the power cell back in. "I turn it on at the stock?"

"Yes," I shouted back. "Wait for it to power up, then aim at a target, preferably far away from us."

We waited a minute, and Dan swore under his breath. "Here goes nothing."

The weapon hummed as the fuel was released. "Dusted ash," he muttered, as the hum got louder, then abruptly stopped.

I peered over the table, though Bo tried to grab me. "What happened?" I asked.

Dan set the weapon down on the table, and glanced at his palms. "It got very hot, and then—it just stopped."

"Did you put it back together correctly?"

"I know how to assemble a weapon," he snapped.

Bo and Jill rose from the table and followed me to Dan. "The power cell is drained," Jo said, motioning to the gauge on the butt. "It did fire up."

"Then it worked. It neutralized itself and stopped the disintegration process after it fired up." I breathed out. "Now to try this on the bombs."

I walked outside, under the Buzzard to where the weaponry was stored in the hull. Once I found the munitions bay with the bombs, I pried open the loading door. After making sure all switches were off, I extracted one. It could still blow if I dropped it.

Bo had followed me outside. He stared at me, a walking bomb. "Open the door," I commanded.

He obeyed, holding open the door to the lab open for me as I carried the deadly weapon inside.

I rotated the bomb over in my hands until I found the release valve for the pressure trigger. It had to be let it out with care, so the trigger would become useless—if I let it out too quickly, it might engage, and we'd all be disintegrated. Unlike the handheld weapon that directed an energy beam, this was a much more dangerous test, with a wider radius.

When the pressure released, I flipped open the trigger as if it were just a simple metal flap and pried open the bomb. Tucked inside lay the fuel cell—a small battery—and on the other side from the battery lay the particle cartridges.

The table rattled. I turned, and Jill was using a shovel to beat down some more of the crops.

"Stop, Jill—that's too much force."

She glared at me. "I thought you wanted it crushed up."

"Yeah, but I'm holding a weapon of mass destruction in my hands and I don't need to slip and trigger it."

Jill froze, then set the shovel down, picking up the smashed crop. "Sorry."

"Dan," I said. "I need a flat-tip screwdriver, small enough to fit in here," I showed him, turning the bomb toward him.

A toolbox was still on the ground, probably from when repairs were made the last time I was here. He fished out the screwdriver and brought it to me.

"This is the tricky part," I announced. "You three ought to leave and get away, in case I'm wrong and this blows."

"I'm not leaving you," Bo promised, his hand on my shoulder. I shrugged away in irritation, and he pulled back.

"I'm serious," I insisted, gritting my teeth. "This could easily explode."

"And I'm not going."

Dan folded his arms across his chest. Jill shrugged. I rolled my eyes.

"Very well. It was going to be hard to do this by myself anyway."

Still holding the bomb, I did the same thing I did

with the handheld weapon, and opened one cartridge, with Bo and Jill helping, and then the other side.

"Now is the part where it might all go very, very bad." I paused, staring into his eyes. "Bo, I love you. And I'm sorry if I kill you with this."

My husband trembled, placing his hand on mine. "I love you too."

"Sorry, Dan," I offered.

He grunted and folded his arms. I took it as an acceptance of my apology.

"Jill."

"It will be okay," she said.

I took a deep breath.

"Okay, here goes nothing."

I picked up the screwdriver Dan brought me. Next to the small battery was the divider between the two cartridges. Normally on detonation from the onboard computer, or upon impact with enough force, the battery would blow the divider. Instead, I needed to remove the divider to make sure this worked now, without an explosion.

I carefully shimmied the screwdriver into the edge of the divider until it was loose enough for me to remove, a flat rectangle between the two cartridges. I pulled with my fingertips, squinting as I half-expected some sort of chemical release or heat, like what happened with the handheld weapon.

Nothing happened. No disintegration, no explosion. I didn't realize I'd been holding my breath until I let it out, the nausea lifting away.

"That ought to do it."

"Do what?" Dan questioned.

"I've taken the pressure out of the trigger, so the bomb won't explode unless its high impact, and all it should do is neutralize the disintegrator. Without the power cell, it didn't heat up the way the weapon did for you. But it will upon impact."

"Do you have to do this to all of them?"

"All of them." And time was fading.

My Buzzard launched with eight bombs. I depressurized them one at a time, added neutralized soil to the particles, removed the divider and closed them back up without disintegrating anything.

But while we sealed up the last bomb—Jill and Dan taking two bombs back to the Buzzard—I stopped, eyeing Bo. He'd put his trust in me, let me take the lead. The immediate danger of blowing ourselves up for now had passed.

Now I needed to know.

"Vance told me it was Sal who purchased the Rupture Device."

Bo almost dropped the soil onto the floor. "What?"

"Is it true?"

Bo hesitated, and that moment's hesitation confirmed all my suspicions. Even if he'd done it to protect me, he'd lied to me. "My father," he began, his eyes downcast, "was involved with the Rebels. He was killed in the war, and I swore never to follow his path."

I glared at him. "You told me your parents were killed in a shuttle crash."

My new husband's face twitched. "My mother died in the shuttle crash, that part was true. She grew up on Richo. Maysa—my mother—wasn't from one of the Twelve nations—she came from the people who lived here before. She worked for the Rebels who were trying to take both Melas and Richo at the time. She was a spy, the way the women at *The Threshing Floor* who worked for us were spies."

I nodded, understanding why he didn't tell me.

"My father—Rachel's brother—was a leader of the Rebels. But after my mother was killed, I went to live with Jonah and Rachel."

My former captain sowed seeds of doubt on purpose. But Bo's admission that he lied still hurt.

"You never heard about the Rupture Device before?"

He fell silent, his lips pursed.

"Don't," I warned him as he stepped closer to me.

"Ami," Bo spoke softly, almost whispering. "I didn't know about the Rupture Device being used here until after you figured out this was disintegrator ash. I heard stories. I knew my father was involved in something bad."

"Did Sal purchase the Rupture Device?"

"Everything we've uncovered points to it. Rachel and Jonah bought the farm after the war, but before the war my father worked here, for Cale Lehem. I didn't know you were related when I met you, and because it was only you and Mara, I never thought about your connection to the Lehems here before. The land was claimed by Dahan, but the Sebuj who were here made a pact with the Jamin. I didn't know about the Sebuj—I was only seven when I came here. Rachel knew Sal was involved in some weapons deal right before the start of the war but didn't know what it was. Now, we know."

"The Rupture Device," I finished.

I gazed into his eye, partially covered by the flap of

skin, and remembered how he hesitated before, telling me how his face burned.

"There was no dog."

Bo averted his gaze. "I went back for my father."

"He was still alive?"

"Yes. Jonah got his scar pulling me away as I was burned."

"Why didn't you tell me?"

He shifted his eyes back to me. "Rachel told me it was a man from Dibon who met with Sal."

We stared at each other, exposed again by the truth, before I went back to finish sealing the bomb. *Dibon*. It was Ramaen technology, but Dibon used it for years. Someone spread neutralizer to try to make it look like it was all rainfire destruction. The puzzle took shape.

"My parents disowned me, when I told them I was marrying Max, because he was Dahan. Nacaen. A Twelve."

"I know," Bo said.

I wiped my eyes, embarrassed at my parents, the prejudices each of our people held, shaping the world we lived in.

"Do you know where the device is now?" I asked, refocusing my eyes on his scars.

"My dad died on Richo after the war started, but we don't know what happened to it."

"What about—what about the bombing on Dibon?" I asked, choosing my words with care.

"We tried to make contact with those refugees we knew lived there. We know some Rebels were among them, but we never found out what happened."

"I saw the transcript," I told him. "Vance showed me,

there was a transmission between you and someone in the bunkers. You said, 'Sorry it has to be this way.' It came from the *Jabbok*."

His lip quivered. "I was trying to get them to stop. I'd gone to the Ramaen system for aid for Dahan, but on my way back, I went to Dibon. There was a group of Dahan refugees that started to work with the Jamin rebels there. One of their contacts had been arrested, and everything was falling apart. I didn't tell you—" he began, then shook his head. "I didn't tell you because I was supposed to join them. I refused to be part of it."

"You said, 'Give them hell.'"

"I said that to Ben. He was a friend, loyal to our cause of unity, and he was going to stop them. I didn't know the bombing happened until after I got here, just as I told you."

Our time was almost up, but I had to make a choice: to choose which version of the truth I would believe. Vance's truth came with manipulation and violence. Bo was not without his faults. But this would all end soon, one way or the other. What truth would I accept, for the rest of my life?

Bo pulled me away from the table. "I became the leader of Dahan to undo the work of my father. But I'd give up leadership, anything, as long as you and I can be together when this is over. I don't care if you're from Dibon. They aren't your people anymore. Dahan is not my people anymore. We are each other's people. And we have to build something greater than Dahan and Dibon, if we're going to survive in this universe."

He gathered me in his arms. "Your people will be my people," he promised.

"Your God, my God," I responded. In that moment, I vowed to not let the deceptions of Vance, or the horrors committed by Sal, come between us any longer.

I kissed him quickly. "We need to load up."

"What now?"

"We go on the offense."

My husband helped me load the last bombs back into the Buzzard's launch tubes. Dan searched the skies, which except for a few wisps of cirrus clouds, shone clear and blue. "The likelihood they've already launched—"

"I know," I interrupted him. "The Sim'ee have hopefully held them off long enough or even taken a few out. But I'll need you to cover me as I go after the Buzzards with disintegrator rays, and the cannons on the *Astarte*."

"What if your neutralized bombs don't work?"

"Then this will be a short mission. At least we can try to slow 'em down."

Bo caught my eye, opening his mouth to speak, but closed it fast. He knew I wouldn't turn back.

I stood in front of him, one last time. "Before I met you, I was only living for Mara. I lost everything when Max died. But when I met you, you made me want to live. Not for you—not even for this baby. I didn't know I was pregnant when I surrendered to Vance. You know— it was only the night before."

Bo's lip quivered.

"I surrendered because I wanted to live. You made me want to live for me again."

He crushed me with his embrace. I squeezed him back fierce, as if I held on to him for life.

I tore away to the Buzzard, climbed in and closed the

hatch. My eyes spotted the shorn metal on the wing, repaired in haste back at the bunker. I prayed it would hold together to complete this mission.

"Ami, it's all yours. You lead," Bo called over the comm.

I fired up the engine on the Buzzard, which purred to life as it did earlier. At least the repairs seemed to be holding. I lifted off from the surface, Dan flanking me on my right.

Hitting the throttle, I led the Jamin pilot to the edge of the atmosphere. When I launched from the *Tristan*, I was too fearful about what might happen. Now, despite the danger and likelihood of failure, the thrill of flying coursed through my blood. I'd thought this part of me died long ago, when I married Max, but those parts of me never disappeared, they changed and grew into who I'd become. I was a pilot, a farmer, a wife. A mother.

Despite what Bo said, I was also Diboni. That part would never die. We valued truth, which was why when the Renegades on Dibon attacked the refugees, we fought for the refugees. Because I was Diboni, I needed to stop the remnant of the Dibon Military Force from destroying everything we stood for.

Dan and I followed the course given from base to intercept Vance's ship. I hoped the ships from Samar and Nidos had arrived, prayed the Sim'ee and Jamin fighters had already done their part by the time we got there, so I could take on the remaining Buzzards.

But when we rose from the atmosphere into orbit, I swore. The gunship from Nidos had taken heavy damage. The *Tristan* occupied the other fighters, but still held its own. Sim'ee Sparrowings tried to draw its fire, as they were more maneuverable around its proton rifles and rail cannons.

However, beyond the *Tristan* hovered the Ramaen hunter *Astarte*. It was older than the Diboni vessel, larger, and with its darkened steel hull, much more difficult to spot visually. It was shaped like a barrel set on its side, but flat on its belly, and long arms of rail guns were open, visible only when the lights from other ships flashed on it.

Pieces of smaller fighters floated nearby, indicating the Ramaen ship had used heavy firepower, but not disintegration. Yet.

That's when I noticed there were no Buzzards in the fight.

"They haven't come out yet," Dan warned me on the comm. "They were waiting for us."

For me. Vance was waiting for me.

34

"Coming on your right," Dan called out.

Eight Buzzards came at us, firing on the mixed Nacaen fleet. I did a tuck and roll maneuver, breaking away. Dan protected me, but I didn't spot any of the Kittiwakes mounted with a disintegrator weapon. They were Gull 2s, the version I once flew, with shorter proton rifles and slightly angled wings.

"On your tail!"

I pulled hard, but the Buzzard near my tail exploded.

"You're welcome," the Sim'ee pilot called on the comm.

Another Sparrowing joined to head off the other oncoming fighters, but there was no sign of the Buzzards with disintegrators. I fired my proton rifles at the incoming Buzzard, enough to annoy the pilot, not cause damage. I needed to save my bombs to hit the disintegrator weapons. With only eight bombs, I had to hope the rest of the Buzzards we came across weren't all armed the same.

"What the hell is that?" Dan asked. Two large cannons rotated into view on the front of the *Astarte*, and I knew they had to be disintegrators. More massive than anything we'd seen before.

"Drop on the Z!" I cried out. My companion obeyed along with the Sim'ee accompanying us, dropping on the Z axis. But when I spun my Buzzard around, the other ships that had been in proximity had disappeared. The Nidos gunship. Two of the Tali cruisers. All that was left were faint outlines, dust disappearing into vacuum. Disintegrated.

How many souls were lost in an instant?

"Dammit!" We would not last long dodging those cannons.

"Buzzards coming 'round," one of the Sim'ee fighters announced on the comm. I spun around, pelting the nearest with rapid fire until its engine burst, Dan going for the one behind it. Two others engaged the Sim'ee.

"Why aren't the cannons firing again?" Dan asked.

"It's an old ship," I replied on the comm, maneuvering under the *Astarte* and away from the attacking ships. "They discontinued them when the Ramaen system unified and they weren't trying to conquer worlds anymore. They were built to destroy surface defense systems. The handheld disintegrator needed at least a minute to charge, I imagine the cannons need more time." Cranking the controls hard, I avoided the Buzzard diving at me under the Ramaen ship. "Dan, cover me. I'm going after the cannons."

"Make it count," he called back.

I piloted around the belly and over the port side of the *Astarte*, avoiding its rail guns, until I maneuvered right below one of the cannons.

"I've gotta wait until they're about to fire—catch it when the barrel is full."

"Ami," Bo interrupted on the comm from the surface, and I cringed. He'd given me away.

"I've got this," I yelled back, annoyed as I swerved out of the way of incoming fire.

"He's got—" The transmission went to static, garbled. I couldn't make out what Bo was trying to say.

Dan moved into position behind me, firing at the Buzzards until the Sparrowings caught up. As soon as I noticed the cannon stop moving, I launched a bomb.

The blast from the disintegrator struck the bomb, and it disappeared in front of me. "Dusted ash!" I'd fired too late for the bomb to be of any use. I launched the next bomb right into the second cannon, hoping this time it wasn't wasted.

The base of the second cannon appeared to fold in on itself, like the bucket did when I fired at it in the lab the first time. It was as if the disintegration was continuing up the barrel. That wasn't supposed to happen. It was supposed to stop the reaction from happening altogether.

"AMI! He's..."

The blasts fired from above me told me the other fighters had managed to break through *Astarte's* shields. We were gaining the edge. I waited for the first cannon to power up again, wondering if I'd done enough damage to the second to destroy both.

"Come on, Vance," I called on the comm. "Come on out with your Buzzards and surrender."

"Ami," a familiar voice called, soft and sweet. I shuddered. The signal came from the *Astarte*.

"*Sheya*," I breathed in shock, my body cold with fear.

My message to her. The images of the ADS and the broken Buzzard. He'd known, he'd known all along.

"If you want to see her alive, you will surrender immediately," my former commander ordered.

"Ami—" Bo interrupted again, but I switched off the universal frequency over to the Diboni comm channel.

"Vance."

"Tell the rest of your attackers to stand down."

"Let her go!"

"You are to land on the *Astarte* and negotiate the terms of your surrender." Static filled the channel.

"Stardust and ashes!"

I switched back to the other channel, in time to hear the rest of Bo's lecture. "Don't surrender!" he shouted.

"Stand down. I need all fighters to stand down."

"Are you crazy?" someone on the comm yelled, ringing my ears.

"The disintegrator cannons are damaged, but he may have something worse on board. Bombs capable of taking out cities."

My instinct as a soldier told me we needed to destroy the ship no matter what. My heart told me I needed to try to get to Sheya.

"I need everyone to stand down!" My voice shook with fear.

I went back to Vance. "I've asked them to stand down. I can't promise anything more."

"If they fire while the load doors are opened, she'll be dead."

I switched back to the main channel. "Dan, listen to me. Don't allow anyone to fire while the doors are open. Protect those loading doors."

Silence prevailed on the channel. Vance might've jammed the transmission. I didn't have a choice.

As the load doors opened, I flew right inside to the landing pad. The load doors closed behind me with a bang. I knew the old ship was similar to the *Tristan*, except for the double airlocks on the launch shaft and the old conveyer system to the flight deck, before our fighters had better hover capabilities and better safety technology on airlocks. I landed on the pad and the belt tugged forward, waiting for the second airlock doors to open.

Bo was right, Sheya was probably already dead and Vance would kill me. But there was no time to second-guess my options. The doors opened as the conveyer system pulled me through the second airlock to the flight deck.

Sparks flew from broken internal mechanisms. The outer hull appeared undamaged, but inside the *Astarte*, I saw distressed support beams and broken panels. Orange warning lights flashed. The ship seemed to be falling apart on the inside.

The conveyer system came to a halt, and the airlock doors closed behind me. Six other Buzzards sat, most of them Gull 2's, but two were Gull 7's. One had the disintegrator ray mounted on its fuselage. Vance's bird. I opened the cockpit of my Buzzard and removed my helmet, expecting soldiers to surround me at any moment. But I spotted no soldiers or crew, no pilots coming to their ships even with the warning lights of attack. A pipe cracked, steam escaping with a hiss.

Stairs led from the flight deck to an open metal balcony. I pulled my weapon from its holster on my hip and climbed the stairs. The balcony hugged the outside of a corridor that ran along the far wall of the flight deck, with doors in the middle. From the corridor, one could access the crew quarters. The remaining layout of the ship was like the *Tristan*, except for its enormous engines in the rear and large munition bay underneath the flight deck.

"Ami."

I spun to my right. On the floor against the railing, Sheya sat, a bullet wound in her side and blood pooling on the floor. I raced to her, forgetting my own safety, forgetting everything that had happened since we said goodbye. I holstered my weapon, dropped to my knees and cradled her face in my hands.

"Sheya—"

"He wants...he wants to kill you." she breathed.

"Shhhh—I know. I know."

I had lost. I brushed her beautiful curls out of her face, smiling through my tears. If I had to die, at least I wouldn't be alone.

"I got away from the guard...tried to contact you..."

That's what Bo tried to warn me.

I unzipped my flight suit and tore part of my under-shirt, placing it on the wound to try to staunch the bleeding. "I'll get you out of here."

The sliding doors behind me hissed open. "You're not going anywhere," Vance said from behind.

I swore, not taking my eyes off my sister-in-law as I placed her hand on top of the covered wound. His steps echoed on the metal balcony. "Whatever you did to your bombs is causing the ship to disintegrate on itself. You may have neutralized the initial blast of the cannon, but the fuel cells won't stop recharging, won't stop filling the barrels. They're leaking into the hull. Or did you not know that before you started playing with toys you shouldn't have?"

I spun around to find Vance's weapon aimed at head. My hand rested on my pistol, but I knew I couldn't draw it fast enough.

"Drop your weapon. Our shields will fail any moment and we'll be done for, unless we escape, now."

I removed the pistol from my holster and placed it on the floor. "Why? Why did you do this?"

"They hit us, we hit back harder," he taunted, repeating a childhood saying from Dibon.

I stood with my hands raised. "So we knock each other out, kill each other, destroy each other's worlds?"

The captain shook his head. "You don't get it! They destroyed *our* planet! We were merciful, only moving in to stop them, to take control so they wouldn't do it again!"

"What threat were they to us? They sent their refugees to us. Why would they be behind the ADS failure? Even among the Rebels, they don't strike refugees! It doesn't make sense, Vance!" I pleaded with him.

His eyes shifted. A large creaking sound erupted from behind the airlock doors.

"What happened with the ADS? You said yourself

the Twelve couldn't have done it. You said it to me the day it happened."

My former commander kept his weapon trained on me.

I recalled the image of the broken ADS satellite, entwined around the Kittiwake fuselage in the middle of the Galactic Ocean. "What happened with the wreckage I found?"

"The Ramaens have it now," Sheya called behind me, her voice raspy. "They've cut off all aid to Dibon. I sent your message to our leadership. Right before he kidnapped me."

Vance's gun didn't waver. "Why did they stop aid?" I asked.

"There were Dibon military exercises taking place in the asteroid field." She swallowed. "The outer alarms were disabled because they were supposed to let an asteroid get closer for practice, but it was too large of a target. Instead, they only broke part of it, sending it to Dibon."

I glared back at Vance. "Did you know when we were in the bunkers?"

"No!" he barked. "I was under orders to evacuate. Admiral Donovan didn't tell anyone what happened."

"Yes," Sheya breathed out. "Donovan ordered the murders of the pilots involved, to cover up the incident. The wreckage you discovered had its entire comm system still intact, all transmissions recorded. The admiral killed himself when they went to arrest him, and Vance kidnapped me."

I gasped. The lies, the cover up. This wasn't the Diboni way.

"Why did you blame Dahan?" I demanded. "The refugees were innocent."

"You sided with them. You made the accident appear to be a cover up."

I furrowed my brow. "What the hell are you talking about?"

Sweat beaded along his forehead. "You said there was a distress call, but there wasn't. You lied. You hid the evidence on the *Ashkelon* until you were far enough in the Galactic Ocean to plant it, send the images back, and sent them to the Ramaens. You destroyed us."

"You're delusional. We all heard the distress call on the *Ashkelon*, we recorded the crew's account in the records. We found the wreckage. I sent a copy to Sheya because I was afraid it would go nowhere. Good thing I did."

"You sided with the refugees," he retorted, peering at me over the barrel of his pistol. "The Rebels bombed the bunkers months later, remember?"

"You said they did it with Baratanium, but you know it's too unstable to be transported that far."

Vance breathed out harshly through his nose. "The Rebels came. They claimed they were coming to help their own refugees, but you saw the transmissions yourself. They had a plan. They set off a bomb. We fought back."

"You used disintegrators. Underground." It all came to me. Bo's friend stopped the Rebels, only to have Vance take them out. "You told me Baratanium because you knew it wouldn't be traced and no one would know for sure who brought it. You decided it was better to take out everyone than let the Rebels take us over, and then framed the Rebels for the ADS failure, hoping the Ramaens would back you. But you didn't think of it until after I left, you were simply trying to cover up the ADS accident."

"I was under orders," my captain admitted. "But they will still try to kill us unless we strike them first."

I shook my head. "The Ramaens wouldn't help you anymore, let alone the Noma System Council. Jahaz and Rabbah and...Kir." I remembered the retired Pinion from Kir. My eyes widened in recognition. "You were in contact with Felix. But he wasn't interested because there wasn't enough money. That's why Aaron was almost kidnapped by the Stiner..."

My head hurt as I relived the memory. "That mercenary wasn't after Aaron, she was after me. You contacted the Stiners before you even replied to my message. You followed me to Bara." I paused, sliding another piece into place. "Esmie knew I was going on to Melas, not to Aza. Did you kill her, too?"

"None of that matters now."

Sparks blazed as a panel on one end of the balcony fell open. The fire suppression system immediately engaged, spraying extinguisher on the panel. A red light flashed.

But Vance didn't move. I'd have to find a way to distract him, if his own ship falling apart wouldn't do it.

"None of it matters? You connived me into rejoining, refused to discharge me, then manipulated me into thinking that despite the fact my husband is dead because of a military cover-up, my planet destroyed because of your ash-dusting need for revenge, somehow I'd help you infiltrate Dahan."

I remembered what Bo discovered, that Sal purchased the Rupture Device not from a Ramaen, but from a Diboni.

"*You* sold the Rupture Device to the Rebels. You came here to get it back. You were using me to get to it."

He didn't respond, but his eyes twitched.

"You did it," I repeated. "Sold it to wipe out Dahan, but instead, it was used on the Sebuj, who had an alliance with the Jamin. Sal started the war there, sending refugees to our system."

"Some of those refugees were Rebels!"

"But we sold the Rupture Device to the Rebels, starting their war. I don't get it, Vance. You were my commanding officer. We were on Dibon's side, protecting the refugees, and fighting against the Renegades."

The captain lowered his weapon slightly, his lip trembling. "I had to kill our own people, because of those gods-dusted Rebels."

"Vance..." My voice drifted off. I couldn't reason with him. He believed his version of the truth and would do anything to uphold it.

"They've won, Ami," he declared, his voice shaking. "Dahan has won, the Twelve have won, and we will be gone. Dibon will be a vague memory in the history of our galaxy. But you—you sided with the enemy. You betrayed your own people when you left, abandoning us for them."

"I left you. That's the real problem, isn't it?" I took a slight step forward, my hands still raised. "I looked up to you. You were the one I trusted. You kept me alive more times than I can count. You liked that I admired you. But this—this is the ultimate betrayal. You betrayed our people's values and principles, and millions were killed." I choked, thinking of Titus, Gene, Natalie, my crew, my friends aboard the *Ashkelon* —even Bricks and Felix. "You used people and discarded them. And you betrayed me, to get to the Rupture Device."

Vance bit his bottom lip.

"The Rupture Device doesn't exist anymore, Vance. It's gone."

I took another step sideways, in front of my weapon.

"You don't know that," he spat. "They lied to you. We made bombs for fighters, even managed to convert the cannons on this piece of junk, but couldn't figure out how to make a weapon of that magnitude. We need the Rupture Device. One capable of wiping out an entire rebellion once and for all. They are hiding it."

"No."

I trusted Bo, believed him. Because as much as I loved him, I also knew the temptation to use it was too great. The militia leader didn't have it.

Lowering my hands, I took another small step forward. The ship rocked in waves. "It's over, Vance. In a few minutes we're both gonna be dead."

"Guess we'll both have to reckon with the gods for our blind faith."

He raised his weapon.

I flinched, but a shot rang out behind me, not in front of me. A blood stain formed in the middle of his chest, right below his heart. Vance slumped to the floor.

Spinning around, I gasped as Sheya lowered the gun —the very pistol Vance gave me. I didn't realize she had the strength to reach for it on the ground, while the captain locked his anger on me.

I dropped to her side. "Let me help you up."

My sister-in-law grimaced, shaking her head. "No. It's too late."

"No, you haven't—"

"Shhh. Look at me, dear sister. Look at me."

I gazed into her bright, brown eyes, full of love and wonder and light.

"I'm going home, to Chip and Max, to your brother and sister. I will tell them the story of their brave and wonderful sister and wife, who brought an end to our war."

I gripped her hand tight. "Don't go."

"It's not your home, but mine. Sister, your home is on Melas, with Mara, with your new husband, with your child."

"How did you—"

"Where you go, I will go; where you stay, I will stay—"

Tears crested, spilling over. "Your people will be my people, your God, my God..."

"Where you die, I will die—" she coughed. "As long as you are alive, I live in you, dear sister. And so do your brother and sister, and Chip, and Max. They live in you."

Her hand slipped from mine. I drew her into my embrace, holding her close as her breathing grew shallow, until it ceased.

Lying her down on the floor, I removed the pistol from her hand. I set her palms up, closing her eyes.

Vance coughed behind me, blood soaking his chest, striving to keep his head up so he could breathe. I made my way over to the stairs. I covered my face as a panel above us broke open, raining sparks.

"Your weapon worked too well," my old captain sputtered.

"I overcompensated." I had expected that the bomb would stop the disintegration process in the cannon, but I hadn't realized that connected to a larger power source, the cannon would keep recharging, and would continue disintegrating. The bomb neutralizer only managed to stop the conversion to the energy beam.

"You always were an overachiever. Top of your class." He swallowed, trying to suck in air, watching my hand on the pistol. His own had fallen out of reach. "Best prospect who ever entered the Dibon Military Force." His hand clutched the wound. "Kill me and get it over with."

"I can't. I wouldn't have shot you before, either." I made my way to the stairs. "First priority for a soldier: save the civilians who cannot save themselves. You taught me that, you know. I still live by it. If you'd let me get Sheya, we could've stopped this."

"How did—how did you find the debris, in the middle of the Galactic Ocean? Donovan said they'd destroyed all evidence that Kittiwakes were involved." His voice had become raspy.

"I told you, but you don't believe it."

My former commander closed his eyes. For a moment I thought he'd passed, until he spoke, his voice soft. "It was a miracle, then. A miracle the transmissions were intact. What is the saying the prophets always declared? 'The truth is the only way to honor ourselves.'

No. Not all truth is equal. Some truth leads only to death. This was a mistake."

"A mistake? Our fellow Pinions, all dead?"

Shaking my head, I started to descend the stairs. But I stopped at the third step, gazing back. Vance's eyes were open again, staring at me, but the hate was gone. Only a sad, dying man remained.

I slid the pistol across the floor, near his reach. In case I underestimated his injuries, I ran down the steps, but I heard nothing besides the twisting and peeling of the ship apart until I reached the flight deck below. A single shot rang through the air.

Climbing into the Buzzard, I pulled the cockpit shut, firing up the engines as pieces of the ship fell around me. I pulled on my helmet and opened the Diboni channel. "All aboard the *Astarte*, abandon ship. Repeat: abandon ship." I didn't know if the crew would listen to me, but I had to try. At this point, there were too many bodies to count. Too much blood on my hands. If I could save at least one...

Four pilots ran onto the balcony from the corridor. One stopped short at the sight of Vance's body, but the others kept going. "Escape protocol engaged," an unfamiliar voice said over the comm. "All hands, abandon ship."

I waited until the other pilots were aboard their Buzzards. The fourth had run back inside. We couldn't wait. The balcony started to collapse.

"Airlocks won't open," one of the other pilots said, appearing as K-11 on my display. "Outer hull breached and safety protocol engaged."

I lifted off from the pad. "We're going to have to blast

our way out, then," I said. Once the other three had their engines engaged, I fired my proton rifles at the doors. As soon as the doors released, all warning lights blazed, and broken pipes and wires flew out the doors ahead of us.

I pushed forward and took the Buzzard out through the broken conveyer belt shaft. Two others followed me, the third Kittiwake crashing into a broken support beam.

The load bay doors were gone, as the ship continued to disintegrate.

"Mind telling me if there were disintegrator bombs on board?" I asked as I flew out of the ship.

"There were—"

I was met with static as the *Astarte* disintegrated behind me. When the disintegration process met the munitions hold, the heat from all the bombs released.

"Get out!"

"Fall back!"

The comm filled with a mess of anger and confusion, as instructions were garbled and shouted. I shut the damn thing off. The *Tristan* was struck by debris from the *Astarte's* destruction. The implosion-turned-explosion pushed my trajectory toward the atmosphere. Ships darted everywhere from the explosion. I had to avoid panicked pilots and stay ahead of the debris field. If I pulled too hard and hit the atmosphere at a weak point on my shields, I'd burn up. Instead, I shifted the angle of my entry, skimming off the outer atmosphere, spinning like a skipped stone: what our Buzzards were known for back in the day.

Vance taught me that maneuver, years ago.

Behind me, fighters burned up, pilots not as quick thinking as they hit the atmosphere at sharp angles. Skimming across the atmosphere flung me far from the explosion. I pulled on the thrusters, flipping over to slow my velocity, and then firing at spurts to stop the spin from getting out of control. An alarm sounded, as I'd been burning at max power since leaving the *Astarte* and my shields had almost overheated. I needed to shut it down for a while to cool off. The alarms ceased, as I kept only life support on, the green light letting me know oxygen and pressurization remained at normal levels.

In the darkness of my Kittiwake, like a burial tube, I fell apart. Sobbing, I grieved Sheya's loss, but also the Vance I once knew, though he'd been gone for some time.

I screamed out my pain, my frustration at everything that had been taken from me. Max. Chip. All our neighbors and friends. Sheya. Our planet, our culture, corrupted and distorted for power. All my friends on the *Ashkelon*. Even Vance.

The desire for revenge turns the best of us into monsters, unleashing us at the people we love, the people we swore to protect. Because revenge, in the end, was about us. It was selfish, our own need to see someone else suffer, because we suffered.

Revenge was what my parents wanted, to the point they were willing to lose me to satisfy their own selfishness over the children who were gone. They only recognized it too late.

There, in the silence, still moving far away from the ships burning, the rest breaking apart, I closed my eyes, breathing out my own hate and rage, letting go. I chanted the Mourner's Prayer for Sheya first, and then for the Vance I'd known, longer than the Vance who killed Sheya. I added the Diboni commission: "To the stars, beyond the edge of the galaxy, we commit to you a warrior of the worlds. Soldier of the gods, knight of the night: greet the stars, lay down your weapons in the peace of light." I recited something similar at Titus' funeral, but now I spoke the full Diboni committal for deceased soldiers.

Then I remembered the words Mara spoke to me once. "There is but one God, Creator of the Universe, blessed is God's name."

Maybe it was God who guided me to the evidence, who led me to unravel the truth of what happened. Vance even said it was a miracle.

I wiped my eyes on my glove and restarted the engines. I considered jettisoning the final bombs into the atmosphere to burn up, but then I realized the best impact would be to use them on the fields of the farm.

Our farm.

I'd shut off the comm in the aftermath of the *Astarte's* destruction.

"Lion One?" I called out, listening for his voice. "Lion One? Bo?"

"Ami? God blast it, where are you?" His voice carried his desperation.

"On my way home."

I re-entered Melas' atmosphere near the southern continent, where the Sim'ee called home. Below me, I saw crowds gathered, flares being sent high into the air, fireworks exploding in brilliant colors as I soared above. The word had spread. Parts of the destroyed ships disintegrated in the atmosphere as white streaks crossed the sky above me.

Flying toward home, near the coastal hills, I spied Dan in the Sparrowing, circling to join me. "Thought we'd lost you."

"Suspected I'd switched sides again?"

He chuckled over the comm. "What's the plan?"

"I'm gonna bomb our home."

"What? Can you repeat that?"

I laughed. "I'm going to bomb the farm with the neutralizer. It should impact most of the fields. We'll have to settle all the soil and replant, but this time, there shouldn't be any problems."

"Copy that, Lioness."

"Is that my call sign?"

Bo jumped in. "If I'm the Lion you're the Lioness. Dan is L-2. Don't have any other female fighter pilots right now."

"You've got to be ash-dusting kidding me. None?"

"I'm almost through training," Jill announced from the shuttle, which I spotted flying to my north on an intercept route, "but Dan kept hogging the only fighter we have."

"Well that's something we definitely have to change."

They laughed on the comm as I dove lower for the bombing run. I dropped my remaining bombs, circling around to make sure most of the farmland was hit. Each one landed like a pebble in a puddle, causing a ripple effect outward on the soil, overturning the few tractors remaining in the fields. But now, the contamination would be neutralized. New life would flourish.

35

"Everything's looking well," Phin told me, moving the wand away from my swollen belly.

Mara squeezed my hand and kissed my forehead. "I'm so happy for you!"

"I'm so happy for us," I assured her.

I feared at first that she would feel left behind when I married Bo. But when we moved back to Lehem farm, first in tents, now in the farmhouse we were building, I made sure we included space for her—on the first floor, next door to the nursery. Across the way, another home was being constructed, for Rachel and Jonah. I kept my promises.

I stayed out of the lab since we returned to the farm, avoiding any chemicals which might still be present. I shouldn't have handled the bombs the way I did, but Phin didn't notice any abnormalities. All tests and scans fell within the normal range for a pregnant mother gestating in a post-war world. The baby was growing as expected at five months along, and now and then I felt something—a kick, a roll.

Bo and I left the infirmary together and walked out over the farm, and I rested my hand on my abdomen, the bump only beginning to be noticed by others. The day laborers were getting ready for the first planting of the new year.

We didn't rebuild the fence. If people were desperate enough to come and take the crops, they needed it, I argued. Before the last battle, fences were built to mark the owner's territory, hiring their own guards, protecting their property. But it was never ours to begin with.

We separated out one section of the farm, on my insistence. Through Jill, we contacted the one Sebuj we knew—the man from the botched arms deal. His name was Ara. We gave him that section of the farm. If any other Sebuj came forward, they were to be given a portion of the farm as their own, in exchange for turning over disintegrator weapons. It was their land first, and as much as possible, I wanted it go back to them. Nacaen custom may have passed the land to me, but I knew the truth. I wanted to do what I could, to repair the damage done.

We still found some spots of contamination the day laborers worked on, and to speed up the process, we dismantled disintegrator weapons. Pulling them apart, we neutralized the cartridges and then the soil. We shared our method through as many channels as possible, though the largest source of contamination was here at Lehem Farm, where we transformed weapons into farming tools.

The Sim'ee, Jamin and Dahan formed a representative council, along with Ara as the Sebuj delegate. Bo presided over the meetings as judge, but included me on the Council, as the representative for refugees. Because that was who I became—a Diboni refugee. Jill became the new leader of the Melas Unified Military. She had enough connections with former Rebels and other outsiders to bring them under one roof, and they had begun a new flight school with Sparrowings and the one Kittiwake which survived it all.

Bo clasped my hand, and we walked along the tire tracks of the land we'd soon plant again. "I can't believe my father did this," he muttered. "He started the war, here."

I stopped, pulling him close to me. I understood how my husband felt. There were days I could look back and see Vance, calling us into line, remembering at one time he did care about saving lives. There were times I didn't want to believe it was really him this past year. My former captain had been too important to me, and it still hurt. "You're not your father. Remember that."

"You know how I told you my father was killed in the war?"

"Yes."

"He died on Richo, where my mother was from, in a place where they found the same kind of ash. I was always told it was a weapons malfunction, but now I know." Bo said. "Sal destroyed the Rupture Device there, taking his own life." Bo's gaze swept out over the place where the old farmhouse stood. "But before he went there, I'm certain he spread out the neutralizer here—after I was burned by the rainfire." My husband's arm tensed, his voice trembling. "I want to think my father was ashamed of what he did. And that when Sal went to Richo, he tried to atone for it by taking his own life. I don't know."

We walked past the copse which had survived a second war. The needle trees waved tall in the wind, unbreakable, undeniable reminders of the land's resilience. The space where the old buildings stood had been bulldozed and cleared.

"Sometimes," I said, my voice just above a whisper, "the only thing we can do, since we can't make sense of it all, is to let go. To forgive. So we can move on."

I snaked my arm around Bo, pulling him tighter, and he rested his new hand on my shoulder.

We stopped in front of the bulldozed land, where the farmhouse once stood. "We'll plant here, too," I promised.

EPILOGUE

Obie whined as I pulled him off my breast. He'd eaten his fill but didn't want to sleep. I rocked him, shushing him, but still he cried.

"Let me take him," Mara offered, and I handed over her grandson.

Right before I gave birth to Obie, I sent a message to my parents in the Ramaen System and told them they'd be grandparents. They sent a message back, asking to come visit. It would take them a long time to get here, but I wanted them to come, for all we'd been through. They were, after all, Obie's Diboni grandparents, and among the few Diboni left in the universe.

And it was time to move on.

People can change. It's hard for the old ways to die, to break the cycle of revenge, but out of death comes new life. Dibon's once great military was no more. The few survivors from escape pods and the two Buzzards that made it out after me had surrendered immediately. Once all weapons and flyers were turned over, they were given clemency. None decided to stay on Melas. We booked transports for the survivors back to the Bara system, to find new lives elsewhere. I was the last here, and wouldn't fight again. That part of me was finished.

For now, I was content to be a farmer and a mother.

Mara cooed to my son, who closed his little blue eyes and stopped crying. He had dark, curly hair and skin almost as brown as mine, but blue eyes like Bo's mother, like Mara's sons.

Bo came outside and moved to sit behind me on the steps of the porch. I gazed out over the fields, and I imagined more dark-haired children. Right now, the full heads of the harvest ruffled in the breeze, born from the soil I bombed. People who were once part of the Dahan militia now prepared to harvest barley and wheat. More folks were building in Ephra, and other farms joined our way—fewer guns and guards, more offering a living wage so their workers would thrive without fear. Thriving in our fields.

There wasn't a day that passed where I didn't have at least one thought, one memory of Max. The ache of his passing faded with time, but the memories remained. Bo slung his arm over my shoulders, as familiar as Max's once had been.

Phin walked up the long driveway, coming to sit by Mara on the front porch. The breeze kicked up, chilling the air but I didn't mind—I'd been cooped up inside for far too long, and Obie was wrapped up. The priest said he needed to check on me, but I suspected he really came to call on the older widow, for whom he seemed to have developed a soft spot.

He lifted Obie from Mara's arms. "The future of our people is here."

I smiled. "We put an awful lot on the next generation, you know. We always expect them to save us from our own sins."

Phin shook his head. "It won't be Obie or his generation, or even his children. But come his grandchildren, and I think we will see a new dawn for us all."

"Why that long?"

He shrugged, pulling Obie closer to his chest, rocking him as if the baby were his own. "It seems it takes us that long to forget the hurt."

"Perhaps," I responded, leaning back into Bo. His arm moved around my waist, his chin tucked over my shoulder, and I watched Obie nestle to sleep in the priest's arms.

I remembered how Phin called out to me, long ago, as I entered the old farmhouse with Rachel: "Childless one shall be mother of all." The old prophet wasn't talking about me, but about Mara, as he held her grandchild. For as much loss as we both experienced, our hearts were full.

War wouldn't leave us be forever. A time would come when my people—our people—would struggle again. But I'd had a lifetime of violence. Time to stop reciting the Mourner's Prayer, and instead cling to life.

Smiling at my child in Phin's arms, I knew he was right. The future of our people was here.

ACKNOWLEDGMENTS

"When Naomi saw that Ruth was determined to go with her, she said no more to her." Ruth 1:18

A long time ago, late at night in the student lounge of Andover Newton Theological School while playing D&D, an idea sparked of retelling Ruth as a space opera. The idea never left me.

Ruth's story was determined to stay with me, and I am grateful to God our Creator.

Thank you to the PitchWars community. This is a book that didn't make it into PitchWars but did snag me two early readers of this manuscript, Karen and Bethany, whose feedback on the earlier drafts was invaluable. Thank you to Hayley Stone whose enthusiasm for Ami's story kept me on the revising track. I am grateful for Ryn Richmond whose edits helped shape this story and made the worldbuilding come alive.

Thank you to Cascade Writers, the most supportive, encouraging community of writers and workshops that have helped me to grow. Thanks to Tammy Deschamps and Emily Papel, my critique partners, who have faithfully read draft after draft of this work. Without them I would have given up on writing many times over, but they would not let me quit.

Many thanks to Spencer Ellsworth whose encouragement and feedback helped me to cross this threshold, and thanks to Kelli Stasi for continued cheering on and coffee, and to Paul Schneider who read this book after I thought it was hopeless and told me he couldn't put it down. Thank you to Laura Anne Gilman for the venting, wine, and chocolate.

Thank you to Scott James Magner for seeing my Facebook post, when I thought all hope was lost, and gave this book another chance with ARUS Entertainment. I am forever grateful. Thank you for your friendship and encouragement in writing.

To my parents, thank you for your love of science fiction that you passed down to me. Thank you for introducing me to both Star Wars and Star Trek, Enemy Mine and Silent Running, even though I cried all night after watching that last one.

To my son AJ, thank you for always making me strive to be a better person. To my husband JC, thank you for your unending love, support, enthusiasm, and baking, and for not letting me give up, ever.

ABOUT THE AUTHOR

Melinda Mitchell grew up in Alaska and has lived all over the United States, currently residing in Wisconsin with her husband and son. Raised by parents who were fans of science fiction and fantasy, NEXT OF KIN is her debut novel. Melinda has written numerous nonfiction articles on the intersection of theology and sci-fi and has co-authored two academic papers on the subject. The greatest truths are in the stories we tell, whether or not the stories are true themselves.

www.melindamitchellcom

Printed in the USA
CPSIA information can be obtained
at www.ICGtesting.com
CBHW022147200524
8867CB00031B/676

9 781954 394117